PRAISE FOR *A STRANGER ON THE BEACH*

One of . . .
Her Campus's "14 Books By Women We Can't Wait to Read This Year"
Frolic Media's "Most Anticipated Beach Reads"
Bookstr's "8 Thrillers For Your Beach Bag This Summer"
Women.com's "15 Most Anticipated Books of Summer by Women"
Brit + Co's "7 Must-Read Books for Fans of True Crime"
The Nerd Daily's "14 Upcoming 2019 Crime Thriller Books"

"Engrossing . . . breezy intrigue on a hot summer day."

—*Publishers Weekly*

"A roller coaster of fear and intrigue."   —*Booklist*

"*A Stranger on the Beach* will keep you reading—and guessing—from one
end of your beach weekend to the other."   —*Coastal Living* magazine

"Prepare for *A Stranger on the Beach* to chill your bones, even if you're
reading it on the beach."   —*Newsweek*

"A twisted story for fans of *Dirty John*."   —Brit + Co

"Master of suspense Michele Campbell is back with a twisted new thriller."
—PopSugar

"Bestselling author Michele Campbell's newest thriller is full of passion,
intrigue, and nail-biting drama."   —The Nerd Daily

"Michele Campbell's latest thriller is full of unexpected moments you
won't see coming."   —Women.com

"Michele Campbell's edge-of-your-seat story of passion and intrigue will
keep you guessing until the very end."   —Bookstr

"*A Stranger on the Beach* rides its rising tide of terror to a finale that blanched
my knuckles. An exceptionally suspenseful thriller."   —A. J. Finn,
#1 New York Times bestselling author of *The Woman in the Window*

ALSO BY MICHELE CAMPBELL

She Was the Quiet One

It's Always the Husband

a stranger
on the beach

MICHELE CAMPBELL

ST. MARTIN'S GRIFFIN
NEW YORK

First published in the United States by St. Martin's Press, an imprint of St. Martin's Publishing Group

A STRANGER ON THE BEACH. Copyright © 2019 by Michele Campbell. All rights reserved. Printed in the United States of America. For information, address St. Martin's Publishing Group, 120 Broadway, New York, NY 10271.

www.stmartins.com

The Library of Congress has cataloged the hardcover edition as follows:

Names: Campbell, Michele, 1962- author.
Title: A stranger on the beach / Michele Campbell.
Description: First edition. | New York: St. Martin's Press, 2019.
Identifiers: LCCN 2019003999| ISBN 9781250202536 (hardcover) |
    ISBN 9781250313324 (trade paperback) | ISBN 9781250240460
    (international, sold outside the U.S., subject to rights availability) |
    ISBN 9781250202543 (ebook)
Classification: LCC PS3613.A78648 S87 2019 | DDC 813/.6—dc23
LC record available at https://lccn.loc.gov/2019003999

Our books may be purchased in bulk for promotional, educational, or business use. Please contact your local bookseller or the Macmillan Corporate and Premium Sales Department at 1-800-221-7945, extension 5442, or by email at MacmillanSpecialMarkets@macmillan.com.

First St. Martin's Griffin Edition: 2020

10 9 8 7 6 5 4 3

For Jack

Acknowledgments

This book was so much fun to write. It started its life at a lunch I had with my editor and agent where we threw around ideas and laughed and drank wine. After that, the book was charmed, and flowed like magic.

I am so grateful to work with Jennifer Enderlin, who is not only the savviest woman in publishing but a true collaborator in the writing process. Her vision lights my way through all the ups and downs of the writing process. Her ideas and influence are apparent on every page of this book. And I could not write, nor would I ever want to, without the guidance, support, and friendship of Meg Ruley, who has always had my back and nurtured my books beyond the call of duty.

I am indebted to the amazing team at St. Martin's Press for publishing my work so brilliantly. Thanks especially to Rachel Diebel, Jordan Hanley, Brant Janeway, Kerry Nordling, Erica Martirano, and Lisa Senz, and to my wonderful publicist Jessica Preeg who works so hard to get my books out there so readers can discover them.

A million thank-yous to the fabulous crew at Jane Rotrosen Agency for being so warm and supportive, and especially to Jess Errera for everything she does to help me.

Thank you also to Crystal Patriarche and her team at BookSparks, who are just so good at publicizing books in the digital age and have brought my work to the attention of countless new readers.

Finally, as always, I'm profoundly grateful to my husband. I couldn't write without him. He is my rock and my inspiration. Plus, he cooks!

We are only as blind as we want to be.

—Maya Angelou

before
the storm

I'd listened to my instincts. I would've turned and run in the opposite direction. But that's not what I did. I walked toward him. And I would later blame joy. Not for what came after.

1

There was a stranger on the beach. He was standing in front of my house, staring at it like he was casing it to rob.

Sometimes fate sneaks up on you. But Aidan Callahan didn't sneak up on me. He was brazen. He stood there in the middle of the sand, staring up at my brand-spanking-new beachfront house, looking like he was up to no good. I saw him clearly as I looked through the wall of windows, over the infinity-edge pool, to the ocean beyond. Yes, he was gorgeous. But I was a married woman of twenty years' standing who loved her husband, and I barely noticed that. What I noticed was that this guy looked strong. Dangerously so. And he dressed like a townie. Baggy athletic shorts, tank top, the glint of a gold chain at his neck. People like him resented people like me, and sometimes, they robbed them. There had been a string of robberies recently, of some of the big houses. The summer people thought the local cops were dragging their feet about solving them, maybe because the culprits were local boys. When I saw Aidan standing there, those robberies were the first thing that leapt to mind, and a chill went down my spine.

I'll tell you everything that happened, starting from the beginning. My first impression of Aidan was that he was a potential thief. If only

I'd listened to my instincts, I would've turned and run in the opposite direction. But that's not what I did. I walked toward him. And I will always blame myself for what came after.

2

It was a hot, sultry day, two weeks past Labor Day, and the bluff had cleared out. The summer people were all back in the city, leaving only me, and my next-door neighbor, old Mrs. Eberhardt. She lives in a salt-box shack on a wide lot that's coveted by every real estate developer in the East End. I live in the type of place that people build after they tear down houses like hers. She has a yappy little dog that wakes me up at five thirty every morning. As you can imagine, we didn't have much to say to one another, so basically, I was at the beach alone.

I'd been waiting around all day for the technician from the burglar alarm company to show up for the installation. The house had that fresh-paint smell. Details were still being attended to, and the alarm was one of the last items on the punch list. The company gave me a window from ten to two for installation, which I said was fine, because I had work to do preparing for the huge housewarming party I would be throwing in a matter of days. Finalizing guest lists, working out catering menus, scheduling the delivery of the tent, negotiating with the valet parking company, angling to get a photographer from *Avenue* magazine to show up and take pictures for the society column. On and on. Hours passed, and the alarm guy still hadn't showed. At four, I called to complain, and they told me the technician was overbooked, and they'd have to reschedule for next week. *Typical.* I thought about reaching for the bottle of gin in the cabinet and mixing myself a nice strong cocktail to ease my frustration. But it was hours till sunset, and I decided to be good. I'd go for a run on the beach instead.

As I laced up my sneakers, I got the urge to text my daughter. Hannah had just left for college, and I was having trouble letting go. I gave the hair elastic on my wrist a good snap to feel the clarifying sting. My sister had taught me that trick. Aversion therapy. She'd used it to quit smoking, and now I was using it so I wouldn't be a helicopter mom. It worked. The urge passed. I walked through the French doors onto the terrace and took a deep breath of the salty air. The ocean was visible beyond the bluff, the crash of the waves audible from here. The surf was rough today, yet it never failed to calm me.

And I needed calming. Hannah's departure had set me adrift, leaving me all too conscious of how alone I felt in my life. My husband, Jason, traveled constantly for business. He'd never actually spent a single night at the beach house, despite the fact that we were pouring all our money into it. The house was a big source of stress between us. It was my dream, not his. We'd stretched to buy the land, which was postage-stamp-sized but in a primo location. We'd stretched even more to build the perfect house on it. Things weren't right between me and Jason, but in all honesty, I didn't fully know that yet. It was just a nagging feeling lurking in my heart, making me antsy and discontented. But I fought it. I told myself, *He works a lot. He's a good provider. A good father. And hey, somebody's got to pay for the house, right? I shouldn't complain.*

I picked up the pace, fighting the pull of the sugary sand against the bottom of my sneakers, legs working, oxygen pumping through my veins. A shaft of light broke through the clouds, illuminating the water to a sparkling green. I lived on the part of the bluff closer in to the main road, where land was "affordable" at a million-plus an acre. (I won't say how much beyond a million.) The route I liked to run took me down the beach away from the road, toward the point, where the true mansions were. There was a house out there that last traded at forty million.

You couldn't see it, though, because of the tall, perfectly groomed hedge that its famous owners installed for privacy. I'd never met those people, and I guessed I never would. Jason and I didn't rate. He was an investment banker, but not one of the famous ones who hung out with celebrities and owned a fleet of jets. I was an interior designer, but not the type with a million Instagram followers and houses featured in *Architectural Digest*. I'd stopped working when Hannah was born and had only recently gone back, trying to get my business off the ground, but facing headwinds. Jason and I moved in well-to-do circles, but we weren't at the top of the heap. The thing about being rich is, there's always someone richer.

I ran a mile-plus down the beach, not letting myself stop till I was out at the point. Then I doubled over, panting and holding my sides, till I caught my breath. I'd be forty-three in November, and I liked to think I still looked good. But lately there were hints of middle age coming on. Fine lines in the mirror that I covered with makeup, gray hairs peeking through that I masked with highlights. But you can't fake exercise. I needed to get back to Pilates class, or hire a trainer. Getting the house finished had taken too much time and energy. With Hannah gone, I should focus on *myself*.

The clouds were rolling in over the water, turning the sky black. I could smell the rain coming. I hadn't checked the forecast before I left, but generally they were saying to expect a stormy fall and a bad hurricane season. My superstitious mother had left me with a fear of electrical storms, to the point that I wouldn't turn on a faucet if it was lightning out. So, when the first peal of thunder sounded, I turned around and headed back.

Ten minutes later, I was back on my stretch of the bluff, with a clear line of sight to my house. A huge thunderclap sounded, and a vivid bolt of lightning split the sky. And there he was again, like some demon who'd materialized from thin air. The stranger I'd seen an hour earlier from my kitchen window. Staring again. The sight of him stopped me short. I could tell he was a townie, that he didn't belong in my neighborhood. Maybe that sounds snobbish. But I don't come from money, and I didn't mean it that way. As a matter of fact, Aidan that day reminded me of my own people. My brothers and their friends, playing street hockey back in the day on hot afternoons in front of our house. I loved those guys, but they were no angels. I know what I'm talking about. I know casing when I see it, and when I saw Aidan, I knew exactly what he was doing.

I'm not a shrinking violet, and I can take care of myself. I walked toward him, determined to say something.

"*Hey!* Hey, can I help you?" I yelled.

The wind took my words away. But somehow he heard, and turned and smiled at me. The smile, I definitely noticed. It was like the sun breaking through the clouds, and all my suspicions melted away. He fooled me. Anybody can get fooled.

"That's your house?"

He spoke as if he already knew the answer. I should have noticed that, and realized it was odd. But I didn't see it. I only saw him.

"Yes," I said.

"She's a beauty."

"Thank you."

"I'm Aidan," he said, and held out his hand. I took it.

"Caroline."

"Caroline. Pretty name."

"Thank you."

His hand was warm. His eyes were very blue. He looked at me searchingly. I felt tongue-tied. He had to be ten or fifteen years younger than me. He seemed like he was about to say something more. But then the skies opened, and it started pouring.

"You should get inside before you get soaked," he said.

"Yes."

That was it, our whole conversation. He gave me a little wave and turned and hurried off. He was so casual about it, so nonchalant, that I forgot all about the idea that he might be a burglar. The beach where he'd been standing was public. He had a right to be there, and I figured he was just a guy who stopped to look at a beautiful house. Twice. Okay.

But that's not a crime. I went inside and tried to put him out of my mind, but I didn't entirely succeed. My interest had been piqued. My guard had been lowered. My life was not in order. The combination of those things would prove to be my downfall.

3

The night after I first saw Aidan on the beach, my twenty-year marriage fell apart. I swear to God, one thing had nothing to do with the other. It was a total freaking coincidence, the worst coincidence of my life.

I was sitting barefoot on the big L-shaped couch in the great room, going over my guest list for the housewarming and feeling pretty good about life, when Jason called to say he wasn't coming to the party. And that's not even the bad part.

"Honey, I'm sorry. I can't make your housewarming thing" was how he put it.

"*My* housewarming? Last time I checked, this house belonged to both of us."

"You know what I mean."

"Seriously, Jason? That's not okay. You have to come. It's not just a housewarming. It's for your birthday, too."

"My birthday isn't until next month."

"But I put it on the invitation. I ordered an expensive cake. I invited people from your firm and your golf club."

"I didn't ask you to do that."

"Well, they're coming. And you know who else is coming? People I need to impress for the design business."

I'd been a successful interior designer once. I could be again, with my beautiful new house as my calling card. Did he not get that?

"You want me to start making money, right?" I said.

"Of course I do."

"The party is important to that, Jason. Magazine people are coming, and decorators and architects. I need you there."

"I'm sorry, hon. I would if I could, but I'm stuck in Cleveland on this deal."

Cleveland? What the hell? He'd told me he was going to Denver.

And that's when it hit me. He was lying.

I cradled the phone against my neck and picked up my iPad from the coffee table. With our family plan, I can track everybody's devices. I'd done it a few times with Hannah, when she was out late, and I was worried she'd been kidnapped by the Uber driver. But I'd never checked up on Jason before—I was that oblivious. Now I hit FIND MY IPHONE, and waited for the map to load showing his location. My heart was in my throat. I could feel that something bad was coming. And boy, was I right.

That little dot loaded like a punch to the stomach. Jason wasn't in Cleveland, or in Denver. He was in the city, a three-hour drive from me. But not at our apartment. At an address near Times Square. At ten thirty at night. I zoomed in on the map. That address—it was the Marriott Marquis. He was in a freaking *hotel* in Manhattan.

Why would a man go to a hotel at that hour, in a city where he owns a perfectly lovely apartment?

To cheat on his wife, obviously.

What an idiot I was. Jason was never home, and yet I never suspected. He was secretive, and hard to reach, and had been for a while now. He'd get a call late at night and walk out of the room to answer. Or rush to close a text or email when I walked up behind him. When he was away on business, it was impossible to get him to call me back. But somehow, I never saw it coming. I was way too trusting. No, wait, I'm letting myself off the hook too easily. The truth, warts and all. It's not just that I'm trusting. I'm too damn full of myself. It never occurred to me that a man would cheat on me—at least, that *Jason* would. I was a cheerleader in high school and student body president in college. I got every guy and every job I ever wanted. Jason always said I was his dream girl. I never doubted him, because I never doubted myself. But I was wrong. His feelings had changed. When had that happened? How long had this been going on?

I was floored.

"Caroline? Are you there?"

I took a deep breath. I wasn't going to cry. I would be calm, and dignified, but call him on his bullshit, because I wasn't a doormat. I would make him tell me the truth.

"What aren't you telling me, Jason?"

"What? Nothing."

"I don't believe you. You're hiding something."

"What are you talking about?"

"Are you cheating on me?"

"Of course not. Don't be ridiculous," he said.

But I had proof. At least, I had proof that he was in a hotel in Times Square right this minute, when he claimed to be in Cleveland. I couldn't tell him that, though. If I confronted him with the evidence, he'd know I was tracking his phone, and I wanted to be able to keep doing it.

Jason sighed, like I was the one causing trouble. "Enough drama, babe. It's late. I'll do my best to get to your party, okay? But no promises. You need to cut me some slack. Things are complicated at work right now."

He was lying to me, and I knew it, but he refused to own up to it. What more could I do?

"Caroline?"

"I have to go," I said, and hung up on him.

I sat there on the sofa, too stunned to cry. It was like I aged twenty years in the space of that one phone call. I hadn't realized until right that minute that I wasn't little Caroline Logan anymore, with my high ponytail, my cute figure, my cheerleader outfit. I was middle-aged Caroline Stark, semi-unemployed housewife, empty nester. And my husband was cheating on me.

4

At seven sharp the band began to play. They were set up in a tent on the lawn, to one side of the swimming pool. The music floated on the ocean breeze as the waiters dashed in and out in white jackets, passing trays of chili-lime shrimp and glasses of rosé. I grabbed a glass off a tray and thought, *I ought to be enjoying myself. This is my big night. I can't let Jason ruin it for me.* Easier said than done. He hadn't shown up yet, and I couldn't stop watching the door.

In the living room, I took up position in front of the sweeping wall of windows that looked out over the ocean. I wore a white dress to match the décor. I could turn in one direction and watch the waves crash. Or turn in the other for a view across the double-height living room to the front door, where guests were arriving, stepping out of their shiny cars and tossing their keys to the valet. I'd been a little worried that nobody would come, that they wouldn't drive out from the city this late in September. But they were showing up in droves. Everybody but the person I was waiting for.

Each time the front door opened, I looked up and plastered a smile on my face so big I felt like my cheeks would crack. And each time, when it wasn't my husband, I had to take a deep breath to fight off the panic. I made excuses about Jason's absence to the guests as we hugged and air-kissed. Important deal, flight delay, missed connection, on his way, yada yada yada. I hate to lie, but I do believe in putting on a good face for company. I couldn't bring myself to tell the world that I didn't know where my own husband was. All I knew was that, with every second that passed, I got angrier, and more insecure, and more hurt.

The guests were too polite to comment on Jason's absence, until my sister Lynn walked in with her husband, Joe. God love her, Lynn's a loudmouth, like all the Logans, but she's not mean. Just oblivious. She's the one sibling I'm close with now. Among the living, that is. It's a long story, but let's say we've had our troubles as a family. Out of three boys and three girls, I was the youngest. Two of the boys died young—one on a motorcycle, the other with a needle in his arm. My parents were hard livers, and they passed it down. Then we fell out over Dad's will. It was ugly. Me and Lynn on one side, Erin and Pat Junior on the other. Mom was dead by then, thank God, she didn't have to see it. That fight brought me closer with Lynn. She's the one person I truly trust in this world other than my daughter. She doesn't fit in with my uptown crowd, with her spray tan and her tight clothes. But like I always tell her, you do you, babe. I love Lynn to death, and I wouldn't've dreamed of throwing a party without her.

"Where's that handsome husband of yours?" Lynn asked, in a booming voice that made the other guests turn to look. She still talked with that old Lawn Guyland brogue, too, that I'd worked hard to get rid of, and that was nails-on-a-blackboard to everybody else in that room.

"Flight delay."

"Yeah, right. Too good to show up for his own party is more like it."

"Somebody has to pay for the house."

"Ahright, I'll zip it. But when I see him, I'm giving him a piece of my mind. Now, which way is the bar?"

Lynn started a trend by asking about Jason. The next guy through the door was Peter Mertz, Jason's boss at the hedge fund, and instead of nodding politely when I said Jason was running late, he started probing. Why wasn't Jason in New York? Why was he stuck in Cleveland? When

I said he was there on a deal, Peter raised an eyebrow and said, *Really? Really?*—like he didn't believe me. He basically implied that Jason was lying, or else I was. And yes, okay, it so happened that we both were lying. But that didn't make it any less rude for Peter to call me on it in front of my guests.

After that, I couldn't stand there watching the door any longer. I made an excuse and went out to the tent. Fresh air, fresh alcohol. But I couldn't get that encounter out of my mind. Was Peter trying to tell me something by calling me out like that? Did he know something I didn't, or more precisely, something I suspected but was praying was not true? In other words, did he know my husband was having an affair? Did *everyone* know but me? My cheeks were burning at this point. I felt humiliated. But little did I know, the festivities were just getting started.

I'm an experienced hostess, and I normally wouldn't drink at my own party. But as time went by, and Jason still didn't show, I guess I had a few more than I intended. By the way, I was drinking the signature cocktail of the night, a Moscow mule, which the caterer offered passed on trays. So, when the waiters walked by, I'd grab one. What I'm saying is, I don't recall going up to the bar in the tent that night. Not once. Aidan tended bar at my party. I found that out later, but I didn't know it at the time. I never saw him there, and I certainly didn't hire him myself. Caterers bring their own staff. Everybody knows that.

Anyway, Jason.

I was talking, probably too loudly, to this woman who was a contributing writer for *Dwell* magazine, when Lynn walked up and snatched the drink right out of my hand.

"*Hey!*"

"Excuse us," Lynn said to the woman, and yanked me away.

"What the hell. I was networking."

"You're not doing yourself any favors, getting sloppy at your own party. But at least now I know why."

"What are you talking about?"

"Jason's here, and he's with a woman. A real piece a' work, too."

The room went dark. I had to grab Lynn's arm to steady myself.

Everything had been so normal until two nights ago. And now my life was in smoldering ruins around me.

"Where?" I asked.

"Inside, in the living room."

"Since when?"

"A few minutes. Why didn't you tell me he's having an affair? You know I'd go after that son of a bitch."

"He actually brought someone *here*? To my house, to my party? I can't believe he'd do that to me."

"I'll have Joe deck him if you want. Or I'll do it myself."

"No. You stay here. Distract people. They can't know about this."

"It's too late, hon. Nobody could miss this chick."

I walked away in a daze, heading for the living room. I had to find Jason, but I had no idea what I'd do when I did. Yell, scream, kick him out? Cry, beg? This didn't feel real. It didn't feel like *us*. Meanwhile, the guests were all watching me. I'd dreamed of throwing a party they'd talk about for years. And now they would, but for all the wrong reasons.

5

Heading for the house was the longest walk of my life. I was thinking, *This can't be happening. We're not those people. We're teammates, best friends. We're inseparable.* But then I thought, *We're not inseparable. We used to be, but not anymore.* This had been a long time coming, actually. Hannah was a preemie, high-strung, not popular in school. I sweated parenting her. Maybe—I'll be honest—maybe I loved her more than I loved my husband. Anyway, she sucked up all the attention. My life revolved around her. Volunteering at her school. Homework and dance lessons and her social life. Her clothes and her hairstyles and whether she'd go to summer camp. Her college applications. On top of that, yes—the house, the apartment, my Pilates class, my nutty sister who had plenty of drama of her own. None of it was about him. Maybe he felt slighted, or ignored, and so he did what men do. He looked elsewhere.

But then I thought, *Hell no. This isn't my fault. I don't deserve this. I made that man.* Jason was nobody when he met me. Meeting him now, you'd think he was born with a silver spoon in his mouth, the way he dresses and talks and carries himself. Well, I've got news for you—that was all me. That was Caroline, telling Jason what to do, and how to behave, over a period of twenty years. It was hard work, too. When I met him, he was working two jobs, scraping by, struggling to pay for school.

He had those dark, chiseled good looks, and he was smart. I saw the potential. But he was rough around the edges. I was the one with the drive, the vision, and, yes, the cold hard cash. I put Jason through business school, or he never would be the tycoon he is today. I used the money Dad left me to do it, blood money, that I lost siblings over. Everything Jason Stark has, every penny, is because of my sacrifice. And yet, he goes and cheats, right when our daughter left, when I'm so alone.

That bastard.

That's how I was feeling as I walked back to the house. I was furious. I admit that.

Inside, I looked around the living room, but there was no sign of him. It was late, and the crowd was starting to thin out. I walked up to my friend Stacey Allen, whose daughter Grace went to high school with my Hannah, and whose lawyer husband, Josh, represents Jason's firm. And I didn't have to say a word. Stacey already knew. She knew who I was looking for, and she pointed at the door.

"He went outside a few minutes ago, with a *woman*. Caroline, what the hell's going on?"

Stacey has one of those very expressive faces—wide-eyed, with big features—and it brimmed with pity for me, mixed with excitement, and a subtle touch of schadenfreude. People thought I had such a perfect life. To have something like this befall me would naturally be titillating, and Stacey could spread gossip like wildfire. By tomorrow morning, my entire social circle would know about Jason's affair, whether I'd invited them to the party or not. As the realization sunk in, my head literally went hot, as if steam was coming out of it, like in the cartoons. *I'll kill that asshole*, I thought. Stacey's eyebrows shot up into her carefully trimmed bangs, and I realized I'd said that out loud. Well, screw her and her ladylike shock. I have the Logan temper. We say things.

"It's a figure of speech," I said.

"Of course."

"Who is she? Do we know her?" I asked, because that was the biggest thing on my mind at that moment. Was Jason doing it with somebody I knew? That would make it so much worse.

Stacey shook her head. "I doubt you'd know her, and you definitely didn't invite her. She crashed."

"How could you tell?"

"Jason showed up first, alone. I tried to say hi, but he was on his phone, and he looked distracted. Less than five minutes later, the front door flies open, and *she* comes in. *Rushes* in. Almost like she'd chased him here. He basically dragged her out the door to get her away from people, but it was too late. Everybody saw. They're probably still out there, it's only been a few minutes," Stacey said, nodding toward the front door.

"Don't tell anybody about this," I said.

"Caroline, they already know."

I turned and rushed out to the driveway. Jason was still there, talking to her. Her back was to me. The first thing I saw was, she had dark hair. It made no sense. Jason likes blondes, or at least he used to. Like me (though I get a little help with the color). But he had her by the arms, like she was trying to run away, and he wanted to stop her. The intimacy of it made me sick.

I marched right up to them. "What the hell is going on?"

They turned in unison, and Jason jumped away from the woman, like he'd been caught. Goddamn right he had, and with a tramp, by the looks of her. And the *smell*. The woman reeked of this cheap gardenia perfume. I nearly gagged on it. I started thinking, *Maybe she's a prostitute. This is who he's cheating with?* She wasn't young, wasn't beautiful. She had one of those faces that's almost catlike from too much plastic surgery. I'm sorry, but she was a big step down from me.

Then she opened her mouth, and it got worse.

"Who is this?" she says to Jason, and she's looking me up and down like I'm dirt. In my own house. But it came out like—*who is zis?* She was Russian, or maybe Czech. Flashy, hard-looking, heavy eyeliner, a tight leather skirt and fuck-me pumps. A younger, more beautiful woman, okay. Or a more educated, a smarter woman, a woman who was powerful in her own right? I'd get that. But to get betrayed for this, this *whore?* I was devastated.

"I'm his *wife,* who the hell are you?" I said.

My hands were twitching, I wanted to slap her so bad. But there were guests within earshot, just inside the door. And I wasn't about to give them more to gossip about than they already had.

Instead of answering my question, she made this contemptuous little noise—the sound of air escaping between gritted teeth. Like I wasn't worth her consideration. A car drove up, a brand-new cobalt-blue Audi coupe that looked like it cost real money. The valet stepped out and handed her the keys. She made another impatient sound at Jason and slid into the front seat.

"I go," she said.

"Galina, wait," Jason said.

"You need to decide," she said. Then she pulled the door closed and took off with a spray of gravel.

My jaw was on the ground.

"Decide what? What is she talking about?" I said.

"I don't know."

"You don't know? Bullshit. You bring another woman to my house, to my party, and let her talk to me that way, and refuse to explain?"

Jason turned to me like he hadn't even noticed I was there till that minute. He was so caught up with this Galina woman that *I* didn't even register. And he got this appalled expression on his face and started sputtering.

"Wait, no, it's not what you're thinking. We work together. There's a problem, a work problem, and she followed me here to discuss it, that's all."

"I know the people at your firm. That woman doesn't work there. They wouldn't even let her through the door." Which was one hundred percent true.

"I didn't say she worked there."

"Yes, you did. You just did. Stop *lying.*" I was about to burst into tears. I mean, people were watching.

"Caroline. You've got this all wrong."

"Then explain it to me."

"I told you, she's a business associate."

"And I told *you* that I don't believe you."

"After twenty years of marriage, you need to give me the benefit of the doubt," he said.

"I don't have to do a goddamn thing."

"You're jumping to conclusions. But I can't fix that right now. I have a crisis situation on my hands. I need to go in to the city."

"What?"

"I'll be back as soon as I can."

"If you leave this party to go after her, don't bother coming back."

I regret saying that. I certainly regret saying it *in front of* people. My threat didn't work anyway. He went after her. And I'm thinking, *Screw him, I'll get the best divorce lawyer in New York and take everything. The beach house, the apartment, the cars, the jewelry. I'll take custody of Hannah, or—since she's too old for custody—I'll make her* hate *him. Hate his guts. He'll never see her on holidays. He won't be invited to her wedding. No walking her down the aisle, I'll do that. He gets shit. He can die alone and see how he likes it.*

I thought all those things. Anybody would, if their husband brought another woman to their big party, and then left to run after her. But never once did I actually think, *I'm gonna go buy a gun and shoot my husband dead.* Okay, well, maybe I *thought* it. But I didn't *do* it.

Swear to God.

6

Jason never came back to the beach house on the night of the party, or on the day or night after that. I must've called his phone twenty times. Finally, he texted me with some lame excuse about a work crisis, but since I was tracking his phone, I could see the lie in real time. His office was in Midtown, but his dot was way the hell out in Brighton Beach. Brighton goddamn Beach, also known as *Little Odessa*. Jason was with the Russian woman.

That night, I turned off my phone and drank myself senseless. Obviously, that's a wrong way to handle stress, but it's also an old family tradition. I learned to drink at Daddy's knee. Pat Logan, Sr.—man, that guy could put away the booze, and he was none too pleasant when he did it, either. And Theresa, my mother—straight gin, I'm not kidding. Is it any wonder that, when my life to fell to pieces, I reached for the bottle? I'm not making excuses. I saw what it did to them, and I should have known better. I *had* known better, when my little girl was home. We like to think our children behave for us, but it's really the other way around. I controlled my drinking around Hannah, to set a better example than my parents set for me. But she wasn't here now, and I swigged blood-colored wine until the empty bottle fell from my hands and I passed out.

On Sunday afternoon, I woke up to the smell of the Russian woman's cheap perfume. I thought I was dreaming, but then I opened my eyes and Jason was standing over me, looking as bad as I felt. Which was very, very bad. He knelt down by the bed, and I could see tears in his eyes. At that point, I would've accepted an apology. Hell, I was praying for one.

"I can smell her on you," I said, and my eyes filled with tears, too. "You can't see her anymore, love. Please. I'm begging you."

"I wish it was as simple as that, Car," he said quietly. "It's worse."

I sat up. The room was spinning, and I had to swallow hard to keep from vomiting.

"Worse, how? Please, don't tell me she's pregnant."

"I never meant to hurt you. Things got out of hand. It's beyond my control now."

"What are you talking about? Stop being so mysterious." I dug my fingers into my temples. My head felt like it would split apart.

"I can't tell you any more without—" He stopped.

"Without what?"

"I can't say."

"Jesus, what am I supposed to make of that, Jason? What am I supposed to do?"

"Honestly? I hate to say this. But you need to find a good divorce lawyer. It's the only plan I have right now."

"Does she have some kind of hold on you?"

From the look on his face, I'd hit the nail on the head.

"Jason, answer me, is she pregnant?"

He pressed his lips together, ignoring my question.

"We have to get a divorce," he said. "I won't contest anything. You take everything. The apartment, the beach house, all the money. I want you to."

Divorce. Maybe at the party I was imagining getting a lawyer and taking him for everything he had. But that was not the outcome I wanted for my marriage. Even after everything that had happened in the past forty-eight hours, I still loved him. We'd been together twenty years.

We had Hannah. And the apartment, and the house, and a life we'd built up from nothing, together. We were happy. Strike that, we were content. Okay, maybe we were treading water, but it was possible that with counseling and effort, we could've been happy again. But he had to go and bring that woman home and completely blindside me.

"Twenty years, and this is how you end it?" I was choking on my tears.

Jason's face was pale, and his eyes burned dark. He made a choking noise in his throat, like he couldn't get the words out.

"It's the only plan I have."

"You don't have to do this."

He grabbed my hands. "Yes, I do. But please know, I love you, and I'm truly sorry."

Then he leapt up and walked out of the room. I heard his car start outside, and he was gone.

I staggered around the house, going from room to room, so dazed with shock that I could barely see what was in front of me. Maybe I cried, but I was too numb to notice. I had no clue how to get through the next hours, the next days—the rest of my life—without him. Or without the stability and continuity he represented. I walked out onto the lawn and listened to the waves crashing on the beach. And I thought, I could go down there and—And what? End it? No. That wasn't me. I wasn't a quitter. And screw him, that would make things too easy for him. I knew I had to get a grip on myself. I ran back inside and called Lynn's cell.

"Jason left me," I blurted, the second Lynn picked up.

Silence.

"Lynn?"

"I can't believe he's that big of an idiot."

"He is. He did. Not five minutes ago. He told me to find a divorce lawyer."

Lynn paused. "Stay there. I'm coming."

"You're coming—?"

"I'm coming out there. Pour yourself a drink, turn on the TV, zone out. I'll be there in an hour, unless the cops get me."

"Thank you, sis. I love you so much."

"Love you, too, babe. You're not going through this alone."

Lynn lived in the same house in Massapequa where we grew up, which was a solid hour and a half away, but she had a fast car and a lead foot. Fifty minutes later, she walked in the front door, carrying a bottle of bourbon and a big glass bowl of spaghetti and meatballs, which she shoved into the microwave. I grabbed the bottle and poured myself a good slug, but the thought of eating was beyond me.

"I can't eat that. I feel sick," I said, as Lynn set a plate on the kitchen table.

"Just the spaghetti. It'll settle your stomach. We have work to do. I have calls in to friends of mine who know all the good attorneys. We're gonna get you squared away."

Lynn stayed the night, slept in my bed with me, stroked my head when I cried. Before she left the next morning, she forced me to make an appointment with one of the divorce lawyers, who came highly recommended by a friend of hers who'd cleaned up in her divorce settlement. I wanted Lynn to come to the appointment with me. God, I wish she had, because then I would've kept it. But she had to leave. Lynn and Joe own a bunch of condos down in Florida that they rent out. The condos got hit with this big storm, and she had to go down to oversee repairs. I understand, it's their livelihood. And I'm a big girl. But damn. I can't help thinking about how different things would be if she'd stayed in the Hamptons with me for those few days. I never would have gone to that bar. I never would have met Aidan again.

7

*Of all the gin joints in all the towns in all the world, she walks into
mine.*

Aidan thought of that line the second Caroline Stark walked into the
bar where he worked. It was a rainy Monday night, with the smell of
woodsmoke in the air. Every time the door opened, he got a cold blast,
and looked up. He recognized her right away. How could he not? She
was the one who threw the party the other night. The one who built that
house on Gramps's land. She tore down their old fishing shack to build
it. That place meant everything to him when he was a kid. It was im-
printed on his brain—the sound of the waves, the salt in the air, the way
the light slanted at the end of a summer day. Her house was the total opposite of Gramps's old place. It was a freaking palace. He couldn't decide if it was a nightmare or a dream, but he was dying to go inside it.
He'd tried to get on the construction crew, but the site manager was a
hard-ass, and wouldn't hire him because of some bad blood that went
back years. (People had long memories in this town.) So, when the bartending gig came along, with the chance to see the inside, he jumped on
it. Then it turned out the bar was set up in a tent on the lawn. He couldn't
even sneak inside pretending to use the john, because they wanted the

catering staff to use the facilities in the pool house. Didn't trust 'em in the main house, apparently.

Here was the star of the show now, though, walking into the Red Anchor. The glow she gave off lit up the place, making it seem like something more than the average local bar and burger joint that it was. She carried herself like a queen. The shoulders thrown back, the tilt of her beautiful head, the thick glossy sweep of her honey-colored hair. The world should bow down. The place was deserted, and she threw a glance his way. She took off her coat. Shook it out. Took a seat at a booth along the wall. Fluffed her hair. Like she was waiting for him to come over and take her order. Did he look like a waitress? She could get her ass up here to the bar, or else wait for Nancy, who was on a cigarette break.

He pretended not to see her, turned his back, wiped down some glasses that were wet from the dishwasher. But then he changed his mind. Maybe because she was beautiful. Maybe because she lived on the land that ought to be his by rights, and he wanted to take her measure. Maybe both. Then there was the fact that the party had been a complete disaster for her. The husband's mistress showed up and caused a scene. It was all anybody was talking about in the big tent that night, as Aidan poured their drinks. He knew what it was like to be gossiped about. People talked behind his back; had since he hit a patch of hard luck at the age of seventeen. The point was, on top of everything, he felt sorry for her. Imagine that—him feeling sorry for the likes of her. It would be funny if it wasn't pathetic.

He mixed up a Moscow mule, walked over to the table and laid it down in front of her.

"On the house," he said, and smiled.

Women rolled over for his smile. But she didn't. She looked down at the drink, then back up at him, like he'd done something weird.

"I'm sorry. Have we met?" she asked.

Now, that was bullshit. She was playing games. Even if she didn't remember him tending bar at the party, they'd met on the beach. She remembered that. He knew she did. Mind games. He didn't need that shit.

"Yeah, we met on the beach. Then I tended bar at your house this past weekend. For the party, remember? That's why I figured you'd like the Moscow mule, because that was the cocktail of the night."

"Oh, right. Well, thank you. I'll take the drink, but I'd prefer to pay."

He nodded, feeling stung. Why should he care what she thought of him, though? Some rich bitch from the city coming out here on weekends, acting like this town and everybody in it belonged to her. They were all like that. It was nothing to him. Rolled off his back.

"Suit yourself. Give a shout if you need anything, ma'am," he said.

She didn't like the "ma'am," he could tell. Probably worried he thought she looked old. Which, to him, meant she wasn't as untouchable as she pretended. Aidan sauntered back behind the bar. He felt her watching him from the safety of her table as she sipped her drink. Time passed. He ignored her. She'd look over at him, though, every few minutes, checking him out.

She wasn't immune.

Wayne Johnson and Mike Castro came in and sat down at one end of the bar. They worked for his brother Tommy.

"Hey, Aidan. Coupla pints," Mike said, stripping off his police department windbreaker. Water ran off it in rivulets.

"Still raining?" Aidan asked.

"Yeah, it's getting worse."

Aidan drew off two pints of Guinness and set them up on the bar. The guys were talking about some warrant they had to serve for the feds. A mobster with a foreign name, wanted by the FBI, holed up in a mansion on Harbor Lane. Aidan listened a little too intently, which made them exchange glances and clam up. They could piss right off. People always had to think the worst. Aidan could sell that information for good money, but that didn't mean he was going to. He'd been on his best behavior for ten years now, and what did it get him? People still shot him suspicious looks just for walking down the street in broad daylight, minding his own business.

Not long after the guys came in, Caroline stood up and put on her coat. That was fast. He hadn't really noticed what she was wearing before. Tight jeans, black boots, a sexy top. Had she come in here looking for company? Had he missed his chance? She had a great body for a woman her age. For any age, really. He caught her eyes, raised an eyebrow as if to say, *Leaving already?* She gave a half smile and a little nod and walked out.

Nancy was busy in the dining room, so Aidan bussed the table. Cocktails were twelve bucks, and the woman had left a twenty. The big tip annoyed him somehow, like she was putting him in his place. He'd offered her a free drink, and then she pulls this? He had half a mind to follow her outside, but she might take that the wrong way. It wasn't worth getting his boss pissed off, or having people say he was up to his old tricks. He pocketed the money and thought, what the hell, if he wanted to see her, he knew where she lived. Right?

8

On Tuesday, I drove in to the city to meet with the divorce attorney. But at the last minute, I got cold feet, and called to cancel from the street in front of her office. My marriage fell apart so fast that I hadn't had a moment to think. Was this the right thing? Could we avoid it somehow? Jason and I had been married for *twenty years*. You don't throw that away without a fight. Shouldn't we try counseling first? Okay, he wasn't exactly giving me that option. He wouldn't even take my calls. You might say that was all the answer I should need, but I couldn't accept it. Beneath my every thought was Hannah. Your average kid who'd gone off to college would be upset if their parents split, but they'd take it in stride. Hannah was fragile. And she was a Daddy's girl. Jason was everything to her. I didn't want to burden her with our marital problems just as she started college. But I also didn't want her blaming me for abandoning her beloved father. That's the truth. That's why I didn't meet with the lawyer. It had nothing to do with Aidan. We'd barely spoken at that point.

I canceled the appointment. I went to our apartment in the city, pulled the blinds, drank an entire bottle of red wine, and passed out on the sofa watching *Gossip Girl* reruns. I was hiding my head in the sand.

At midnight, the shriek of the phone woke me. I grabbed it, hoping it would be Jason. But it was the alarm company calling, to say that a motion sensor had been tripped back at the beach house. The police had been dispatched, and found no evidence of a break-in. The guy thought maybe the system wasn't calibrated properly, which didn't surprise me. I'd had it installed the day before, and I'd chased the technician out prematurely, so I could go sob in the bathroom.

But this meant I needed to go back out to the beach. It was raining on Wednesday morning, and traffic on the LIE was a nightmare. But I was grateful to be back in my beautiful house, even if it had been the scene of my recent humiliation. I opened the French doors and sat listening to the rain, waiting for the technician to show up. I'd canceled the appointment with the lawyer, but I was obsessing over the thought of divorce. If we split up, I'd never go back to our apartment in the city. Jason could have it. I wouldn't want the reminders of our life together, of raising our daughter. This house would be my future. I'd live here full-time. He claimed he wanted to play nice. Fine, then. He could give me a big settlement, one I could live well on. I'd walk on the beach, get a dog, plant a garden. Divorce wouldn't be the end of the world. I'd survive. That was the Logan in me talking. We're survivors.

When the alarm company didn't show, it took me hours to figure out that something was wrong. They'd given me a window of noon to two o'clock for the technician to arrive. When he wasn't there by three, I called the alarm company and got the runaround from the receptionist. At four I called back and demanded to speak to a manager. At six, the manager finally returned my call.

"I'm afraid we've had an issue with the payment, so I can't dispatch a service provider at this time," the manager, whose name was Shelley, explained.

"Wait a minute. I was told you accept personal checks. I wrote a check for the installation fee and first year of service."

"Yes. But that check bounced."

"It—?"

"It *bounced*. It was not honored by your bank," Shelley said loudly.

"I *know* what 'bounced' means."

Why the hell did the check bounce? As of Monday, when I wrote it, there was plenty of money in the account to cover that payment, and more. I was absolutely certain. This woman had to be wrong.

Right?

"No need to get snippy, ma'am," Shelley said. "As soon as we receive payment, we'll reinstate service and dispatch the technician."

"Reinstate service? You mean the alarm's not working now?"

"The sensors installed in your home should still function—"

"It wasn't functioning. It was going off for no reason."

"It will function to the level of installation."

"You mean it's still broken."

"We're no longer monitoring your signal, sending alerts or calling alerts in to the police. If your motion sensors get tripped, the alarm will go off in your home, but we won't respond or relay the signal to the police. I'm sure you understand, we can't provide service we're not paid for."

"Look, I don't know why the check bounced. It must be an error. Can I pay you some other way?"

"Certainly. I can take a valid credit card over the phone."

"Well, why didn't you say so? Hold on."

I went to get my wallet, telling myself to stay calm. But as I read off my Amex number and waited for the charge to go through, I had a sick pit of fear in my stomach. I'd logged into the joint checking account Monday, and there was over a hundred grand in there. Jason couldn't possibly have spent so much in that short a time. For it to disappear, he would've had to move it somewhere. He'd told me I could have the money. But men lied to their soon-to-be-ex-wives all the time. They drained bank accounts, hid cash, ran off with mistresses. Was Jason better than other men? I'd thought so. But I was afraid to find out.

"Ma'am?" Shelley said. "I'm sorry, that card was declined."

I went cold. I handled our household bills, and I saw to it that credit card balances were paid off monthly. No card of mine was ever declined. Something had happened, and Jason had to be behind it.

"I'm so sorry. Would you mind trying a different one?" I said.

We tried three more cards, and all three were declined. By the end, I was crying. When I hung up, it was nearly seven, getting dark, pouring rain, and the windows were all open. I got up to close them; then I sat at the kitchen table and logged onto my laptop in the darkness of the kitchen. My hands were shaking as I went through all the accounts. The brokerage account, the savings account, his IRA, my IRA—gone, gone, gone. He'd left me destitute, completely. Took every penny he could get his hands on, with one exception. He didn't touch Hannah's 529 plan. Her college tuition was still there.

At least he had the basic decency not to rob his own child. But he'd robbed me. Jason telling me I could have everything—that was a lie. A ploy so I would let my guard down. I trusted him. I fell for it. I didn't rush to see the divorce lawyer, or to freeze our joint accounts. I gave him the breathing room he needed to take everything we had.

I called Jason's phone. Got voicemail. I said a lot of things. I said I was going to kill him, but I didn't mean it literally. The only person I was in danger of killing in that moment was myself. I could imagine life without my husband, but not if I was destitute. What would I do? How would I survive? My fabulous career as an interior designer existed only in my dreams. In real life, I didn't have a single client. I didn't have one red cent except for the money he'd just taken. I couldn't bear it. I threw the phone down. I screamed. I pulled my own hair. I slapped myself across the face. I looked out the window at the dark waves and imagined walking into them. Imagined the briny water tugging at my clothes, up to my waist, then my chest, then over my head. I would die, and that would show him.

But Hannah.

I couldn't stay in the house alone for one more second, or I would hurt myself. And I wouldn't do that to my daughter.

I picked up the phone to call Lynn; then I remembered she was in Florida. I thought of the bar in town, where I'd gone a couple of nights earlier. There would be people there. And a stiff drink. I put a jacket on and got my car keys.

If I thought things were bad, I was about to make them much worse.

9

The bar at the Red Anchor hosted a two-for-one happy hour on Wednesday nights. The place was packed by seven, and Aidan was hustling to keep up when chief of police Tommy Callahan walked in. Even in the midst of the crowd, Tommy was hard to miss, with his bulk, his booming voice, and his ruddy face. The Irish sunburn, they called it. The bar at the front of the Red Anchor restaurant was Tommy's favorite place to hold court, and if he was here, his men weren't far behind. They'd sit around for hours, the guys laughing at Tommy's jokes and generally licking his boots, all of them expecting a couple of rounds on the house. But Aidan knew better than to complain. His big brother had gotten him this job and bailed him out of trouble more times than he could count. Acting like a devoted kid brother was small price to pay for the cover he got from Tommy. He never knew when he might need that cover again.

As Tommy approached, Aidan reached across the bar and clasped his brother's hand.

"Good to see ya, bro. The usual?" Aidan said, grabbing a beer stein.

"No. I got something to say to you. Outside," Tommy said, jerking his head toward the door.

"Uh, I'm working here."

"Don't backtalk, Aidan. I'm not in the mood."

The flash of anger was like heat in his blood. But he held his tongue. "All right. Give me a minute."

He called out to Nancy, the waitress. A huge smile lit up her tired face as she caught sight of Tommy. She hurried over, wiping her hands on her apron.

"Chief!" Nancy said.

"Nance, you're looking fine tonight," Tommy said, and gave her a hug.

"Aww, thanks," Nancy said, blushing with pleasure. "We got shepherd's pie for the special. Want me to grab a plate for you?"

"You know I do."

"Tommy needs to talk to me outside," Aidan said. "Cover the bar for a few?"

"No problem," Nancy said.

Yeah, right. She would've screamed bloody murder if Aidan ever asked that for himself.

Aidan followed Tommy out to the parking lot, which backed up onto the ocean. It was a blustery evening, with the tang of salt in the air. Clouds scudded across the dark sky, and gulls cawed around the trash cans. Tommy's cruiser was parked in front of the restaurant in a spot reserved for the owner, who wasn't in yet. If he did come in, what the hell, he could find himself another spot.

Tommy leaned against the cruiser and took out a pack of cigarettes. He lit one, and offered the pack to Aidan, who shook his head.

"I quit."

"Yeah? Good for you," Tommy said, with a cynical half laugh that implied it wouldn't last.

"What's up?" Aidan said. "Ma complaining about me again?"

"No. But you really ought to call her."

"I do call. It's never enough."

"You could come for dinner on Sunday."

"I work Sundays. Some of us don't make our own hours."

Tommy shrugged and took a few drags off his cigarette before grinding it out under his shoe. Then he reached into his pocket and pulled out something. Aidan saw a glitter of gold, and his heart skipped.

"What's this?" Tommy said, dangling the St. Christopher's medal so it swung in the breeze.

Aidan took the medal and put it in his pocket. "You know what it is," he said.

Tommy had given that medal to Aidan when he graduated high school, the year after their dad died. *For protection on your journey*, the card had read. Trouble was, Aidan's journey never took him out of this shitty town.

"The clasp is loose. I've been meaning to get it fixed," he said in a defensive tone.

Tommy watched him with cynical eyes.

"Why did I find that on the bluff the other night, when I was checking out an alarm at the new house?" Tommy asked.

They both knew which house he was talking about. The one built on land that had once belonged to their family. Tommy pretended like that didn't bother him. But Aidan knew better.

"I worked a job there," Aidan said, gazing out at the oily, black water. Moments like this felt like déjà vu. For good reason. They seemed to come over and over again. Tommy questioning him, acting aggrieved and disappointed, Aidan having to defend himself against the accusations. He was exhausted by it.

"What kind of job?" Tommy asked.

Aidan sighed. Like it or not, he was going to have to explain himself to his brother.

"What do you think, teaching astrophysics? I was tending bar at a party. Remember Brittany Pulaski, Samantha's sister? She's the manager for Harbor Gourmet now. She hooked me up with the gig."

"Brittany Pulaski hooked you up? Why would she do that? She hates you."

"I was surprised, too. The lady who owns that house threw a big party. Harbor Gourmet was catering. Who knows, they must've been short-staffed, because Brittany reached out to me. You don't believe me, ask her."

"Look, I believe you were there. I believe you were working. But that doesn't set my fears to rest. Where was the bar?"

"What?"

"The bar, for this party. Where was it set up? Inside the house, outside?"

"The bar was outside, in a tent on the lawn, next to the pool house."

"Then explain to me how this medal ended up under the window of the master bedroom around the side of the house."

"How should I know, Tommy? There must've been a hundred people there that night. The medal falls off, somebody picks it up, drops it, drags it on their shoe. Or maybe I have a thing going on with the lady of the house and I dropped it climbing out her bedroom window, so her husband wouldn't see me."

"Like she'd ever be interested in you."

"She likes me. We met before, on the beach. She came looking for me after that."

"Bullshit. And why the hell were you on her beach?"

"It's not *her* beach. It's public. I got as much right to be there as anybody."

"Gramps is dead. Let it go already," Tommy said, shaking his head.

"I don't know what you're talking about."

"Yes, you do. Don't lie. You're not making it easy to help you, Aidan."

"Look, I appreciate everything you do for me. And I work hard to stay on track, so I don't let you down. Give me some credit. Stop riding me when I didn't do anything wrong."

"I can't stand to see you backslide. That's all."

"I'm not backsliding. I wouldn't do that to you. Don't worry. Please, Tommy," he said.

"Fine, I'll back off. But you need to stay away from that woman's house. You got it?"

A second police cruiser drove up, sparing Aidan from having to answer. Wayne Johnson and Mike Castro got out.

Tommy punched Aidan on the shoulder lightly. "You heard what I said. Now be a good kid, and set up a round for me and the boys, all right?"

For the next hour, Aidan hung around the edges of his brother's party, keeping the drinks flowing, and basking in the reflected glory. When Tommy was around, Aidan became everybody's kid brother. He felt almost included, almost like he belonged. But who was he kidding? Tommy's guys thought he was dirt, and no matter what he did, they always would.

Then *she* walked in. Second time in two days, and he thought, *She's looking for something. Maybe she's looking for me.* Why else come to this place? Someone like her has got to feel a townie bar is beneath her. But maybe she didn't. Or else she liked him enough to ignore that. It was possible, given the way she'd looked at him that day on the beach. His luck could still change. All he needed was one good break, and he had a funny feeling that this woman might be it. She hadn't given him the time of day when she came in here the other night, and he offered to comp her drink. But then again, he hadn't really tried.

He leaned over to his brother. "That's her. That's the woman who owns the house," he said, under his breath.

"Yeah? So?"

"Watch, you're gonna see I was telling the truth before. This lady likes me."

"That rich chick likes *you*?" Tommy said, raising an eyebrow.

"I'm not lying. Watch. You'll see."

10

The bar was crowded and noisy, and all the booths were taken. I was lucky to find an empty barstool at the far end, near the bathrooms. The bathroom doors kept opening and closing, letting out powerful blasts of air freshener. The place was a dive, with kitschy beach décor— all anchors and ropes and fake lobster traps. I'd just taken off my coat, and I was already tempted to put it back on and leave. But then the bartender came over. I remembered him from the beach. I remembered thinking he'd seemed dangerous at first, then deciding I was wrong. But that moment was when I noticed him for real. I noticed that he had one of those perfect, lazy smiles that make the world seem warmer and more welcoming. There was even a dimple in one cheek. He was wearing this deep-blue chambray shirt that matched his eyes, and khaki pants. His hair was brushed. He didn't look thuggish tonight. He looked like a college guy, the one in your dorm that all the girls had a crush on.

"Hey, you. I was hoping you'd come back," he said.

I practically looked over my shoulder to see if he was talking to someone else.

"Seriously?"

"Yeah. You ran off last time, before we got a chance to talk."

"Um. Well. Doesn't look like we'll get much chance to talk tonight. Busy in here for a Wednesday."

Stupid line. But I was feeling self-conscious. I'm not generally the sort of woman who goes to bars alone, and to have the hot bartender start flirting me up right away—it threw me.

"We have our two-for-one happy hour on Wednesdays. Everybody likes a cheap drink," he said.

"I could use a cheap drink myself tonight. I'm Caroline, by the way."

"I know your name. You told me on the beach, and then I tended bar at your party. I wouldn't forget a woman like you."

He had a sexy voice, gravelly, a little rough. I extended my hand. He gripped it for half a second too long, gazing into my eyes. He was extremely handsome. Sandy hair gone blond at the ends, blue eyes that crinkled at the edges from staring into the sun, tall and broad-shouldered, perfect white teeth. Like a surfer from a beach movie, or an underwear model. I should have gotten up and walked out right then. But things were so messed up, and I needed to dull the pain. So instead, I asked his name.

God, was I stupid.

"You forgot my name?"

He actually looked hurt. I told myself he was probably pretending, and anyway, I secretly liked it. His reaction should've been a warning sign. Instead, it gave me a cheap thrill.

"I'm sorry. I'm not good with names."

He nodded. "Aidan Callahan. Nice to meet for real this time, Caroline—?"

"Stark."

"Can I get you a Moscow mule, Caroline Stark?"

"Oh. No. Those were just for the party. I'll take a vodka and soda, if you don't mind. That's my drink."

"Good to know. Be right back."

But he didn't come right back. A lot of the customers seemed to know one another, and they all knew *him*. I liked that. I like a guy who's outgoing. Jason's reserved, even sullen sometimes. I can't always tell what he's thinking. But I watched Aidan glad-handing the cops at the other end of the bar and thought, *That's a simple, down-home, easygoing guy. And easy on the eyes. If only I were ten years younger, or not married, I'd . . . No.* I'd better stop thinking like that, or I'd end up acting on it when I shouldn't. I absolutely shouldn't.

They were teasing him as he poured another round, calling his name. *Aidan*. Aidan Callahan. An Irishman, obviously; we had that in common.

Aidan came back smiling, carrying two drinks and a dish of mixed nuts.

"Are those both for me? Do I look like that much of a lush?" I said.

I gave him a seductive laugh, and thought, *Where the hell did that come from?* It had been a long time since I flirted. I wasn't sure I'd remember how, but apparently it was like riding a bicycle. As he slid one of the drinks closer, his hand brushed mine, and I got this *thrill*. He was looking at me with—I have to say it—*lust* in his eyes. It was blatant. And I'm thinking, this could be my chance for revenge on Jason. Not to murder him, okay? To sleep with the hot bartender, like any red-blooded betrayed American wife would do in similar circumstances.

"Nope, one of 'em's for me," Aidan said. "You don't mind if I drink with you, do you? Or would you rather not associate with the riffraff?"

"Are you the riffraff in that scenario?"

"The *help*."

To be honest, on any other night, I might have been above having a drink with him. Not because I'm a snob, but because it's pretty low to walk into a bar and start drinking with some random guy you barely know. But that night, I was willing to lower my standards of behavior. That night, I was not proud.

"If you're the help, then count me in," I said, and raised my glass.

He clinked his glass against mine.

"*Sláinte*," he said.

"*Cin cin.*"

We both took a swig. He'd made the drink powerful. I liked feeling it burn going down. I liked feeling the room fade away and start swaying. I needed to forget, and this guy was helping me do it.

He leaned down and put his elbows on the slick wooden surface, his face a foot from mine. Even in the dim light, his eyes were very blue.

"*Cin cin?* That's Italian, right?" he asked.

"My mom's side. And boy, did she like to drink. I get that from both sides actually."

"The other side——?"

"Irish."

"Ah, that explains the freckles," he said, and traced a finger gently across the bridge of my nose.

Wow. His touch was so unexpected, so forward, it made me squirm on my barstool.

"Drat, thought I covered those with makeup," I said, and my voice came out several octaves lower than normal. My breathing was quicker. I flashed on this movie I'd seen years ago. A woman picks up a guy in a bar and within minutes they're screwing like animals up against the fence in the alley. I told myself, *That's crazy, stop this, calm down, act your age.* I picked up my glass and downed the rest of it in one gulp. Then I held it against my cheek, and my neck, hoping the icy coldness of the glass would still the throbbing in my blood and make me behave. But no.

"Never cover those freckles. They're perfect. Irish and Italian together is the most beautiful combination. But I bet you've heard that all your life."

I was not entirely certain whether he was flirting with me for real, like he truly found me attractive. Or whether he was joke-flirting with an older woman, to get a tip or something. Not that I cared. But I was conscious of the gap between us——age-wise, class-wise, whatever-you-want-to-call-it-wise. I wasn't taking myself too seriously, and I wasn't sure yet that I'd be taking Aidan home. In fact, I was still telling myself not to go there. But I hadn't thought about Jason and the crash-and-burn disaster of my marriage in at least three minutes, which had to be some kind of miracle.

"Your glass is empty. Hold on, let me get you another."

He went away and came right back with a fresh vodka. If nothing else, I'd be giving him one helluva tip for the drinks. But thinking about cash reminded me about the missing money, and I got upset all over again.

Then he started asking me about myself, and that distracted me.

"So, do you live here full-time, or are you a weekender, like everybody else in town these days?"

"It was supposed to be just weekends. But . . . I don't know. My life is up in the air right now. I'm taking things one day at a time."

"Yeah? That doesn't sound good. Anything you want to talk about?"

He sounded so sincere that it's possible I teared up. I was very vulnerable right then.

"No. Thank you. My life is a mess, but I shouldn't impose. We barely know each other."

"It's fine, really. Listen, I've been there. I've had troubles of my own. The temptation is to keep everything in and go through it alone. But it can help to talk. It can especially help to talk to the bartender."

That got a laugh out of me.

"No joke," Aidan said. "We're like priests. We hear confessions, and we give our own special absolution. It comes in a bottle, though."

"I like that. Sounds like more fun than the kind the church doles out."

"For sure. Freshen your drink?"

My glass was empty already. I handed it to him, and he walked away. I started wondering how much he knew about me. He claimed he'd tended bar at my party. I didn't recall seeing him that night, but the party had been crowded, and the catering staff large. If he was there, did he hear about Jason and the Russian woman? Were the other guests gossiping about me, about the epic fail of my marriage, in front of him? Did he think that's why I was here, flirting him up? I thought I was being all sexy and mysterious, but instead I was a pathetic old cougar, dumped by her husband for another woman, hitting on a guy young enough to be my son. No, wait—I wasn't *that* old. My much younger brother.

He came back with fresh drinks for both of us.

"So," I said. "Are you from around here?"

That line was corny as hell. I started thinking maybe I *was* a pathetic drunken cougar coming on to a hot young guy after all. But the nice thing about Aidan was, he didn't seem to mind. He took a swig of his drink and gave me that slow, sexy grin.

"Born and raised, never made it out. Prob'ly gonna die here."

"You could do a lot worse than this place. It's beautiful. The water, the sky. The town is adorable."

"The part you go to, maybe. Guys like me, we're on the outside looking in. I meet a woman like you. Beautiful, sophisticated. I can imagine what your life is like, but I can never really touch it, you know."

"I'm not sure what you mean. Here we are right now, having a conversation."

He shrugged. "I think you *do* know what I mean. We could have this conversation. We could even have chemistry. But you're out of my league. And I know that, so I would never take it further."

I was thinking about telling him to give it a try and see what happened. But before I could decide to, somebody called his name, and he stood up. The rush of disappointment I felt was intense, and I was drunk enough to give it voice.

"Don't go," I said.

Aidan's eyes widened.

"Hey, hold your horses. I'm busy here," he said, over his shoulder, to whoever'd called him.

He leaned back down to me, his face inches from mine. I was looking at his mouth, and then he smiled again. His smile was killer.

"Hey, see those guys at the other end of the bar?"

"The cops?"

"Yeah. The chief there, sitting near the door—he's my brother. He's gonna order another round and expect me to put it on the house. Then he's gonna want me to stand there and entertain him, even though I'd rather stay here talking to you."

"That bum."

"I know, family's a bitch, right? Would you consider doing me a favor?"

"Anything. Name it."

Yes, all right, I was down to do whatever he asked. Already.

"Let's make Chief Callahan wait for his next round. I'm gonna go over there, and you call me right back."

"You mean, like, order another drink?"

"No, it should be more than that, or I'll have to top them up first. Pretend like you and me are close, and you don't want to let me out of your sight. Can you do that?"

"Aidan, get your ass over here," the big cop called out.

The summons was almost nasty, and I felt for Aidan, the kid brother to this jerk of a cop who obviously ruled the roost. I didn't stop to think. I took Aidan's side.

"Go. I've got your back," I said.

He winked at me as he retreated. I waited until Aidan was right in front of his brother, then raised my hand and waved.

"Aidan? Aidan!"

My voice vanished into the din, and Aidan didn't turn around. Why not? He'd asked me to call him. Did he want a bigger show? I hesitated, but what the hell, I'd agreed to play the game. He was taking my mind off my pain, anyway.

I walked over to where the brother sat and tapped him on the shoulder.

"Hey, sorry to interrupt, Chief, but I need Aidan to come back and talk to me. I *need* him, badly."

I leaned on the word "need," so it sounded sexy as hell, and got a kick out of the shocked look on the brother's face. This was so much fun that I decided to run with it.

"Aidan, please, come back. I have to talk to you, baby. It's so important."

The brother looked so flummoxed that I started to think I'd gone too far. But, c'mon. He couldn't possibly believe there was something between us. Right? That was so implausible.

"I'm coming, baby," Aidan said, and turned to his brother. "Tommy, give me a minute here. Caroline needs me."

I went back to my barstool, and Aidan followed, convulsing with laughter. His dimple was showing, his eyes were crinkling, and I was tingling down to my toes.

"Hah, did you get a load of the expression on his face? Hilarious."

"Did he know I was joking?" I asked.

"Who knows? Tommy's not too bright," Aidan said.

I felt a little uneasy about the practical joke. But Aidan soon distracted me, regaling me with gossip about the people in the bar. To hear him tell it, half of them were degenerates, and the other half were fools. They were constantly beefing with each other, trashing each other's cars, falling off the dock, and generally causing mischief. We drank and laughed like old friends. He fetched another round, and then another. (Somehow, the drinks kept vanishing.) And I . . . relaxed. I let go. He had this laid-back, adorable, stoner cowboy vibe about him. Like he didn't take the world too seriously, so I shouldn't either. God, did I need that right then. Meanwhile, the brother and his fellow cops were looking on, scandalized.

"Your brother and his friends are staring at us," I said.

"He's shocked a woman like you would be with me."

"He thinks I'm *with* you?" I giggled. The vodka had gone to my head.

"Why you laughing?" Aidan said, looking almost hurt.

"Honey, I'm way too old for you."

"What are you talking about? You're hot as hell. Trust me, if I was gonna get with one woman in this bar tonight, it would be you. You blow everybody else away."

The boy knew how to sweet-talk, and he was getting in my head. I looked around the bar and decided, *Hell yeah, I* am *the best-looking woman in here tonight*. If I was the woman in the bar he most wanted to sleep with, then he should have me, right? He'd made his choice, and I was flattered enough that I wanted to honor it. It made sense, in that crazy moment. The room was warm and pulsating with light. I was feeling no pain. Jason was somewhere in Brighton Beach, screwing his Russian whore, and I didn't care, because I had Aidan to distract me. I wasn't thinking about my declined credit cards, my empty bank accounts, the silent house awaiting me. I was flying, and I wanted it to last forever.

Time passed. I can't count how many vodkas I drank. A bunch of people got up to leave, and Aidan went to settle their tabs. I followed him with my eyes as he worked the crowd. He had a lot of fans. The women in the bar lit up under his attention, poor saps. It never occurred to me that I was one of them.

I watched him taking people's money, and it came rushing back for the umpteenth time that I had no money to pay my tab. Just then, Aidan returned, carrying two more drinks and an antipasti plate—which I couldn't pay for.

"Something wrong? You look upset," he said, his face full of sweet concern.

"I forgot my wallet."

"No worries. I know you're good for it. Here, eat something or I'll have to carry you out of here."

He smiled at me, then took a toothpick, speared an olive, and held it up for me to eat. And I ate out of his hand. In the bar. In front of people. What the hell was I thinking?

The din had died down. When Aidan's brother called his name, the sound carried across the empty room. The cops were standing up to leave, waving money at Aidan. He went over to take it and shook hands all around. I drained what was left in my glass—vodka-flavored melted ice. My body felt loose; my face felt numb. My vision was doubled. Bands of light reflected off the mirror behind the bar and seemed to vibrate in the air. I knew I was drunk, and I didn't give a shit. The booze held Jason at bay, at the edge of my consciousness where I could tolerate him. I got up and went to the bathroom and peed for a really long time. I thought about sticking my finger down my throat to get rid of the liquor but decided not to. My face in the bathroom mirror was puffy, and my eyes were too bright. I didn't recognize myself, so I redid my lipstick as fast as I could and got the hell out of there.

When I got back to my seat, the bar was nearly empty, and people were talking about me.

"—your lady friend?" one of the cops said to Aidan.

"She's waiting for me to close up shop," Aidan said.

That made no sense, since I was not actually waiting for him. Well, I was waiting, in my own mind, but he'd be pretty full of himself to assume that. We had no understanding. It hadn't remotely been discussed.

For all he knew I was about to stiff him for a night's worth of drinks and run out the door. But I didn't say anything to contradict him in front of his brother.

I should've, probably. I realize that now.

I looked at my phone. It was almost midnight. How had that happened? Aidan wiped down the bar, took the money from the cash register and placed it in a light-colored fabric envelope. The people on either side of me had left. Aidan looked my way.

"You okay, Caroline?"

"I think so."

"I have to give the till to my manager. I'll be right back. Stay there. Okay?"

"Okay."

I closed my eyes, letting the room spin around me. It seemed like he was gone for a long time.

"Hey. You okay?"

I opened my eyes to see that Aidan had returned. He was pulling on a beat-up leather bomber jacket. It must be time to go. I tried to stand, and nearly fell off the stool. Magically, he was behind me. He caught me as I tumbled. His arms were like iron around my waist.

"Whoa, easy there. Let me drive you home, sweetheart," he said.

I thought, *What the hell, I've got nothing to lose.*

Wrong.

11

I lowered the window and let the cold night air blow on my face. Aidan was driving me home in my own car. He asked me once or twice if I was all right, and I managed a nod. Otherwise we didn't speak. I was grateful for his silence, and for the comfort of his presence. I couldn't stand the thought of being alone tonight in that big house that I'd built for my husband and me.

He pulled into the circular driveway and turned off the engine. Jumping out of the car, he came around and opened the door for me. Such a gentleman.

The distance from the Escalade's passenger seat to the ground seemed impossible.

"Here," he said, in a gentle tone, "put your hands on my shoulders."

I stepped down, and his arms went around me.

"Okay?" he whispered, his lips against my hair.

"Yes."

I leaned into him, my head swimming, savoring the feel of his long, hard body against mine. A vision flashed into my mind of us in bed together. Lying naked, our limbs intertwined, his hands running over my body. The thought of it took my breath away.

I leaned on Aidan's arm as we walked up the front steps. At the door, he took my keys from my hands and inserted them in the lock, as I crumpled sideways, my face against his shoulder. He smelled like the ocean, mixed with the tang of leather from his jacket. I'd been warned over the course of an entire female lifetime never to let a strange man into my house. But somehow every bit of caution I possessed had deserted me. Here I was—on a dark, deserted stretch of beach, my neighbors fled to the city—inviting the stranger inside. And not just any stranger. The one I'd seen a week earlier, possibly casing my house. I won't blame the vodka. My dad used drink as an excuse for every wrong thing he did, and my mom's excuse was my dad. I was drunk, yes, but I knew what I was doing. I felt awake, alive, fully conscious—more conscious than I'd felt in years.

Inside, I flipped on the lights and headed for the front of the house, stumbling slightly over the corner of a thick Tibetan carpet. Aidan was right there to grab me, and the grip of his hand on my upper arm sent warm waves through my body. In the kitchen, Aidan gazed around like a kid on Christmas morning. I was glad for how awestruck he seemed. He'd been taking care of me, and I'd been helpless. But now we could switch roles. In my house, I was in charge.

"I'll give you a tour," I said, and in my own mind, it was an invitation to more than that.

He lit up. "I'd like that. When I worked your party, I wasn't allowed inside."

I shrugged out of my coat and hung it in the hall closet, then held out my hand for his.

"Take off your jacket," I said.

He stripped it off and handed it to me, and I thought, *First piece of clothing, off.* My heart was beating so loud I thought he would hear it. I couldn't help it—my eyes went up and down his body, taking in the broad shoulders in a soft blue button-down, the flat stomach and narrow waist, the long legs. I took a deep breath, and met his eyes, only to find him watching *me,* appraisingly, like he knew what I was thinking. I felt a blush spread across my face. But I had no intention of turning back.

"Come," I said, and took his hand.

I led him through the living room, over to the wall of windows that faced the ocean. "The water's right there."

"I know. I can visualize it even at night. I love this place."

It was full dark outside, and our own reflections stared back at us. Aidan stood behind me, a full head taller, his outline blurred—or was that double vision from the drink? Our eyes met, and he put his hands on my waist. I leaned back against him, feeling his hot breath on my hair. He kissed my neck, and I shivered.

"Show me more," he said.

Show him *more*? Did that mean what I thought it did? I imagined undressing for him, unbuttoning my top, taking off my bra, my jeans, my panties, while he watched me in the window. The vision sent a sweet ache right down to my thighs. I would have done it then and there, but he took my hand and led me toward the living room, and I realized, no— he actually wants to see more of *the house*. For a second, I wondered if I'd gone crazy, imagining that a man so much younger, so good-looking, wanted me. But he did want me. If he also wanted my house, those two things didn't have to be mutually exclusive.

We made a circuit of the room, and I demonstrated its features like Vanna White showing off prizes. Touchscreens ran the lights and the blinds and the music. A soaring French limestone fireplace dominated the great room. I touched a button and flames sprang to life in the grate. We stepped through the French doors onto the terrace, and I flicked on the outdoor lights. The pool sparkled invitingly, but it was too chilly for a dip tonight, and certainly for a skinny-dip. The deck had its own built-in kitchen complete with pizza oven, enormous grill, hidden beverage drawers, and firepit. He admired it extravagantly, as the wind caught his words, and cut through the filmy fabric of my shirt.

"It's cold," I said. "Come back inside."

The media room featured a wet bar and a giant television screen, surround sound and two rows of leather recliners. He was a very appreciative audience, but I was getting impatient. If he didn't want to do anything, I'd rather that he leave, so I could retreat to my bed and wallow in my sorrows. But how to find out what he had in mind, short of coming out and asking?

I had an idea.

"I even have a light show. Come on, it's in the master," I said.

I took him by the hand and led him up the dramatic hanging staircase to my bedroom. We lay down side by side in the dark, on the enormous bed, with its mountain of pillows, and looked up at the ceiling. I pointed the remote, intensely aware of his body, inches from mine.

"Watch."

My voice was full of barely suppressed excitement. I pressed a button, and the ceiling above us began to change slowly, from black to indigo to bluish gray to glowing pink. The sound effects moved in sync with the dawn, evolving from the soft whoosh of the night breeze to the first stirrings of the birds to joyful chirping at the break of day. I shifted closer to Aidan, so our legs were touching. My body against the bed was liquid and melting, thrumming with the thought of what would happen next.

"That's incredible," he said.

"Just wait. Sunset's so beautiful, it'll make you cry."

We lived a perfect day together watching the colors wash across the ceiling. From the fresh light of early morning through the beaming radiance of noon, through the gathering of shadows as the day waned, our fingers intertwined. He raised my hand to his lips and turned it over, kissing my wrist, then my palm, slowly, lingeringly. The brush of his lips against the skin of my hand made me dizzy, and I thought, *It's been too long*. And, *Why shouldn't I?* And, *I deserve this*. At sunset, rapturous colors—pinks and lavenders, ochers and golds—cascaded across the ceiling accompanied by soft music and the sound of lapping waves. The round, red orb of the sun was beginning to touch the water. As we watched it sink into the waves, he moved his right leg until it rested between my two, and I knew then it would happen. I paused the display at the moment the sun disappeared into the water, then looked into Aidan's eyes. His face was bathed in the spectral glow, his eyes dark with lust.

"Isn't it magic?" I whispered.

"You're magic," he said.

The line was corny, but I ate it up. He pulled me toward him and took my face in his hands. I was conscious of my own heartbeat, of this singular moment in time. In bed with a complete stranger, I could forget who I was. I could become a different woman. My lips parted. He kissed me, and I kissed back harder. His tongue tasted sweet and tangy, of limes and vodka. He pulled my head back, kissing me with such fury that it was almost a bite, then moved his mouth to my neck, my ears. I thought, *I'll have marks in the morning,* and I loved the thought of that. My insides turned to mush, and I arched my back, quivering with need, pressing into him until I felt the bulge in his pants. I moaned and reached down for his belt buckle. No hesitation, no shame. I wanted him that badly.

He grabbed me and pulled me on top of him, so I was straddling him. His eyes were locked on my face, the pupils dark, as he grabbed me by the butt and pressed himself against me through our clothes. I rocked and squirmed, aching with need.

"Is this what you want?" he whispered.

"Yes."

"What do you want me to do to you? Say it."

"I want you to fuck me."

"Say please."

"Please."

"Strip for me first," he said, and his voice was rough. "Go ahead. Start with the shirt."

I leaned back and undid the top button of my filmy blouse, taking my time going down the row of buttons, loving the way his eyes were glued to my fingers. I let the blouse slip from my shoulders, luxuriating in the tickle of the fabric against my bare skin. Every sensation was heightened. I'd worn my sexiest bra tonight—sheer, push-up, black. I must've been planning ahead, without fully realizing it, or admitting it to myself. My breasts swelled out of it now like an invitation. He reached out and yanked the bra lower, so my nipples showed, and made this primitive grunting sound at the sight of them. I thought I would faint.

He pulled me toward him. His mouth found my breasts, and he grazed them with his teeth, first one, then the other. I was panting with pleasure. Then he grabbed my waist and flipped me, so he was on top. He hovered there, the front of his jeans tented with his hard-on, as I writhed. To be wanted like this, by this gorgeous guy—I was swooning. My eyes closed, and my head swam.

"Look at me," he commanded, as he grabbed my arms and pinned them to the bed.

I opened my eyes. He let go and took a step back, yanking his pants down and his shirt over his head. Then he ripped my jeans and panties off and stared down at me. Instead of plunging into me then and there like I expected—like I wanted, *needed*—he got down on his knees. He leaned forward and blew softly on the sensitive spot between my legs, and I shuddered with desire. He moved higher up, kissing my abdomen, then my navel, his lips caressing, his tongue licking and teasing as he moved slowly back down. My legs went rigid, and drunken, rapturous tears leaked from my eyes. Then he slipped two fingers inside me, and I moaned in bliss.

"Mmm, so wet," he said, as his fingers moved slowly in and out.

By the time I finally felt his tongue down there, I was panting and bathed in sweat. My hands grasped the duvet, and I screamed at him not to stop. He took his time, and I cried out, shuddering, as the orgasm washed over me in intense waves. Then he stood up and grabbed me by the ankles, yanking my legs toward his shoulders, and plunging into me hard, stroking in and out with perfect control. I cried out with every thrust, holding on to his arms, mesmerized. I couldn't remember the last time I'd had sex like this. Maybe I never had. Just when it was about to become too much, when I was about to beg him to stop, he started groaning. He bucked and twisted, gripping my thighs, and collapsed against me.

I was so happy I laughed. His skin was warm and slick with sweat. I breathed in the musky scent of sex, closed my eyes, and sighed. The perfect one-night stand, to distract me from my marriage troubles.

"That was great. Thank you," I said.

"I love you," he whispered, as he kissed my neck.

My eyes flew open.

12

I woke in semidarkness to feel the room spinning and vomit rising in my throat. Aidan had flung his arm across my chest as he slept, pinning me to the bed. I threw it off and ran to the bathroom, where I spent the next five minutes on my knees on the cold tile floor, heaving into the toilet. When I was finished, I went to the sink and rinsed my mouth. I'd woken up hungover more than once in recent days, after drinking myself senseless to forget Jason's betrayal. But this was the mother of all hangovers. My skin was clammy, my legs were shaking, and my whole body ached. There was a throbbing behind my left eye so bad it felt like someone had plunged an icepick in there. I gulped down some Advil, drank an entire glass of water, then stood completely still, waiting to see if they would stay down. When it seemed likely I wasn't going to hurl again, I took a deep breath, and only then did I realize how much I reeked. Of *sex*.

The gravity of the situation hit home. I'd picked up the local bartender and brought him to my house, to my bed, for a one-night stand, and everybody in the bar saw me do it. I barely knew this man, and he was still here, fast asleep and snoring. I wished to God this hadn't happened. But it had, and now I had to face him—in my bedroom. At least I wasn't worried that he was dangerous. But the shame of it made me feel like jumping out of my skin. Ugh, I wanted him gone, out. I wanted to take a shower, talk to my daughter on the phone, drink a cup of tea, pretend everything was normal and that I hadn't just violated every rule of decent behavior that my Italian Catholic mother raised me with. I wanted to get rid of this guy—*now*.

Wait. Did he say he loved me last night?

The thought was crazy. I must've hallucinated it in a drunken stupor.

Okay, deep breath. I'd wake Aidan up and ask him to leave. Simple. No problem. Working in that bar, I imagined he was the king of the casual hookup, going home with a different woman every night. He wouldn't expect breakfast and sweet nothings. Not even a kiss good-bye. Just a pat on the butt, a thank-you, maybe a cup of coffee in a to-go mug if he was on his way somewhere.

I could handle that.

Wait. He drove here in my car. How would he leave?

I would call him an Uber.

None of my credit cards worked.

Fuck.

I needed to take a shower before I could solve this problem. Right now, my body felt like it was held together with Scotch tape and rubber bands, and my fuzzy tongue could barely form words. The hot water would revive me. There was a pink glow around the bathroom blinds. The sun was rising, and if I wanted to get Aidan out of here without being seen, I needed to do it in the next half hour. After that, the gardeners and caretakers and housekeepers would start showing up. Any stray neighbor who'd happened to venture out here past Labor Day would be heading into town for their morning Starbucks and a copy of the *Times*. And Mrs. Eberhardt, the neighborhood busybody, would be sure to look out her window at the least opportune moment. Francine Eberhardt was a retired school teacher who lived in the one old-time beach shack on the bluff that hadn't been pulled down and replaced with a palace yet. When my house was under construction, Francine called often to complain about the noise, or how many vehicles were parked on the street, or the fact that the construction workers were smoking in public. I did my best to handle her complaints with good grace, but we didn't have an easy relationship. The thought of Francine knowing my darkest secret made me distinctly uncomfortable.

I flipped the lights on, then winced and turned them off again. The master bath was massive, with acres of shining white tile, gleaming glass, brushed nickel—altogether too much glitter for my tender eyes at the moment. I turned the shower to full force, made it as hot as I could bear, then stepped through the glass door into the deluge. There was an enormous rain showerhead and jets spraying from both sides. I let the water pound me, but it couldn't wash away what I'd done last night, or how much my life had changed in the space of a week. My marriage had imploded. My husband took our money and ran. And I morphed into some drunken cougar who picked up men in bars and brought them home for sex. Panic overwhelmed me. I felt like I couldn't breathe. I started to cry, the harsh sound of my sobs filling the steamy stall. Then, with a sudden rush of cold air, Aidan stepped into the shower, naked, and pulled me into his arms.

"Hey, hey. Don't cry. What's the matter, baby? I'm here. Everything's okay," he whispered, pushing my sodden hair back from my face, looking down at me tenderly. His body was sleek and hard under the rush of water. In that moment, even though I wanted him gone, I wanted him to stay even more. At least *somebody* was here, to hold me, to listen to my troubles.

"What is it? You can tell me anything," he said.

I was crying so hard that I could barely force the words out.

"My . . . husband . . . left me."

God, it hurt to admit that. Aidan was the first person I'd told other than Lynn. I cried even louder.

"I know," he said.

He kissed my forehead and stroked my back.

"How did you know?"

"I heard it at your party. People were talking. Look, you'll be fine. I promise. I'm gonna take care of you."

"How can you say I'll be fine? We've been married twenty years. Out of the blue, he left me for some Russian whore. She's not even pretty. He broke my heart. And took all my money."

"He took the *money?*"

"Yes."

"Well, shit. That *is* a problem. We have to get that back."

We? I let the weirdness of that slip by, so desperate was I to believe it was possible to get my money back. I imagined he had some legitimate plan in mind, involving lawyers and court orders and such. Why I thought that, I can't explain. I was assuming he was normal, I guess. In fact, Aidan's experience with the law was all from the wrong side, but I didn't know that then.

"*How?*" I asked. "How can you get it back?"

"Don't worry. I know what to do. I'll take care of your husband for you," he said.

I'll take care of your husband. Those words should have terrified me. But they went right by me, because of what he did next.

Aidan kissed me deeply, his tongue finding its way into my mouth. Then he took me by the shoulders and spun me around, so I faced the tile wall. The water cascaded over us as he grabbed my hips and thrust into me from behind. I should have known that Aidan was bad news. I should have heard the meaning behind his words. Not, *I'm sorry to hear about your problems.* Not, *I sympathize,* or even, *I have a smart lawyer friend you can call.* But, *I want you, I want your money, and I'll kill your husband to get it if that's what it takes.* I didn't hear any of that. I couldn't, over the sound of rushing water, of my own moans of pleasure. There's no pretty way to say this. I wanted to feel better. I wanted the sex. At that moment, nothing else mattered.

13

She looked beautiful wrapped in a bathrobe, sitting at the kitchen table, so beautiful it was a crime. Even the bathrobe was beautiful. White terry cloth, thick as a rug, like you'd get in a five-star hotel. Not that Aidan had ever stayed in such a place, but he could imagine. The kitchen table was beautiful, too. Rustic oak, built by a skilled carpenter, with a sparkly chandelier hanging over it, and a view of the ocean waves rolling in the distance. And not just any view, but the view he'd loved since he was a little kid and first realized that the world could be beautiful. So, yeah, the robe and the table and the view of the ocean had moved him this morning. But it was the woman who made the real magic. *Caroline*. She was his good-luck charm, come to rescue him, and he loved her for it. Hell, he plain loved her, as she sat there laughing, her skin glowing, tendrils of golden hair curling around her face.

"I haven't had this much fun in a long time," she said, and he leaned down to kiss her on the mouth.

They'd had sex in the shower, then fallen back into the big bed, with the down comforter, and done it for a long time. Every position. He made her come three times, screaming like a banshee. She was starved for it. Then they slept till noon, and he woke up with her tangled in his arms, her hair cascading onto his chest, and he thought, *This is what I've been waiting for.* He loved this place, this house, this woman—completely. It scared him how much. He was almost embarrassed to think it, but meeting Caroline felt like destiny. The bad times were a trial, a test that he must've passed, or how else would he have graduated to this incredible reward.

He lived it again in his mind. Watching her sleep. How she woke up and smiled. And how they made love again, till his cock was raw, and his heart so full that he didn't know how he could ever pay her back. He'd worked as a short-order cook before the bartending gig. He learned at the halfway house, and he was damn good at it, would've kept at it except it was hard work and the pay wasn't as good as tending bar, where he made mad tips. But cooking was one way he could thank her. He was hungry anyway, after all the sex. When he offered to make breakfast, she lit up at the idea, and they wound up down here in the kitchen with Aidan standing at the fancy stove.

"You like your eggs scrambled or fried?" he said.

"Mmm. Scrambled. Thank you for taking care of me. You make me feel good, Aidan."

"Yeah, I noticed," he said, and she blushed adorably. In the misty morning light, she looked like a girl, like they could have been the same age.

He got out a pan and took the eggs from the giant Sub-Zero fridge. Even the eggs were magical here. Blue-green beauties from the organic farm, they shone like jewels. He cracked one into a bowl. The yolk was vivid orange, and Aidan thought, *Take me out in a box, I'm never fucking leaving this place.*

He brought plates to the table. She smiled up at him, grabbed his hand, kissed it, and he thought about having sex with her again. But this thing between them was more than sex. He didn't want her to think of him as just some stud. He wanted to get to know her, and for her to know him. Well, not everything about him, not yet. He'd be nervous telling her about his past. He would start with the good things, and there *were* good things. He'd make her see.

He turned on the burner, and the blue flame was beautiful to him.

Scrambled eggs and toast—simple, you'd think, but he had a special technique involving butter and a long, slow cook over low heat that made them extra creamy. He took his time, humming as he worked, enjoying the feel of her eyes on him. When the eggs were perfect, he carried the pan over to the table and turned them out onto her plate.

She took a bite and closed her eyes, savoring.

"Mmm. These are the best eggs I've ever had," she said.

He served himself, sat down and tasted. He couldn't disagree.

"I'm all right at a couple of things," he said, ducking his head modestly.

"All right? More like amazing." She raised an eyebrow suggestively.

Now it was his turn to blush. But he couldn't stand it if this was only about sex for her. People refusing to take him seriously was the story of his life. He wanted more from Caroline, and she kind of owed him, didn't she? After the way he took care of her last night. Maybe she didn't owe him love, or even gratitude, but she owed him respect. He hoped she wouldn't turn into some stuck-up bitch, or he'd be really sad. He ate his eggs in silence, staring down at the plate, until she teased him with her bare foot on his leg.

"Cat got your tongue? I didn't take you for the silent type," she said, nudging him playfully. Her toes were painted the color of blood.

Her legs where they emerged from the bathrobe were perfect and shapely. An hour ago, those legs had been wrapped around his neck. He could take her back to bed and make her beg for it. He had power here. He needed to be more confident, and not be cowed by her beauty or her money.

"I'm feeling cooped up," he said. "It would be nice to get outside. What if we went for a walk on the beach?"

"Oh." She put her fork down. "That's not such a good idea."

Figures, uh-huh. Should he be surprised if she was like everyone else?

"You're embarrassed to be seen with me," he said.

"*No.* If I was, would I have been hanging all over you in the bar last night?"

"Maybe. You were pretty drunk."

She leaned toward him, taking his hands and looking into his eyes. "Stop it, okay? I want to be with you. I want us to go places together. Just not right in front of my house where my neighbors can see. I'm married, you know."

He had this funny buzzing feeling in his head. He got it sometimes, like a warning bell, a bullshit detector. Was she playing him somehow? But she was saying all the right things. Things he wanted to hear.

"All right. Where, then?" he asked.

"What about your place? I'd love to see where you live."

He turned away, so she wouldn't see how her request unnerved him. The two of them lived in different worlds, and he'd been ignoring it, hoping she would, too, or better yet, that she hadn't noticed. He was working on changing his situation. Taking her to that shithole would blow the illusion, would make her see him for someone he wasn't—or someone he was, but only temporarily, because of a string of rotten luck that she was going to help him reverse.

"Ah, it's messy. You know, guy living alone, and all," he said.

That was a lie. Aidan was a neat freak who cared for his few possessions meticulously. He did his laundry at the Wash N' Go every Monday like clockwork, and never left a dirty dish in the sink. But his run-down studio apartment near the edge of town wasn't much better than an SRO, with a hot plate and a mini-fridge standing in for a real kitchen, and a cramped bathroom with a cheap plastic shower. The furniture consisted of a sofa he got for free off Craigslist, a plastic table and chairs from Walmart, and a twin bed from his mother's attic that smelled like piss and mothballs. Aidan's paycheck went to his clothes and his car, the restitution payments from his conviction, and the rent. When he got done with all that, he was so broke that he scrounged his meals at work.

Caroline would hate him if she knew how he really lived, and he'd hate her right back for knowing. He was already walking that thin line with her, the one between love and hate. He loved Caroline, but he hated city people. They were the reason guys like him couldn't live in this town anymore. Coming in with their millions, buying up every shotgun shack to build their mega-mansions. Gramps saw how it was going and sold, but that was years ago, and the land changed hands two or three times since then. It made the speculators rich, and Aidan and his brother never saw a penny. Then Caroline came in like a queen, riding in her golden carriage. Aidan was the guy running along behind, cleaning up the horse shit. If she didn't know that, he wasn't about to enlighten her by letting her see his crappy apartment.

"I know somewhere better," he said. "A place you would never find on your own, that's really special. Come on, get dressed, I'm taking you out."

14

"Where are we going?" I asked.

"You'll see," Aidan said, his mouth set in a hard line.

We were in my car, speeding along the main road. Aidan was driving. The sky had clouded over. The wind had picked up, and the trees swayed. In the gaps between the houses, the surf pounded the beach like it was angry. A storm was coming.

"I thought you needed to go back to the Red Anchor to pick up your car. But we're headed in the opposite direction," I said.

He stared out the window, stone-faced, and didn't reply. A cold knot of fear gathered in my stomach. The first time I saw Aidan, I knew he was trouble. But I was so desperate for distraction, and he was so tempting, that I ignored the warning signs. When we were in the shower together, and he said he'd *take care of* Jason for me, I knew I should have kicked him out. But I wanted the sex. When he offered to make me scrambled eggs for breakfast this morning, I should have asked him to leave instead. But the sight of him, standing shirtless and barefoot in my kitchen, the morning sun illuminating his perfect body, silenced my doubts. After breakfast, when he leaned over to kiss me, I should have pulled away. Instead, my lips parted, and I kissed him back. He drew

me to my feet and pulled me tight against him. We were on the verge of
going to bed again when he said something that made my blood run cold.

"Once your husband's out of the picture, we can do this all day."

I pulled back.

"Out of the picture? What's that supposed to mean?" I'd said, looking him in the eye.

"Nothing," he replied.

His arms tightened around my waist. It took an effort to break loose
from that grip.

"*Nothing?* Aidan, I don't know what you're suggesting, but you have
no right to get involved in my marriage."

"Too late. I'm already involved."

"No, you're not. You barely know me."

His eyes narrowed, and his entire body tensed.

"We spent the night in bed together. I'd say I know you pretty well.
You think you can use me and show me the door? Well, I got news for
you. That's not gonna happen."

"You're scaring me," I said, and backed away. "Please leave."

His face changed. "Hey, I'm sorry. That was dumb. I say stupid things
sometimes. I apologize. Forgive me, okay?"

I didn't entirely trust the change in his tone, not after that display.
But I wanted to end this quickly, with a friendly goodbye, and Aidan
out of my house—and my life. So, I appeased him. It's what women do.

"Apology accepted. But I do have a busy day."

"C'mon, Caroline, lighten up. It was a joke."

"Okay. So . . . we should get together again soon. Let me call you
an Uber—"

"An *Uber?* If you insist on making me leave because I said one wrong
thing—"

"No, no, not at all. I accept your apology, totally. But I'm going
through a divorce. I have to see the lawyer today."

"At least give me a ride back to my truck. Like I did for you. Is that
too much to ask?"

If I gave him a ride to the restaurant, he'd be gone, and we'd be done. That seemed like a reasonable price to pay to get rid of him.

"I'd be happy to. Get dressed. I'll get the keys," I said.

While Aidan went upstairs to get his clothes, I looked everywhere for my car keys but couldn't find them. I heard a jingling sound and turned around. He stood there holding the keys by a fingertip, a sly grin on his face.

"Looking for these?" he said.

The grin that had struck me as so laid-back, so surfer-cool last night, gave me a chill in the light of day. But, I told myself, the keys were in his coat pocket from before. That's all. I walked toward him, holding out my hand. He just laughed and shook his head and ducked out the door. By the time I got to the car, he was in the driver's seat. When he headed in the opposite direction from the Red Anchor, there was nothing I could do but try to remain calm and look for my cue to exit.

Aidan turned at the sign for Glenhampton Town Beach. At least he was taking me to a public place, I thought. Then I saw that the ticket booth at the entrance was deserted, with a sign posted that said, CLOSED FOR SEASON. Aidan pulled into a spot up front, near the boardwalk, and turned off the car.

"What are we doing here?" I asked.

"I have a hankering to walk on the beach with you."

There was a note of sarcasm in his voice that made me wonder if he was playing with me. His hands on the steering wheel looked coiled and tense.

"Not today, Aidan. The beach is closed. The weather's awful. And like I said, I have a lot to do."

"You don't have anything that can't wait. Let's go."

That was a command, not a request. He got out and slammed the door. He had my car keys, so I didn't have much choice. My chest tight with anxiety, I followed him.

The parking lot was built on top of a rocky outcropping that overlooked the ocean. We walked past bathrooms and a snack bar locked up tight for the season and descended a rough wooden staircase down to the beach. The wind pressed against me, whipping my hair into my face and making the descent precarious on the slippery steps. The beach was deserted, studded with rocks and driftwood, backed by rugged cliffs. A red flag snapped in the wind, signaling dangerous conditions. A couple of surfers tempted fate out on the water. I kept expecting them to go tumbling and get sucked under. But they were remarkably resilient, disappearing behind a wave only to reappear moments later closer to shore.

Taking my hand, Aidan led me down the beach, away from where the surfers were coming ashore. His face was determined, his eyes fixed on the far distance, his grip on my hand so tight that it hurt. A fine spray of sand blew into my eyes, and I had to raise my voice to be heard over the wind.

"I don't like this. Let's go back."

"There's something I want to show you. Come on."

He nodded toward the horizon and kept marching. We came to a second rock outcropping that jutted into the water. At low tide, you could presumably walk around it and continue down the beach without getting your feet wet. But now, with the surf pounding, the rock divided the beach in two, leaving only a thin sliver of sand exposed to walk on. If you tried to go around the rock, you might get hit by a wave and pulled under. But Aidan headed right for it.

"Is this safe?"

"I wouldn't take you here if it wasn't. Come on, it's worth it."

A wave crashed against the rocks, foaming and swirling. Aidan watched it, and, timing the movement precisely, pulled me forward into the receding water. It came up to my ankles, soaking through my suede boots. We rounded the rock, reaching the other side just as the next wave hit. The spray from it hit me in the face, soaking my hair and my clothes, the cold such a shock that I gasped.

A new stretch of beach spread out before us, magnificently empty under the cloudy sky. But Aidan ignored it and made a beeline for a large boulder that rose from the sand, close up against the rock outcropping. He ducked behind the boulder, which was as tall as a man. When he didn't reemerge after a minute or two, I walked up to it. No Aidan. He'd disappeared into thin air. With my car keys.

"Aidan?"

The boulder was blocking an opening in the rock. The mouth of the cave was narrow, its sandy floor covered with an inch or so of seawater and speckled with foam and bits of seaweed. A strong smell of brine and damp emanated from inside.

I had a bad feeling about this place.

15

Caroline offered to give him a lift home. On the way, he would show her a special place. There were things he knew that she didn't. Things only a local would know, someone who lived closer to the ground than she did. Maybe he was rough around the edges, but she liked that, or else, why be with him? He suspected it was nostalgia. The harshness of her accent in unguarded moments gave her away. She hadn't always been the lady of the manor.

They got all the way to the cave, and she didn't want to go inside.

"Don't be afraid," he said, as they stood side by side, staring into the entrance.

He could understand why she'd hesitate. It was dark in there, and she didn't have the history with the place that Aidan did. He used to run away to there when things were hard at home, pretending he was like Butch Cassidy at the hole in the wall. The first time he got drunk, the first time he got high, and the first time he had sex were all in that cave. Good times. Bad times, too. The one girl he'd ever loved had spent time with him in there. Then she'd shared the place with someone else, and the aftermath was so ugly that Aidan was paying for it to this day. But that wouldn't happen with Caroline. She was better than Samantha. She was a lady.

He took her by the hand. "It gets wider in a few feet. Light comes in from a hole in the roof. It's magical, you'll see. You have to trust me."

He let her go first, creeping along behind her. Within a few feet, the narrow entrance fed into a space the size of a small bedroom. Rough rock walls slanted up to a peaked ceiling, where the hole revealed a patch of sky. The light filtering through was delicate and shimmering, like the inside of a seashell. And it smelled like the ocean. Aidan took off his jacket and used it to sweep sand off a low, flat boulder.

"Your chair, my lady," he said.

She hesitated, hanging back near the opening.

"What's the matter?"

"Nothing."

"It's okay, promise. Come here, I'll protect you."

She walked toward him, but stopped short of the rock, seeming so shy all of a sudden that she reminded him of the deer he'd seen this morning from her kitchen window, drinking from the swimming pool. Caroline's house, on his grandfather's land. It was a magic combination, and it was within his grasp. Like the woman herself. He reached out and put his hands on her waist, pulling her closer, holding her eyes with his. She stopped resisting, and her body relaxed. Then he slid a hand between her legs and felt her up through her jeans until she moaned. He stood up, drew her closer, grazed her lips with his.

"I used to come here in high school," he said, kissing her neck, her ear. She trembled in his arms.

"Matter of fact, I lost my virginity on this rock," he said.

"Really? How old were you?"

"Fifteen. She was twenty-two. My boss at the Food Mart."

"Another older woman? Seriously?"

"Yeah, she was married, too."

"Wow."

He looked into her eyes. "Is that weird? What was your first time like? Wait, let me guess. You were in college, and you ended up married to the guy?"

"How'd you know?"

"Because you're such a rich girl."

"I'm a *nice* girl."

He laughed. "Not if you're hanging out with me, you're not."

He kissed the freckles on the bridge of her nose. Those freckles were like a promise. That she was the girl next door. That she could be his. Then he kissed her again and knew it was true.

16

Waves crashed on the sand. Gulls spiraled overhead, their shrill cries making the empty beach feel desolate. Nobody knew where I was, except for Aidan. My daughter, my sister—they believed I was safe at home. My faithless husband, if he bothered to think of me at all, wouldn't know to worry. These things occurred to me as I hesitated at the entrance to the cave. Where had Aidan gone? Was he inside there? I needed my car keys. I stepped forward to take a closer look. Suddenly he was behind me, and I jumped. He'd walked around the boulder and snuck up behind me like an immature kid.

"What the *hell*, Aidan."

"Go in," he said, looming over me.

"What? No."

"I said, get in there," he said, and gave me a shove.

My stomach flipped as he pushed me through the narrow entrance into a larger, wider space. It was dank and claustrophobic, with dripping rock walls as thick as the cliff itself. He guided me toward a low rock that was covered with sand, the ground around it strewn with cigarette butts and used condoms.

"What the hell are you doing?" I said, my voice quavering.

"I didn't want you to miss this place."

"So you *shoved* me?"

"I wanted you to see. Magic, isn't it?"

"It's—dirty," I said.

Aidan's face tightened.

"Not fancy enough for you, princess?"

"It's not that."

"Then what?"

I knew what he was after. But I was put off by him now, even anxious about what he might do. I didn't want sex. What I wanted was to tell him this was over. That it had been a wonderful distraction, but now it needed to end so we could go back to our real lives. The trouble was—crazy as it sounds, since I was a forty-three-year-old housewife, and Aidan was a gorgeous young guy—I was convinced he'd take it badly. You'd think it would be the other way around. That I'd be the one to get overly attached after a one-night stand. But I hadn't, and it was beginning to seem like he had. We were alone in a cave on a deserted beach. Aidan stood between me and the exit. Making him upset in this confined space was not a smart idea. I floundered around for an excuse.

"I'm—I'm claustrophobic," I said. "I'll have an anxiety attack if I stay here."

He came up to me, took me by the shoulders, and looked down into my eyes.

"Nothing bad will happen to you while I'm around. Promise. I won't let it, okay? Come sit down."

He took off his jacket and brushed sand from the big rock, then kicked some of the detritus that surrounded the rock into the corner. I'd made it clear that I wanted to go. It was beginning to worry me that he wouldn't listen. While his back was turned, I edged toward the exit.

"I'm nervous in here, Aidan. Can we go, please?"

"Give it a chance."

"You showed me the place, now I need to leave. I've been telling you all morning I have things to do."

His face fell. "You're mad at me. What did I do wrong?"

"I'm—I'm stressed, okay? My life is a mess. I don't have time for this right now."

I moved toward the exit. He blocked me.

"Let me take your mind off it."

"That only works for so long."

"It'll work again. I promise."

He kissed me on the mouth. I didn't kiss back. His teeth ground against my lips as he pushed me backward toward the rock. My legs hit it, and I sat down hard. I felt the rock, rough and cold, through my jeans. Aidan sat beside me and started groping, his hands rough on my body, my breasts.

"I want you so much," he whispered, his breath hot against my neck.

He reached for the buttons of my shirt. I pushed his hands away.

"Aidan, no. Stop it."

He pulled back momentarily. His expression had changed again, this time to fury. His face was red, his mouth screwed up like he wanted to spit.

"What's the problem? I was good enough for you last night."

He grabbed my hand and pressed it to the bulge in his pants. I pulled away.

"I said no."

"You don't mean it."

We wrestled. He was bigger and stronger. My heart beat wildly. Before I could get up and run, he'd unzipped. His hands tugged at the waist of my jeans. He pulled me under him, stood above me, yanked his jeans down to his knees. There was no point in screaming. The rock walls were too thick, the wind and the surf too loud on the beach. If I yelled, or fought, or resisted in any way, I'd only make him angrier. I couldn't predict how he'd react, because I barely knew him, but he might hurt me. The Catholic girl inside my head, the one my mother had raised to feel responsible when men misbehaved, was saying, *What the hell did you expect? He's not gonna to take no for an answer when you already told him yes.*

I was about to give in when I heard a noise. Above the sound of

Aidan's rushed breathing, there was a scrambling, a dislodging of pebbles near the cave entrance that attracted my attention. Aidan jumped off me, pulling up his pants. The two surfer dudes we'd seen before out on the water stood there in dripping wet suits, staring at us.

17

When the surfers barged in, I saw my chance. Gathering my clothes around me, I pushed past them out of the cave. Outside, I gulped the salty air in relief, but the feeling only lasted a second. The tide had come roaring in. Waves pounded the rock cliff, completely obscuring the narrow strip of sand that Aidan and I had crossed twenty minutes earlier. If I tried to make it to the other side of the beach now, I'd be swept out to sea. Before I could figure out what to do, Aidan hurtled out of the cave after me, buttoning his shirt as he came. The surfers had stayed behind in the cave, and he was by himself, which meant I was alone with him again. As he approached, I took a step back toward the crashing surf, my heart pounding.

"Hey, babe, I'm really sorry," he said. "I never thought we'd get interrupted in there. I know that was embarrassing. Are you okay?"

Aidan smiled—a gentle, laid-back smile that said he was the nicest guy in the world. I might have believed it, if he hadn't tried to assault me in there. He was acting like nothing was wrong. I wanted to find my car and get the hell away from this place. And from him. But how could I, when the escape route was blocked?

He caught my nervous glance at the waves.

"No worries," Aidan said. "Tide comes in on the regular. There's another path to the parking lot, c'mon."

He tried to grab my hand, but I dodged him. He gave me a funny look, then squinted up at the thick, black clouds.

"If you don't want to get soaked, you'd better come along," he said. "Sky's about to open."

He knew what he was talking about. As I watched him walk away, fat drops of icy rain began to fall, making plopping sounds in the sand. The chill came up through my shoes immediately. The damp penetrated my light jacket, and I started to shiver. Aidan sped up, throwing a last glance over his shoulder to see if I would follow. I didn't want to. But I got worried that he'd take his secret shortcut to the parking lot and drive away with my car, leaving me stranded on this desolate beach in a storm. I walked after him, breaking into a jog as the rain fell harder. Water streamed into my eyes as he disappeared into a narrow break in the rocks. By the time I got there, he was gone. The steep, sandy trail twisted upward between rock walls. Behind me, the rain pounded, and the surf was wild. I stepped onto the path and began climbing. By the time I made it to the parking lot, my dripping hair plastered to my head and my lungs burning, Aidan was in the driver's seat of my car, with the engine running and the wipers going. I sank into the passenger seat, grateful for the blasting heater.

I was praying we'd go to the restaurant now, and that would be that. But he drove me to his apartment instead. Aidan lived at the Sea Breeze Cottages. The name was a lie. There were no cottages, only a long, low apartment building with a crumbling parking lot, painted a dull tan that looked dirty in the rain. And for a sea breeze, you'd have to use your imagination, since we were miles from the beach. I remembered places like this from my Long Island girlhood. Once upon a time, my friends lived in them. I'd worked hard to avoid that fate, and I had no intention of looking back.

There were ten apartments, each with a small concrete stoop, a metal door, and a parking space in front. Aidan pulled into a parking space in the middle of the complex.

"Come inside, I'll make us some coffee," he said.

My phone buzzed in my jacket pocket, giving me an excuse to stall. I pulled it out to see a text from Hannah lighting up the screen, all in caps.

WTF MOM DAD TOLD ME YOU'RE SPLITTING??

I hadn't spoken to my daughter in two days. I'd been putting off breaking the awful news about the divorce. It never occurred to me that Jason would tell her first. He hadn't been returning my calls, so I assumed he wasn't talking to Hannah either. But they always talked. I should realize that. They were closer to each other than either one of them was to me.

Aidan frowned. "Who's it from?" he said, and I heard jealousy in his tone.

"My daughter."

"You have a daughter? Why didn't you tell me that before?"

"It didn't come up."

"That's a pretty big thing to leave out. Don't you think I'm entitled to know?"

Entitled? My jaw dropped. I was tempted to utter a few choice words, but doing that would only delay the moment where Aidan got out of my car, and out of my life.

"It's hardly like we've told each other our life stories," I said. "I need to call her back."

"How old is she? Does she live with you? What's her name?"

The prospect of discussing Hannah with Aidan made me nervous. It had been a mistake to mention her at all. Aidan had threatened Jason, in so many words. I didn't know him well enough to know whether to take the threat seriously. But I didn't trust him, and I certainly wasn't about to give him details about my daughter. I wanted my car keys and then I wanted Aidan out of my life. But he wasn't going easily. He stared at me with arms crossed, waiting for an answer.

"Aidan. I need to speak to my daughter, and I'd like some privacy. *Please.*"

The "please" seemed to help.

"All right," he said, grudgingly.

He stepped out into the rain, then stuck his head back in the car.

"Come inside when you're done." He slammed the door.

He'd taken my car keys again, of course. As the rain pounded the windshield, I dropped my head into my hands wearily. I was sick of this game and annoyed at myself. I'd dodged a bullet. If the surfers hadn't stumbled into the cave when they did, Aidan would likely have forced himself on me. He could try that again if we were alone in his apartment. But my keys—I had to get them back. I could call the cops. I didn't want to; it would be embarrassing for both of us. But he wasn't leaving me much choice.

I opened my phone, contemplating whether to call 911. Then I remembered. The police would never help me. Aidan's brother was the chief. It was my own fault for getting involved with a complete stranger. I wanted to scream. But the phone rang in my hands, startling me into dropping it and catching it again. It was Hannah.

"Hi, sweetheart," I said. "I was about to call you."

I heard soft snuffling on the other end of the line, and my stomach dropped.

"Oh, baby," I said. "Hannah. Honey, please, don't cry."

"Mom? How could you do this?"

I paused. Was she taking Jason's side, when he was the one who cheated?

"Me? What did *I* do?" I asked.

"How could you not tell me, Mom?" she said, her voice rising in grief.

"Oh. Well, I was working up to telling you."

"If you guys split, it's like my whole life was a lie."

"This has nothing to do with you. It's about Dad and me."

"Were you purposely staying together until I left home? That makes me feel lied to."

"No. Nothing like that."

"Why didn't you tell me you were having problems?"

"I didn't know, until the party."

"You were going to let him leave the country, and not even tell me?"

"Leave the country? What are you talking about?"

"He said he's going away on business for a while."

"But—out of the country? *Where?*"

Hell, no. Not with my money, he wasn't.

"I don't know. Mexico or something? He's coming here tonight to say goodbye to me."

Mexico? I needed to see a lawyer, immediately.

"He's coming to your dorm?"

"No. I don't want to talk in front of my roommate. We're going to a restaurant."

"Which restaurant?"

"Why does that matter?"

"Hannah, I'm coming to that dinner," I said.

"You're not invited. He doesn't want to talk to you."

"He's not allowed to decide that."

She paused. "I mean, I think he is."

I know that all the parenting books say don't air your dirty laundry with your kids. Well, screw that. Jason betrayed me. Hannah deserved to know what sort of man her father was, so she could make an informed decision about whose side to take. Otherwise, she'd automatically take his side. I knew their relationship, and I could predict that with certainty.

"Hannah, listen to me. Your dad is treating me very badly. He's *cheating* on me, and he refuses to see me or answer my calls. And he's cut off all the bank accounts," I said.

There was silence at the end of the line.

"Hannah?"

"I can't believe he'd do that."

"Well, he did."

"What did *you* do to him?"

"Whose side are you on?"

But it was obvious. Hannah had always been a Daddy's girl. It hurt me terribly, since I was the one who sacrificed everything for her, but I'd never been able to compete with their bond.

"I'm not on anybody's side. It's not about sides," she said, but she was wrong. Or lying. Hannah knew it was about sides, and she was taking Jason's.

"Did you know he brought his girlfriend to the party at the beach house? I bet he didn't tell you that, huh? She's a real piece of work, too, so slutty—"

"Mom, stop. I don't want to hear it. I don't even believe you."

"You have to let me come to this dinner, Hannah."

"Stop it. Can't you see how awful this is for me? Dad isn't acting crazy like this."

"No, because he's the one who left. He's the guilty party. Don't you see—"

"I have to go."

"*Hannah*—"

"Goodbye, Mom."

The phone said CALL ENDED. I stared at it, shell-shocked. My own daughter had hung up on me. And there it was. The ugly truth. Not only had Jason taken my money. He was taking my daughter, too.

There was a knock on the window. I looked up to see Aidan standing in the pouring rain, holding a bedraggled umbrella. He motioned to me to come inside. Insane as it was, I opened the door. I was hurting so badly from the phone call with Hannah. And Aidan was the only person in my life right now who seemed to want my company. Nothing so terrible had really happened in the cave. I didn't actually know what he would have done if those surfers hadn't showed up. If I kept saying no, he probably would've backed off.

As I watched, a middle-aged woman stepped out of the apartment next to his, letting out a scraggly-looking dog. The dog ran over and lifted his leg at the dumpster, while the woman retreated inside the metal screen door.

What was I so worried about? Aidan had neighbors. The walls in a place like this were paper-thin. If he tried to hurt me, I would scream. Nothing bad could happen.

I was wrong about that, too.

18

Aidan's apartment was as bad inside as the outside foretold. A single room with a tiny kitchenette, it was shabby to the point of being squalid. But he took my coat like a gentleman. A coffeemaker perked cheerily on the kitchen counter.

"I know what you're thinking," he said. "This apartment is a dump. The thing is, I don't spend much time here. It's just a place to crash. I got all my money tied up in investments."

Investments? Right. Like I believed that.

"That's smart," I said. "And the apartment's fine."

The coffeemaker beeped. Aidan poured me a cup. I cradled it in my hands for warmth, then sipped carefully. The coffee was hot and strong, and my fingers began to defrost. Aidan rummaged in a closet and pulled out a fresh towel, which he draped around my shoulders. It smelled surprisingly clean. I put the coffee down and dried my hair.

"You look like a drowned rat," he said, affection in his voice.

I hadn't entirely forgotten his behavior in the cave. But if he continued to take care of me like this, I might be willing to forgive it, or at least view it as an anomaly.

"I feel like one," I said. "Listen, thanks for the coffee, but I really need to go. I'm having dinner with my daughter tonight, and I need to see a lawyer first."

I wasn't making phony excuses. Hannah hadn't invited me to her dinner with Jason, but I had every intention of showing up anyway, with legal papers in my hand if I could swing it. Jason was planning to flee the country with my money. If I had any hope of stopping him, I needed to act fast. I didn't have time to get to that lawyer I'd canceled the appointment with in the city. But there was another lawyer on Lynn's list whose office was much closer, in Port Jefferson, not far from Hannah's school. I'd call and beg for an appointment and see if I could get papers drawn up quickly. I knew where Jason was going to be tonight—having dinner with our daughter at a restaurant near Stony Brook, where she went to school. I could track both their phones to get the exact location. From the sound of it, I'd better hurry, before he got on that plane to Mexico.

"Okay, I have to be at work, anyways," Aidan said. "But the thing is, my car's still in the lot at the Red Anchor."

"I can drop you there on my way," I said, feeling suddenly generous.

I'd insist on being in the driver's seat, of course. And when we got to the Red Anchor, he was damn well getting out.

"Yeah, all right. Let me take a quick shower and change."

He opened a door across from the bed, revealing a minuscule bathroom.

"You're welcome to join me," he said, smiling over his shoulder.

In that pokey shower? We'd never fit. I kept my expression neutral and said nothing, and he looked disappointed. He let the door swing shut behind him. I heard the shower turn on.

While Aidan showered, I took the opportunity to make the rounds of the small room and examine his things. Given the circumstances, snooping felt urgent and necessary, like a matter of self-defense. I wanted to reclaim my car keys, to make sure he didn't pull a fast one again and drive me where he liked.

On the narrow single bed, Aidan had laid out a fresh set of clothes, his bartending uniform for the night presumably. Jeans and a deep-green flannel shirt. *That color will look nice with his eyes,* I found myself thinking as I rifled through his pockets. Hmm, no keys. They weren't on the bedside table, which held a rickety lamp and an ancient clock radio, along with Aidan's wallet.

The wallet caught my eye. Here was an opportunity to do some investigating of the man I'd just spent the night with. *Better late than never.* The bathroom door was firmly shut, and the sound of running water came from behind it. My breath quickening, I picked up the wallet. It was thin and light—for a reason, it turned out. Inside, I found only a driver's license, a debit card from the local bank, and seventeen dollars in cash. *Investments.* Right. This guy didn't have two dimes to rub together. But that didn't surprise me, nor did it tell me anything about Aidan that I didn't already know. I looked at his driver's license. Aidan had the same August birthday as my mother. He was twenty-seven—sixteen years younger than me.

I turned the wallet inside out, poking my finger into an interior slot until I hit cardboard. I worked the items out and examined them. A loyalty card from a pizza place in town with four holes punched in it. A faded photo of a middle-aged man who, from his resemblance to the police chief and to Aidan himself, was probably Aidan's father. I turned it over. On the back, an inscription in boxy handwriting read simply, "Love, Dad." There was a school photo of a pretty, dark-haired teenager in the fashion of ten years past; nothing written on the back of that one. And one business card. STEVEN M. FIGUEROA, it said. SUFFOLK COUNTY DEPARTMENT OF PROBATION.

Aidan had a probation officer.

Shit.

The water stopped. He was done showering. I took my phone from my pocket and snapped a picture of the card, then replaced it as fast as I could and put the wallet back where I'd found it. I still hadn't found the car keys. My eyes darted around the room. Aidan's coat hung on a hook by the front door. Of course: My keys were in his coat pocket. I started to cross to it, but something shiny caught my gaze. The drawer of the bedside table sat slightly ajar, a silver gleam emanating from inside. I pulled the drawer open, cringing at its loud squeak. Luckily the water from the sink had gone on at that moment, drowning out my snooping.

I eased the drawer all the way open, and my breath caught in my throat. The shine wasn't coming from my car keys. A gun stared back at me—big, silver, angular, deadly-looking. I picked it up, and it was heavy in my hand. I turned it this way and that, holding it up to the light from the window, careful not to touch the trigger or point it at myself. Was it loaded? I was no expert. There was clearly a—a what do you call it?—a *clip,* in the handle, that could be removed, but I was afraid to take it out to check.

The water stopped. Blood pounding in my ears, I shoved the gun in the drawer and eased it closed, holding my breath for fear that I'd give myself away.

But the bathroom door stayed shut. I went over and searched the pockets of Aidan's coat, breathing a sigh of deep relief as I pulled out my keys. When Aidan emerged from the bathroom a moment later, a towel cinched around his narrow waist, I had my coat on, my keys in hand, and I was ready to bolt out the door at the first sign of trouble.

"You're in a hurry," he said, and he didn't look pleased.

He stood by the bedside table, inches from the gun. If he reached for it, I would run.

"Yes, I've been saying that. I'm meeting my daughter. Remember?" I said.

"Right."

He seemed angry with me, but he didn't say anything more. He dropped the towel and reached for his jeans. Despite my best intentions, I watched. Even now, with my deepening doubts about him, I couldn't deny that he was gorgeous.

"Let's go," he said.

A few minutes later, I was driving him to work like everything was normal. We rode in comfortable silence like old acquaintances, friends even. Or like an older woman whose one-night stand with a younger guy was coming to a close, and they were both fine with it. We'd had our fun. It was over. Nobody was upset.

I worried it wouldn't last.

19

Aidan couldn't give Caroline riches. He couldn't give her gold or diamonds or cars or designer handbags, not without robbing somebody anyway. Her shitty ex had an advantage on him there. But he could give her himself, his love, the things he was good at, the places he knew.

He took her to the cave, and she didn't love it the way he did. He tried to see it through her eyes, and he understood. The place was his from way back, and the secretness of it was what made it precious. The things that had happened to him there over the years. The memories. Naturally she didn't feel any of that. He tried to explain it to her, but she was too distracted by the lack of creature comforts. Yes, it was damp in there. The rock wasn't a feather bed, even when he took off his jacket and laid it down for her like a blanket. She was used to the finer things, to always being safe and warm. He had to remember that.

"C'mere," he said. "I'll warm you up."

He was gentle with her, like he'd never been with any woman. He was shocked at the depth of his feelings, but he'd fallen, hard and fast. He kissed her eyes, her lips, the hollow of her throat. He stroked her hair and removed just enough of her clothing so they could make love without exposing her velvet skin to the elements. She trembled under his hands. They stared into each other's eyes, touched the deepest places in each other. The light filtered in from above. Water shimmered in reflection on the walls like they were inside an aquarium. He held her, with tears in his eyes. He belonged to her now, and she to him.

Then the surfers had to go and interrupt them and break the spell. It wasn't until later, at Aidan's apartment, that he realized how upset she was about being discovered. She must be, from the way she went all distant on him. He got it, kind of. She'd been seen, half naked. She had a reputation to maintain. Aidan admired that, envied it actually. His reputation had been shot to hell years ago, and he'd give his right arm to have it back now. He hadn't known what it was worth till he lost it. Year after year of people giving him side-eye, never cutting him any slack. Refusing to forgive and forget. People who paid lip service to Jesus at church on Sunday, too, but that was a big fucking lie. Bunch of hypocrites, all of them.

It was on toward October, and the East End was wet and cold. Their fingers and lips were blue as they sat in her big, beautiful Escalade blasting the heater, trying to warm up. Aidan didn't want to take Caroline to his apartment. He was afraid of what she'd think. But the rain beat on the windshield, and she was soaked and shivering. She wanted coffee, and she didn't want to go to a restaurant. Afraid to be seen with him, probably. She had her reasons. He felt close enough to her now to brave her judgment. She knew him. She could see the soul in him, see through the stupid surfaces of things. She wouldn't be troubled by the difference in their status in the world. She was better than that. So, he drove her to his apartment, and waited while she talked to her daughter on the phone. Then he took a leap of faith and led her inside, full of hope and anxiety at the same time.

The second they walked in, he saw he'd made a terrible mistake. It was there in her eyes. Pity. Disgust. His worst nightmare. He'd been imagining they'd warm up in bed, picking up where they left off before the surfers barged in. But Caroline immediately started talking about leaving.

"What is it? Is it the apartment? It's bad, right? I know I'm not rich, but I was hoping maybe you could get past it."

"I would never hold that against you," she said, her expression softening. "I didn't come from money, you know."

"I wondered. You seem like you do, but—"

"Not at all. I grew up more like you than you could imagine. Thank you for bringing me here. It shows your honesty."

"Honesty is the only way to get close to someone, you know?"

She nodded. Her skin up close was luminous, her mouth lush. She was like a dream to him. He pulled her into his arms, and a minute later, they were back together, the way they should be. The way they belonged.

When it was over, they lay entangled in the sheets, and he caressed her hair, her face. He felt like he could tell her anything. He felt like he wanted to, so there would be no secrets between them. He couldn't bear it if she heard the bad stuff from somebody else, and thought he'd lied to her, even by omission.

"You say you like that I was honest with you by bringing you here," he began.

"Yes."

"I want you to know me, Caroline. I want you to know everything about me."

"That takes time," she said. "No need to rush things."

"Yeah, but there's something I think you should know up front. Something about my past. So you don't hear it from someone else."

She raised herself on an elbow and looked at him quizzically. "Okay."

With her eyes on him, he hesitated. What if it was too much? What if it drove her away? But she sensed his anxiety, reached out and squeezed his arm reassuringly.

"It's all right. Whatever you say, I promise, I can handle it."

He nodded. "I feel like I can tell you anything."

"You can, Aidan. Don't worry."

He took a deep breath.

"I served time for manslaughter. But it's not how it sounds."

"Go on."

"A long time ago, in high school, I had a girlfriend. Her name was

Samantha. I thought she was the one. Turned out, she was sleeping with my best friend."

He stopped. How could he ever explain what came next, without sounding like he was lying?

"There was—"

He looked away.

"Please. Tell me," she said, and took his hand.

"There was a fight, between me and my friend Matthew. This was ten years ago now. I was seventeen. Matthew had been my best friend since we were kids, until I found out what happened with him and Samantha. I was the one who ought to be mad. But Matthew threw the first punch. She'd got back with me, see. He was upset that she ditched him. The fight started in that cave where I took you. But it didn't end there. We ended up in the parking lot. He hit his head. It . . . we . . . ugh, I don't want to get into the details. I want you to know that it wasn't my fault."

She lay back down, warm against him, her arms around his neck. Her face was a breath from his as she looked into his eyes.

"It wasn't your fault. You did what you needed to do to defend yourself. That's all I need to know."

"Yes. That's it. That's it exactly. I defended myself."

Caroline accepted him for who he was. She took his darkest secret with an air of calm and peace, like she knew what had happened without him needing to say a word. And she was on his side. Other women would have been scared off. Maybe she should have been. Caroline was like the lady in the castle, and he was the hired hand. You'd think he'd have to do something crazy to win her—an act of bravery, or of strength. Fighting a duel or something. But all he had to do was be honest with her, let her see who he truly was. Now she knew the worst thing about him, and still wanted to be with him.

"Thank you. I'm really grateful for your understanding," he said.

"It's not only that I understand. I admire that part of you. Because I know that you would defend me the same way you defended yourself," she said.

"Always. I'll protect you. I'll do anything you need."

"You mean it?"

"Of course. Say the word, and I'll be there."

"Okay. I'm going to trust you, then."

"Yes. You can, absolutely."

"I told you the terrible way my husband treats me."

"I know."

"He brought his mistress to my party. I couldn't stand for that, so I asked him to leave, and then he left me for her."

"It's insane. What a fool he is."

"He didn't just leave me, Aidan. He stole my money. He left me destitute. With nothing."

"You told me that. What an asshole."

"But even more. I don't know the extent of it, but I think he may be involved in criminal dealings."

"What kind of criminal dealings?"

"I don't know. That's why it's so scary. I'm afraid of him. Afraid he could end up hurting me or my daughter, maybe without intending to. Because he doesn't care enough to protect us."

"What can I do to help?"

"I need him gone."

"Okay. I understand that you're afraid of him. Do you want me to be there when you tell him it's over?"

"No. That wouldn't be enough, you see."

They were sitting up, looking at each other, serious now.

"What then?" he asked.

She leaned over and put her hand to his cheek.

"I need him dead."

Aidan jumped out of the bed. His boxers were lying on the floor, and he pulled them on, then his pants. *Jesus.* She'd just asked him to kill her husband. He'd said he'd do anything, but he never expected her to ask for *that.* Why did she think he'd do it? Because of his past, that's why. She thought of him as some outlaw, some lowlife. He was so shaken that he didn't know what to say.

Caroline watched him warily. He must look as stricken as he felt.

"What's the matter?" she asked, as he buttoned his shirt with trembling fingers. "Where are you going? Don't leave."

"Did I hear you right? You just asked me to kill your husband."

"Okay, no. You're right. That's crazy."

"Is that what you meant?"

"I want him out of my life so badly. And I have to keep the money. We could be together, Aidan. You and me."

He sat on the edge of the bed and took her hands.

"I want that, too. More than anything. But I can't do what you asked. I'm not like that. I need you to understand. This one terrible thing that happened years ago—it wrecked me. I can't go through that again."

"Okay, I understand," she said. "I've been so stressed with Jason leaving, I'm talking crazy. I got crazy there for a minute. That's all. I apologize."

He leaned in and kissed her. The sheet was draped across her body, but it couldn't hide the beautiful curve of her breast, the elegant slant of her neck, the lustrous fall of her hair. She looked up into his eyes. He said he'd do anything, and she took him up on it. She'd placed her faith in him. What she'd asked was too much. But he forgave her. How could he not?

"Of course I forgive you."

"You won't tell anyone I said that?" she said, laughing nervously.

"I'm no snitch, and even if I was, I'd never tell on you."

"I know."

"But I want you to know, I'll do anything else in my power to protect you. Other than that. I swear it. I'll have your back, now and forever. You have to believe me."

"I do believe you," she said. And she melted into his arms.

20

The parking lot of Red Anchor was surprisingly full for three o'clock on a rainy Thursday afternoon. Just as I cruised in with Aidan in the passenger seat of my very recognizable white Escalade, a group of women spilled out of the restaurant and ran through the raindrops toward their cars. One of them looked directly at me, through my windshield. With a jolt, I recognized her. Julie owned a boutique in town that I frequented. I'd been there with Hannah a couple of weeks before, looking for a dress to wear to the housewarming party. Julie knew me, and worse, she knew my daughter.

"Get down," I said to Aidan.

"What?"

"Ach, forget it. Too late."

I sped past her, around the side of the building, stopping in the alley between the restaurant and the strip mall next door.

"What are you doing?" Aidan said.

The rain came down hard, and the wipers swished. I was so unnerved at being spotted by someone I knew that my heart was skittering. I looked in the rearview mirror, trying to see if Julie was still there. But from that angle, in the heavy rain, the parking lot was hidden from view. If I couldn't see the parking lot, then people in the parking lot couldn't see me.

"You should get out now."

"Here? It's pouring. Can you drop me at the front door?"

"Isn't that the back entrance right there?" I said, nodding toward a blank-looking door across from a collection of trash bins.

"I don't go in that way."

"I'm sorry, but there's a woman I know in the parking lot, and where there's one, there're others."

"So?"

"*So,* people talk. If she sees me dropping you off, she'll think we spent the night together. She could blab that all over town."

"We did spend the night together."

"I don't need everybody knowing that. It could hurt me in the divorce case. Jason is supposed to be the bad guy. Not me."

I could see him getting mad again. His eyes clouded over, and his jaw tensed. His hands clenched into fists, and I started to get nervous.

"I get it," he said. "You took a walk on the wild side, and now you're done. I get tossed aside. I'm expendable."

"I don't understand why you're taking this so personally," I said.

"It *was* personal. It sure seemed that way when you had your legs wrapped around my neck."

"Please don't talk like that."

"Too rough for your dainty ears? Don't lie to yourself, Caroline. You wanted it. You still want it."

"All I mean is, keeping this on the down low for now is not a judgment on you, or my feelings for you. It's about my own situation. I never lied to you, Aidan. You know I'm married."

"You're not married, not for long anyway. He left you for a Russian hooker. He took your money. You need to wake up and face the facts."

I wanted to appease him, but anger flashed through me. Who the hell did this kid think he was, talking to me like that?

"Whether I'm married or not, and how I handle it, that's my business. It has nothing to do with you."

"Then, what is this?" he said, moving his hand back and forth in the space between us.

"What is what?"

"What do we have together? How do you feel about me?"

"I think we had a nice time."

"That's it?"

"It was one night."

"I don't like the sound of that. It sounds like you're blowing me off."

"How can I say where this is going at this point? We hardly know each other."

"Hardly know each other? What the fuck, Caroline."

He slammed his fist against the passenger window so hard that I jumped.

"Stop that! You'll break it."

My heart was pounding. I had plenty of evidence at this point that my first impression of Aidan had been right, and my alcohol-and-lust-fueled second impression had been very, very wrong. Aidan had a probation officer. And a gun. And he was in my car, in an alley where no one could see us, on the edge of becoming violent.

"You're going to see him now, aren't you?" he said.

"Who?"

"Your husband."

Had he eavesdropped, back at his apartment complex? It seemed impossible, given that I was sitting in the car when I spoke to Hannah about the dinner, and Aidan was inside.

"I told you, I'm going to visit my daughter," I said.

"But he's gonna be there, isn't he?"

I could lie and tell him he was wrong. But Aidan's behavior was so possessive, and so over-the-top given the nature of our relationship that I felt like I had to talk some sense into him.

"Aidan, no offense," I said, trying to sound reasonable, "but if I choose to see my husband, that's not your business."

Without warning, he threw himself forward and slammed his head against the dashboard three times in quick succession. I screamed.

"What are you doing? Are you crazy?"

A smear of deep red stood out on the rich beige leather. I looked at Aidan in horror and saw blood trickling from a cut on his temple.

"You're bleeding. Oh, my God."

"You hurt my feelings, Caroline," he said, his eyes wet with unshed tears.

Every woman likes to be desired. But it was completely bizarre that Aidan would be so into me after one night. Something was off with this guy. At the same time, maybe I bore some responsibility. I thought we were having a no-strings fling, but had I made that sufficiently clear to him? Had I led him on? He was a grown man, but he was so much younger than me. I had the impression he'd been with lots of women, but it was possible he hadn't had many serious relationships. Maybe he wasn't a player after all. Maybe he was vulnerable. Maybe he had a tender heart, and I'd bruised it.

Leaning across Aidan, I grabbed a pack of Kleenex from the glove box.

"C'mere and let me fix that," I said.

The skin around the cut was rapidly purpling. I dabbed at the blood with the tissue, and he flinched.

"I'm sorry, did that hurt?"

"Yes."

He looked at me with blue eyes that swam with tears. I felt a strange flash of that feeling I'd get when Hannah was little and skinned her knee. Pity and protectiveness at once.

"Restaurants always have first-aid kits," I said, in a firm, motherly tone. "I want you to go inside and put some disinfectant on this right away. You hear me?"

"Yes," he said. "I'm sorry I freaked out."

"It's okay. We're both tired. It was a crazy night, right?"

I smiled, and he gave me a sad smile back.

"That it was, Caroline. That it was."

"You need to take care of yourself. So, do like I said, and get that cut cleaned up. Okay?"

"Okay."

"Promise?"

"Yeah, sure. When will I see you again?"

"Very soon," I said. But I was lying, and I suspected he knew that.

I leaned forward and kissed him lightly on the lips. That seemed to mollify him. He got out and ran through the rain to the restaurant's back door. As he disappeared inside, I exhaled a long breath, then pulled out of that parking lot so fast that my tires squealed.

21

Aidan's plan when he set out that afternoon was simple reconnaissance. He'd promised Caroline he would protect her, and he intended to keep that promise. The husband was ruthless and abusive. Caroline had told him that much, but he needed to understand the full extent of the threat. How far would the guy go? He'd stolen her money, and that suggested he had no conscience. Would he hurt her physically? Aidan had brought binoculars. He planned to follow the husband, find out where he went, who he met, what he was up to. He had to make sure Caroline was not in any danger. Maybe there was even a way to get some leverage on the guy, to force him to return Caroline's money. If Aidan could swing that, he'd be her hero. And he wanted that, more than anything.

Caroline had let slip enough information that Aidan was able to figure out the restaurant where they'd be meeting. It was an Italian place not far from the daughter's college. He got there early to scope it out. The building was fake limestone with a green awning out front, set back from the street in its own parking lot. The lot was brightly lit on this chill, drizzly evening, and mostly empty—a bad combination. He decided not to wait in the parking lot, where his bright red truck might draw attention. He didn't need anybody asking questions, didn't need

some Good Samaritan deciding he was a threat and calling his probation officer. He drove around for a while, stopped at a convenience store,
bought a Red Bull and a pack of Twizzlers to keep focused. He returned
an hour later with his senses on high alert and parked behind a tree at
the far end of the lot, away from the lights, hunkering down in the front
seat to wait.

Time passed. He closed his eyes and saw Caroline's face. He visual-
ized kissing her brow, her perfect cheekbones. He remembered the eggs
at breakfast, the view from her bedroom. The rain started up again, tat-
tooing on the windshield. His heart beat steadily. His luck had turned
that night Caroline walked into the bar at the Red Anchor. His life was
good now, with her in it.

Everybody was late, and Aidan was getting antsy. Had they changed
the location since he found out about this dinner? There was nothing to
do but wait some more. He ran the wipers briefly so he could see out the
windshield.

The daughter showed up first, emerging from the backseat of a silver
Toyota that sported an Uber decal in its front window. He recognized
her from the photos on Caroline's phone. He felt bad about snooping,
but he'd done it almost by accident. He'd seen Caroline type her code
into the phone that night in the bar, and it stuck in his head because
she used all sevens. Seven was his lucky number, too. He almost said
something, how they were alike, but then he didn't. Good thing, because
later, when he was in her bed, and she was fast asleep, he'd picked the
phone up to look at her screensaver, which was a picture of the beach in
front of her house. He'd recognize that strip of sand anywhere, and he
was mesmerized, looking at it. Once the phone was in his hand, he'd
typed in her code almost without thinking. Just to see what he saw.
Once he started scrolling, it was hard to stop, even though he knew
that he was doing something wrong. The impulse to learn about her was
too powerful.

He wouldn't recognize the daughter now if he hadn't done that.
Hannah Elizabeth Stark, age eighteen. She'd be nineteen in November.
It was a bit awkward how close they were in age, closer than he was to

Caroline. He'd be more like a big brother to Hannah than a stepfather, but they'd make it work. She was average height, average weight, long dark hair, nice face. Not beautiful like her mother, but pleasant-looking. She wore jeans and ankle boots and a sweater. Hannah went inside the restaurant.

Fifteen minutes later, the husband's car pulled into the lot. A real dick move, letting his daughter show up first, making her wait that long for him. This guy didn't have a clue about how to treat women. The car was dickish, too, a Mercedes E-Class with New York plates, navy blue and sleek. It was the type of car you might expect a chauffeur to drive, the kind you saw idling outside fancy office buildings in the city every night, waiting for the masters to emerge and get driven to their expense-account dinners. Caroline's husband was driving himself tonight, though. Jason Stark pulled into a spot right in front of the restaurant and got out. Aidan raised the binoculars and checked the guy out. Stark walked like someone used to getting his way in this world. A confident strut, his broad shoulders in a well-cut blazer tapering to tailored slacks, a hundred-dollar haircut. He didn't even hurry out of the rain. Why should he? Raindrops couldn't touch a guy like that. Aidan hated the dude on sight.

Jason went inside. Five minutes later, he came out again, his phone to his ear. Just then, Caroline's Escalade pulled into the lot. Aidan had been in that car a couple of hours earlier. He sniffed his shirt, trying to recapture the scent of her perfume and feel how it felt when she'd touched him. But it was already a fading memory.

Caroline parked, then walked to the spot under the awning where her husband stood. Aidan expected to see a cold welcome, possibly even a confrontation. He was ready to spring into action if the need arose. Instead they embraced. As he watched, that dickwad took the woman Aidan loved into his arms and kissed her on the lips. It wasn't a passionate kiss. *Still*. The guy's hand was on the small of her back, her head tilting up toward him. A jealous fury bubbled in his blood. He opened the door of the truck and got out. His hands instinctively balled into fists, he was itching so bad to break them up. But uncertainty kept him from going in closer. This could be a ploy on Caroline's part to lure the husband into letting down his guard and revealing where he'd stashed the money. If so, Aidan shouldn't screw it up. But what if what he was seeing between them was real? What if she'd lied to him for some reason, and she was still in love with the guy? But no. That wasn't possible. He was doubting, because this thing with Caroline seemed too good to be true. Because he didn't believe in himself enough to buy that she really cared for him. He needed to have more faith.

The rain had finally stopped, but the blacktop was shiny and slick. The air smelled of fall. Wet leaves, a tang of woodsmoke. Water dripped from the tree beside him onto the shoulders of his leather jacket as Aidan watched the husband open the restaurant door for Caroline. She went inside. But the husband stayed behind under the awning, on his phone again. He was pacing, waving his arms, looking increasingly agitated. Must be an interesting call. Aidan was too far away to hear. He crept closer, maneuvering between the cars, wishing he had a smoke in his hand. Dirty habit, but it made for a good cover. A man lurking in a parking lot could seem like a threat; a man smoking a cigarette was taking an innocent break.

As Aidan drew within earshot, Stark glanced in his direction and hunched over, shielding his phone, his expression wary.

"Hold on a second," he said, and stepped out from under the cover of the awning.

Stark slunk around the side of the building until he was out of Aidan's line of sight and earshot. If the dude was willing to stand in the rain to avoid being overheard by a complete stranger, this call must be something sketchy. Was he talking to the mistress? Were they scheming about the money? Or was it something even worse? Shady dealings that might affect Caroline? Aidan would love to be able to give her a detailed report.

A row of tall bushes along the front of the building gave off a heady smell of wet mulch. Aidan glanced over his shoulder to make sure nobody was looking, then ducked behind them. He brushed against the branches, darkening his clothes with the rain, as he made his way to the corner of the building. He could hear the conversation clearly now. Stark was talking about money, all right. He mentioned a number—half a million. That was a lot of cash, more than a guy would spend on a mistress. This had to be something else, something bigger than cheating. Maybe it was what Caroline had alluded to, that her husband was mixed up in criminal activity of some kind. Aidan moved closer, straining to hear more.

"—at the warehouse?" Stark asked, then paused. "I'm not stupid, Galina. . . . I'm doing what I can, but I told you, she's giving me a problem. . . . You have my word. I'll call you as soon as it's done."

Galina. That had to be the Russian woman. Stark said that someone—somebody *female*—was giving him a problem. Was it Caroline he referred to? The talking stopped abruptly. Had the asshole moved away again? Aidan couldn't see. He took a step out from behind the bushes, around the side and—

Pain exploded in the side of his head. He was lying on the wet pavement, on his back, seeing stars.

"*What the fuck?*"

The guy had sucker-punched him. Aidan touched his temple. His fingers came away bloody. Jason Stark stood over him.

"I don't know who you are or why you're following me. But stay away from me, or I'll kill you," Stark said.

Then he walked away nonchalantly, like nothing had happened.

Fuck that.

This ain't over, pal. Not hardly.

22

As I walked into the restaurant, I spotted Jason and Hannah at the corner table, their dark heads together, deep in conversation. The sight of them made me stop and catch my breath. How many restaurant dinners had we shared, the three of us, since Hannah was a baby in her carrier? I could still picture her as a little girl, thin and pale, with big brown eyes. What a picky eater she'd been, and then later, what a junk-food junkie. As much of a struggle as it had been to raise her, with Jason gone so much and everything on me, I'd give my right arm to have those days back. I'd loved being a wife, and a mom. Now our little family was shattered.

I had a piece of paper in my handbag that was sure to make everything worse. It would take what Jason had started and make it permanent. I didn't want to use it, but he'd left me no choice. He'd cheated and lied. He'd drained the bank accounts and left me destitute. Now—if what Hannah told me was right—he was planning to skip town. As much as part of me still loved him, it was time to face facts.

I sighed and started toward them. Jason and Hannah looked up simultaneously, with identical dismayed expressions, and I saw that my first impression of a cozy tête-à-tête had been mistaken. In her first weeks of college, Hannah should be glowing and full of adventure. Instead she looked pale and worried, her skin acting up, her hair stringy. And Jason, beside her, looked haggard, like he'd lost ten pounds in the few days since I'd seen him.

"Caroline."

"Mom, I said this wasn't a good idea."

"I wish I didn't have to barge in like this, but your father left me no choice. He—"

"Can we please leave Hannah out of this?" Jason said. "She doesn't need to hear the ugly details."

"Don't blame me. Hannah told me you're planning to leave the country. And you won't return my calls. Where's the money, Jason?"

In spite of my best intentions, my voice rose. People were turning to look. A waiter stepped up behind me with a chair. Jason waved him off.

"She's not staying."

"Don't tell me what to do."

"Mom, Dad, please," Hannah said, red-faced with embarrassment. She was looking around the restaurant, obviously worried that someone from her school might be in attendance to witness her family drama. I felt terrible that her parents' problems were hurting her at this important moment in her life. But, come on. I was the victim here. If Jason didn't put the money back immediately, I'd have to start pawning jewelry in order to eat. Hannah wouldn't wish that for me.

Jason stood up. "Caroline, come outside. Hannah, your mother and I need to talk."

Jason took my elbow and steered me toward the exit. My cheeks were burning. I hated scenes, and I never meant to shame my daughter. But I refused to let him mistreat me with impunity. I had my payback planned. Out in the parking lot, I reached into my handbag and pulled out a manila envelope.

"You've been served," I said, and thrust it at his chest.

The lawyer Lynn recommended had done quick work, drafting a divorce complaint and a court order in the space of an hour to stop Jason from stealing any more of my—*our*—money. It might be too little, too late. What he'd taken, I might never see again. But the divorce papers at least made me feel that I was sticking up for myself. They included every salacious detail I could think of to make Jason look bad. The Russian woman. The lies about his business trips—let his partners suck on that. How he'd left his devoted wife destitute after twenty years of marriage. I'd humiliate him in front of the world, like he'd done to me. It didn't feel good, but nothing felt good since I'd discovered his betrayal.

"What is this?" he said.

"Divorce papers. My lawyer's filing the complaint in court tomorrow. It has all the dirt about you and that Russian woman, and your so-called business trips. I know you're lying about where you go. Everybody will know that now. They'll see what a rat you are, Jason."

"That's not a good idea."

"Maybe not for *you*."

My voice rang out in the silence of the dark, empty parking lot. A misty rain had been falling all evening. The chill got in my bones, making me shiver. I longed for an apology. I'd settle for shock, or even anger. Instead, Jason looked dejected, and his unhappiness gave me no satisfaction.

"It'll be hard on Hannah," he said.

"I don't want to do this. But you told me you would take care of me, then you took all the money, and you're planning to flee the country. How am I supposed to react?"

"I know. I'm sorry."

In the light from the streetlamp, I gazed at his familiar face, and my heart flooded with regret. I didn't want revenge. All I wanted was for the past week never to have happened, for our marriage to be warm and cozy, for Jason to be my rock, like he'd always been.

"It kills me to put you through this," he said.

"Then don't," I said, my voice thick with unshed tears. "It's not too late."

To my intense relief, he opened his arms, and I walked right into them.

When Jason and I returned to the table fifteen minutes later, we were holding hands. He pulled up a chair for me, and I gazed at him over my shoulder as I took a seat. Hannah looked back and forth between us in wonder.

"Looks like you guys had a good talk," she said, and the hope in her face tugged at my heart. I had hope, too, even if it was last-ditch and desperate.

"Your mother and I made up," Jason said. "But let's not talk about it too much, because I don't want to jinx it. Hand me the menu. I hear they have great carbonara."

He signaled the waiter. I felt hungry suddenly and realized I hadn't eaten since the scrambled eggs this morning. Scrambled eggs . . .

Aidan.

Was that really today? Was it even this lifetime? Thank God that ridiculous fling was over. What a crazy mistake. Now that I was back with my family, where I belonged, I could put it out of my mind and never think of it again.

From behind me, a man's hand, holding a pitcher, reached to fill my water glass. Something in the hand was so familiar that I held my breath, afraid of what I'd see if I turned around. Could it be? I stared straight ahead.

I saw Jason look up, and his eyes widen.

"You're the guy from the parking lot," he said. "You work here?"

"Yes, sir. Can I get you anything else?"

At the sound of Aidan's voice, I froze. Had he followed me here? I could tell that he was standing right behind me. In a terrible moment of suspended animation, I waited for him to say something that acknowledged our connection. To call me by name. To spill the truth about our affair to my husband, with whom I'd now—I hoped and prayed—reconciled. Instead, he circled to the other side of the table, coming close enough to brush against the back of my chair. I saw that he was wearing a black apron embroidered with the name of the restaurant and carrying a pitcher of ice water. *What the hell?* Either this was the most bizarre coincidence of all time, or he was masquerading as a waiter. It was the latter; I knew it in my gut. He'd followed me to this restaurant, stolen the apron and the pitcher, and walked up to our table, in some deranged attempt to make contact, to barge into my dinner with my family. I had no idea why. But he could only mean harm.

I watched in horror as Aidan filled first Hannah's water glass, then Jason's. He lifted a hand to push back his hair, and I saw that the left side of his forehead had turned a deep purple, marked by a dark red gash where he'd bashed it against the dashboard of my car. Aidan finally met my horror-stricken gaze. And *smiled*. What did he hope to gain by sneaking up on me like this? I wanted to ask him. I wanted to demand that he leave me and my family alone. But my voice died in my throat. The only thing that mattered right now was saving my marriage. If Jason knew I'd cheated, even though he'd done exactly the same, our fragile reconciliation would be at risk. So, I sat completely still, praying in silent horror that—whatever his intentions—Aidan would leave us without giving me away.

The elderly, white-jacketed waiter returned to check on us. He looked Aidan up and down in confusion.

"Who are you?" he said. "You don't work here."

"I'm new," Aidan said. But he set the water pitcher down on the table and hurried away.

"Uh, folks, could you give me a minute," the elderly waiter said, and rushed to follow Aidan.

I watched as Aidan ran out the front door of the restaurant. The elderly waiter stopped at the maître d's station. He and the maître d' stepped outside, then came back in moments later and engaged in an animated conversation.

"That's odd, don't you think?" Jason said, watching them, too.

My voice was rusty with shock, to the point that I had to clear my throat before I could get out a reply.

"What—what do you mean?"

"That guy who brought the water. I don't believe he works here."

"Who knows," I said.

The elderly waiter shrugged, then headed back in our direction.

"Here comes the waiter," I said. "Forget about that guy. I'm starving. Let's order."

Aidan was gone, thank God. But for how long?

23

I opened my eyes to feel the delicate morning light kissing my face. The drapes were open, and the smell of fresh coffee wafted from the kitchen. I rolled over and sighed with happiness to be in my own bed in our New York apartment, with the pillow on Jason's side dented from where his head had rested last night. Then I remembered—and sat up so fast I saw spots.

Aidan.

Aidan had followed me to the restaurant last night, and—bizarrely—pretended to be a waiter and approached our table. I didn't understand why. He hadn't acknowledged our relationship, or even said anything to indicate he knew me. Thank God for that, yet it made his behavior seem even more bizarre. Was he trying to get close to me, after I'd said good-bye? Or threaten me with the prospect of ratting me out to my family? I'd managed to escape without Jason or Hannah finding out about our fling—this time. But if Aidan followed me again, next time I might not be so lucky.

My gaze traveled around the familiar bedroom. It felt suddenly precious to me, and precarious, like my home of over a decade might vanish in the blink of an eye. We'd lived in this apartment since Hannah started kindergarten. I vividly remembered the day we moved in, what a palace it'd felt like at the time. We'd scraped and saved to afford it. A two-bedroom prewar with high ceilings and good light, on a pretty block within walking distance of Hannah's school. Over the years, as Jason became more successful, I tried to convince him to upgrade. We could use more space. The kitchen and bathrooms were dated. There were more exclusive buildings, with better-connected neighbors who could've opened social doors. But Jason refused, and now I was grateful we hadn't. This was home. This was where we'd raised our daughter together. I wanted to get down on my hands and knees and kiss the faded carpet. But I couldn't take for granted my return to paradise. Not with Aidan out there, plotting who knows what. He was the snake in the garden.

Uneasily, I put my feet in my slippers. I pulled on my silk robe and made my way to the kitchen. Jason sat at the island, the newspaper open in front of him, dressed for the day in suit and tie. I'd forgotten how distinguished he could look, with his chiseled features, his dark hair graying at the temples. I remembered seeing Aidan on the beach that first day, looking like some goombah thug. Not just looking like one. He *was* a thug. He owned a gun and had a probation officer. I didn't know what crime Aidan had committed, but now that he'd shown up to haunt me at the restaurant, I'd damn well better find out. Was I dealing with a petty thief or a killer?

Jason saw me, glanced at his watch, and stood up.

"Better get going. It's later than I thought," he said.

"Oh. I wanted us to have breakfast together. You should've woken me."

"You looked so peaceful, I didn't want to bother you."

He leaned down and gave me a quick peck on the cheek. The familiar scent of the shaving cream and hair pomade he'd been using for decades made me want to cry. I grabbed his arm and kissed him on the lips, but he didn't respond.

"Don't go," I said.

"Have to. Important meeting today," he said.

But his eyes were shadowed, and his face looked strained. I felt like he was avoiding me. He was certainly keeping something from me.

"What's wrong?" I asked.

"Nothing. Everything's fine, hon."

Jason's words didn't ring true. Was I imagining it? Could I trust him? Was this reconciliation for real? I was afraid to ask him whether he'd broken things off with the Russian woman. What if the answer was no?

"You seem . . . distant," I said.

"I have a lot on my mind."

I wanted to ask him about the bank accounts. He'd promised to put the money back in. There were bills to pay. But I didn't want to seem like a nag or make him think that my only motivation for getting back together was cold, hard cash.

"Okay," I said in a small voice, and let go of his arm.

If he left now, if we parted like this, I'd brood over it for the rest of the day. I had to ask.

"Jason——"

"What is it?" he said, sounding annoyed.

"I have to ask. That woman who came to the party? Is she—are you still—?"

"I told you, that wasn't what you think. It was business. And the thing I'm working with her on is coming to an end. I promise. After that, believe me, I never want to see her again."

"It was only business? You swear?"

"I've never cheated on you, Caroline," he said, in a cold, angry tone. "I wonder if you can say the same. You might want to check your phone."

My hands felt icy cold as Jason trained his gaze on me.

"Why?"

"It was ringing like crazy before. I put it to silent, so I could read the paper in peace. Repeat phone calls from someone named Aidan."

"Aidan?"

"Yeah, who is he?"

"I'm not sure. What did he say?"

"I didn't *talk* to him. He was calling you. That's the name that showed up on your phone, anyway. Aidan with a heart."

"Aidan with a *heart*?"

"Yes. Is there an echo in here? Who is he?"

Aidan's name—not just his number—came up on my phone? With a heart? I was flummoxed. I'd never put Aidan's number in my phone. And certainly not with some stupid heart.

"I—I."

"You don't know who that is?" Jason asked.

"The only Aidan I know is a friend of Lynn's," I said.

"Why's he calling you ten times in the last hour?"

"Um, because, she's in Florida. I was supposed to—uh, to let him into her house. He's staying there while she's gone, but he doesn't have a key."

"Why is his number in your phone?"

"Maybe because Lynn shared her contacts with me? Phones are weird like that."

Jason nodded, but I could tell he didn't believe me. I tried to organize my features into some semblance of calm expression as my heart pounded with guilt and the fear of being found out. Though God knows why I felt so bad. I didn't buy for one minute Jason's story that the Russian woman was a business associate—which meant he'd cheated first. Now that we were back in our apartment together, I was prepared to forgive and forget. Was he?

"Will you be home for dinner?" I asked.

"I don't know. I'll call you."

He walked out, without any further goodbye, and my heart sank. This reconciliation was twelve hours old and already on shaky ground.

As soon as I heard the front door slam, I grabbed my handbag from the counter and pulled out my phone. When I saw the call log, my legs buckled, and I had to sit down. It was insane. There were fourteen missed calls and three voicemails since last night. And Jason was right. The calls registered as coming from "Aidan♥," as if I'd entered his number with a cutesy heart beside it into my contacts. But I hadn't. We'd never once talked on the phone; I didn't even know his number. Frantically, I pulled up my contacts. There it was, under "A"—Aidan♥, with a cell number listed that I didn't recognize. How the hell—? Well, of course. He'd gone into my phone and entered himself into my contacts during that wild night we spent together. I'd been drunk, passed out, hungover. It was my own fault. I had a distinct memory of Aidan watching me intently as I typed in my passcode. I remembered thinking that was odd and wondering if I should shield the phone from his view. But I didn't, because I was afraid of seeming paranoid or condescending. I didn't want him ragging on me for being a snob, so I let him watch. I basically gave him the code. How foolish was that? Then I left my phone lying in plain view on the bedside table. All Aidan would've had to do was wait for the right moment to type in my code and put his number in my contacts. I'd left myself completely vulnerable to a man I barely knew.

As the implications dawned on me, I started to sweat. My entire life was on that phone. Pictures of my family. My calendar, with every doctor's appointment and lunch date and exercise class I had scheduled for months to come. The addresses and phone numbers of my loved ones—my daughter, my sister, my husband. My emails and texts, waiting to be plundered for personal details. All sorts of financial information. On and on. Aidan had uninterrupted time with my phone while I slept. He could know a lot.

Shit. He could know *everything about me.*

There was no telling how much damage he could do with that information, if he chose to.

24

Tommy was taking Aidan out on his boat, supposedly fishing, but Aidan knew better. They never spent time together for its own sake. There was always some ulterior motive on Tommy's part, usually a lecture, or something he wanted Aidan to do that would supposedly be good for him in the long run. Tommy's big-brothering got old sometimes. But the weather was fine for the first time in a week, and Aidan loved the ocean. Tommy always stocked a cooler full of beer and his wife Kelly's excellent meat loaf sandwiches. What the hell, if Aidan said no to the boat, he'd get lectured anyway. Might as well say yes and enjoy a day on the water.

Tommy was coming off an overnight shift and asked Aidan to meet him at the marina in Port Jeff at nine thirty that morning. It was a bit of a haul to the North Shore. Tommy only docked there because he got the slip on the cheap from a friend in town. The boat was an old bay, small and wheezing, fragrant with gasoline, that he got for a song after it was seized from a drug dealer. Aidan wondered why his brother didn't take better advantage of his position. Tommy, Kelly, and their three kids lived in a cramped raised ranch on the same street where Tommy and Aidan grew up, which meant Ma dropping in to supper constantly. Tommy drove his work cruiser, and Kelly drove an eight-year-old Toyota. Vacation was splurging on the Holiday Inn for the kids' travel soccer games. If it was him, he might consider cashing in. But that was Tommy, always the stickler. Aidan had to admire it, really.

Tommy was waiting for him on the boat, gassed up and ready to cast off. As Aidan hopped on board, Tommy touched his own forehead in the spot where Aidan had the bruise from getting slugged by Caroline's husband last night.

"What happened to your head?" he asked.

"I, uh, had a few too many the other night at work. Walked into a door. Professional hazard."

"I hope you don't drive under the influence."

"Never."

"I heard you missed work last night."

Aidan was annoyed with the direction of the conversation. But he was hardly surprised.

"Already with the interrogation? I just stepped foot on the boat."

"Okay, you're right. Get that line?"

The sun glittered on the water. The wind was in Aidan's hair as he cast off the dock lines and joined his brother at the helm. If the only lecture was one small mention of his truancy last night, then he'd gotten off easy, and they could enjoy the day. Tommy steered the boat expertly out of the crowded marina, picking up speed as they hit the open water. They cruised for a while, not talking, squinting through their sunglasses at the waves. Eventually they reached a sheltered cove that was known for its striped bass. Tommy cut the engine, and they dropped anchor.

The wind died down. They sat there for half an hour without a single bite, enjoying the sunshine, a couple of morning beers, shooting the shit about football and the like, before Tommy finally got to the real point.

"This woman you've been hanging out with," Tommy said, his eyes on the horizon. "The chick from the bar."

"I knew it," Aidan said, shaking his head.

"Knew what?"

"That you had some ulterior motive for taking me out here. It's never that you want to hang with me."

"I do want to hang out with you, and there is no motive. We're together, so I'm asking about your life."

"About Caroline?"

"Yeah. What's up with that?"

"What do you mean, what's up?"

"Are you seeing her? Is this something ongoing?"

"Why is that your business?"

Tommy shot him a look, which was easy enough to decipher. Tommy thought that anything Aidan touched was his business. And Aidan had touched Caroline.

"Because I care. I worry about you. How much do you know about this woman?" Tommy said.

"I know enough. I know what I need to."

"Did you know she stiffed every contractor on the island? Unpaid bills from here to Kalamazoo."

"I don't believe it. That's not even possible. Those guys don't run balances. They take their pound of flesh along the way."

"I'm telling you what I heard. Plus, I heard some concerning things about her husband."

Aidan looked at his brother sharply. "*Concerning*, in what way?"

"That he might be mixed up with some bad characters. Involved in some crooked business dealings. That sort of thing. And if he is, and you're getting with his wife, the guy could go medieval on you."

"Have you seen him?"

"No. I haven't. Have you?"

"He's some uptight Wall Street type in a fancy suit. I'm not afraid of him."

"Maybe you should be."

"If there's something I should be worried about, then tell me. You say you have information that this guy is involved in something criminal. So, tell me the details."

Tommy met his gaze. "I don't know any details, and if I did, I wouldn't tell you. I know you, Aidan. And I don't need you going vigilante out of some foolish sense of chivalry. Forget this woman. She's bad news."

"Come on, Tommy, please," Aidan begged, worried now. "I need to know what Stark is mixed up in. If there's something shady with the guy, I have to protect her."

"Protect her from her own husband? What are you even talking about? This is a married woman."

"She's getting a divorce."

Now, based on what he'd seen at the restaurant last night, Aidan had his doubts whether Caroline was really getting divorced. Watching her greet her husband with that kiss shook him. If the divorce was off, that was a serious setback for their relationship. But it was only a setback. There were steps Aidan could take to change it. He could be her savior, her defender, like he'd promised, like she'd asked. From what he'd over-heard at the restaurant last night, Stark was dealing in big money with this Russian woman. And now here was Tommy suggesting that Stark was mixed up in shady business. It added up to something that could pose a threat to Caroline, or even to her daughter. He had no intention of letting her get hurt, or of letting her slip through his fingers, either. They were destined to be together, and this was his route to winning her, forever.

"Whether she's getting divorced or not," Tommy said, "you don't have a frigging clue what you're walking into. You're gonna end up screwing up your life again, and I won't have it."

"Do you know how you sound, trying to scare me off her? What are you, jealous? You can't let me have a relationship."

"I'm trying to protect you."

"I can take care of myself."

"Can you?" Tommy said.

"Yes, I can, but you refuse to see that. You can't stop thinking of me as a screwup. Finally, after all these years, I meet a woman that I feel something for, that I can build a relationship with. Why can't you let me live my life?"

"Maybe because the last time you fell for someone, I had to get you out from under a murder rap."

Murder? It wasn't *murder*. Tommy knew that.

"Manslaughter, Tom. I was convicted of manslaughter. It's not the same. You're a cop. You know that."

"Yeah, well whatever they call it, someone died, and you went to jail. I don't ever want to go through that again."

"You think I do?"

Aidan's mind flew back to the past, to the event that had ruined his life. The day he found out the love of his life and his best friend had been together behind his back. There had been a fight. A fight between two guys over a girl. Happens so often it's almost a cliché. Aidan didn't even throw the first punch. Matthew did. Then Aidan fought back, and Matthew wound up on the ground, unmoving, having hit his head on a rock. Aidan would never forget the panic when he realized that Matthew wasn't breathing, that there was blood on the back of his head. It was a terrible tragedy that Matthew died that day. A tragedy for Matthew and his family. A tragedy for Aidan, too. He'd loved his friend. He hadn't meant for him to die. It happened in the blink of an eye. Every day since, Aidan wished he could take it back. Hell, he wished it had been him who took the punch and hit his head, him who died.

Aidan crushed his beer can and threw it hard against the water, where it bobbed in the waves. The wind had picked up, and clouds were rolling in. The water looked cold and threatening, even in the shelter of the cove. Aidan's mood swung with the wind. It seemed impossible to stay caged up on this boat with his brother, listening to the litany of his sins for the thousandth time.

He tore off his shirt, kicked off his sneakers, and stepped up onto the gunwale.

"What are you doing?" Tommy said.

"Getting out of here. I'm done with this bullshit," he said, and dived overboard.

25

I sat at the kitchen table with a cup of coffee in front of me, working up the courage to listen to Aidan's voicemails. My hands were shaking, and I'd double-locked the doors. In the past twenty-four hours, this man I did not know well, with whom I'd shared a single night of passion, and who had a probation officer and a gun, had: been borderline violent at the beach, refused to leave my car, bashed his head bloody on my dashboard, followed me to the restaurant and posed as a waiter in front of my family, entered his number into my phone and done God knows what else while he had possession of it, called my phone a total of seventeen times, leaving three voicemails. The voicemails were likely to be threats. I dreaded hearing them. But I had to listen. If I didn't know what I was facing, how could I protect myself?

The ticking of the clock on the wall was loud in the silence of the kitchen. I picked up my phone, feeling very alone. I'd love to talk to Lynn, who was coming back from Florida today, and get her advice. But Lynn told her husband Joe everything. And Jason and Joe were golfing buddies. Jason was already suspicious because of the repeat phone calls. If he thought about it for two seconds, he might connect Aidan♥ to the intrusive waiter at the restaurant last night. I couldn't risk sharing this burden with my sister. I was too worried that telling her would lead to blowing my secret to my husband. I'd have to handle this alone.

The first voicemail had been left late last night. I squared my shoulders and pressed play.

"Hey, uh, Caroline," Aidan said.

The sound of his voice had an oddly calming effect at first. I remembered his smile at the bar, his laid-back ways. This guy was chill, right? He wouldn't hurt me.

"Sorry for getting into it with your husband last night," he said. "I promised to protect you, and help you get your money back. So, I followed him, and the bastard got wise to it and slugged me. That's why my head was cut up last night. Did he say anything to you? Give me a call. Also, uh, when can I see you?"

Aidan's head was cut because he bashed it against my dashboard, not because Jason punched him. That couldn't've happened. Jason would have said something. Wouldn't he? What did Aidan mean, that he'd followed Jason? Followed him to the restaurant? I assumed Aidan had gotten to the restaurant by following me. This guy was out of touch with reality. I remembered crying to him in the shower about Jason taking my money. God help me if Aidan had taken it upon himself to go after my husband out of some misguided sense of chivalry. If that was true, I had to call off the dogs before Aidan did something crazy.

But there were two more voicemails still to listen to. I queued up the next one.

"Hey, we have things to discuss. I need to hear from you, Caroline. Don't freeze me out, or I'm gonna get upset."

And the third: "Why aren't you returning my calls? I don't like the way you're treating me. I go out on a limb for you, and this is what I get. It's not okay. I'll be out on the water this morning with my brother. Then I'm coming to find you."

I'm coming to find you. Oh, my God. I'd been warned. I should have listened to my mother's nagging voice. I should have paid attention to the accumulated horror stories of forty-three years of life as a woman.

Never trust a stranger. Never let a man you don't know into your house, your car, your pants. I'd ignored them all, and picked Aidan up instead, for a night of wild sex. Now an obviously mentally unstable felon with a gun in his drawer was coming for me. It was no better than I deserved.

My only option was to appease him somehow.

I pulled up Aidan♥ in my contacts and pressed call. He answered before the first ring was even completed.

"*Finally.*"

"Did I catch you at a bad time? You sound out of breath," I said.

"I went for a swim."

"Oh." I looked out the kitchen window at the gray sky. It was like fifty degrees outside. Didn't really seem like the weather for that, but then he was an odd guy.

"I'm returning your call," I said. "Your *many* calls."

There was an awkward pause.

"What do you expect when you don't call me back?" he said.

"How about, wait? Also, how did your number get in my phone?"

"I thought you'd want it."

At least he admitted to messing with my phone, though he hardly sounded remorseful. I wanted to ask him what else he'd done with the phone while I was sleeping. But I was afraid of the answer.

"You shouldn't mess with another person's phone," I said.

"Jeez. *Sorry*. Why didn't you call?"

"My husband was here."

"With you?"

"Yes, with me. What do you think?"

"You said you were getting a divorce."

"I said I wasn't sure."

"That's not what I heard, Caroline."

I sighed. "Look. I need to ask you to back off and give me space to figure things out. Can you do that for me, Aidan?"

"Are you saying you *might* be getting a divorce?"

"I don't know. Maybe."

"Where are you now?"

"Why?" I asked, my heart skittering with alarm. I did *not* want him coming to this apartment.

"I want to see you. When can I see you?"

"Not today. I have a lot of things to do."

"What about our agreement?"

Agreement? What the hell was he talking about? We'd never agreed to anything. The only thing I could think of was that conversation in the shower about Jason taking the money. He'd made noises about getting it back for me, which, naturally, I didn't take seriously. He wasn't a lawyer, after all. Hardly. If he had some crazy notion about that, I needed to disabuse him of it, fast.

"Look, I appreciate your concern. But my husband and I are working things out amicably, as far as the money is concerned. So, I won't be needing any help."

"I don't buy that."

"You don't buy what?"

"You can't trust him. He's not reliable. He's possibly even dangerous. I have some information to give you. Things you're not aware of. When can I see you?"

"That's not a good idea right now."

"Then *when?*"

He'd nearly shouted into the phone. This guy's temper was on a hair trigger. Did I need to get the police involved? But that would blow my secret, probably without doing much to protect me. I had to remember that Aidan's brother was a cop. My father always said, cops stick together.

"When I get back out to the beach, I'll give you a call," I said, to put him off, and calm him down.

"When will that be?"

"I'm not sure. I'll call you when I know."

"I'm gonna hold you to that."

If he'd been listening, he would've realized that I hadn't actually committed to anything specific. But he seemed less agitated, so if he wanted to think I'd made him some kind of promise, then fine. I ought to get off the phone while I was ahead.

"Okay, talk soon," I said cheerily, and hung up.

I immediately deleted Aidan's number from my contacts and blocked it. That gave me more satisfaction than it should, given that I knew it was useless. Aidan was not the type of guy you could get rid of just by blocking his number.

26

My friend Stacey Allen was waiting for me in front of the spin studio. I watched her from across Third Avenue as I waited for the light to change, steeling myself for this encounter. It was a cool, crystalline fall morning, and I was trying to get my life together. Stacey was on my to-do list.

The light changed, and I ran up to her breathlessly.

"I'm not late, am I?" I said, giving her a hug.

"Not at all. I'm glad you called. I've missed our spin classes together. But I didn't want to press, since I know you've been going through a tough time," Stacey said, in a syrupy voice, holding the door open for me.

We hadn't seen each other since the night of the housewarming party, when Jason brought the Russian woman to the house. Stacey had acted so sympathetic then, but she was a terrible gossip. Sure enough, mutual friends in the city had been pity-texting me about my marriage troubles ever since. Stacey had obviously blabbed my business all over town. Jason and I were patching things up, but the truce was fragile. Gossip would make things harder. I'd invited Stacey to spin class to tell her to back off.

"I'm not sure what you mean, Stacey. Things are great with me," I said, in a cheery tone, as we presented our cards to the girl at the desk.

Stacey looked confused. "What about that big upset at your house-warming party? That woman, with your husband?"

"Right. Well, I can understand why you might've jumped to the wrong conclusion. I did myself, at first. But that woman was a disgruntled worker. She'd screwed up some paperwork, he complained, and they fired her. She was harassing him."

"Is that what Jason told you?" Stacey said. "Because I'm pretty sure I would have heard about that if it was true."

Crap. I'd forgotten that Stacey's husband's law firm represented Jason's company. If my white lie had been true, her husband would indeed know about it, and might well have told Stacey. By repeating Jason's explanation that the Russian woman was a coworker, I'd ended up confirming for myself that my husband was lying.

"Oh, you poor thing," Stacey said. Which pissed me off.

"I don't need your pity."

"It's *sympathy*. And maybe you need some honesty. Look, I can't really say much, but I think Jason has issues at work. You should ask him about them."

"What kind of issues?"

Stacey made a zippering motion across her lips. Class was about to start. We headed for the spin classroom.

"Stacey, look, we've been friends for a long time, right?" I said.

"Since Gracie and Hannah were little. I love you, Caroline. You can trust me. You don't have to pretend to be okay when you're not."

"That's the thing. I can't trust you. I know you've been gossiping about my marriage. And now you're trying to make me doubt my husband."

Stacey flushed bright red and put her hand over her heart. "No, you've got it all wrong," she said. "I was *not* gossiping. I would never gossip. I wasn't trying to do anything except look out for you."

"Well, thanks, but I'm fine, and I'm asking you to stop talking about me to our mutual friends. Jason and I are doing great together. It's hurtful and damaging to have people say otherwise."

"Look, if that's how you want to play it, I'll butt out. I was only trying to be helpful."

"I hear that, but it's not helpful."

"Fine. Message received," Stacey said, holding up her hands defensively.

We took bikes side by side but didn't look at one another. I wasn't sure what my diatribe had accomplished. Would Stacey stop gossiping, or would she simply stop talking to me? Maybe I *wanted* her to stop talking to me. Her vague insinuations about Jason having trouble at work only caused me more anxiety. I remembered Jason's boss, Peter Mertz, acting so skeptical at the party when I talked about Jason's business trip. I'd had a feeling for a while now that something was off at Jason's work. But I was hesitant to confront him about it when our reconciliation was so new. Not without more information, anyway.

Gabrielle, the spin instructor, mounted a bike at the front of the room, adjusted her headset, and fiddled with the controls. An image of a road winding through hills by the sea popped up on the video screen behind her, and the overhead lights dimmed. The music swelled, and I started to pedal. From the corner of my eye, I noticed a straggler entering the studio. Gabrielle paused the music. She hated tardiness, and I'd seen her eject latecomers. I was expecting her to say something nasty, but to my surprise, she gave a big smile.

"Hey, new student. Awesome, we need more guys in this class. Come on in, take a bike."

I turned to look, gasped, and grabbed the bike handles. It was *Aidan*, and he was walking right toward me. He wore biking shorts and a cut-off sweatshirt, like he actually planned to take this class. It wasn't a coincidence. It couldn't be. He was stalking me.

Aidan held my gaze as he walked up to the cycle next to mine.

"Hello, Caroline," he said, with a chilling grin, as he got on the bike.

Stacey's head whipped around. She couldn't believe that this good-looking young guy knew me.

"Hey, I could use some help with my settings," Aidan said.

I had a terrible urge to run. But I needed to stay cool, and act like nothing was out of the ordinary, so Stacey didn't get suspicious. She was gossiping about my marriage enough already.

I dismounted and stepped over to Aidan's cycle. The music came back on, loudly enough that I wouldn't be overheard. I leaned down, my mouth at his ear.

"*Stop following me*," I said, the words coming out like I'd spit them.

"I'm not following you."

"Then how did you know I'd be here? You went through my phone, didn't you?"

Aidan looked hurt, even bewildered.

"You told me a lot of things when we were together. You told me how much you love this class, and that I should try it."

"No, I didn't. You're making that up. I never told you about this class. And I certainly never said you should come to it."

"Maybe you don't remember all the things you said."

From the front of the room, Gabrielle spoke into her headset.

"Everything okay over there, folks?"

I gave Gabrielle a thumbs-up and climbed back on my cycle. I forced myself to do the class, but the entire time, I was flooded with panic at Aidan's presence. I couldn't have him making a scene in front of Stacey. I was afraid that he might follow me home. (Though I realized he could already know my apartment address from my phone.) I had no idea how to defuse the situation. I pedaled maniacally, dreading the end of class.

Forty minutes later, the lights came up. I was bathed in sweat and my legs were shaky, but I jumped off the bike, ready to bolt for the door. Stacey stood in the aisle, blocking my escape and eyeing Aidan with open curiosity.

"You *know* him?" she asked.

"Caroline. Wait, don't go," Aidan said, dismounting.

"I guess so," she said.

Aidan came over to us, and I caught Stacey looking him up and down. He was buff in his workout clothes, his hair damp, his arms glistening with sweat.

"Hey, thanks for your help with the bike," Aidan said. "Is this your friend?"

"I've got to get going."

They both ignored me. Aidan stuck his hand out, and Stacey took it, her eyes lighting up.

"I'm Aidan."

"Stacey. What did you think of the class?"

"Great. Caroline's been telling me this class is an awesome workout, so I decided to check it out for myself."

Stacey looked back and forth between us, her eyebrows shooting up. "How do you two know each other?"

"I tend bar at a restaurant near her beach house."

"*Oh.* So you're from out on the island. What brings you into the city?" Stacey asked.

"I'm here to visit Caroline."

"That's not true," I insisted. "He's a friend of my sister's. Of Lynn's. *Right?* He's here to see Lynn."

"He said he was a bartender near your beach house," Stacey said.

"He's also a friend of Lynn's, which is why he's in the city."

"Really? How do you know Lynn?" Stacey asked, turning to Aidan.

He laughed. "Whatever Caroline says. Nice to meet you, Stacey. Come on, let's go, babe."

Aidan grabbed my arm and steered me firmly toward the door, as Stacey stared after us slack-jawed. I gave it thirty seconds till she opened her phone and started texting everyone I knew.

Outside, I yanked my arm from Aidan's grasp.

"Get away from me," I said.

I turned and ran, dodging traffic on Third Avenue. But he was in much better shape than me, and within a block, he'd fallen into step beside me. I slowed to a fast walk, my heart hammering in my chest as I realized I couldn't outrun him.

"Leave me alone," I said, staring straight ahead.

"Don't be like this."

"Go away, or I'll scream."

"What do you expect when you block my number? I call and call, and it goes straight to voicemail, so I came to find you."

I whirled on him. "A normal person would take no for an answer."

He looked hurt and bewildered. "You never told me no. You said you would call. You said you were coming to the beach. And you didn't. I want to see you, that's all."

"*I* don't want to see *you*. You're screwing up my life. I'm trying to make my marriage work. You told my friend that we're having an affair."

"I never said that."

"Yes, you did. You might as well have."

"You're ashamed to have her know? You think I'm not good enough for you, is that it?"

"Aidan, how many times do I have to say this? I'm *married*. Is that a concept you understand? Do you know what you did? Stacey's the biggest gossip in town. She's going to tell everyone I have a hot young boyfriend now. My husband will hear."

"Good."

"Good? You're *trying* to ruin my life?"

"I'm trying to help you get away from him. He cheated on you. He took your money."

"He put the money back."

In fact, Jason had only restored a fraction of the funds he'd taken from the accounts, leaving me with just enough to cover our immediate bills. When I asked where the rest of the money went, he made excuses. Deals that went south. A "cushion" he needed for his business accounts. It was possible that he was lying to me, and that he planned to use the money for his Russian girlfriend. Or maybe Stacey Allen was right, and Jason was in serious trouble at work. That prospect was just as worrying, frankly.

"You're lying. He didn't put the money back. Did he?" Aidan said, watching me knowingly.

"None of your business."

"You made it my business when you asked for my help, Caroline."

"I *never* asked for your help. Stop saying that. We spent one night together. It was fun, it was great even, but now it's over, and I'm asking you, nicely, to leave me alone. If you can't do that, then there's something wrong with you. If you won't do it, you'll force me to go to the police. Are we clear?"

His face fell. "You feel the same way I do. I know it. He's *making* you say these things."

"That's crazy."

"I'm going to free you from him."

"*Free me?* Do you know how that sounds?"

"You think I'm not serious? I am serious."

I looked into Aidan's blue eyes and saw a glassiness there, a vacancy. Fear licked my bones. I'd had moments of thinking something was off with Aidan, but now I saw that he was truly detached from reality. We stood at the busy intersection of Second Avenue and Seventy-ninth Street. The whole time we'd been talking, people and cars and taxis had been whizzing by, giving me a false sense of security. I must be safe, because this was Manhattan, in the middle of the day, with a million people all around. But no. I wasn't safe with Aidan, any time, any place.

I held up my hand, and a taxi screeched to a halt in front of me.

"What are you doing?" he said.

"I'm leaving. If you follow me, I swear to God, I'll call the police," I said.

I jumped in the backseat and slammed the door.

"Drive!"

The cab sped away. When I looked out the rear window and saw Aidan fading into the distance, getting smaller and smaller, my eyes filled with tears of relief. But this was a temporary escape. I hadn't seen the last of him, and I knew it.

"Where to, miss?" the cabdriver asked.

Where would I be safe? If he'd gone through my phone, then Aidan knew the address of my apartment in the city. He knew my comings and goings, my spin class, restaurants I liked, my friends' addresses. Anywhere I normally went, he would find me. I'd held off going to the police out of fear that my fling with Aidan would become public knowledge. But given what gossipy Stacey had seen in spin class, it already had. I needed to worry less about my reputation and more about my safety.

"Take me to the nearest police station," I said.

27

The Nineteenth Precinct was housed in a quaint brick-and-limestone building on a quiet side street. Inside, it was standard government issue, with scuffed linoleum floors and garish fluorescent lighting. When I explained why I'd come, the gruff old guy behind the desk took my name and told me to have a seat.

The waiting room was crowded, and from the look of it, I could be sitting here all day. While I waited, I texted Hannah. Seeing her at dinner the other night had reminded me how much I missed her. Some quality mom-daughter time would make me feel better about everything. I suggested picking her up at school this weekend to take her shopping and to lunch.

Ten minutes later, Hannah still hadn't texted me back, and a young woman stepped into the waiting room, holding a clipboard, and called my name.

"Follow me, please," she said.

She introduced herself as Officer Sanchez. She was short and stocky, with a pretty face and dark hair pulled back in a bun. I followed her through the door to an open area crowded with rows of desks. Uniformed officers bustled all around us. A large, tattooed man was being led away in handcuffs, and a police dog stood obediently in a corner. Officer Sanchez led me to the back of a room, to a desk that was separated from the others by a partition. The desk was covered with folders and paperwork and strewn with half-filled coffee cups. We sat down, and she pulled a keyboard toward her and pulled up a form on the screen. She typed in my name and address.

"First," she said, "do you require medical attention?"

"Medical attention? No."

"You were not injured physically in the incident?"

"I mean, he grabbed my arm. Maybe I have a bruise or something. But no."

"Name of perpetrator?" she asked, evenly, holding my gaze.

And I froze.

This was the moment of truth. If I gave Aidan's name, this officer would presumably interview him, possibly even arrest him. I would have to face Aidan in court. My one-night stand would become public knowledge. My indiscretion might even make the news. It would be so much worse than Stacey's gossip. But wasn't it better to risk humiliation and public shame than—than *what*? Aidan had followed me, but would he really hurt me? I found myself denying, rethinking—chickening out.

"I—I don't know if I can."

"This is always the hard part," Officer Sanchez said. She glanced down at my wedding and engagement bands. "It's your husband, right? A lot of women get to this moment, and they can't bring themselves to file charges. No matter how long he's been hurting them, they still love him. But you wouldn't be here if you didn't know in your heart it's the right thing."

"No. You see, that's the problem. It's not my husband."

"*Oh*. Another man?"

"Yes."

"An intimate partner?"

"An—?"

"Somebody you had sex with?"

I hesitated.

"Ma'am, no judgments. This situation comes up more than you'd think, where the abuse was by—you know—someone on the side. I always advise complainants to put their safety ahead of any embarrassment."

"But why do you need to know if we were intimate? You're not going to write that in the computer, are you?"

"It's relevant to whether you can file for an order of protection in family court. You can only do that if the perpetrator is an intimate partner or family member. So, yes, I do need to know, and it will go in the record."

That gave me pause. But the officer had a point—it said something that I'd even come here. I was afraid of Aidan, and with good reason. I had to be brave and protect myself.

"Okay. Yes. We had sex."

"Name of perpetrator?"

"His name is Aidan Callahan," I said.

"Spell it?"

I did and watched her type it into the computer.

"Do you have his date of birth or social security number?"

"I know his birthday. Why?"

"There could be twenty Aidan Callahans. I need to make sure we get the right one. Plus, with a DOB, I can run him for priors."

Prior arrests, she meant. Aidan must've been arrested before, because of the card in his wallet from the probation officer. I didn't know when, where, or for what. Maybe this officer could tell me.

I gave her his date of birth, which I remembered from his driver's license because it was the same as my mother's. She typed it into her system. Her eyebrows lifted as she stared at the screen.

"What?" I said, my heart slamming in my chest.

"Were you aware that he has a prior conviction for manslaughter?"

"He killed someone? He's a *murderer*?"

"Manslaughter isn't murder. It means someone died, but it could be a lot of different things. It could be he was provoked, like in a fight. Could be he was driving drunk and he killed someone. Or even, sometimes, it was an actual murder, but they can't prove it, so they plead it down to manslaughter. There's no way for me to know from what's in the computer. It does say he's still on probation. When you file the domestic violence complaint, I'll inform his probation officer, and I can ask for the details then."

"Okay."

"All right, now the complaint. Please describe the act of violence Aidan Callahan committed against you. When and where it occurred, and exactly what he did," she said, like she'd uttered those same words a thousand times before.

"Um, there hasn't been any actual violence yet. I'm worried there might be, but so far, it's just stalking."

"Stalking? What do you mean by that?"

"He followed me. He came to a restaurant where I was eating dinner. Then he came to my spin class."

"Okay, but what did he *do*? I can only help if there's a crime, ma'am. And family court can only issue a protective order if there's an express threat. Did he do something threatening, violent, disorderly, unruly?"

"He hasn't done anything yet. But he's acting crazy."

"What do you mean, crazy? Be specific."

I paused, sighing. "There isn't anything that you might typically call crazy. We had a one-night stand, and now he's showing up everywhere I go. I told him I don't want to see him anymore, but he's following me. Leaving messages on my phone. It's freaking me out."

I was expecting her to show me the door, but she nodded sympathetically.

"I understand. But is it possible you're overreacting? The messages on the phone are not a crime unless he makes a verbal threat. And if he hasn't said or done anything threatening, how do you know his presence isn't a coincidence, like he happened to be in those places at the same time as you?"

"Because he doesn't live here. He lives in Glenhampton, where we met. He came in to the city specifically to find me. He even said so."

She frowned, her eyes flicking back and forth at the computer screen.

"Ma'am, I wish I could be more help. But I'm looking at my categories here, and what you've described so far is not criminal behavior. He hasn't raised a hand to you?"

"No."

"Hasn't made any explicit threats of violence? I'm talking verbal threats of violence?"

"No."

"Did he brandish a weapon?"

"He has a weapon. A gun. I saw it in his apartment. But he didn't use it."

"Hmm. He's probably not supposed to have a gun while he's on probation. We could try to get him charged with a probation violation, and they might remand him."

"Remand?"

"Lock him up, for some period of time. I can't promise how long, or even if they'd really do it. Depends on the terms of his probation. But it might be your best option, since you have no case on domestic violence."

"Would he find out it was me who told on him?"

"He might. They'd have to search his house and seize the gun in order to violate him. And they're generally not gonna search based on an anonymous complaint. So, yeah, you'd probably have to come forward and give your name."

I looked away, torn about what to do. If I filed a complaint about the gun, she couldn't promise me that Aidan would go to jail. On the other hand, he might go to jail, but only for a short period of time, and he might find out it was because of me. When he got released, he'd be furious. So far, he'd followed me, but he hadn't tried to hurt me. If I filed charges, I could end up escalating the situation. He might flip out and retaliate. Would the police be able to protect me? I doubted it.

"I'm not sure it's worth it. I don't think I should do it." I dropped my head into my hands.

"I know it's frustrating," she said. "The system is built to respond after violence already happened, and it can leave women vulnerable. If you want, I'll give you a referral downtown to family court for an order of protection. In all honestly, it's a waste of time. You'll get denied there for lack of a verbal threat."

"There's nothing I can do, then."

"You can watch your back. Don't walk alone at night. Carry a whistle or some pepper spray. If he does threaten you verbally—I'm talking a direct, specific threat—or if you believe he's about to become violent, call nine-one-one. I'll give you this information sheet for the domestic violence hotline, and the number for family court protective services. It explains what they do. Who knows, maybe they can help more than I think they can."

She jotted some notes. I took the paper she held out; then she walked me to the exit.

"Thank you," I said, sincerely, and shook her hand.

"No problem. Stay safe. And maybe—"

She hesitated.

"What?" I asked.

"Not to be judgmental or anything. But you should be more careful who you associate with. A one-night stand, who knows what you're getting into. Could be a nice guy, could be a nutjob who likes to hurt women."

She walked away before I had a chance to protest that I'd never done anything like that before, and never would again.

28

Caroline had told Aidan they couldn't be seen together in public. She freaked out when her friend with the big mouth saw him at spin class. He hadn't even wanted to go to the stupid class. He did it to be with her. And now she was using it as an excuse to avoid going places together, at a point when their relationship should be taking off, going public, turning into something long-term.

Sometimes he wondered if she loved him as much as he loved her.

"You shouldn't hang out with Stacey. I can tell she's not your true friend," Aidan had told Caroline afterward, out on the street.

"True friend? What are you, in eighth grade?" she'd said, laughing.

That lilt in her voice when she was amused was so adorable, he didn't even mind being the object of her laughter.

"I'm just saying, you deserve better."

"I agree, but what can I do? My circle is full of catty people like Stacey. She saw what she saw, and she'll talk. She knows everybody I know. It was an unforced error. I can't afford any more of those."

She was worried about her divorce case. He got that; he felt the same way. The last thing Aidan wanted was to screw up her divorce. He wanted her free, sooner than later, so they could be together for real. And he wanted her to get the money back, and keep the beach house, so they could live the life he dreamed of. The two of them together in that house on Gramps's land, for all the world to see.

"These people in your life treat you so bad," he'd said. "Not only your friend, but your husband. I worry about him. About what he's mixed up in. I want to protect you."

"How can you help me? Jason is so volatile, and you're not around," she said.

"I can make sure he doesn't hurt you."

"How? You heard what I said. You can't be seen with me, without having it damage my case."

"What if I were to follow him, to see what I can find out? To get some leverage?"

The city passed them by on all sides as Caroline held his gaze. Cars honking their horns, sirens blaring, people rushing. It was nothing to him. All he saw was her. He would do anything for this woman.

"Okay," she said, finally. "But Jason can't see you. And it's better if we don't communicate for a while."

She glanced around to make sure nobody was watching. Then she stepped up to kiss him lightly on the lips and walked away. He would miss her terribly if they didn't communicate, even if it was only tempo-rary. But he had to do this—for their future, for her safety. The conver-sation he'd overheard in the parking lot before the husband slugged him weighed on Aidan's mind. Half a million dollars, and the Russian chick. That jerk was up to something, and Aidan feared that Caroline could be in danger. He would find out, one way or the other, and put a stop to it.

29

Manhattan was an easy place to follow someone. On every block, at all hours, there were people out and about. Aidan spent days on the husband's tail and got good at melting into crowds. He would find that perfect doorway to duck into. Or step into a bus shelter, drop behind a parked delivery van, peek out from behind a dumpster, lurk behind some scaffolding, you name it. Nobody ever noticed a thing. He would find a diner, or worst-case scenario a Starbucks (friggin' coffee cost enough to fix his car), with a big window, and sit and wait forever, nursing the one coffee he was willing to pay for. It was easy, though granted, the hours were long. He would do that all day, then drive out to the island for the late shift. Clock in at the Red Anchor at four, clock out at midnight. Up at dawn the next morning, get in the car, drive back to the city, take up his spot outside Caroline's apartment by eight thirty, when the husband would leave. And do it all over again the next day. It took its toll. The time, the money. Gas, parking, coffee while he sat and watched. So far, he hadn't seen much. But he did it for Caroline.

It was a warm, blustery day. The winds were out of the south, smelling of summer still, but picking up yellow leaves that had fallen from the trees and swirling them on the sidewalk. He pulled Caroline into an alley between two buildings. She tilted her head back and closed her eyes, and his tongue found hers. The kiss was so intense that he was hard in a second.

She pulled away, eyeing the bulge in his pants.

"Oh, my," she said, glancing up and down the street, giggling in a way that sent chills through Aidan. Like she wanted him. Thank God, too, because he was starting to wonder.

"Can we go back to your place?" he said, reaching for her again.

She dodged his hands. "No. You know that's not smart."

"How about a hotel then?"

She'd have to pay, though. That did bother him. The man should always pay, but he couldn't.

"We have to be careful. I told you. Have you found out anything about Jason yet?"

"Nothing concrete. But I'm on it."

She nodded. "Good."

"He's living with you. In your apartment. I don't understand."

"It's part of my strategy. The lawyer says not to move out because I might give up my claim to the property."

"But it's the beach house you really want, right?"

She put a finger to his lips. "Don't you worry about those things. I have it under control. We'll be together soon, I promise."

"When?"

"Once the divorce is resolved."

"Okay, I guess."

"You need to keep doing what you're doing."

"I am."

"Good. Now, I have to go. I'm going to walk away. Don't leave here until I get to the end of the block."

"I miss you," he said.

She stepped out of the alley and was gone.

That was four days ago, and it was the last time he'd touched her. He'd seen her, since. He saw her every day, from a distance. Watched her. Imagined his hands on her body, his mouth on hers. He was getting antsy.

Now he sat in a mostly empty Starbucks, eyes trained on the entrance to the building across the street. He looked up, and the barista smiled. She'd flirted with him before when he bought his drink. A goth girl with dark eyes, blue streaks in her hair, and a tattoo of a snake crawling up her arm. Before Caroline, he would've been all over that. All over any attractive woman who let him know that she was interested. But not anymore. Amazing how Caroline had changed him, and in such a short time. He felt different. He felt alive. She'd given him hope, and now he couldn't imagine being with anyone but her. What was it about her? Only everything. The way she made him feel. That crystalline beauty—the eyes and cheekbones, the body. All her ways. That plummy, rich-bitch voice, the way she moved, the classy clothes, the luxury car, her discreet perfume that he wished would linger on his clothes longer than it did, but it wasn't some cheap drugstore pisswater. Her house, of course. So, yeah, it was her life, and all the things that came with her. Caroline's life was the one he'd dreamed for himself, always, watching from the other side of town as the weekend people came and went as they pleased. They were untouchable, and free, like he ought to be. He was tired of sucking up to everyone in the world—his brother, the cops, his boss, the customers at the restaurant. He was the better man, but they never would see that. Well, Caroline would make them see. She would make things happen for him, once the obstacles were out of the way. He had to earn it. But it would be worth whatever it took. He wouldn't shrink when the time came.

The barista was coming toward him with a cup in her hand.

"I made you a fresh one. On the house," she said, smiling.

The name written on the cup wasn't Aidan, like the one he'd paid for. It was Samantha, with a phone number. He stared at it, disbelieving. She set it down on the table before him, and then she caught the expression on his face.

"Is something wrong? Not cool to give you my number?" the girl said, shuffling her feet nervously.

"Oh. Right, that's your number. It's fine."

"I wasn't trying to harass you. I thought you were cute. I'm sorry. Don't tell my manager?"

"No, really, it's nice of you," he said, but he choked on the words. "See, Samantha was my girlfriend's name, and she—we . . . things didn't work out."

"Like I said, I apologize. Keep the drink."

From the corner of his eye, he saw Stark emerge from a building across the street.

"Gotta go," he said, jumping up.

"Okay, well, enjoy the drink. And have a great day."

He left the drink behind, even though it was free, and he wanted it. The name on the cup was an evil omen. Samantha had cheated with his best friend, and the aftermath of that left Matthew dead. It wasn't Aidan's fault what happened, but it destroyed his life as sure as it did Matthew's. He'd lost hope that he'd ever recover—until Caroline. She was like the pot of gold, out of reach at the end of the rainbow. If this chance slipped through his fingers, it would never come around again. There'd be nothing left for him on this green earth. He might as well walk into the ocean and not come out.

But no. He was letting the dark feelings suck him under. And why, because some idiot blue-haired girl hit on him with her poisoned name? No. Today was a *good* day. The sky was brighter, the wind was warmer. Things were different now. Caroline was loyal and kind; she had class. Nothing like Samantha. And *he* was different than he had been. He wasn't a dimwit pushover like he'd been as a kid. He was somebody who reached out and grabbed life and took what he wanted.

"Thanks," he said, and hurried out the door before he lost Jason Stark in the crowd.

30

Lynn and I were sitting in an Italian place near my apartment, sipping glasses of pinot grigio and waiting for our Caesar salads to arrive.

"Jason and I are renewing our vows for our anniversary," I said, "and I'm thinking about doing it up. Maybe the Rainbow Room, with a band and a champagne fountain. The works. What do you think?"

It was the first time I'd seen my sister since her return from Florida a couple of days earlier. She'd come in to the city to meet with her lawyer about some real estate business, and suggested we meet for lunch, so she could catch up on my marital drama. I tried to beg off. I worried that Aidan might ambush me again, the way he had at the spin class. On the other hand, I was too keyed up to be alone, and dying for the comfort of Lynn's company. I had half a mind to tell her about Aidan anyway, to get her advice.

"Renewing your vows? Are you sure?" Lynn said. "When I left, you were on the verge of divorce. I come back a week later, and everything's roses? Shouldn't you wait for the reunion to take before you throw some big expensive party?"

"I thought you'd be happy for me."

Lynn flicked her blond hair back over her shoulder. Her deep tan and coral lipstick clashed with the grim expression on her face.

"I want to be happy for you, sis, but I'm not sure that's justified yet. I've been hearing some gossip that I hope isn't true. I didn't want to have to repeat it to you," she said.

I knew what was coming.

"You don't have to repeat it," I said.

"Because you already know what it is."

"I can guess. I know you play tennis down in Boca with that—what's her name?"

"Andrea Grassi. She's friends with your girlfriend Stacey."

"Stacey's not my friend."

"Apparently not, since she talks behind your back something awful. Anyway, I told Andrea it was impossible. That she must be misinformed. Am I right?"

Lynn gazed at me intently. I kept my expression neutral.

"Caroline?"

"Hold on."

The waiter was walking toward our table, carrying our salads—mine with shrimp, Lynn's with chicken. We waited while he worked the long pepper grinder. I loved the food here, but today I had no appetite. A large plate-glass window faced the street, and I sat where I could look out, constantly glancing over Lynn's shoulder, scanning for him. He'd been following me. I hadn't seen him yet today, and I was praying he was gone. That he'd given up, lost interest in me. But what if he hadn't? This man was a killer. I knew that from what the police officer told me. Manslaughter. It could mean anything. And Aidan Callahan was now focused on me. My nerves were taut, my stomach unsettled from the stress. I worried every minute that I would turn around and see him behind me.

"Tell me what you heard, and I'll tell you if it's true," I said, once the waiter was gone.

"I *heard*, you got yourself a boy toy. A bartender named Aidan who goes to spin class with you. And he's a hunk and a half. But obviously this isn't possible, right? A few days ago, I was holding your hand while you sobbed about your rat of a husband."

"Aidan followed me to spin class. I didn't bring him."

"He's real? I can't believe it. What the hell is going on, Caroline?"

"*Nothing's* going on. I'm not cheating. Not exactly, not currently."

"Whoa, a lot of hedging there, babe. Listen, let me say up front, if you did it, I understand. Jason cheated first."

"Jason didn't cheat. He told me all about it. She's a—a work colleague."

"The Russian tart in the leather skirt? Please. You can't even say that with a straight face."

"It's true."

"Don't tell me that. I *saw* her."

"Well, I believe him. My marriage is fine. Stacey Allen should shut her trap."

"If your marriage is so fine, who's this bartender, and why did he follow you to spin class?"

"Okay," I said, glancing around the restaurant to check one last time that nobody I knew was present. I lowered my voice. "You have to promise not to tell."

Lynn eyed me with interest. I took a swig of wine and then a deep breath.

"Cross my heart," she said.

"Not even Joe."

"I won't tell my husband, promise," Lynn said.

"Thank you. Now. You remember how I was when you left?"

"You were a wreck."

"It got worse from there. I found out Jason drained the bank accounts."

"Shit, you're kidding me. That prick. I told you to go to the lawyer."

"I did. I actually filed papers. But then I withdrew them."

"Why?"

"It's a long story."

"Did he put the money back?"

"Some. Not all of it. But he's going to."

She made a clucking noise. "Why would you trust him at this point? With everything he's done?"

"I'm choosing to trust him. I mean, it's Jason. Twenty years of marriage, right?"

"I guess. He always seemed like a good guy."

"Yes, he did. Anyway, in the middle of all this mess, you were in Florida, I was freaking out—"

"Oh, so it's my fault now?"

"I'm just explaining. I was really upset. There's nothing to drink in the house, nobody to talk to. I go to the bar in town."

"Which bar?"

"The Red Anchor."

"Oh, I've been there."

"Yeah, it's halfway decent, and it was open. I had to get out of the house or I'd go crazy."

"Wait a minute, are you talking about that guy, blondish hair, built, looks like Brad Pitt?"

"Brad Pitt? Really? I don't see that."

"Come on. They're like twins. He's freaking gorgeous. You didn't—?"

"I did. I was drunk off my ass. It was a one-night stand. And I regret it terribly."

Lynn threw her head back and laughed. "Oh, my God. I didn't know you had it in you. Seriously. How was it?"

"How was it? It was a huge mistake."

"Uh, hello, that's not what I'm asking."

I leaned forward. "I know what you're asking, but this isn't funny," I said. "It's not some schoolgirl prank. It's a nightmare. We did it *once*. I told him goodbye, and now he won't leave me alone. He's been *following* me."

She sobered instantly. "Is he blackmailing you?"

"No."

"How much does he want?"

"I said no. It's not about money."

"What then?"

"He's, like, obsessed with me."

"That hot bartender—obsessed with you?"

"Yes."

"No, really."

"Is that so implausible?" I said, huffily.

"I mean, you're a beautiful woman, Car. But aren't you like twenty years older than him?"

"More like fifteen. Look, I agree, it's weird. It's freaking me out. The first time I tried to get rid of him, he slammed his head against the dashboard of my car till it was bloody."

"Holy shit, really? Is something *wrong* with him?"

"I don't know. But that's not all. Then he starts turning up in the city. Telling me he can't live without me. After a one-night stand, can you believe it? I thought it would be a big nothing to a guy like that."

"What did you say when he showed up?"

"I told him to stay away from me, or I'd go to the police."

"Good for you. And did he? Stay away?"

"No. I've seen him a bunch of times since then. He follows me, always at a distance."

"That's so creepy."

"I know."

"You *should* go to the police."

"Here's the thing. I did, after the spin class. And they told me unless he hurts me or threatens me with a weapon, it's not a crime, and there's nothing they can do."

Lynn put her fork down. I could tell she believed me now.

"I'm worried about Hannah," she said.

"Hannah? Why? It's me you should worry about."

"If this guy is a psycho, how do you know he won't go after your daughter?"

"Because this has nothing to do with her," I said, and sighed with irritation. "I swear, you're obsessed with Hannah."

"Somebody needs to be. You don't think enough about how your actions affect other people."

"Thank you for your concern. But I can take care of my own daughter," I said, coldly.

"Sorry, I didn't mean to offend you."

Well, she had. Lynn didn't have kids of her own, so she'd glommed on to my daughter. The two of them were thick as thieves. Despite everything I did for Hannah, not only did she prefer her father to me, she preferred her aunt. Kids act out against the parent who provides the tough love. I understood that, but it still hurt my feelings. I resented their tight bond, and I didn't need Lynn acting like she knew what was good for Hannah better than I did. But Lynn couldn't let it go.

"It's just—" she said.

"*What?*"

"How do you know he's not violent?"

I wanted to confide in her. I really did. By making this about Hannah, she'd made it impossible. I couldn't tell her about the manslaughter without risking having her do something crazy, like telling Hannah about my affair.

"Since I threatened to go to the police, he's kept his distance. Stop worrying."

"But you said this guy's still following you."

"No. I said he *did* follow me, but now I think he won't bother me again."

"That's not what you said."

"Lynn, back off. Let's talk about something else. Renewing my vows. How to celebrate Hannah's birthday next month. Visiting you in Florida this winter. I don't want to think about Aidan Callahan anymore. I'm done with him."

"I hope he's done with you, too."

31

Aidan watched Jason Stark emerge from the office building across the street. Stark was on his phone, and from the way he surveyed the traffic, he was waiting for a ride. Aidan got anxious when he had to follow by vehicle. On foot, he could blend into the crowd. But his old red pickup with its rusted-out, banged-up passenger door stood out too much among the sleek black SUVs and grimy yellow cabs that made up the bulk of Manhattan traffic. He had no choice if he wanted to follow the guy, though, and he'd better move it. Heart racing, Aidan turned the corner and sprinted to where he'd parked his truck. *Shit.* He grabbed the parking ticket off the windshield. Sixty bucks for blocking the alley by a few frigging inches. Sixty bucks he couldn't spare.

He pulled out onto the avenue in time to see Jason Stark slide into the passenger seat of a sporty blue Audi. There was a woman at the wheel. He couldn't see her face, but she had black hair. The Audi edged into traffic and took off. Following was nerve-racking. He had to stay far enough back that they didn't spot his truck but not so far that he got stuck at a light and lost them. It was stop-and-go all the way to the Midtown Tunnel. Halfway through the tunnel, traffic started moving for no apparent reason. He emerged into daylight and the traffic soon disappeared. The surface streets in Queens were wide-open and empty, and he stayed as far back as he could without losing them. Aidan didn't know Queens at all. From the street signs, it looked like they were heading in the general direction of Kennedy Airport. Maybe these two had a plane to catch. Maybe Stark was running off with her and taking Caroline's money.

After several turns deeper into Queens, he realized that wasn't happening. They were in a warehouse district now. Parking lots and low-rise buildings, all grimy and looking like they'd be full of junk inside. He turned a corner and came upon the Audi already pulled over in front of an auto parts store. The two of them were getting out of the car. He eyed them as he drove past. Stark wore a gray business suit. The woman was in stiletto heels and a short skirt topped off with a leather jacket. She was attractive in a hard sort of way, but how any man could betray Caroline for her—for anyone—he couldn't fathom.

Aidan parked around the corner and walked back toward the auto parts store, hands in his pockets, huddling into his jacket against the wind. There wasn't a single person on the street except for him. A car cruised slowly toward him. It was nondescript—an old Ford in a muddy color—but he could've sworn he'd seen it before. He felt eyes on him, and the hair on the back of his neck stood up. Something felt off here. He strolled past the auto parts store and glanced through the plate-glass window. The aisles were full of cables and batteries and chains. An older woman stood behind a counter with a cash register. But Stark and his girlfriend were nowhere in sight.

Aidan walked past the store and turned down the alley, heading around the back, hugging the side of the building. He poked his head around the corner and there they were, about fifty feet away, standing in front of an open garage bay where a mechanic worked on a car raised on a lift. It wasn't the sort of place you imagined Jason Stark going to get his car serviced. Then again, that hard-looking Russian woman was more mobster moll than the girlfriend of a one-percenter finance bro like Jason Stark. None of this fit, which was why Aidan was so worried.

The small parking area was decrepit and full of debris and reeked of burning oil. The mistress was stamping her feet and blowing on her hands in the unseasonably cold air. They waited there for about five minutes, and Aidan watched, deeply confused about what was going on. Then a man emerged from the open garage bay. Not the mechanic, a different guy, and the look of him made Aidan gasp. He looked like a hardened killer. Built like a prizefighter, with a scar on his cheek, dressed all in black, a knit cap pulled down low to his eyes. It was shocking to think that Stark, with his establishment aura, his air of wealth and privilege, would associate with a man the likes of this. The fact that they were meeting was suspicious on its own.

Aidan watched with his own eyes as the bruiser walked up to Stark and shook his hand like they were acquainted. Stark took a thick envelope from his jacket and passed it to the man, who opened it and rifled through a substantial wad of cash. A payoff of some kind. Jesus, this was some shady stuff. Aidan moved in closer to listen. The bruiser opened his mouth, and as if on cue, a horrible screeching sound started up inside the garage. Whether or not it was specifically designed to cover up their conversation from potential eavesdroppers, it had that effect. The wind was blowing in Aidan's direction, and if not for the noise, he would've been able to hear what they said in its entirety. Instead he only managed to pick up a few words here and there. He heard "money," "no good," and "problem." Stark looked agitated. The wind shifted, and for a few minutes, Aidan heard nothing. The mistress lit a cigarette and looked away. She backed up a few steps. Aidan got the impression that what was being said was so ugly that she wanted to stay out of it.

The wind shifted back. Aidan heard Stark say his wife's name. He wasn't imagining things. Stark clearly said "Caroline," and a film of anger dropped down over Aidan's eyes. He wanted to go over and punch that smug asshole Jason Stark in the face, yell at him to get Caroline's name out of his dirty mouth, to keep her away from this wretched company. What the hell was he doing talking to this evil thug about a beautiful woman like Caroline? Whatever he was doing, it was not good. Aidan took a deep breath and sharpened his ears. The bruiser had moved on to talking about Hannah. He distinctly heard that name. Hannah was Caroline's daughter. The thug not only said her name; he said Stony

Brook, too, which Aidan knew from Caroline's phone was where her daughter went to college. That couldn't be a coincidence. Was this—

"*—gonna die,*" the bruiser said, and that confirmed Aidan's worst fears.

What had he witnessed? Stark and his mistress meeting with some lowlife underworld hit-man type. Stark paying off the thug with an envelope full of cash. The two men speaking about Caroline and Hannah. Then the thug saying someone was gonna die. What could that be, except a contract for a hit? Jason Stark wanted to be free to live with his trashy girlfriend and not have to share the money with his ex-wife. He'd taken out a hit on his wife and daughter.

Aidan was the only one who knew. He was the only one who could protect them.

32

Aidan called Caroline's phone to warn her, but the call went straight to voicemail, and he worried that she'd blocked his number. She wouldn't do that, would she? But she'd been so insistent that he not contact her. He understood the concept of hiding their affair to protect her reputation for the divorce proceeding. That was the least of their worries right now. Her husband posed a real, imminent threat. He left a message telling her so. But if she'd blocked him, she would never receive it. In order to warn her, he'd be forced to visit her in person, which she'd specifically told him not to do. It was goddamn frustrating.

He was late for work at the Red Anchor, where he was on shaky ground for missing several shifts in the last month. Aidan went to work and called her from the phone there, which she hadn't blocked. When she didn't pick up, he left another voice mail. Hopefully, this one she would get.

"Hey, Caroline, there's something important I need to tell you. I'm worried your husband is—well, that he's a danger to you and your daughter. I have some specific information. It's too much to go into on a voicemail. Call me back. Please."

At the bar that evening, Aidan tried to act like nothing was off. He poured and mixed, he smiled and cracked jokes and bickered with Nancy, the waitress. The whole time, he was obsessing about Caroline, and Hannah, and the thug from the auto parts store.

The woman sat alone at the far end of the bar. She'd been there a few minutes, watching him from the corners of her eyes. He didn't think much of it. Women like that—middle-aged, overdressed, flashy—they hit on him all the time. Tonight, he had no patience. He let her sit longer than normal. Then he took a swig of Johnnie Walker to fortify himself and went over to her.

"What can I get you tonight?" he said. But he couldn't a muster a smile.

"I'm not here to drink," she said.

"The restaurant's in the back, ma'am," he said warily.

He was on high alert now. He recognized her, but he couldn't place her. In Queens this afternoon he'd seen that nondescript Ford and felt like he was being followed.

"Are you Aidan Callahan?" she said.

What the hell? Involuntarily, he took a step backward.

"Who's asking?"

"Never mind that. I'm here to deliver a message. Stay away from Caroline Stark."

"You were in that Ford today, weren't you?"

She looked at him like he was crazy.

"What are you talking about? I don't drive a Ford."

"Yes, you do. You followed me," he said.

"Listen, I don't know what's wrong with you. You're obviously mentally disturbed. But you don't scare me. You stay away from my sister, or you'll regret it. You hear?"

Sister.

Of course. He recognized her now—Caroline's sister. She'd been in the tent at the party when he was tending bar. And he'd seen her picture in Caroline's phone. He'd wanted to meet her. But now he'd screwed it up by accusing her of following him. It was an honest mistake, though, and he couldn't let her talk to him like that. Aidan glanced down the bar. It was still early, and they were half empty, but that was a mixed blessing. Not as many ears to hear, not as much noise to cover up the sensitive things he needed to say.

"You're Lynn, right?" he said.

She reeled back in surprise. Not expecting him to know her name, surprised that he was on the inside already? But he was, and he wanted to make sure that she understood that.

"Look, not to be disrespectful, Lynn. I appreciate your concern for Caroline's welfare. But you've got it all wrong. She and I are together, we're involved. She cares for me."

He wanted to say, "She loves me," but he ought to take that slow, out of respect for Caroline's position.

"That's a lie," Lynn said.

"I'm not lying."

"She said she told you to get lost, but you're harassing her, following her around like some crazy stalker. She wants you gone."

"She doesn't. If Caroline wanted me gone, she'd tell me that herself."

"She *did* tell you. She threatened to go the police. Now it's time for you to listen."

"You don't know what you're talking about. Caroline loves me."

Lynn's expression morphed from shocked to horrified. Aidan thought his face must look the same way. What this woman was saying could *not* be true. Yet, judging by her expression, she believed it was.

"Wow, she wasn't kidding," Lynn said. "You really are crazy. She told me you two had a one-night stand, and she regrets it. She loves her husband. She wants you out of her life, *forever*. But you won't listen. I'm here to tell you that you better."

"Lies. You're lying."

"I'm not lying. I'm telling you the truth. Get it through that messed-up head of yours and leave my sister alone. You understand me? Or I'll get somebody to teach you a lesson. I can, you know. My husband has connections. *Back off.*"

Lynn rapped her knuckles on the bar to underline her words. Then she got up and marched out the door. Aidan's breath was coming fast. He staggered out from behind the bar. He could feel people's eyes on him, but he didn't care. What Lynn had said was so wrong. It had to be. He needed to convince her of that, or else he'd start to worry it was true. And he couldn't believe it. He refused. He would not accept that Caroline felt the way her sister claimed. Caroline was not Samantha. This relationship was beautiful, it was the real deal.

Right?

In the parking lot, the sea air hit him in the face and cleared his mind. Lynn was getting into a BMW. He ran toward her, waving his arms, and saw a look of alarm blossom on her face.

"*No*," he said. "Wait."

He came up to her car and reached for her door handle. She put the car in gear, backed up, and stepped on the gas. The car lurched forward, barreling toward him. He stood his ground till the last minute, then sprang out of the way, hitting the ground and rolling, the wet pavement tearing at his skin. Jesus, she could have killed him. She seemed like she wanted to. The knee of his jeans was ripped and bloody.

He jumped in his truck and screeched out of the parking lot. Five miles down the road, he saw her taillights, and floored it. She didn't recognize his truck, didn't know it was him closing in on her, didn't speed up to get away like he expected. When he was right on top of her, she looked in the rearview mirror and saw him. Her eyes bugged out in terror. It was a two-lane road, narrow and curving. He pulled alongside her, lowered the passenger window. They were both doing sixty in a thirty-five.

"Pull over," he yelled, over the roaring wind. "I have to talk to you."

Her mouth moved frantically behind the tinted glass of her window, but he couldn't tell what she was saying. A horn blared. A car was coming at him head-on, its headlights blinding against his wet windshield. He swerved, slotting back into the right lane, deciding not to kill the person in the other car just because Caroline's sister was a goddamn liar. Deciding not to die for fear that what she said was true.

He could kill the sister for what she said. For her lies. But *was* she lying? What Lynn had said had the awful ring of truth. He hit the brakes and let her pull ahead, then watched her disappear around a bend. He pulled into a turnoff and sat there with his head in his hands. Warm blood from his knee trickled down his leg. It was like his heart bleeding. He'd had such faith in Caroline. He'd put his trust in her, believed she wasn't the kind to say one thing to his face and another behind his back. Yet he'd felt something from Lynn. He could tell that she believed her own words as they came out of her mouth. She was telling the truth as she knew it. What could that mean, except that Caroline was lying to one of them? But which one?

If the barista had never given Aidan the cup with Samantha's name on it, he might believe that Caroline was true to him, and that it was her sister she'd lied to. But the cup was a vivid reminder that the people you love most in this world are the very ones you should never trust. They will cheat on you and use you. They will ruin you, even kill you, if they can. He'd hoped he'd found something different with Caroline, but had he? Would she betray him, the way Samantha had, the way Matthew had? He needed to know. But how, when she refused to see him? Screw it, he was done listening to that. He would try to storm her apartment. But no, she had doormen. They'd stop him and call the police. He could try to follow her on the street. But if Lynn was to be believed, Caroline planned to rat him out for that.

No. It made no sense. Why would she turn on him?

He had to see her. Had to warn her. Had to get to the truth. And yet, if she called the police and claimed he was harassing her, he could get in trouble. In his situation, a call to the police could land him back in jail on a probation violation. And Aidan was terrified of going back to jail. Of course, there was also the possibility that the sister was lying, and that Caroline had never said that. He couldn't stand the confusion. He needed to know what was real. He needed to see Caroline, to talk to her. And more than anything, he needed to warn her about the possible hit on her—and her daughter.

Maybe the right way to handle this was through Hannah.

If Lynn was right, and Aidan showed up unannounced at Caroline's apartment, there was at least some chance, much as he hated to admit it, that Caroline would call the police and inadvertently end up sending him to jail. But Caroline's daughter didn't know him from Adam. He could sneak up on her. Not in a sketchy way. But make contact, make sure she was safe. Try to find a way to warn her that she was in danger. He knew where she went to school, and it was less than an hour's drive from his apartment. He would be doing it out of love for her mother. If Aidan could protect Hannah, that would show Caroline how much he cared, and bring her running back into his arms.

33

Jason came home from work and announced that we were meeting Peter Mertz and his wife at a restaurant in Midtown for dinner in twenty minutes.

"I'm sorry for the short notice, but this is important," he said. "You need to get changed, and wear something nice."

He wouldn't look at me. His eyes shifted as he spoke, and there was something tight and forced in his manner. I couldn't help but remember Stacey Allen's mysterious insinuations that Jason was in trouble at work. I'd tried to get him to discuss that with me, but to no avail. At the housewarming party, Peter had seemed so skeptical when I told that white lie about Jason's whereabouts, almost like he was on to Jason's lies himself. At the time, I'd assumed that was about the Russian woman, but was it?

"What's going on, Jason? Are you in trouble at work?"

"Honey, there's always trouble at work. It's not worth bothering yourself over. The car's waiting downstairs. We need to leave in five minutes. Please."

I was in the bedroom at the vanity table, doing my eyes, when my phone rang. Every time it rang now, I jumped, terrified it would be Aidan.

But it was Lynn. I declined the call, and she called right back, so I picked up.

"I'm getting ready to go out to dinner. Can I call you back?"

"He tried to run me off the road."

She was breathing hard, her voice panicky. I knew instantly who she meant, but I couldn't admit that—not to her, not to myself. What had I brought into the lives of the people I loved?

"Who did what?" I said. "Are you okay? You sound bad."

"I'm still shaking. Your boyfriend tried to sideswipe my car. No joke. Thank God a car was coming the other way. He was going to collide with it head-on, so he had to back off. It must've freaked him out, because he stopped chasing me."

"Wait, *who?*"

"Who do you think? That fucking bartender."

"Aidan?"

"Yes, Aidan. He's as crazy as you said, Caroline. We need to go to the police. I didn't get the plate number, but I can describe the truck to a T. Red, rusted out, banged-up door."

"Why would Aidan go after you? That makes no sense."

"You don't believe me?"

"I didn't say that. But I do think you should calm down and ask yourself if it was really him, or some maniac who happened to look like him. Come on, what motive does Aidan have to go after you? How would he even know who you are?"

"He would go after me to get to you. And I don't know how he knew. But he knew, and he said a lot of stuff. He claimed to be close to you, Caroline. Is there something you're not telling me?"

"He said this while he was chasing you in his truck?"

"No. Before."

"He came to your house, and said these things?" I said, stunned.

My phone. Aidan must've found Lynn's address on my phone, tracked her down, and attacked her. My worst fears were coming true.

"No, not my house," she said.

"Then where did this happen?"

"Near the bar where he works."

"Why were you at the bar where he works?"

"Because. I told him to back off."

"Ugh, Lynn. What did you do?"

"You're being so passive that I felt I had to step in. I went there, and I told him to leave you alone."

"Are you insane? That's guaranteed to set him off."

"Well, it did. You should thank me, because now we have enough to go to the police."

"But you created the situation. Don't you see? Now Aidan has an excuse. The police won't do anything."

"What are you talking about? How does telling him to back off you give him an excuse to try to kill me?"

"The police won't take it seriously."

"Of course they will. You're not making any sense. Are you covering for this guy, Caroline?"

I was about to tell her that Aidan's brother was the chief of police. I heard a noise and turned to see Jason standing right behind me. When had he gotten there, how much had he heard?

"Who's that?" he said.

I held the phone away from me and covered the microphone.

"It's Lynn."

"What does she want?"

"Nothing. It's nothing."

"Did I hear you say something about going to the police?"

"Someone stole something from her. Or, she thinks they did. Hold on, okay?" I said, putting the phone back to my ear. "*Lynn,* listen. Jason and I are late to dinner. I'll have to call you back."

"What are we going to do?" she demanded.

"Let me think about it. I'll call you later."

I hung up, then I turned my back to him. "Zip me up, and let's go," I said.

The Uber was waiting downstairs, a black SUV. When we were

buckled into the backseat, Jason asked me again if he hadn't heard me talking to Lynn about going to the police over something.

"She can't find a piece of jewelry, and she's wondering if her housekeeper took it," I said.

"Rosario? Hasn't she been with them for, like, twenty years?"

"It couldn't be Rosario, right? I told her to look around. She probably misplaced it. You know how people hide their jewelry, like if a workman's coming or something, and then they forget where they put it? That's probably what happened."

Fifth Avenue was clogged with traffic. I felt bad lying to Jason when we were trying to find our way back into one another's hearts. But I couldn't tell him about Aidan without risking our reconciliation, especially not now that Aidan might be volatile, even dangerous. Jason would blame me for bringing this element of instability into our lives. He might even start thinking that we should separate again. I stared at the reflections of the buildings on the window of the SUV and felt so alone. I was keeping secrets from my husband. And I wondered what secrets he was keeping from me.

Peter Mertz was sitting alone in the dimly lit bar area at the restaurant, a martini on the table in front of him. Where was his wife? He stood up when we came in. But there was no smile of greeting on his face, no move to kiss or even greet me at all.

"What's this?" he said to Jason, but he was looking at me.

"Did I misunderstand?" Jason said. "I thought wives were included."

"We never said that."

I saw what was going on, and my stomach cratered. I had not been invited to this meal. There was something very serious going on between Jason and Peter that was meant to be discussed tonight, and whatever it was, it was bad enough that Jason was trying to avoid it. I was being used. My presence here was a shield.

"My mistake," Jason said. "I do apologize. But since Caroline is here, why don't we sit down and eat? Pete, you and I can talk at the office tomorrow."

I had to hand it to him. Jason was smooth under pressure. The guileless expression, the even tone of his voice. Every word out of his mouth sounded so reasonable that the listener would ask themselves if they were the crazy one. I'd taught Jason well. The student had become the master, and now he used his powers of persuasion to keep me in the dark about what increasingly seemed like very important matters. First the Russian woman, now whatever this discord was between him and Peter. Maybe I was the one who should reconsider our reconciliation.

"If you two need to talk, I can always go home," I said. "Honestly, I don't mind."

"Or, Pete could call Donna, tell her to hop in a car and come join us," Jason said.

"I believe the reservation is only for two people," Peter said.

"It's for four. My secretary made it," Jason replied.

Peter looked back and forth between Jason and me, presumably weighing his need to have it out with Jason against his reluctance to be rude to me.

"This isn't really the place to have our business discussion," Jason said.

"Yes. I said that when you suggested it."

Jason shrugged.

Peter took out his phone.

"Fine, let me see if she can get down here."

The four of us ended up having a lovely meal, despite a discernible undercurrent of tension between Jason and Peter. I'd put my phone to silent, so I didn't know until later how many times Lynn had called, in a frenzy of anxiety, asking what I planned to do about Aidan. Nor did I know that Aidan had called me several times from an unfamiliar number, one I hadn't blocked, demanding to speak to me right away. He claimed he had information that Jason was a danger to me in some way, and even a danger to Hannah. Not only was that ridiculous, it was a downright creepy thing to suggest. Luckily, I didn't listen to that voicemail until the next day.

The four of us—the Starks and the Mertzes—sat together in the exquisite, airy dining room, under glittering chandeliers, toasting and chatting like the old friends we supposedly were. I ordered the duck, and drank two glasses of a fine cabernet, and had what appeared on the surface to be a roaring good time. I admired my husband's good looks, laughed at Peter's jokes, gossiped with Donna, commented on the elegant outfits of the women at the next table. It was a night I'd look back on like it belonged to a distant, untroubled century. Because the reckoning was coming for all of us. I could feel it.

34

The morning after Lynn's run-in with Aidan on the road, she called my phone. I hesitated before picking up. I knew she'd be mad that I hadn't called her back last night to address what she perceived as a major crisis. I couldn't handle an argument right now. After that strange dinner with Peter Mertz and his wife, Jason had gone "to the office," and hadn't come home till three o'clock in the morning. I'd pretended to be asleep when he came in. But in reality, I'd barely slept all night.

"You never called me back last night," she said, and she sounded genuinely angry.

"I'm sorry," I said, flustered. "Our dinner went late. It was a business dinner, so I couldn't get away to call back. I'm on my way out now, so—"

"Whatever you're doing can wait. I'm going to the police about your bartender, and you're coming with me. No excuses."

I was in the bedroom. Jason was in the shower in the master bath. As Lynn spoke, I heard the water turn off. He'd be standing right behind the door next to me, drying off. I couldn't let him overhear this conversation. Jason still hadn't found out about my fling with Aidan, and I wanted very much to keep it that way.

I walked out into the hall.

"Lynn, it's not a good time," I said, in a low tone. "Can I call you back?"

"No. What's the problem? Don't you want to get this guy?"

"*Jason is here,*" I whispered.

"Come to my house as soon as you can. We'll go to the police station in Glenhampton, together. We don't have to say a word to Jason about any of this."

"It won't do any good to go to the police. I wanted to explain to you last night, but we got interrupted. His brother is the chief."

"The chief of what?"

"Aidan's brother is the chief of police in Glenhampton."

"You're kidding."

"I'm not. If we go to his brother, it'll get back to Aidan for sure, and piss him off more. That's why I talked to the police in the city. But they told me I had no case. I don't think that what happened to you last night changes that."

"Maybe you're right. The cops in the city'll say since it happened in Glenhampton, it's not their problem."

"Exactly. Nobody's going to help."

"What do we do, then?"

"Nothing," I said. "Stop antagonizing Aidan, and hope he fades away."

"*Antagonizing?* I almost get killed trying to get this maniac to lay off you, and you imply it's my fault for *antagonizing* him?"

"I didn't say that."

"Yes, you did. That's what you meant, anyway."

I could hear Jason moving around in the bedroom now, mere feet away. I needed to get off the phone ASAP. But I didn't want to leave things like this with Lynn. Not only was she worried about me, but she honestly believed that Aidan had tried to run her off the road.

"Lynnie, I'm sorry. Please, don't get upset. Let's discuss this in person, okay?"

"That's all I'm asking. When and where?"

"I'll drive out there. I'll be there by lunchtime."

"Okay. I'll see you then. And don't you dare stand me up," she said, and hung up.

I'd been planning to talk to Jason this morning about where the hell he'd been last night, and what was going on between him and Peter Mertz. Peter clearly wanted to have it out with Jason over something, and I was brought along to dinner to prevent that from happening. When the dinner ended, Jason took me home in an Uber, then claimed he needed to go deal with a crisis in his office. Maybe that was true, or maybe he was back with the Russian woman. When I tried to track his phone, it was off. I was dying to hash things out with him.

"Jason, we need to talk," I said.

"I've got an Uber waiting downstairs, honey. Gotta run," he said, and kissed my cheek.

"Wait one minute," I said, grabbing his arm as he tried to pass by me to leave. "You owe me an explanation. Where were you last night until three o'clock in the morning? If you have any hope of saving this marriage, and convincing me you're not having an affair, you'll tell me the truth."

He looked me in the eye. "That is the truth. Maybe you could tell last night that Peter is upset with me."

"Yes. What was that about?"

"There's a problem with one of my funds. A big problem. He referred me to the SEC for investigation."

I gasped. "*Criminal* investigation?"

"I'm afraid so, honey. But I didn't do anything wrong, I swear it. I'm going to hire a lawyer and clear my name. I'm sorry I haven't told you until now. I didn't want you to worry. I may be hard to reach in the next few days because I'm busy with this. I hope you'll understand."

"I'm so sorry I doubted you," I said, and threw myself into Jason's arms.

He pressed his lips to my hair. "Don't worry. It'll be okay. I promise. Now, I have to go."

After Jason left, I was at loose ends, fearful that he was in trouble, knowing there wasn't much I could do to help. The most productive use of my time would be to face up to my other big problem—Aidan. I would go see my sister and try to convince her to stay out of that situation. Lynn's interference would only stir things up, and I had to make her understand that.

I went to the garage where we parked, three blocks from the apartment, to get my car.

It was rush hour, and I hadn't called ahead. When I got to the garage, the line of customers waiting for their cars to be brought up from the depths was five deep, and there was only one valet on duty. He was the older of the two valets who worked there, soft-spoken and slow-moving, with a shiny, bald head. Jason sometimes drove himself to work in the morning, and when he did, he made sure to call the night before to ask that the car be brought out by the night valet. Otherwise, he said, don't even bother, because the old guy on duty was slower than molasses. Turned out Jason was right. I waited and waited. Half an hour passed. Finally, I was the next customer. The valet took my car number and went off in search of my car. More time passed. I saw my white Escalade nosing up the ramp. It came to a stop in front of me. I slapped my hand over my mouth to stifle my cry. In the pearlescent paint of the passenger door, the words "DIE BITCH" had been scratched in deeply, presumably with a key.

The valet stepped tentatively out of the car, scratching his head.

"How did this happen?" I said, barely getting the words out, close to tears as I stared at my beautiful car in horror.

"I can't say. Never seen nothing like it before in all the years I worked here," he said.

I walked around, barely believing my eyes as I saw the same words scratched a second time on the driver's side, with deep scoring scratches on the rear door and the tailgate.

"Who did this?" I asked, turning on the valet.

My voice shook with fear, because I knew who did it. Lynn's visit to the bar had set Aidan off. He wasn't just following me anymore, creepily confessing his adoration, begging to spend time with me, making ridiculous insinuations that my husband was a threat to me. The threat was Aidan himself. He'd turned to violence. He'd tried to run my sister off the road. And now, if this message was to be believed, he was coming for me.

"I don't know. You got enemies? Maybe somebody's mad at you, maybe it's random. Either way, I didn't see a thing."

"Well, don't try to tell me it didn't happen here. This car was *not* like this when I brought it in."

"I believe you," the valet said.

"How would somebody even get in here to do this?" I asked.

"To be honest, that's not hard. I'm the only one working days. At night, it's only José. Somebody comes in when we're down below getting a car, we don't see them. They could hide, sneak around, do some damage. I told management we need more staff, but they don't listen. You should complain."

"Oh, I plan to. The least you could do is help me figure out who did this. Is there a surveillance camera?"

"The only camera we got is outside where the buzzer is. It shows who comes and goes, but only if they go legit. If they sneak in, you won't see nothing on the tape. When José comes on duty at four, I'll ask him if he saw anybody sketchy hanging around. If he knows something, I'll give you a call. Otherwise, you can fill out the form to claim damages. The garage got insurance. They'll pay to fix your paint, no worries."

No worries. If only this were as simple as a new paint job.

I took the form and got behind the wheel, feeling queasy. I was completely overwhelmed at the thought of driving to Lynn's house right now. This was her fault. I'd told her to stay out of it, but no. She had to go and provoke him. She couldn't help herself; she was a hothead, like our father. I could only imagine how she'd react when she saw "DIE BITCH" scratched all over my car. She'd do something crazy and wind up getting us both killed.

I wouldn't be like Lynn. I would stop and consider my next step.

In order to get the police to take me seriously, I needed proof. I'd blocked Aidan's calls and ignored the ones that had managed to sneak through from other numbers. But I should call him now and do my best to trick him into confessing that he was stalking me. If I recorded the phone call and got him on tape admitting to anything—following me, following Lynn, trying to run her off the road, damaging my car—then I'd have proof. Would it be enough to arrest him? I wasn't sure, but it was worth a shot.

I got out of the car and walked around it, photographing the damage with my phone. The pictures would help make my case to the police.

I handed my keys back to the valet.

"I changed my mind. I'm not taking the car out now. I'll call when I want it."

And I walked back to my apartment, looking over my shoulder every step of the way, terrified of seeing him behind me.

35

Caroline hadn't returned Aidan's calls, even after he left a message explaining that she and her daughter were in danger. She'd told her sister that she'd call the police if Aidan came anywhere near her. He wanted to believe the sister was lying. But he had to face the possibility that she wasn't, that something had gone very wrong in his relationship with Caroline. Jason Stark had gotten to her somehow. The image of the two of them kissing outside that restaurant haunted him. It shook his faith. He felt her slipping away, and he couldn't stand it. He had to do something dramatic to bring her back to him.

He decided to approach Hannah Stark and offer his protection in some way. Or maybe wile his way into her confidence enough that he could gauge whether she was in any danger. How much did she know about her father's secret life? Was her dorm secure? Was she a partier, or a druggie, with shady connections of her own? He had to get close to her to find out.

But how could he do that without setting off alarm bells? Hannah might recognize him from the restaurant the other night, decide he was a stalker and call the police. He could try to stop her from doing that by telling her the truth. But how would that work? Just come right out and say that he was involved with her mother and had followed her father because he was worried Jason Stark was dangerous? First off, he couldn't tell her about his relationship with Caroline. And second, she'd never believe him anyway. It sounded bizarre even to Aidan. No, he'd have to pretend to be a stranger and arrange to meet her by happenstance. Strike up a conversation, try to gain her confidence. As for their encounter in the restaurant, he'd have to hope that she didn't remember. People's eyes passed over the faces of waiters and delivery boys and checkout clerks. They were part of the scenery. A rich girl like Hannah wouldn't register the face of the guy who poured her water at a restaurant. And if, somehow, she did, he'd pass it off as coincidence.

Aidan knew what Caroline's daughter looked like. He'd seen Hannah Stark at the restaurant. He had a photo of her that clearly showed her face, lifted from the camera roll on Caroline's iPhone. But it turned out that finding one particular girl on a campus as big as Stony Brook, even if you knew what she looked like, was a bigger challenge than he'd imagined. Uploading the campus map to his phone told him nothing about where to find Hannah. He didn't know which dorm she lived in and didn't know his way around. He couldn't go up to someone and ask without risking getting noticed by campus security. Aidan stood out because of his age. Even with his youthful face, dressed in a sweatshirt and jeans, he was pushing it to pass for a student. He'd never been to college himself, and he felt like an impostor. The place bustled. Space-age modern buildings, Asian kids with expensive backpacks hurrying along the wide paths like they were going someplace important. Aidan didn't belong. They'd know, they'd smell it on him. He'd get himself in trouble.

He wandered and tried to blend in, keeping his eyes peeled. He sat on a bench, looking at her photo on his phone. The paths were empty now. Everyone was in class. He would need to get inside the buildings in order to have any hope of finding her. But which building, and how? He walked up to the nearest one, glanced around, tried the door. It was locked. The map said it was a dorm. He'd better hope other buildings were open, or his brilliant plan had failed before it could get off the ground.

He drifted across the campus, crossing his arms over his sweatshirt against the wind, which was picking up. Dark clouds were blowing in. Suddenly the paths were full of students changing classes. His hopes lifted, till he realized that half the girls looked like Hannah. Eliminate the Asian ones, the black girls, the blondes, the heavy ones, the skinny ones—and what do you get? A lot of girls with long brown hair, average build, pleasant face, jeans and sweater, boots and backpack. A couple were dead ringers, to the point that he checked their faces against the photo, only to see that he'd remembered wrong.

After a couple of hours of nothing, he was cold, hungry, and frustrated. The weather had taken a serious turn for the worse, like it was threatening to storm, hard. He started telling himself he should quit while he was ahead, get out before the rain hit, or at least before some interfering employee recognized him for the vagrant he was and called the cops. But he couldn't bring himself to leave empty-handed. This girl was his ticket to Caroline, to his future. Quitters never win, right, and winners never quit? His dad used to say that, probably because he thought of Aidan as a quitter. Well, he wasn't quitting this time. He wanted Caroline too damn much for that. His hands were going numb from the chill, so he followed a wave of kids into a campus coffee shop, looking to get out of the wind. He'd wring a couple more hours out of this venture, hoping for his luck to change.

Wouldn't you know, she was right there, sitting at a corner table with a latte and a laptop open in front of her. He didn't even need to check his phone to make sure. It was definitely her.

He got in line and paid for yet another stupid-expensive coffee drink that he didn't even want. The whole time his mind was working, trying to figure out his approach. Once the drink was in his hand, instinct took over. The place was full. The seat next to Hannah was empty. She was a girl. Girls liked him. He walked up to her and smiled, like she was anyone.

"Hey, mind if I sit here?"

Her eyes flicked up tentatively. "No, go ahead," she said, and looked down again, blushing.

All right, she was shy. This would be easy. Piece of cake. He almost felt bad, lying to her. He reminded himself that he was here to help, and he shouldn't let himself feel intimidated. Hannah Stark wasn't better than him. Everything she possessed had been handed to her on a silver platter. This impressive campus. The freedom to sit around a coffee shop with a four-buck latte and a two-grand MacBook Pro in front of her in the middle of the afternoon. Not because she worked nights like he did, but because she didn't work at all. At Hannah's age, Aidan was—well, at her age, he was locked up, that was the ugly truth. But later, when he got out, he'd swabbed floors and cleaned grease off the grill at the diner while waiting patiently for a promotion to waiting tables.

It wouldn't be smart to seem overeager. That would only creep her out and chase her away. He looked at his phone, sipped his coffee, and waited for her to notice him.

Ten minutes had passed, and she still hadn't spoken to him. Either she was shy, or else she thought he was a lowlife and had no intention of speaking to him. Didn't really matter which. The place was clearing out. She was starting to gather her things. It must be coming up on time for the next class. He had to make his move.

"Uh, excuse me, miss. Do you go to school here?" he asked.

She looked at him like, *Duh, why else would I be sitting here?*

"Yeah, sure," she said. "Don't you?"

"I don't."

"You're not a student here? Because you look really familiar."

"You look familiar, too. Maybe we met in a past life."

She laughed. A positive sign.

"Actually," he said, "I'm here for a tour. Thinking about coming here next year."

Her brows knit skeptically. "I thought I saw an email that they cancelled the tours today, because of the storm that's coming."

Aidan thought quickly. "Yeah, but I didn't get the message in time, so I drove all the way out here for nothing. I hope you don't mind me interrupting your studying. It's just, if I could ask you a few questions, I could maybe get something out of this trip."

"Sure. But wait, are you in high school? You don't look like it."

"No. I'm a vet. Pulled two tours in Afghanistan. Now Uncle Sam's gonna send me to college on the GI Bill. Law school, too, or even medical school if I want. I'm here checking this place out, wondering if it would be a good fit for someone like me. Someone who's been around, seen things. You know?"

He had her interested now. She sat up straight, closed her computer, played with her hair.

"I'm Aidan, by the way."

He held out his hand. She shook it awkwardly. Her hand was warm and slightly damp.

"Hannah," she said, leaning closer and lowering her voice. "Honestly, I *don't* know if this would be the right place for you. Everyone here is super boring. And it's kind of a commuter school. Dead on the weekends."

"Really? What are you doing here, then? You don't seem boring."

She colored. "Really? Thanks. The thing is, I haven't made many friends yet. People are cold. They keep to themselves, you know?"

"I do know. That's why I miss the military. The closeness, the solidarity. I've felt really alone since I got out."

He looked off into the far distance, putting on his best damaged-young-man-who-needs-rescuing expression.

"I can't even imagine," she said. "I've barely been anywhere outside New York. Just to Florida a few times to visit my aunt, because she goes there in the winter, and I'm super close to her."

"That must be nice."

"It's really nice. We hang out and do girl stuff. You'd probably think it's boring, since you're used to more excitement. What was it like, being in Afghanistan?"

There was an announcement that the café would close early, in half an hour, because of the storm. But they stayed and talked as the place emptied out around them. He regaled her with war stories, convincing ones, borrowed from tales he'd heard Mike Castro tell during long nights at the bar, after he'd had a few. Mike was one of Tommy's guys, and he'd had a tough war, but Aidan didn't see any reason not to profit from that. He'd used Mike's stories on women before, often enough to have perfected the telling of them. He knew the right note to strike. Be humble. Don't be a hero. Au contraire, the hero was your buddy who caught the IED. That weighed on a man, watching his best friend make the ultimate sacrifice. He managed to seem brave and heroic, but wise and sad at the same time. It was the perfect recipe to convince the girl to take him into her confidence. Eventually, he started asking her the questions that weighed on his mind, and she answered willingly.

"What are your parents like? Are they still together? Are they happy?" he asked.

"They used to be so happy together. I don't know what went wrong. They split up recently, but now they're back together, and I can't tell if it's for real."

"They're back together?" he said, and his throat tightened, so the words came out hoarse. The thing he feared was true.

"Yeah, they reconciled. I don't know if it will last, though."

"Did your father cheat on her?"

Hannah squinted at him. "What makes you ask that?"

Aidan cleared his throat and smoothed his features into a better poker face. "It's the most common reason couples split, isn't it?" he said.

"You hit the nail on the head. She claims he cheated. But I know my dad, and he wouldn't do that. If anyone would cheat, it's her."

"I'm surprised you'd say that about your own mother."

"My mom's not very maternal."

"No? She's not a good mother to you?"

"I don't mean to sound ungrateful. Sometimes I think I'm not the right daughter for her. I'm not smart or pretty enough. She's not abusive or anything. She doesn't say mean things, but she's always trying to fix me. You know, like Hannah, you should take this class, go on that diet, get a makeover. She constantly buys me clothes that aren't my style. That kind of thing."

"I'm sure she does it out of love."

"You might be right. But my aunt Lynn accepts me for who I am. So does my dad, and that feels better, you know?"

Aidan didn't like listening to criticism of Caroline. But he couldn't rush to her defense without giving himself away.

"What's your dad like?" he said, changing the subject.

"He's awesome. Really kind and loving. He works hard to take care of us. My mom digs the lavish lifestyle. I think he went into finance to support her in the style to which she's accustomed, you know? He'd probably rather be doing something more worthwhile, but he needs to bring home the bucks for her, so he's stuck."

Poor Hannah had it all wrong. She had no idea what kind of man her father really was. Judging by the stars in her eyes when she spoke of Jason Stark, Aidan had better tread carefully. He couldn't come out and tell her what he knew, because she'd never accept it. He needed to take a roundabout approach.

"What about his friends?" he asked.

"What about them?"

"Have you met them? Do they seem like decent people?"

She looked him in the eye. "That's a weird question. Why are you so interested in my parents? Do you know them, or something?"

"No, of course not," Aidan said, flustered. "I'm not interested in them. I'm interested in *you*."

That made her blush and flutter her lashes. "Wow. Thank you. I have to say, I'm kind of surprised. Guys don't always get me right away. But I really like you, too," she said.

Crap. He'd made a serious mistake. He couldn't have Hannah thinking he was coming on to her, not if he planned to be her stepfather someday. But before he could correct his error, there was announcement that the café was officially closed, and they had to leave.

"I feel so bad that they canceled the tour on you," she said, standing up and gathering her things. "The least I can do is show you around. My dorm's on Roosevelt Quad. It's like the most happening part of campus, so we should go to my room." She lowered her voice. "Plus, I know where my roommate keeps her vodka."

Should he tell her he didn't like her *like that?* He couldn't correct this awful misimpression without alienating Hannah completely. She'd feel humiliated and drop him. The thing was, he actually did want to see her dorm room, to check whether it was secure. Was she on the ground floor, so that Russian thug could climb in her window? Were there security cameras in the building? A lock on her bedroom door? He could let her think he was interested long enough to get a look. He'd refuse the vodka, of course, and keep things strictly friendly. He didn't like leading her on, but he had to make sure she was safe. Once his very brief reconnaissance was complete, he'd make an excuse and slip away.

"Sure, I'd love to see your dorm room," he said to Hannah. "Lead the way."

36

I walked in to the empty apartment, still shaky from seeing that ugly threat scratched into the paint of my car. *DIE BITCH*. Would Aidan really hurt me? The signs were beginning to point to yes.

Jason's briefcase was gone from the front hall bench, and his raincoat was missing from the coat stand.

"Hello? Jason?" I called out.

Silence. I double-locked the door behind me. As afraid as I was to be alone, I was relieved to find the apartment empty. A woman about to phone her lover and get him to implicate himself in a crime didn't need a suspicious husband breathing down her neck. I had things to do that Jason couldn't see.

To make certain he was gone, I went through each room, checking. I even looked in the bathrooms. In the master bath, I caught sight of myself in the mirror and stopped short, startled. I looked haunted, exhausted, with pinched cheeks and shadows under my eyes. If I saw myself from a distance, I would think, *That woman is hiding something.* You could see the deception in my eyes. Jason was no longer the only party to this marriage who had secrets. Now I was the one retreating to other rooms to take phone calls, lying about where I'd been, sneaking time alone to conduct my shady business. What had happened to me? When did I become this horrible person? Mere weeks ago, Hannah, Jason, and I were a happy family. I slept easy at night. I wasn't afraid. I didn't tell lies. Then the Russian woman came to the party, and everything changed. In a moment of weakness, I slept with Aidan, and the dominoes began to fall. Now I was as bad as Jason, as bad as the Russian woman. I wanted my old life back. I wanted my family back.

I wandered into Hannah's room and sat down on her bed. My little girl had left for college, and I missed her with a terrible, stabbing pain. I toppled over sideways, pressing my face into her pillows, tears flooding my eyes. I was tired, and I was sad. I hugged Hannah's stuffed puppy dog to my chest and rocked him like a baby. His name was Benji, after the dog in the movie that she loved when she was a little girl. I whispered his name over and over again, kissing his raggedy head. Poor Hannah—she'd wanted a dog so bad, but she was allergic. I should have tried harder, looked at hypoallergenic breeds, taken her in for allergy shots. A pet would have made a difference to a lonely kid like her, but it had seemed like too much bother. Was I a bad mother? I remembered dropping her off at school when she was little, how she'd cling to me, afraid of the mean girls. That exquisite agony of protecting a child from harm, the awful wrench when you had to let them go. I was the one alone now, and I wanted Hannah back. I wanted her little again. I snuggled deeper into her pillows, shifted to pull her down comforter close around me. The smell of the bed brought her back so vividly. That organic perfume she'd mixed up in the shop, with its notes of vanilla and spice. The smell of her peppermint chewing gum, her floral shampoo. I lay there and closed my eyes, sinking into the bed, the coziness of the memories.

I closed my eyes and gave in to the fatigue.

The sound of a ringing phone woke me. I sat up, groggy and disoriented, confused at finding myself in Hannah's bed. The ringing was coming from the front hall, where I'd left my bag when I got back from the parking garage. It all came back to me in a rush. Aidan's threat, scratched into the paint of my car. Coming home to find Jason gone and feeling so relieved. The mess that was my marriage. No wonder I'd given in to sleep. My troubles were beginning to feel overwhelming.

How long had I been sleeping? The sun slanting through Hannah's blinds was much lower in the sky. I went to find my phone, and saw it was 2:40. Hours had passed while I hid from my problems. I took the phone with me to the kitchen, where I splashed water on my face and drank thirstily from my hands, then poured a cup of cold coffee from the carafe. I smoothed my hair and sat down at the kitchen table to check my phone. The missed call was from Lynn. I'd never shown up to her house as promised. She'd left a voicemail. I winced as I listened.

"What the hell, Caroline. You said you'd be here by lunchtime. It's two thirty, and I'm worried. Are you okay, or are you ditching me? I'm not waiting around any more. I'm gonna go talk to my lawyer friend about your situation. Call me when you get this."

Lawyer friend? I had no idea who she meant. Lynn was dragging some random lawyer into my conflict with Aidan? No way. I had to stop her. I hit her number.

"I'm fine," I said, the second she answered.

"Where the hell are you? You were supposed to be here hours ago."

"I had car trouble."

"You couldn't call and tell me? I was freaking out."

"I'm sorry. I came home and fell asleep."

"Seriously, Caroline? What's with the excuses? Are you avoiding me?"

"I practically passed out in Hannah's bed. Look, things are complicated here, with Jason. I'm depressed, I'm upset. And it doesn't help to have you talking to people I don't know about my personal problems. Don't do that. Okay?"

"We need advice. This Aidan guy is nuts, and he's dangerous."

"I don't want advice from some rando."

"It's my friend Jodi Avergun. She's a lawyer, and she's very smart. A criminal lawyer, not divorce like those other names I gave you. She used to be a prosecutor."

"*No.* This is a sensitive situation, Lynn. I want to keep it quiet. If I need your help, I'll ask. Do you understand? It's my life."

"Better to say it's your funeral."

"Thanks a lot."

"I'm serious. I'm worried about you. But if that's how you want to play it—"

"It is. You don't have my permission to speak to anyone about this. And if you do, I'll know I can't trust you, and I'll stop confiding in you."

"All right, fine. But promise you'll tell me if you're really in danger."

"Of course. I'm not stupid."

"That's debatable."

Nobody but Lynn could get away with talking to me like that. Of course, she'd been doing it since we were kids.

"When are you coming out here then?" she asked.

"I'm not coming. There's too much going on in the city. Jason's got some kind of . . . *thing* at work—"

"You should come. You should check on your house."

"My house? Why?"

"Hurricane Oswald is why. Don't you watch the weather? Category Four. They're saying it's gonna make landfall as far north as Delaware. Usually it hits a lot farther south, and it's nothing by the time it gets to Long Island. We could get hit bad this time. I'd be worried about your beautiful house if I was you."

"I've got enough problems without bothering about some storm."

"Do you know what I went through, repairing damage on the condos from the last big one? Eighty thousand out of pocket and counting, and my insurance is saying they won't pay. Board up your windows at least. An ounce of prevention is worth—"

"Okay, okay, I will. You promise you won't tell anybody about Aidan."

"I said I won't."

"Thank you. I'll talk to you later."

I hung up, glad to be done with her. I loved Lynn, but she could be such a meddler.

The coffee had cleared away some of the cobwebs. It was around three o'clock. Aidan wouldn't've left for work yet, and I should try to catch him. I couldn't afford to put this off one more day. I would call his phone, get him to admit to what he'd done, and record the call. Then I'd have proof to bring to the police. Problem solved, right?

Nothing was ever that easy. My phone lacked the capability to record phone calls without installing a special app. I was the least technically inclined person on the planet, but I told myself I could figure this out. I spent half an hour reading reviews of the various recording apps. Most of them got terrible reviews, with the major complaint being that they actually failed to record calls. Just what I needed—to blow my one shot at getting Aidan to confess with some malfunctioning recording app. On top of that, it turned out that recording phone calls without the other party's consent was illegal in many states. Great. I'd bring the recording of Aidan's confession to the police, and wind up getting arrested for illegal wiretapping.

I tried downloading the best-rated app anyway. But it wouldn't open on my phone. Typical. I threw up my hands.

Should I try meeting Aidan in person? I could set the meeting for a public place, where I'd feel safe. I'd confront him about his scary behavior, with my phone in my bag set to record.

No, too risky.

I gave up in frustration.

I wandered back into Hannah's room, stopping to remake the bed. As I picked up Benji the stuffed pup, nostalgia hit me hard again. Suddenly the need to hear my daughter's voice was overpowering.

I dialed Hannah's number. It rang and rang. Right before it went to voicemail, she picked up.

"Hello?"

"Hi, sweetheart, it's Mom. You sound out of breath. Did I catch you at a bad time?"

"Yeah, kind of. I'm . . . I'm with someone."

"With who? Your roommate?"

"Um, no, Mom."

She paused. And I understood. My stomach lurched.

"You're with a *boy*?"

"Yeah, can I call you back?"

"Yes. But, soon, okay? Promise?"

"Sure, Mom," she said, dismissively, and hung up.

I stared at my phone, feeling stung and surprised at this unexpected turn of events. Not that it *should* be unexpected. Hannah was eighteen years old and away at college. But somehow, dating had seemed like a remote contingency, something to worry about far off in the future. I could be forgiven for thinking that, since Hannah had never so much as gone to a dance in high school. She went stag to her prom, with a couple of girlfriends who were so not-into-it that they left after an hour and went to the movies. Despite Hannah's lack of experience with the opposite sex—or maybe because of it—I'd insisted on having those awkward conversations before she left home. Hannah knew about STDs, birth control, staying safe at parties, though she'd blushed through the whole thing, and acted like I was torturing her. She was prepared for the practical aspects of dating. But did she know how to protect her heart?

The thought of my daughter with a boy worried me. But I took a deep breath and told myself to relax. On the list of things I had to fear right now, Hannah dating barely cracked the top ten.

37

That night, the rain finally started.

It was past seven, and I was alone in the apartment. I heard a thunderclap and went over to the living room window. Looking straight down, I could see drops beginning to hit the pavement, and people walking below opening their umbrellas. Our apartment was on the tenth floor, with a view south of the tops of surrounding buildings and open sky above. Lurid purple clouds hung low and thick in the sky, reflecting the lights of the buildings back at me. It felt claustrophobic, like the clouds might strangle me.

Jason's secretary had left for the day, and he wasn't picking up in the office or on his cell. It felt like the days right after the Russian woman had come to the party. He'd promised that was over for good. Was he lying? I'd tried to track his phone, with no success. Maybe he was onto me, and my clever little trick, and he'd somehow disabled my ability to track. Or maybe I was being paranoid, and his cell reception was poor simply because of the storm. I left him a pathetic voicemail, begging him to come home for dinner tonight. I wanted to sit him down and figure out what was really going on, and whether this reconciliation was a masquerade. But he remained stubbornly out of reach.

It was hours since I'd interrupted Hannah with that boy and begged her to call me back soon. But so far, nothing. Could she possibly still be with him? Was she avoiding me because she didn't want to talk about her sex life with her mother? Or was he a psycho, and had he done something to her? I had to stop myself from imagining the worst. The point was, I had too much on my mind to worry about the weather.

An hour later, the rain pounded against the living room windows so loudly that I looked out again. On the street below, people were running for shelter, their umbrellas turned inside out in the wind. Only then did I take seriously what Lynn had said, and bother turning on the television.

The networks were predicting catastrophe. The reporters, in matching jackets, standing in front of swaying trees in the driving rain, in Virginia, along the Chesapeake, at the Jersey shore, talked in urgent voices. *Eighty million people in harm's way. Category Four and strengthening. Landfall projected in mid-Atlantic region by midnight. Mandatory evacuation orders as far north as Cape May.* But they always did that, to pump up the ratings. They'd cried wolf so many times that I couldn't take it seriously.

Then my next-door neighbor from out at the beach called.

Francine was a complainer, but I always took her calls. I had no choice. She was the sort of person who had no problem calling the zoning board on you, or even the cops, if she felt you weren't taking her concerns seriously.

"Hello?"

"Caroline, this is your neighbor, Francine Eberhardt."

"Hello, Francine. Are you okay out there in this awful weather?"

"I am not okay. Your burglar alarm has been going off for the past fifteen minutes, and it's driving me *nuts*."

The alarm going off? But I'd never gotten an alert, and I'd paid the bill in full as soon as Jason put money back into the account.

"It can't be mine. The security company didn't call me," I said.

"It's yours, all right. I should know. I'm right next door, and it's *shrieking*."

"If it is my house, I apologize. The wind must have set it off," I said.

"It wasn't the wind. Someone broke in. The front door is wide open."

The front door had a dead bolt. Unless I'd left the door unlocked, it couldn't blow open.

"The lights are on, too," Francine said.

A cold fear rippled through me.

It couldn't be the housekeeper. She didn't have a key. Was it possible that, in my frazzled state of mind, I'd left the house without bolting the door or turning off the lights? I wanted very much to believe that, because the alternative was terrifying. The alternative was, somebody broke in. And that somebody was probably Aidan.

"Is there any way you could check on it for me?"

"I'm not going in there. They might still be inside. Besides, the wind is so strong it would knock me down."

"I'm sure there's no one in there. I'd give you my alarm code, so you could turn the alarm off and stop the noise."

"I said no. I'm battening down the hatches, not stepping outside my door till the storm's over. If you're smart you'll get out here yourself and take care of your property before it's destroyed. But if you can't be bothered, at least call the alarm company and have them shut off that awful noise."

She hung up.

I called the burglar alarm company and sat on hold for ten minutes. When I got through, I was told they hadn't received any alert but that it was possible the phone lines had been damaged by the storm and weren't transmitting.

"My neighbor says my front door is open. Can't you send someone to check?" I demanded.

"I'm sorry, ma'am. We are not dispatching technicians at the moment because of the severity of the storm."

"Then call the police."

"Our policy is to relay alarms that we receive to local authorities. We have not received an alarm in this case."

I threw my phone down in frustration. My dream house, that I'd worked and slaved for, that I'd put blood, sweat, and most of my money into, sat directly in the path of a raging hurricane. The front door was wide open, leaving the house exposed to the elements. I wanted to rush out there and do something about it. But if I did, I could be walking into a trap. I had a strange tingling sensation on the back of my neck that I couldn't ignore. Sometimes paranoia was justified by the facts. Aidan had been stalking me for days now. It wasn't crazy to think he'd broken into my house. He might be lurking there right this minute, lying in wait to ambush me. I couldn't take that risk.

But I *could* call the police, without ever mentioning Aidan's name. I'd simply report that the alarm had been triggered. They'd have to believe me. If Aidan was in the house, they'd find him, and they'd have no choice but to arrest him, right?

I found the number for the Glenhampton Police Department and dialed.

"Police dispatch," a woman's voice answered.

"I'd like to report a break-in at my house."

"What's the address?"

I gave it to her.

"Can you see the intruder?"

"No. I'm not at the house. My neighbor called to tell me my burglar alarm is going off."

"You are not currently the house?"

"That's what I said."

"Is anybody else in there?"

"The burglar."

"Your neighbor saw this individual break in?"

"Not exactly. She heard the alarm go off, and she says the front door is open."

"Are there signs of forced entry? Broken windows, or the like?"

"I don't know."

"We've got sustained winds over fifty miles per hour and rising. That could account for the open door and the alarm."

"Maybe, but shouldn't somebody check it out?"

"All right. Name of the reporting party, please?"

"Me? I'm Caroline Stark."

"Ms. Stark, I'm radioing this to all patrol officers so if there's a car in the area, they can swing by and take a look."

"Can you send somebody over there right away?"

"Ma'am, all vehicles are busy responding to emergencies related to the storm."

"But this *is* an emergency. My house is getting robbed."

"Property crimes come after emergencies that threaten loss of life. Once the other calls are completed, they will turn to this one."

"But somebody broke into my house."

"Ma'am, to set your mind at ease, the majority of calls we get about alarms being triggered are false. You got your animals, the wind, systems malfunction. In all likelihood, this is nothing."

"Really? That's funny. I've heard there've been a ton of burglaries in Glenhampton lately, and the police haven't made a single arrest."

"Ma'am, your call was sent out, and now I need to take another call," the dispatcher said, and hung up.

So much for my tax dollars at work.

My phone lit up, and a message from Hannah appeared on the screen.

Hey sorry I hung up on u before, she wrote.

I wanted to yell at her. I wanted information. Who was the boy? What were his intentions? How were his grades? Did he drink or do drugs? How far had they gone? But I restrained myself. If I acted too eager, she'd shut me down.

That's okay honey. How was your date? I texted back.

Three little dots appeared. She was answering.

Great, Hannah wrote. We hung out for a long time. He's a little older. Super sensitive and smart. Oh, and he's gorgeous, check out this selfie we took.

I smiled. If Hannah was happy, then something was going right in the world.

As the photo loaded, I saw her, sitting on the edge of her bed in her dorm room, with the pink and orange tie-dyed bedspread we'd chosen together that matched her pink and orange throw pillows. The so-called smart, sensitive, older guy sat right beside her, his arm thrown loosely around her shoulders. And my heart stopped.

It was Aidan.

38

My first instinct was to warn her.

Are you still with him? I typed, fingers flying over my phone. Get away! He's dangerous.

I stopped typing. Aidan couldn't be with Hannah now. My house was an hour's drive from her school, and I was ninety-nine percent sure he'd just broken into it and set off the alarm. Maybe this photo was from earlier tonight? But I couldn't take that risk.

Is he with you now? I texted, and waited for her reply, my heart in my throat.

When she didn't respond, I started pacing, climbing the walls, my mind racing. I stared at the picture she'd sent me. Aidan looked indifferent, bored, almost annoyed. He didn't care about Hannah. He was with her to taunt me, using her to get to me. He could end up hurting her—emotionally, even physically. Maybe he wasn't the one who'd set off the alarm. Maybe he was still with her. The thought was terrifying. I had to do something.

I typed the beginnings of multiple texts, then deleted them. In order to explain why Hannah should fear Aidan, I'd have to confess my one-night stand. I'd be telling her that a guy she liked—the *first* guy she'd *ever* liked, as far as I knew—was playing her in order to get to me. To get to her own *mother*. The very idea was so sick, so twisted, that it made me nauseous. I'd also be confessing that I cheated on her father. Even though Jason cheated first, Hannah would blame me. She loved Jason best. It wasn't fair, but it was true. He could do no wrong in her eyes. What would it do to Hannah to know all that? Destroy her self-esteem? Destroy our relationship? I had to think this through.

I'd call her instead and make up an excuse get her away from him. Say there was an emergency, that a hurricane was coming, that I needed to come get her and take her home.

The call rang forever and rolled over to voicemail. I called back. Same result. I started to panic. I left a voicemail.

"Hannah, it's Mom. Call me right away. I'm worried about your safety."

I hung up, my hands shaking. If Aidan was still there, I had to get her away from him. Even if he wasn't still there, I had to warn her never to go near him again. I could tell her about his arrest record.

He's too old for you, I wrote. He has a criminal record—

I stopped myself.

That was saying too much. I'd end up revealing that I knew him. Not just that I knew him—how *well* I knew him. I should tell her that she wasn't allowed to date anybody I hadn't met and vetted. But no, that would never work. Hannah was eighteen years old and away at college. When I was that age, if my mother told me to do something, I'd make a point of doing the opposite. Nothing like forbidden fruit. I could end up driving Hannah into Aidan's arms.

There was no good way to warn her without revealing the whole truth. And I couldn't bring myself to do that for fear of destroying my relationship with her. I thought about calling the police. But that meant Aidan's brother, Tommy. What would I say? *Hello, Chief Callahan, I'm the woman who screwed your brother. I need you to get him away from my daughter right now.* Tommy would laugh, then he'd probably give Aidan a high five.

My chest was tight with panic. Time was passing with no response from Hannah. I could tell her I was worried about the storm and that I was coming to pick her up. For a moment, that seemed like the answer; then I realized. On the off chance that Aidan was still with her, seeing me could trigger him to act out, even to get violent.

I would send Lynn. That was it. When Lynn told Hannah to do something, Hannah listened. Yes, I would ask my sister to intervene, to get Hannah away from school immediately. There was a terrible storm coming. It was plausible that I would be worried about Hannah in this weather. As a matter of fact, now that I thought about it, I *was* worried about Hannah in this weather.

I dialed Lynn's number. She picked up on the first ring.

"I was about to call you," she said.

"Lynn, I'm worried about Hannah with the hurricane."

"Me, too, hon. Don't worry. I'm on my way to get Hannah right now. She told me you were calling. She was on with me, arranging to get picked up."

"Oh, that's wonderful. Thank you so much."

"Don't thank me," Lynn said. "You know I love that girl like she's my own. I don't want her in that high-rise dorm with all those windows when the storm hits. You need to take care of your house. Let me handle this. Hannah will be safe with us."

"How long will it take you to get there?"

"I'm fifteen minutes away from her right now."

"I'm so glad to hear that."

Then it occurred to me. In my panic, I'd forgotten that Lynn and Aidan knew each other, that they'd had that awful confrontation. What if he was still there? What if they saw one another when Lynn went to Hannah's dorm? That would be a nightmare.

"*Lynn?*"

"Yes?"

"When you talked to her, was she alone?"

"No, her roommate was there. That girl Olivia? She's a bit of a flake, but at least Hannah isn't alone."

I breathed out in relief. Aidan had left. He wouldn't see my sister. Most important of all, Hannah was unharmed. He'd paid her a visit as some sort of sick threat to me, then gone on to break into my house, where he probably lurked still, waiting to hurt me directly. But at least my daughter was safe, and I was free to deal with Aidan as I saw fit. I could no longer dismiss the serious threat he posed to me and my family. Aidan was stalking me. He was getting progressively more violent. Trying to run my sister's car off the road. Scratching a death threat into the paint of my Escalade. And now, going after my daughter. There was no room for compromise here. I had to stop him, even if it meant killing him.

"Thank you, Lynn," I said into the phone. "I'm heading out to the house now. Whatever happens, you keep Hannah safe."

"I will, hon. You stay safe, too."

She hung up. *Stay safe* was right. Aidan could be lying in wait for me. I had to be careful. I might have to defend myself. I needed a weapon. I walked into the kitchen and took a knife from the knife block. I didn't cook much, and it was dull. I got out the sharpener and worked on the blade. When it was honed to a perfect edge, I looked at it, and instead of feeling reassured, I realized what a fool I was. Aidan had a gun. All I had was this stupid kitchen knife. He was bigger and stronger than me. He was a felon, a violent one, with a manslaughter conviction to his name. I was a woman who'd never so much as taken a kickboxing class. If I attacked him, and somebody ended up dead, that somebody would probably be me.

And yet, what else could I do? He was going after my *daughter*. I put the knife in my bag, grabbed an umbrella, and ran out into the storm.

39

Rain lashed my windshield. I peered out at an apocalyptic landscape of stalled vehicles, accidents, flashing blue lights. My hands clenched the steering wheel, knuckles white, my head pounding from the strain of concentrating so hard on the road. On the LIE, traffic was bumper-to-bumper. The cars inched forward. After half an hour, I hadn't gone more than a few miles. At this rate, I'd be out here all night. I could die in a terrible car accident. Or I could reach the house safely and then be attacked by my stalker. Either way, in the chaos of the storm, it could take hours, days, before my family was notified of my death. In my stress and exhaustion, my throat tightened with tears, and I dialed Jason's number. My heart lifted at the sound of his recorded voice, and I missed him terribly.

"Jason, honey," I said to his voicemail. "I'm on my way to the beach house. The neighbor says the alarm's going off and the front door blew open. The police are too busy with other calls to respond. The roads are terrible. I wanted you to know where I was. I'm scared of what I might find, and I wish you were with me. Is there any way you could come out here? Hannah is with Lynn, and she's safe. Call me. I love you. Bye."

It took two hours longer than usual to get to Montauk Highway, which normally would have been deserted at this time of night in October. But traffic was backed up here, too. The closer I got to Glenhampton, the slower I went, but I couldn't turn around, because there were cars in front and behind going in both directions. When eventually I got to the front of the line and saw what the obstacle was, I broke out in a cold sweat. The road ahead was completely flooded. Around me, several vehicles had washed out. In front of me, a man jumped out of his stalled car and sank into waist-deep water as the car beached itself on the side of the road. A man in a rain poncho waving a flashlight beckoned me forward. He wasn't a cop as far as I could tell. And I wasn't driving into a flood at the behest of some bystander. I shook my head, and he walked right up to my car and pounded on the window.

"Go!" he screamed.

I did, only because I was more afraid of him than of the flood. I hit the accelerator, and the Escalade lurched forward. Water lapped at my tires, and the engine started making choking noises, like it was about to die. For a terrifying moment, I felt the Escalade float. I ripped off my seat belt, heart pounding, getting ready to abandon ship. But a second later I felt the tires gain traction again and saw pavement. The road ahead was clear. I stepped on the gas and got the hell out of there.

Twenty minutes later, I pulled into the circular driveway at the beach house. The rain was coming down hard. Trees were swaying in the wind, and leaves were blowing wildly. I was limp with nerves and bathed in sweat after the awful drive. The condition of the house was as Francine had described. The front door stood open. Lights blazed from inside the house. The burglar alarm was still shrieking. The local police must still be occupied responding to the storm, since, despite my earlier phone call, they obviously hadn't made it out here.

I stopped to ask myself whether I could possibly have left the house like this: lights on, door unlocked, so it could blow open and trigger the alarm? I thought back to when I last left here. That was the night Aidan followed me to the restaurant and barged in on our family dinner. But that came later. At the time I left the house, I'd been running out to see the divorce lawyer, to get the papers to serve on Jason. I was calm about my decision. I was running late, but I wasn't flustered, and I didn't panic. I locked up properly, like I always did. I was sure of it.

It wasn't me who'd left the house in this condition. Somebody had been in there since, without my permission. An intruder. An intruder who wanted to send a message. Why else leave the door wide open and the lights on? Who could it be but Aidan? My house blazed with light, but the rest of the street was dark. Nobody was home on the bluff. They were smarter than me and had cleared out in the face of the storm, with the exception of my neighbor, Francine, who would be of little help if Aidan was inside waiting for me. I knew I had to confront him. His behavior was escalating, to the point where he'd contacted my daughter. Hannah was safe with Lynn for now, but he could try that again. And next time, he might hurt her.

I stepped out of the car into driving wind and rain, my legs rubbery after the hellish five-hour trip. Here at the ocean, the storm was more powerful than ever, and I was soaked instantly, my raincoat plastered against my legs, my hair streaming, water running into my eyes. I staggered up to the wide-open front door, stopping on the threshold to take in the damage. The beautiful Tibetan carpet was soaked and matted. A lamp had been knocked over, and framed photos from the side tables had blown down and lay scattered across the floor. There were streaks of mud everywhere, and shards of glass, from the lamp or maybe the picture frames. A gust blew through the room, sending light fixtures swaying, and leaves and twigs skittering across the white-oak floors. Was this damage done deliberately, or was it simply the wind that had blown in the door and knocked things around?

The alarm was so loud that I couldn't think straight. From habit, I reached in and tapped the code into the keypad beside the door. The shrieking stopped instantly, but then I realized what I'd done. If Aidan was in the house and heard the alarm shut off, he'd know I was here. I'd given myself away.

Panicking, I backed out the door. But as I turned toward my car, a gust of wind hit so hard that it sent me staggering. Simultaneously, a loud crack sounded. I watched in horror as an enormous tree limb came crashing down onto my car, shattering the windshield into a thousand tiny pieces. I turned and ran back inside, grabbing the front doorknob with both hands, using my body as a counterweight to yank it shut. The wind died from a howl to a dull roar, and I turned and leaned against the door, panting. I couldn't go back out there. The wind was tossing around debris big enough to kill me. But the car was undrivable with a shattered windshield.

I was trapped here.

The house was not safe. Aidan could be hiding anywhere. He knew his way around, and I had nobody to blame for that but myself. My nerves tight as a drum, my heart beating frantically, I took out my phone to call the police. They hadn't responded to my earlier call because nobody was in danger. I could very well be in danger now.

I stared at my cell phone in dismay. No reception. And we hadn't bothered installing a landline. Not only was I trapped, I was cut off from all help.

I rifled through my bag until I found the kitchen knife. It gave me the comforting illusion that I could defend myself if Aidan jumped me. I hurried through the living room to the kitchen, my eyes sweeping left and right as I took inventory of the damage. A vase had been knocked over on the kitchen table. A pile of newspapers sat on the white marble top of the kitchen island. What the hell? I hadn't left those there.

And then I saw them—and froze. Muddy footprints on the white-oak floors. No footprints had been visible on the living room rug, which was itself muddy and soaked from the storm. But here in the kitchen they stood out in terrifying relief. The prints were large and serrated. A man's footprints, made by heavy boots. The wind didn't do this. A person did. A man. Aidan had been here. He might be here still. I felt sick realizing it.

I followed the footprints, clutching the knife in my sweating hand as they led me toward the terrace door. Was he outside? I caught a movement from the corner of my eye. Something was moving around, low to the ground, out on the terrace. Heart pounding, I raised the knife and moved toward the French doors. I squinted out but couldn't see clearly through the glass, which was fogged with rain and condensation. If Aidan was out there, I could surprise him. I could attack him with the knife. Did I have the nerve? I was reaching for the door handle with my right hand, holding the knife in my left, when a thick, dark thing crashed against the glass and fell to the ground.

"*Aagh.*"

I staggered backward, the knife slipping from my hand and clattering to the floor. I grabbed it up again, panting with fear. But when I peered through the glass, I saw only a cushion from the chaise longue, lying on the ground. That thing had hit the door—it wasn't Aidan. The terrace furniture was blowing around like so many matchsticks out there, and the cushion had knocked up against the glass, terrifying me so much that I felt my heart would come through my chest.

Nobody there, nobody there, calm down.

Maybe he'd left. Maybe he'd gone out through the terrace door. I was shaking so hard. I had to get ahold of myself or I wouldn't be able to continue. I went to the cabinet and grabbed the bourbon Lynn had brought me that night when I despaired over my marriage. That worry felt so quaint to me now. I took a swig right from the bottle. It burned going down, warming my blood, stilling the trembling of my hands. I left the bottle out on the counter and set off to search the rooms.

The first floor consisted of the enormous great room that combined kitchen, living room, and dining area, a powder room, a laundry room, and a media room. The overhead lights were on in the great room, but I walked the perimeter of the cavernous space, turning on every lamp, even switching on the gas fireplace to illuminate shadowy corners. I threw open closet doors and pawed through to make sure nobody was hiding inside. I tiptoed to the powder room, yanked open the door, and switched on the lights. Nothing. In the media room, I hunched down to see under the seats, but Aidan wasn't hiding there. Everywhere I went, I saw Aidan's muddy footprints, but they grew fainter the farther I walked from the kitchen. That didn't mean he wasn't here. It simply meant the mud had worn off his shoes as he walked. I crept up to the second floor and searched all the bedrooms. The whole time I was clutching my kitchen knife, mentally preparing to defend myself, but I checked room after room, and there was nobody.

Aidan had been here. I was certain. Now he was gone, and I was alone, but I didn't feel safe. He might come back. I had to do what I could to prevent him from getting in again. I went downstairs. I stripped off my wet raincoat, which I'd been wearing all this time. I felt so weak. I stood at the kitchen island with some crackers and a jar of peanut butter and wolfed down a makeshift dinner, eating until I felt my strength coming back. Then I went around and checked the locks on every door and window and pulled all the shades. It was the best I could do, but it wasn't much. He'd broken in through the same security before. I'd just have to pray that he was done terrorizing me for the night, that he would wait out the storm before trying anything more.

I grabbed the bourbon and the knife and went upstairs to change out of my wet things. The wind was so strong that my brand-new, supposedly hurricane-proof bedroom windows rattled with every fresh gust. I propped myself up against the down pillows, bourbon in hand, and clicked on the TV for a weather report. The screen lit up for a second, then displayed a floating graphic saying No SIGNAL. Between that and my phone not working, I had no way to monitor the storm. I went to the window, looked out at the beach, and gasped. In the lurid light, the surf was higher than I'd ever seen it. It crashed against the dunes that formed the last bulwark sheltering the house from the ocean. And the dunes looked smaller than before. Hours ago, the Weather Channel people were projecting landfall at midnight along Maryland's Eastern Shore or even as far north as Delaware or New Jersey. If the storm turned sharply north, Long Island and the Hamptons could take a devastating hit. This was just the outer edge of the storm, and things were bound to get a lot worse before they got better—a terrifying thought.

As I contemplated that, the lights in the bedroom flickered—once, twice, three times—and went out. I gasped. Now I was alone here in the dark. Was it possible a breaker switch had tripped? I grabbed my phone from the bedside table and flicked on the flashlight, sweeping it around the room jerkily. The furniture took on lurid shapes, and seemed to lurch at me like an attacker. I cowered in my bed, too afraid to go downstairs and look for the breaker box. I couldn't remember where it was, and I wasn't handy anyway. I pulled the covers tight around me. The bottle of bourbon was on the bedside table. I could see its outline in the watery light shining through the windows. I downed what was left in one gulp and reached out to touch the handle of the kitchen knife, reassuring myself that it was within easy reach. Then I closed my eyes and surrendered to exhaustion.

The music was coming from very far away. It felt like a dream. Sinatra, crooning. *I've got you under my skin. I've got you deep in the heart of me.* The richness of his voice, the swing of the beat, was muffled by my heavy sleep. But it didn't stop, and after a minute, my reptilian brain realized that was weird, and my eyes popped open.

The music was real. The power had come back on while I was sleeping. It was still dark outside the windows, but light blazed in the bedroom. I shut my eyes and pulled the blanket over my head, too bleary to get up and turn it off. But, wait a minute. I hadn't played that song last night. I wasn't playing any music at all when the power went off. So why would this music play when the power came back on?

My heart turned over in my chest, and I couldn't breathe. The lights coming back on I could explain. But the music could only mean one thing. *Aidan was here.*

Slowly, I lowered the blanket, my hand creeping out, reaching for the knife. But it was gone. Of course. Don't allow the target access to a weapon. That was Stalking 101.

Aidan sat in a chair that he'd positioned right in front of the closed bedroom door. In his lap was the big silver gun I'd seen at his apartment.

He smiled. "Morning, sleepyhead."

40

Aidan was still in Hannah Stark's dorm room when he got the text that the bar was closing for the storm, and he shouldn't come to work tonight. The Red Anchor never closed, not even for blizzards. He scrolled through the weather alerts on his phone. This storm looked serious.

He sat beside Hannah on her bed, keeping a safe distance. He'd been trying for a while to make an excuse to get away. Hannah liked him more than he was comfortable with. She'd offered him vodka (he'd declined), leaned her thigh against his until he'd inched away, taken cute selfies of the two of them. He'd kept things polite, but she was sure to be upset when they met again at some future date, and she learned that he was her mother's boyfriend. Any points he earned with Caroline for conducting a safety check on her daughter would get erased then. But Aidan would cross that bridge when he came to it. For now, he needed to escape without hurting the girl's feelings. The storm gave him the excuse he'd been looking for.

"This storm they've been making the announcements about?" Aidan said, standing up and pulling on his coat. "It's a Category Four hurricane. That's serious. I have to go take care of things at home. You should go, too. I'm not convinced your dorm is safe."

"It's so sweet of you to worry," she said, and came to stand a bit too close to him. "This dorm is brand-new and super well constructed. I'll be fine."

"The security isn't as good as you probably think," he said. "Anybody could get in simply by following someone with a key."

"The campus police are everywhere. It's not a problem, really."

What more could he do? He'd tried his best to warn Hannah of her vulnerable position. There was nothing else he could say without revealing that he'd followed her father and watched him meet with some street thug to contract hits on his own family. She'd never believe it— at least, not unless he explained *why* he'd followed Jason Stark, which in turn would reveal his relationship with Caroline. Aidan knew better than to do that. Caroline would never forgive him for telling her daughter about them without her permission. And he could hardly ask permission when she refused to return his phone calls.

"When will I see you again?" Hannah asked.

"I'm not sure. I'll call you."

"Can I get a kiss goodbye?" she asked shyly.

He kissed her on the forehead, in a fatherly sort of way.

"Stay safe," he said.

Then he crossed the campus, bracing himself against stiff winds, to find his truck.

On the LIE, the rain started coming down hard, and visibility was poor. His truck was so big that folks deferred to him on the highway. But it was so old that the brakes acted up in heavy rain. A guy cut him off, and he slammed on the brakes and fishtailed, correcting course at the very last minute. His heart pounded. He kept his eyes on the road, the radio tuned to the weather, but he thought only of Caroline. He worried about her safety, and fought against the urge to call her again. It galled him that he wasn't allowed to. All he wanted was to help her, but she'd constructed this phony wall between the two of them, making that impossible.

It took Aidan an hour to get to his apartment. He arrived to find Ron, the super, boarding up windows. Ron was an old guy with a big belly and arthritic fingers. When he begged for help, Aidan had a hard time saying no, even though his thoughts were elsewhere. He let himself be dragged into helping Ron secure the apartment complex, getting soaked in the ever-worsening storm. The whole time, thoughts of Caroline's house in the path of the storm weighed on his mind. She'd be devastated if that house was damaged, or God forbid, destroyed. He'd ridden out lesser storms on his grandfather's land as a child, and remembered how the wind could howl, how the surf could pound against the dunes. She must be crazy with worry. Maybe she was even driving in this mess right this minute, trying to get there to secure her place. The more Aidan thought about it, the more certain he became that Caroline was out in this evil weather right now, heading to her house. He wouldn't be able to stand it if something happened to her, something he could have prevented. All he had to do was go take care of her house for her, and let her know she didn't have to worry. How hard would that be? How terrible would he feel if he didn't, and then something happened? Aidan lived with so much guilt already, from old wounds. Samantha. Matthew. The worry he caused Tommy on a daily basis. Tommy's blood pressure was high because of him. If Caroline got into a car accident driving out from the city, when Aidan could spare her the risk by looking after her house for her, he would never forgive himself.

"Ron," he said, "listen, buddy, I just realized. My girlfriend's house is sitting empty right in the path of the storm. I have to go check it for her."

"Now? But we're not done."

"Hey, man, that's what they pay you for. Nobody's paying me, and I got other obligations."

"What if the place gets damaged?"

"Then maybe the landlord can get some insurance money and finally fix this dump up. I'm sorry. This is too important. Good luck, my friend. See you later."

Aidan sat in his truck and dialed Caroline's number. His number was still blocked and went straight to voicemail.

"Caroline, it's Aidan. I don't know if you blocked my number, or whether you'll even get this message or not. But I want you to know, I'm heading to your house now to make sure it's okay in the storm. There's no need for you to come out here in this weather. I'm praying this gets to you. Stay safe, baby. I'm thinking about you."

Then he took off in the direction of Caroline's house. Aidan knew that what he was doing was risky. He wasn't worried about the storm. He was worried about getting caught. Because, if Caroline wasn't there, he planned to break in to secure the place. He knew he shouldn't. If Tommy found him, he'd be so disappointed, especially since he'd read Aidan the riot act after finding the St. Christopher medal at Caroline's house. Tommy had been right, of course: Aidan was the one responsible for setting off the alarm at Caroline's house that night. Tommy knew the score, because back in the day, Aidan and Matthew had gone through a phase of breaking into the big houses along the beach. They were stupid kids, sowing their wild oats. They'd go into places they knew were empty, taking only enough to pay for a good time on a Saturday night. It was only after they got caught that Aidan realized how much harm he'd caused. Their families were devastated. They would have gone to jail if not for Tommy. Aidan never did anything like that again. Not even after he got out of prison, when he was broke and desperate and a pariah. He'd stayed out of trouble—until Caroline came along.

He'd never seriously thought about breaking into Caroline's house before. But the fascination had been there, ever since the night she came into the Red Anchor and dissed him with that insultingly big tip. The insult infuriated him, and yet afterward the thought of her consumed him. She was beautiful and rich and beyond his reach. And she owned that house, on that land. The house became a siren song to Aidan. He would go there at night, look up at the light shining from the windows, and dream of her. He would walk around, peek in through the glass, imagine her life there. One night, he'd made the mistake of reaching for a door handle on the terrace. Not because he planned to break in. But to make sure she'd locked it, that she was safe from those who would do her harm. That one enthusiastic jiggle of the handle wound up setting off the burglar alarm. Aidan had run away so fast that he'd dropped the

St. Christopher medal, which led to that big lecture from Tommy. Now, tonight, he would break in for real. But only for the purpose of protecting her house. He didn't have the material with him to board up the windows, but he would use whatever he found inside. He knew breaking in was wrong. But he was acting out of concern for Caroline. He just hoped to hell his brother never learned of it.

When he arrived at the house, it was raining buckets. As Aidan pulled into the driveway, he noticed the light on next door, and worried Mrs. Eberhardt would see him and call the cops. Back when he was a kid, and Gramps was alive, Mrs. Eberhardt gave them hell from dawn to dusk. Aidan and Tommy and their cousins could do no right in her eyes. Hard to imagine she was home tonight, since anybody with half a brain would evacuate that rickety beach shack at the first sign of a storm. But she was stubborn, and if she was there, she'd make trouble.

He turned off the engine. He could barely see out the windshield of the truck, that's how hard it was coming down. Climbing through Caroline's bedroom window would have a certain Romeo-and-Juliet quality, but scaling the building in this weather would be too risky. He'd have to go in the front door. He kept a toolbox in the bed of the truck. He rifled through it in the rain, pulling out anything that might help him—a screwdriver, a bolt cutter, some wire that he could use to pick the lock. The deluge made the ground look like it was boiling. He pulled his hood forward, but the rain streamed into his eyes anyway, making it hard to see as he ran to the front door. He stood in the midst of the downpour, trying to work the lock with a stiff piece of wire. But he couldn't see, and couldn't hear the click of the tumblers beneath the roar of the wind.

He was about to quit when the lock finally gave, and he stumbled into Caroline's living room. The screeching started immediately. He had to shut the damn thing off before Eberhardt heard it and called the police. The keypad was right inside the door. Aidan held his flashlight in his mouth, shining it on the keypad as he popped the plastic surround off with his screwdriver. He eased the bundle of wires from the wall and aimed the flashlight at them. He couldn't make heads or tails of the writhing mess of wires, and besides, he didn't want to damage anything. He'd come here to help, not to destroy her burglar alarm. He pushed the wires back into the wall and snapped the plastic cover of the keypad back into place. Even if Eberhardt heard the alarm and called the cops, it would be a while before they'd show. In weather this bad, cops had other, more pressing concerns. He'd do what he could to protect the house, then get out before he got caught.

Aidan walked around flipping on lights, checking things out, trying not to get distracted by the beauty of the place. This house was magic. It glowed with light and smelled of flowers. He wanted to protect it, to keep it safe, for when he could live here openly with the woman he adored. The windows and the terrace doors were locked, but there were no storm shutters and no boards up. He went to the mudroom and found some newspapers in a pile near the trash bin. It was the best he could do. There was no wood here, not even any cardboard boxes. He brought the newspapers to the kitchen and tossed them on the island, planning to look for tape and then cover the windows with newspaper. Then he heard a sound behind him, turned around, and saw his brother standing there.

Fuck.

"You fucking idiot," Tommy said. "I knew it was you."

Tommy grabbed Aidan by the back of the neck and forced him toward the door. In a second, they were out in the pouring rain grappling and wrestling, trying to force one another to the ground. They were the same height, but Tommy had fifty pounds on Aidan. Aidan was strong, Tommy was stronger. It had always been that way. Tommy shoved and kicked him toward his truck. He slammed him up against the truck bed and grabbed him by the hair.

"You get out of here now and don't come back," Tommy spat out, his face screwed up with rage. "If I find you here again, I'm arresting you and you're going in. This is your last chance. Do you understand?"

"I was only—"

"I don't care what you were doing. That call went out to every patrol car. You're lucky I was five minutes away, or you could be dealing with

Mike Castro right now, who thinks you're a piece of shit and would love nothing more than to lock you up."

"Fine," he said.

"What?"

He raised his voice to be heard over the pounding rain. "I'll leave."

"Yes, you will. And you're going straight to my house."

"What?"

"You're driving away from here, Aidan, and you're not looking back. You're going to my house to watch over Kelly and the kids. Ma's down in Pittsburgh visiting Aunt Joan, and my family's all alone tonight. With everything I've done for you, I think you owe it to me to look after them through the storm. And to give me the peace of mind that I know where you are. Don't you agree?"

Aidan couldn't quarrel with that. The storm was intensifying. He and his brother were soaked to the skin, and the sound from the ocean was like a roar. He was worried about Kelly and the kids, too, if he was honest with himself. Only, he couldn't really feel that, because his worry for Caroline got in the way. It was so much bigger.

"Yeah, you're right," he said.

"Okay, then. Go."

Aidan gestured toward the house, where the alarm still shrieked, and the door gaped open.

"We have to close up."

"If I go in there and turn off the lights and the alarm, she'll know we were here. I'll have to file a report, the whole nine yards, and I'm not doing that, because it would mean lying on duty."

"But the house."

"Screw this lady and her goddamn house. She's poison to you. We were never here. You got it? It's for your own good. You understand me?"

"Yes."

"Now get the hell out. Or I swear to God, kid, I'm done with you."

41

Aidan felt the weight of the responsibility that his brother had placed upon him. He loved his sister-in-law and his niece and nephew. Their safety was in his hands. Tommy had caught him doing something he shouldn't yet still took that leap of faith. He hadn't given up on Aidan yet, and Aidan needed to live up to his brother's trust.

Tommy's house was five miles from the ocean. But Aidan worked like hell to secure the house as if it were oceanfront, facing a direct hit. Tommy had only had time to board up a couple of windows before getting called away, so Aidan finished the job up on a high ladder, lashed by wind and rain. Anything that wasn't nailed down in the backyard, he moved into the garage. He put rolled-up towels along the bottom of the door to stop the water flooding in the crack. It was two long hours of work in the cold rain before he dragged himself inside, wet and exhausted.

Kelly gave him some clothes of Tommy's to change into while she threw his wet things in the dryer. He gratefully slurped down the bowl of chicken noodle soup she'd left him on the kitchen table. They still had power, but that wouldn't last with the winds like this. Too many trees to blow down onto the electric lines. He thought they ought to prepare. Kelly filled the bathtub with water in case the pump went out, and Aidan brought the camping gear down from the attic. Lanterns, a propane stove, coolers to fill with ice and food from the fridge if they lost electricity. It was past eleven by the time Aidan sank down onto the living room sofa with a sigh. Kelly came in, her arms piled high with blankets and pillows.

"Let me make up the couch for you," she said, as the wind roared outside. "It would be nuts for you to drive home in this."

Aidan was torn. He wanted to stay and look after his brother's family through the night, but he had another place he needed to protect. Kelly and the kids were safe, their house secured. But Caroline's house was right in the path of the storm. Not only had he completely failed to secure the windows before Tommy kicked him out; he'd made things worse. The front door was now wide open, exposing everything inside to the elements. He'd left Caroline that voicemail promising to look after her house, and he'd failed to follow through. He couldn't leave things like that.

"Thanks, Kel," he said. "But I should be going."

Kelly studied him with concern. "Where exactly are you going, Aidan?"

Kelly tried to manage Aidan's life for him like Tommy did. He took it better from her than from him. He and Kelly had a big-sister/kid-brother type of friendship that meant a lot to him. She treated him with kindness rather than the scolding Tommy defaulted to. And she had this wide-open face—round and serene, with freckles and big hazel eyes. He was never able to lie to her, and he couldn't now.

"A friend of mind has a house. It's right in the path of the storm. I told her I'd check it out for her."

Her face scrunched with disappointment. "I know about your *friend*. From what Tom says, she's bad news, and you got in trouble once already tonight going in her house. Is it really smart to go back there?"

Aidan wanted to explain. Caroline was a flame to him, and he was the moth. If he ended as a pile of ash, that was the risk he took. His only regret would be the disappointment he caused his brother and Kelly.

"Maybe not. But I promised her," he said.

"Promises are important. But I still think it would be better if you stayed here with us. We're your family, Aidan. We don't want to see anything bad happen to you. And I'm not only talking about the weather. Will you stay? Please?"

He couldn't deny Kelly's claim on his loyalty. He'd always been welcome in her house, even at his lowest. She'd picked him up and dusted him off more times than he could count over the years. He had a place at her table for every holiday. She was asking him to stay. As much as it pained him, he felt obligated to say yes.

"All right, I'll stay, Kel. For you."

"Thank you. Now get up and let me make your bed."

She made up the sofa quickly, then pecked him on the cheek and went off to bed. Aidan tossed and turned in the darkened living room, listening to the shifts in the wind. He tried, but he couldn't get comfortable with the decision to stay here and leave Caroline's house undefended. Not just that, though. He was afraid that she hadn't listened. That she was driving through this mess on her way to the beach. That she might be harmed. Half an hour passed. He got up and wandered to the kitchen, where he looked in the refrigerator. But nothing in there appealed to him. He felt too worried to eat. He went back to the living room, where his phone was buzzing on the coffee table, lighting up with Caroline's number. He grabbed it breathlessly.

"Caroline. Are you all right? Where are you?" he said.

"At my house. It's a disaster. Somebody broke in, set off the alarm, and ran away. Was that you? Don't lie to me."

This was the worst outcome imaginable. She'd driven out from the city despite his warning, only to find the place abandoned and thrown open to the storm. She'd never trust him again.

"It *was* me. But I can explain," he said.

"Explain?" she said. "What the hell—"

The line began to crackle and pop. The next words out of Caroline's mouth were garbled into a tinny, incomprehensible squawk.

"What?" he said. "You're cutting out. Caroline? Caroline, are you there?"

Nothing.

"Caroline?"

But the phone was dead in his hand. Caroline was all alone on that wild, exposed stretch of beach, facing down the storm with no protection, believing that Aidan had betrayed her. He couldn't stay here, protected from the storm, cozy with his family, and leave her alone to face the hurricane. He had to go to her, or he would never be able to live with himself.

42

It was after midnight, and the streets were empty, littered with downed branches and debris. The traffic lights at the intersection swayed like crazy, and Aidan had to fight the wind gusts to keep the truck going straight. When he crossed the highway, he saw a live power wire down, throwing off sparks. The drive seemed endless, because he didn't know what he'd find at the other end. Would Caroline be safe? Would her beautiful house be reduced to a pile of rubble? If she was safe, would she allow him back into her life? Or would she close her heart and mind against him because of the very things he'd done to protect her?

He drove down her road with his heart in his throat, peering through the sheets of rain. When he reached her house and saw her car in the driveway, he jumped out of the truck, crazed with fear. A branch had landed on the Escalade, a big one, and Aidan got it in his mind somehow that she might still be inside, crushed and bleeding. He ran over, playing his flashlight across crumpled glass in the pounding rain. When he saw that the car was empty, he nearly cried with relief. Then the flashlight beam caught graffiti scratched into the side of the SUV. "DIE BITCH," it said, and his blood went cold all over again.

This vandalism must be the work of that thug Jason Stark had hired. Was he here? Caroline's house was completely dark. Had he tracked her to this place, defaced her car, hurt her? Aidan ran up to the front of the house and looked in through the glass sidelights that ran on either side of the mahogany door. It was dark inside. The rain streaming off the hood of his jacket made it even harder to see. He swept the flashlight beam from his phone back and forth, and gasped when he caught a movement. Caroline materialized out of the darkness and floated toward him like an apparition. She came up to the door, looking through the glass at him.

"Let me in," he shouted over the rain and the wind, but she shook her head firmly.

"Go away," she said.

"Are you all right? Is anybody there with you? Please, you have to let me in."

Caroline took a step back, away from the door, looking pale and afraid. Was it possible that the thug was already inside the house?

"Caroline," Aidan said, and pounded on the door frantically. "You have to let me in. I'm here to protect you. Somebody is coming to hurt you. Your daughter, too."

Her eyes widened. She came back to the glass. "What are you talking about?"

"It's your husband. He's mixed up in something dirty. Let me in, and I'll explain."

The rain came down sideways in sheets, and the wind shook the trees. She opened the door a few inches to hear him better over the racket. A gust kicked up and pushed at the door. He took the opportunity to press his way in. In the foyer, she backed away, grabbing an umbrella and brandishing it at him.

"Stay back," she said, looking frantic.

"Are you all right?"

"I don't want you here."

"I'm here to help."

"What was that you said? Something about Jason?" she demanded.

"Yes. I'm going to tell you. I'm dripping on your floor. Put that down. Please?"

Grudgingly, she lowered the umbrella, placing it on a bench, still within arm's reach. He held up his hands placatingly.

"Is it okay if I take my coat off?"

"Why should I trust you, after what you did to my daughter and my sister?"

"I was trying to help. If I could come in for five minutes, I'll explain everything."

She studied his face.

"I would never hurt you. You know that," he said.

She sighed and nodded.

"Thank you for trusting me," he said.

"I *don't* trust you."

He stood by the door, stripping off his jacket and shoes, then followed her into the great room. The fire had been turned on in the gas fireplace, and candles placed around the room, which glowed with a warm light.

"The power's out, as you can see. Sit over there and don't come any closer," she said, pointing at a leather club chair.

She sat down cross-legged on the sofa opposite and folded her arms, glaring at him. He was taken aback by her hostility. Everything he'd done was for her. How could she not understand that?

"I don't know what you think you know about my husband, Aidan," she said. "But I can assure you, he's not mixed up in anything dirty."

"He is. And he's a danger to you and your daughter."

"That's ridiculous."

"From what you told me about him, I was worried, so I followed him."

"You *what*?"

"Why is that so crazy? You asked me to *kill* him for you."

"Okay, that was a mistake. I said so. After Jason left and took the money, I was very, very upset. I said that to you out of desperation, then I immediately took it back. You promised not to mention it again."

"I know, I'm sorry. I only said it to point out that you can't trust him."

"It's you I can't trust. You scare me, Aidan. You went after my family."

"No, I didn't. You don't understand. I was trying to help."

"What are you talking about? You approached my daughter like you wanted to date her. You—"

"Wait a minute, that's completely untrue. I never wanted to date her."

"She sent me this selfie of the two of you looking like two lovebirds."

"I'm sorry if she misunderstood. But I never came on to her in any way. It was totally friendly and on the up-and-up."

"What were you even doing there? She's eighteen years old, Aidan. She's my little girl. What were you thinking, going anywhere near her? And you tried to run my sister off the road. These are the people I care about, that I love. If you hurt them—"

"I never tried to hurt anybody, swear to God. Your sister came to the bar and threatened *me*, then she drove away. All I did was try to catch up to her. Maybe that looked like I was attacking her but I was only trying to talk to her."

"Even if I accept your explanation about what you did to my sister, what about Hannah?"

"Okay, I see now maybe that was a mistake. But I made it because of my love for you. I wanted to make sure she was safe. Your husband is dangerous. He wants to have you killed, and your daughter, too."

She laughed in shock. "That's insane. Either you're making it up, or there's something wrong with you."

He really thought that, once they were together, she'd see his loyalty and his love, but he wasn't getting through. He had to try harder, to say whatever it took to convince her.

"I swear it's true. I told you, Caroline, I followed him. Jason and his girlfriend went to Queens, where they met with a guy who looked like some kind of mobster. I watched Jason hand the guy an envelope full of cash. I heard them mention your name, and Hannah's. Don't you see? Jason wants to be with this other woman. I don't understand how anyone could feel that way, but there it is. And he's taking extreme steps to make it happen. You're in danger."

She stared at him with a horror-stuck expression, saying nothing. He had to make her understand.

"I didn't seek this out," he said. "All I did was offer you a ride home when you weren't safe to drive. And yes, I thought you were beautiful. I thought you were incredible to talk to. But I would never have made a move because you were too far above me. I never thought a woman like you would go for a guy like me. *You* came on to *me* first, you can't deny that."

She didn't deny it. She didn't say anything. She continued to stare in disbelief, and Aidan kept talking to fill the silence.

"Normally, I wouldn't mess with a married woman. But I knew your story. I knew that your husband had mistreated you, and that you deserved better. And I thought, when will I ever get a chance at a woman this amazing again? We slept together, and I fell for you, Caroline. I fell for you hard. As we got to know each other, I saw that your problems were even worse than I imagined. But I didn't run. I stayed. I'm here to fight for you. Everything I did—following your husband, going to see Hannah, breaking into this house to save it from the storm. It was done to protect you, because of how I felt about you. I'm sorry if I frightened you. But you stopped talking to me. You wouldn't see me or take my calls. So, there was no way for me to explain. Please, tell me you understand."

As they gazed at each other, the lights came on suddenly. She looked around in amazement.

"Look at that," she said. "I wonder if it will last."

"Answer me. Do you understand why I did what I did?" he said.

"Aidan, whatever you think you saw, you're wrong. I need you to stay away from my family. Do you hear me?"

"From your daughter, your sister, okay. But your husband—"

"Jason and I are trying to reconcile. He wouldn't hurt me, and he would certainly never hurt his daughter."

"Reconcile? No. That's messed up. I won't let you."

"It's not up to you," she said.

"Tell me something, Caroline. Who vandalized your car, huh? Was that him? Or the thug he hired? Be honest."

She wouldn't meet his eyes.

"You're letting him abuse you," Aidan said.

She sighed and stood up. "I'm exhausted after the drive out here. I need a drink. Do you want one?"

He nodded. If they had a drink together, she would relax and let down her guard. He could bring her around. She couldn't be serious about going back to the man who'd cheated on her and robbed her and threatened her life. Jason Stark was a menace. An animal in a fancy suit. Aidan had to make her see that.

Caroline walked into the kitchen and came back with two glasses. Aidan took a swallow and grimaced.

"What is this?" he said.

"Bourbon. You don't like it?"

"It's fine. Cheers."

They clinked glasses and drank.

"You should to listen to me," he said. "I have your best interests at heart. I'm the only one who does. Why would I lie?"

"Maybe you're not lying. Maybe you're mistaken. But you go too far. I need you to back off and give me some space."

"And then we can be together."

She sighed. "Maybe."

"Caroline, please. You're all I think about. Night and day. Only you. I'm yours, completely."

He took her hand and brought it to his lips. At the touch of her flesh, the room seemed to tilt. He felt a hot shiver run up and down his spine. He put his hand over his heart.

"I'm sorry for the way I approached your daughter and your sister. Please forgive me for my bad judgment. It won't happen again."

She didn't absolve him. She didn't say a word. But when he turned her hand over and kissed the palm of her hand, and then the inside of her wrist, she didn't stop him. Her pulse was racing. He laid his hand over her breast and felt her heart jackhammering. The knowledge that she wanted him made him dizzy.

"Can I stay?" he said.

"It's not a good idea."

"Please? We'll be together through the storm. That's all I ask. Let me protect you until morning."

She looked searchingly into his eyes and sighed. "All right."

"Would you dance with me? You don't have to commit to anything more. Just one song. Let me hold you."

She leaned forward and picked up a remote from a docking station on the coffee table. Everything was moving in slow motion. Sinatra started crooning from hidden speakers in the walls around them, and the music flowed through his bloodstream like he'd injected it. He took her in his arms, and they melted together, swaying to the luscious sound. Aidan understood in that moment that his love for Caroline was fated, ordained. This song was proof. It had been written a hundred years ago, just so they could hear it tonight. He closed his eyes and breathed in the scent of her hair. Was this how true love felt? Her closeness made him unsteady on his feet. As long as they kept dancing, whatever happened to him, he wouldn't mind. He would welcome his downfall if she was the cause of it.

The song ended. A fist pounded on the front door.

"It's Jason," Caroline said, her eyes wide with panic.

Aidan had been expecting the worst, and yet when the moment came, he wasn't prepared. He broke out in a cold sweat, made a move for the door, and stumbled over his own two feet. He must be more tired than he'd realized after his hours of labor in the storm. Caroline grabbed him by the elbows.

"You have to leave, Aidan. Go out the back, down to the beach. He can't know you're here."

"He *will* know. My truck's in the driveway."

"I'll think of a way to explain the truck. He doesn't know who you are. He'd never know it's yours."

"I can't leave you alone with him."

The husband pounded on the door. "Caroline! Let me in, *now!*"

"Please, I'm begging you," she said. "Let me handle him. I don't think he'd hurt me. But if he sees you here, I don't know what he'll do."

Aidan felt wrong abandoning her to that brute at the door. But his thoughts were scrambled, and he felt confused and exhausted at the same time. He'd go outside and let the rain lash his face and wake him up. Then he'd sneak around to the front door and jump that asshole from behind.

His coat and shoes were back near the front door.

"My shoes——"

"There's no time. Go!" Caroline said.

She opened the French doors and shoved him from behind. Aidan stumbled out into the stormy night, barefoot, fighting against the wind.

43

The power had come back on. The lights were on in my bedroom, and Frank Sinatra crooned from the speakers in the ceiling. I was afraid to speak or move. I lay paralyzed, the blood pounding in my veins, my eyes glued to the gun that Aidan cradled in his lap. I remembered picking it up that day at his apartment, the deadly weight of it in my hands. It was pitch-dark outside. The wind shook the windows, and the thought crossed my mind that I might die here tonight. Was Aidan capable of killing me, or did he merely want to frighten me into submission? I couldn't know for sure, but I had to assume the threat was real. Failing to take him seriously could mean my death.

I moved to get out of the bed and he shifted suddenly in the chair, thrusting the gun toward me.

"Stay there," he said.

His eyes seemed unfocused, like something was knocked loose inside. How had I ever found this man attractive? I looked at him now and all I saw was crazy. And crazy was a problem—a big problem. A regular guy who got rejected might come after me. He might hurt me, even kill me. But Aidan had gone after my family. My sister. My *daughter*. That he knew about them at all, that he had a motive to hurt them— that was on me. In order to protect them, to make this up to them, I had to take responsibility for stopping him, even at the risk of my life. But how? I was unarmed and helpless. He was bigger than me. He was blocking the door. And he had a gun. My only hope was to get him talking and play for time, until I found an opening to escape.

I cleared my throat, which was dry with fear.

"How—how did you get in here?" I asked Aidan.

The answer was obvious. He'd broken in, and not for the first time. My alarm went off earlier tonight. It went off last week, and the police supposedly were dispatched and found nothing amiss. The police, right. Tommy Callahan. The cavalry wasn't going to burst in and save me. They were on the gunman's side.

"How did I get in?" Aidan said. "*You* let me in."

"No, I didn't. I was sleeping."

"You invited me in, Caroline. You left the door open for me. You want me here. Admit it to yourself."

My face flushed with the effort of controlling my temper. *I don't want you here. I hate you, you lunatic. You belong in jail, or in the psych ward. Or better yet, dead.* I had to take a deep breath before I could speak.

"Maybe I did leave the door unlocked. It wasn't intentional. I'm not sorry you're here, though. There are things I need to say to you."

"Oh, now you talk to me. After you ignored me for so long? How many messages did I leave? You blocked my number. That's disrespectful."

"I'm sorry. It wasn't nice of me to block your calls. I should have been up front with you and told you that your conduct was unacceptable. You did some terrible things—"

"Shut up. I'm not interested in hearing you trash me. That's over."

"Aidan—"

"I'm done listening. I hold the gun. I'm the boss now, and I say what happens. Take the blanket off. Show me what you're wearing. I want to see your body."

I didn't move. He pointed the gun at me.

"Do what I say," he said.

I drew the covers back, showing off my sweatpants and loose-fitting T-shirt.

"Happy now?"

"Don't provoke me. Take it off."

His mouth was a grim line. If I didn't figure out a way to distract him, he'd be on me in seconds. In the heat of the moment, I heard my father's voice. *The best defense is a good offense.* I had to stop cooperating in my own destruction. I needed to stop acting afraid, to assert control, to throw him off balance. Most of all, I had to figure out a way to get out of this room.

"Why should I, you pervert?" I said. "You went after my daughter. Something's wrong with you. You're sick."

The surprise in his eyes was gratifying to see.

"Don't talk to me like that," he said. "I didn't go after her. She came on to me."

"A mother and daughter. What is that, some kind of perverted fetish?"

His face went deep red. "It wasn't sexual at all. I was only there to help her."

"Oh, please. You expect me to believe that?"

"It's the truth."

"If it's true, prove it. This is my daughter's welfare we're talking about. You can't expect me to take your word for it. I'm calling her."

I picked up my cell phone from the bedside table. I knew there was no service, but he didn't.

He looked at me with suspicion. "What are you doing? Put that down."

"I'm going to call Hannah right now. If you didn't lay a finger on her, she'll tell me that, and then I'll believe you. I'll admit I was wrong. But if you won't let me do that, it says something, doesn't it? It tells me you're lying."

I moved slowly, sitting up, putting my feet on the floor, pulling up Hannah's number on my phone.

"Give me that!" Aidan said, and lunged for my phone.

I threw myself sideways and tried to run around him. He body-checked me, and I tried to grab the gun. He saw that coming, and grabbed me by the hair, yanking me down onto the bed and straddling me. He leveled the gun at my forehead and gave me that same chilling, empty smile he wore when I woke up to find myself his prisoner.

"Stupid move, Caroline," he said. "Now I'm mad."

We paused there, staring at each other, breathing heavily, and I flashed back to the last time we were together in this bed. In pursuit of one night of mindless fun, I'd found my own destruction.

"You need to apologize and make it up to me," he said.

I stared down the barrel of the silver gun, and my courage deserted me.

"Please," I said, my voice shaking. "Don't hurt me."

"I don't want to hurt you. If you treat me with the respect and love I showed you, I won't need to."

"No. Please. I can't. I'm married. What we did was wrong."

"Then we can go another way. I can pull this trigger. You won't even feel it. Either way, I win. You'll belong to me, and you won't hurt me anymore."

"If I hurt you, I'm sorry. I won't do it again."

"You're a liar, Caroline. You can't help yourself."

He thrust the barrel of the gun hard against my forehead. Tears of desperation flooded my eyes.

"Please. Please, don't shoot," I whispered.

Suddenly, downstairs, a crash rang out. Aidan's head whipped around. He stared at the closed bedroom door. Then, to my amazement and gratitude, he got off me, and stood up, listening.

"It must be the wind," he said.

The wind rumbled like a freight train outside the bedroom windows, but it was a steady sound. That had been a crash. If it had come from outside the house, I might've taken it for a tree limb falling. But it came from inside.

"That's not the wind," I said. "Somebody's downstairs. They knocked over furniture, or kicked the door in. Looters come out in a hurricane, Aidan. They could make off with the TV. You claim to be the big man. If that's true, go stop them."

He grabbed my arm and yanked me up.

"You're coming with me," he said, poking the gun into my ribs. "Stay quiet and do what I tell you."

Aidan's grip was like a vise as we moved to the door. He opened it slowly, careful not to make a sound. We stopped on the landing and listened. It was hard to hear anything over the roar of the wind and the thumping of my heart. Aidan dropped my arm and put a finger to his lips. Then I caught it—the sound of footsteps. It was unmistakable. The tread of shoes against the wood of the floor. Someone was downstairs. Aidan knew it, too. I saw the alarm in his eyes.

"Caroline? Are you here?" the voice called out.

It was *Jason*. My husband had come to rescue me. I was so overwhelmed with relief that I wanted to burst into tears. But I held my breath, too anxious to make a sound. Because I realized: Now his life was in danger as well, and it was all my fault.

44

C aroline? Where are you?"

"Answer him," Aidan whispered. "Say you're up here, tell him to come."

Aidan pointed the gun at the stairs. The second-floor landing where we stood was shrouded in darkness. But the lights blazed downstairs. If I called out to Jason like Aidan said, my husband would walk to the foot of the stairs and head up into the dark, the perfect target. Like a fish in a barrel. He wouldn't stand a chance. And Jason would have been lured to his death by *me*, his wife of twenty years. Because he trusted me. It didn't matter what was wrong between us. It didn't matter that we'd grown apart. Or that he'd commandeered our money, or even that he'd cheated. In that moment, I remembered the love we shared, the daughter we raised, the life we built together. And I had to save him, even if it killed me.

"Call him *now*," Aidan said between gritted teeth.

I racked my brain for what to do next, but I had no brilliant plan. The only option was to call out, to do my best to warn my husband, even if it meant Aidan shooting me. It was now or never.

"There's a man up here and he's got a gun! *Run!*" I screamed.

That gun turned on me. Aidan took a step back in order to get the space to fire, and in that moment, I saw what to do. I kicked him with all my strength, and the momentum sent him flying toward the staircase. A boom rang out. The bullet whizzed by my ear like a deadly insect, and plaster rained down from the ceiling. Aidan fell backward and skidded halfway down the stairs before arresting his descent. He hauled himself to standing and started up the stairs for me with murder in his eyes. I ran to the bedroom, slammed the door, and locked it, panting in fear. Then I sank down behind the dresser and waited for him to start shooting.

Nothing happened. I sat there shaking.

A raft of rain sluiced against the windows, so powerful that I jumped.

I strained my ears, too terrified to move. Far below, I heard a cry. Then I realized—Aidan had gone after Jason instead. I'd left my husband alone and unarmed, at the mercy of my stalker and his gun. Jason only showed up here because of my message, begging him to come out to the beach and help me protect the house. Despite the shaky state of our marriage, he'd driven through a hurricane to answer my call. Now I was hiding out in the relative safety of this room while Aidan hunted him down like an animal. Aidan was in our lives, and in this house, only because of my weakness. If he shot Jason—God forbid, if he killed him—I'd have blood on my hands. Jason's death would be on my conscience for the rest of my life.

The kitchen knife I'd brought with me from the city sat on the top of the dresser. Aidan must have moved it from the bedside table while I slept to keep it from my reach. They say don't bring a knife to a gunfight. But the knife was all I had. I clutched it close and pressed my ear to the door. I could hear the squalling of wind and crashing of surf outside my windows; but nothing to tell me where Aidan was. Of course, it was possible his silence was a fake-out. That he was standing right outside this door waiting for me to walk into his trap. I might do that. Not because I was stupid, but because I wasn't a coward, or selfish enough to let my husband march to slaughter without trying to save him.

I held my breath and turned the lock, listening. Still, nothing but the wind, which seemed to be intensifying, if that was even possible. Knife poised, I crept out to the landing, every nerve tense with fear, expecting to get jumped any second. But Aidan didn't come. He wasn't up here. He and Jason must both be downstairs, yet I couldn't hear them.

A powerful blast of wind shook the walls. The house shifted and creaked with every gust, as if it would collapse in on itself. I wondered if the glass in the windows would hold. Outside, all was darkness. Inside, the lights flickered and dimmed and then brightened again. With the next gust, they went out completely. We'd lost power for the second time at just the wrong moment.

I stole down the stairs in my bare feet, hugging the wall. I couldn't quiet my ragged, terrified breathing, and prayed it faded into the deafening wind. I tiptoed into the living room. Earlier tonight, I'd turned on the gas fireplace. Its glowing light suffused the first floor, throwing off shadows that played tricks on my eyes. They were here somewhere, they had to be. But my senses were on such high alert that every piece of furniture seemed like a mortal threat.

Outside the terrace doors, moonlight shone eerily behind the clouds, lighting the sky over the ocean. The world was a writhing mass, with debris swirling in the blinding rain. A movement drew my eye. I watched openmouthed as a tree branch came sailing toward the terrace doors like a torpedo. Glass exploded everywhere, and suddenly the raging wind was inside the house. The tree branch sat on my beautiful floors as water poured in around it. I reeled back, right into Aidan's grasp.

I was too shocked to fight. In a second, he'd stripped the knife from my hand and twisted my arm painfully behind my back. The tip of my own knife was poised against my throat as I cowered, cursing myself for letting down my guard.

"I came down here, and he was gone," Aidan said, raising his voice to be heard over the ruckus of the storm. "Fucking coward. He ran. He doesn't give a shit about you, Caroline. Now you're gonna pay for choosing him over me."

He dragged me back toward the stairs. I went limp as a rag doll, dragging my feet on the floor, using my body weight to stop him.

"Move," he said, and punched me in the side.

I cried out in pain. From the corner of my eye I saw a movement. Not debris—it was Jason, running. But not toward us, around the stairs, so he could come up from behind. Aidan saw him, too, and whirled. While he was distracted, I grabbed for the knife. The blade sliced deep into the flesh of my palm, burning like acid. I screamed, long and shrill, and Aidan let go of me. He dropped the knife and kicked it across the room, so I couldn't get to it. Just then, the wind hit mercilessly, and what was left of the terrace doors flew open, flapping and banging. I stumbled toward them. But the wind was so powerful that it pushed me back into the house. The storm was all around me. Water and wind and pieces of trees flying through the air. I could barely breathe from the force of it pressing down on me.

A strange calm settled over the house. The wind died down completely, and the rain stopped with the suddenness of a faucet shutting off. Time seemed to stop, as I turned to see Aidan and Jason, struggling over the gun.

In the eerie silence, a shot rang out, deafening and final. Jason grunted and crumpled to the floor. Thick crimson blood blossomed on his shirt and spread in a shiny pool out from his body. I saw the light fade from in his eyes, and in that moment, I realized how much I loved him, and how I would live the rest of my life in the horror of this moment. A scream that I couldn't imagine was inside me rose into the air.

"Shut up," Aidan said. "This was your idea. You wanted it."

"No," I whispered, and I was sobbing.

I tried to kneel beside my husband, but Aidan shoved me away.

"Yes, you did. You said you wanted him dead."

"I did not. I never said that."

"Try telling that to the cops. You're in the middle of a divorce. You wanted all the money. You're the one with the motive to shoot him, not me. I only did what you asked."

"It's not true. And *you* shot him. It's your gun."

"Nobody knows that. People will believe me. If you don't want to fry for this crime, you better help me clean up the mess. Help me get him to my truck. We'll dump him in the ocean. In this storm, he'll get washed out to sea. They'll never find him."

"No!"

My face was wet, with rain, with tears. I started pummeling Aidan with my fists. He laughed and shoved me away again, but I came back at him. His face went dark.

"Enough. Stop it."

"*No!*"

He reeled back, raising his hand. I saw the silver flash of the gun coming toward me. Pain exploded in my head. The world went black, and I was in hell.

after
the storm

45

Aidan woke with the taste of metal in his mouth and the worst headache he'd had in his life. Flies buzzed around his face, and a bright light shone in his eyes. It was the beam of a flashlight, he realized, used purposely to blind him. What the hell? He squinted and saw that he was in the front seat of his truck. The light felt like it was splitting his head apart, and a bitch of a hangover was making him nauseous. The windows were rolled down, and rain was coming in, but it stank to high heaven in the truck, like something had died in here. The seat was wet and slick. Someone pounded on the driver's-side door, and he winced at the sound as it reverberated inside his skull. But that made him look out the window, and he was astonished to see two guns pointed at his forehead.

"Put your hands up and get out of the truck."

He couldn't see their faces because of the blinding flashlight beam. But from the voice he knew Mike Castro was out there.

"What's going on?"

"Both hands up or we shoot! Now!"

He raised his other hand.

"You open the door then," he said.

God, the smell. He looked down at himself, and he was covered in blood. That's why the seat was wet, not from the rain. Blood, everywhere. What the hell was happening? He started to shake, and his breath came in shallow gasps. Mike popped the door, and Aidan fell over himself trying to get out, to get away from all the blood. Was it his own?

"What happened?" he said, and his bowels felt liquid.

So much blood. Was he shot? He went to touch his stomach to look for the wound, and Mike tackled him to the ground and cuffed his hands behind him.

"Stop it! What the fuck, Mike. I'm hurt."

Mike patted him down roughly.

"What did you reach for? Where's the gun? Is it on you?"

"I don't have a gun. I saw the blood and freaked. Did I get shot?"

There was sand under Aidan's face and in his mouth. He spit it out. They were on a beach. But which beach, and how the hell did his *truck* get here? It was daylight, early morning. It rained steadily, and the sand was wet and soggy. The remnants of the hurricane. Was that last night? It felt like a hundred years ago. But what had happened between then and now?

"The weapon isn't on him. Wayne, search the truck," Mike said.

Mike's knee was in Aidan's back, unrelenting, like he wanted to cause pain.

"Please, can you ease up?" Aidan said. "I think I might be cut or something."

But Mike pressed harder, which made Aidan panic for real. He couldn't breathe and thought he might black out. He couldn't believe this was actually happening. Was this real, or a nightmare?

"Follow protocol," Mike said, but he wasn't talking to Aidan. "Wear your gloves. This is a crime scene. The gun could be loaded."

Crime scene. Weapon. What the fuck? What day was it? What had happened? His mind was a fog. He remembered being at Tommy's house, boarding up windows, the storm closing in. Kelly making him soup, making up the couch. Then Caroline called. He went to her house, and she let him in. He held her in his arms. They danced to Sinatra, and it was beautiful.

Was *that* real? Or did he dream it?

"Shouldn't we call the chief?"

That was Wayne Johnson's voice. Aidan tried to look up, but Mike shoved his head back down, and he took another mouthful of sand.

"No. He's not getting away with this, like he did with the Bostick kid."

Bostick. Matthew. Was Aidan being punished for what happened back then? Mike had always hated him over that. But to the point where he'd frame him? And frame him for what? What gun? Whose blood?

"Not even a courtesy call?" Wayne said.

"I'm the senior officer on the scene, and I say we handle this by the book. Look in the car, use the gloves. Once we know what we have, we'll call the chief, and if it's what I think, we'll call in the staties, too. Chief's gonna have to recuse himself."

"All right, but if the boss gets pissed, I'm blaming you. I'm not taking the heat for this."

"You're a stand-up guy, Johnson."

"I'm loyal to the man who hired me. And I don't have a chip on my shoulder about Junior here the way you do."

"Do what I say."

Listening to them talk, Aidan felt bile rise in his throat. He vomited a little into the sand under his face and lay there with his nose in it, his chest constricted with panic. His hands tingled and went numb from the cuffs. He tried desperately to remember how he got here. Bits and pieces came back to him. The pounding on the door as they danced in the storm. The look of fear on Caroline's face. There was something important there. He followed the train of thought, and then he knew—the husband had shown up to interrupt their beautiful moment. Aidan saw the words scratched into her car. *DIE BITCH*. He remembered Stark meeting with that thug out in Queens. He'd vowed to protect Caroline from her husband. He remembered a flash of anger like a white heat, the overpowering urge to fight. He was going to come around from behind and jump the guy, beat him bloody. He remembered stumbling out into the storm, the wind and rain on his face. Then his mind went blank. Whose blood was on his hands? Was it Stark's? What had he done?

"What did I do?" he said aloud.

Mike released the pressure on Aidan's back. He felt stupidly grateful for the sensation of air in his lungs, like he loved Mike for not torturing him anymore. Mike knelt down beside him and spoke into Aidan's ear in a calm, reasonable voice.

"You want to tell me, kid? Confession is good for the soul. What did you do? Did you shoot someone? Kill somebody? You can tell me."

"I don't know. I'm not sure," Aidan said, and then he squeezed his eyes shut. He was trying to see what happened after he went outside. But all he saw was the rain.

"Think about it. Tell me what you remember."

"Can I talk to my brother?"

"Talk to *me*, Aidan. We go back. I've known you since you were a kid."

This was a trick. Mike Castro was not his friend. Mike lived down the street from the Bosticks. The Bosticks blamed Aidan for Matthew's death. Mike thought Tommy rigged the case, making it so Aidan barely did any time. But that wasn't true. Aidan was blameless. He didn't sleep with Matthew's girlfriend. He didn't pick a fight to impress Samantha. He didn't throw the first punch. Matthew did that. Yet Aidan's life got ruined. He got punished worse than he deserved. He went to jail. He missed out on going to college. He couldn't get a decent job. All that suffering, and Mike still couldn't forgive him. Mike resented Tommy, too, and coveted his job. He'd love to see Tommy fired and Aidan locked up for good, whether he deserved it or not. Maybe this was some kind of frame-up job. Then again, there was the real possibility that Aidan had murdered Jason Stark in cold blood and didn't remember. Aidan was covered in blood. So much blood that someone must have died. If this was a frame job based on Mike Castro's grudge against him, Mike would have actually had to kill somebody to make it look right. That made no sense. Aidan knew Mike, and he knew himself. Mike was a straight arrow, a rule-follower. If Aidan had to put money on one of them being a killer, he'd definitely pick himself.

If he killed Jason Stark, he was in deep shit.

"I need to talk to Tommy," Aidan said.

"He's not here."

"Then I want a lawyer," Aidan said.

"If that's how you're gonna play it, shithead," Mike said, and put his knee on Aidan's back again.

A pair of boots marched over to them.

"The inside of the truck is covered in blood," Wayne said. "Like, drenched. I don't see a weapon from a visual inspection. You want me to start ripping the truck apart?"

The wind was picking up, and the rain coming down harder. Aidan shivered on the wet ground.

"No. Secure the vehicle and get it towed right away. We don't want to risk losing evidence to the elements out here. The forensics team can finish the search."

"What do we do with Junior?"

"We bring him in."

"On what charge?"

"Murder. What do you think?" Mike said, and then he hauled Aidan to his feet. "You have the right to remain silent. . . ."

46

Aidan shivered in the holding cell. They'd brought him in and fingerprinted him and made him recite his information. Name, address, date of birth, et cetera, even though every person in that station knew him for years. None of them would meet his eyes. They took his mug shot and photographed every square inch of him, so they'd have proof that he was drenched in blood when he was found. His hands, his face, his clothes, even his boots were full of it, and the stench was in his nostrils. They took samples of his own blood, swabbed DNA from his cheek, scraped under his fingernails. Everything was carefully sealed and catalogued. They took his clothes for evidence, folding them away in brown paper bags because that preserved the bodily fluids best. An officer he poured drinks for on Friday nights took him in a back room and made him squat for a body cavity search, then handed him a set of thin, scratchy prison blues that did nothing to keep out the cold.

And now he was alone in this cell, drained and shaky and confused about his own guilt. He'd washed up at a sink after the processing, but the smell of the blood was still on him. Jason Stark's blood? He honestly didn't remember shooting Caroline's husband. But he remembered *wanting* to kill him. And he remembered waking up covered in blood. *You do the math.* If he wasn't a killer, where did all the blood come from?

This was as bad as anything that had ever happened to him, and a lot of bad things had happened in his life. But Tommy had never abandoned him before, no matter how much trouble he'd been in. Ever since their father died, Tommy was there, the one constant in Aidan's life, the guiding light. But not now. Aidan had been at his brother's station house for hours, repeatedly asked to see him, and Tommy had not appeared. Aidan couldn't blame him. He deserved to be abandoned. He hadn't appreciated his brother's support when he had it. Whining, complaining, rejecting help, resisting advice. Well, now he'd gotten his wish. Tommy was off his back. And he'd never felt so alone. He reached up to touch the St. Christopher medal his brother had given him, but it was gone—confiscated, sealed in a plastic bag, to be returned when he got out. *If* he got out.

He wondered where Caroline was right now. She must know what happened last night. She was there. That much he remembered. Their beautiful dance, he'd never forget. How much had she seen, and how did she feel about him now—after *that*? Whatever he'd done was done out of love for her. But she wouldn't understand. She'd be too horrified. The crime must have been brutal to spill so much blood. Mike Castro thought so. Tommy probably did, too, or else he'd be here now. Caroline would curse his name. She'd asked him to kill her husband. He'd been shocked. He'd refused. But after all that, had he done it anyway? And if he had, would she hate him, rather than thanking him? Would she tell? Turn state's evidence against him? He wouldn't blame her if she did.

An alert sounded, and the door between the cellblock and the rest of the station swung open. Wayne Johnson stepped into the hallway, holding a pair of manacles. He opened the cell door and came toward Aidan.

"Step all the way to the back, please."

Wayne cuffed Aidan's hands in front of him, then led him through two sets of locked doors and down a hallway to a brightly lit interview room. It was cramped, with dingy beige carpeting, and smelled of disinfectant. Aidan sat down, and Wayne attached his manacles to a hook on the metal desk. The desk was bolted to the floor.

"Wait here," he said, as if Aidan had any choice in the matter. Then he stepped out, and the key turned in the lock.

Aidan heard voices in the hall. One of them was Tommy's, and his stomach flipped. He longed to see his brother yet dreaded facing him. But when the door opened, the person who walked in was a woman he'd never seen before. Tall and regal, with dark hair, dramatically cut, wearing a sharp black business suit and sky-high heels. She shook Aidan's manacled hand vigorously.

"I'm Lisa Walters. I'm here to represent you."

"You're the public defender?"

"No. Your family hired me."

"My family?"

"Your brother."

Aidan huffed out a shocked breath, then pressed his knuckles to his eyes, which were strangely wet all of a sudden. He couldn't believe Tommy would pony up for this sharp defense lawyer, after everything. He still thought Aidan was worth saving. Too bad Aidan didn't believe that himself.

"You can go with the PD if you prefer," she said. "But I'll tell you straight up, you'd be making a mistake. I'm better. Chief Callahan knows me from prior cases and has enough confidence in me to pay my not insubstantial fee."

"Whatever Tommy thinks is good enough for me, ma'am," Aidan said. "I'm surprised, though. I figured he washed his hands of me."

"I can't speak for your brother, but if he's paying my bill, he must care. You should know, he's in a delicate position. His own brother is accused of a brutal murder in his jurisdiction. That's a conflict of interest if ever I saw one. The state police are stepping in, with an assist from the arresting officer, who was . . ." She perched ruby-red reading glasses on her nose and flipped open a notebook. "Deputy Michael Castro. They'll be watching Castro like a hawk to make sure he doesn't cut you any breaks."

"No worries there. Mike hates my guts."

"Hmm, that's not good, but I'll make a note of it. Personal grudge. We can use it to undermine his credibility when he testifies against you.

Okay, now. I'm going to ask you not to say anything about guilt or innocence until I explain the process, okay?"

Aidan nodded. "You're the expert."

"Good. I like a client who listens. The state has forty-eight hours from the time of arrest to bring you before a judge and charge you. If they don't charge you in that time, they have to cut you loose. Right now, as I understand it, this case is based on a single witness. A woman named Caroline Stark claims that she witnessed you kill her husband last night. Do you know her?"

Aidan gasped. "Caroline says I did it? Shit. Maybe I did. See—"

The lawyer held up her hand.

"Stop right there. I'll take that as yes, you know her, then you close your mouth. Only speak in response to specific questions. I'm going to give you a big, important rule here. *Do. Not. Confess.* Got that? There's plenty of time for confession later. It's early days of the case right now, and I'd like to keep your options open. If you confess to me, I won't tell anyone, because it's covered by attorney-client privilege. But ethics rules would prevent me from continuing to represent you if you later decide to take the stand and testify that you're innocent. Got it? I don't have to tell on you, but I can't help you lie. And that would be a problem for you, because I'm the lawyer you want in your corner. So, keep your guilt or innocence to yourself until I get a handle on this case, okay?"

"Yes, ma'am."

"Good. Now. Based on the bare-bones information given to me by Deputy Castro, Mrs. Stark claims—and this is only what she claims, doesn't make it true—that you broke into her mansion on the bluff last night and shot her husband in the stomach. She claims you told her you planned to dump his body in the ocean. You pistol-whipped her. She lost consciousness. When she woke up—"

"Whoa, whoa. Wait a minute. There's a couple problems with that. One, I don't own a gun. And two, I would never hurt Caroline. Never in a million years."

"Please, Mr. Callahan. Or, Aidan, if I may. I thought I made this very clear. Hold your comments till the end."

"Sorry, Ms. Walters."

"Call me Lisa. Your defense lawyer is your only friend. We might as well be on a first-name basis."

She looked back down at her notebook.

"When Mrs. Stark woke up, she says that both you and her husband's body were gone. And that's all they're telling me right now. I think they're still interviewing her."

"Caroline says I'm guilty. Then I'm done, right? I might as well give up?"

"*No.* She says you're guilty, that's where we start. I go to work to undermine her testimony and earn my paycheck. Right now, this case is based on a single witness. That's great for the defense. A witness's credibility can always be destroyed. *Unless* there's other evidence to corroborate what Mrs. Stark says. Understand?"

"Not exactly."

"If it's your word against hers, I can dirty her up and make her look bad. That creates reasonable doubt. But if the prosecution has forensic evidence against you, we could be in trouble, unless we discredit it somehow. In murder cases, there are two types of forensic evidence that really matter. The victim's body. And the murder weapon. And here's the interesting part. I asked Mike Castro if I could get the reports on the victim's body and the murder weapon, and he hemmed and hawed and made noises about hurricane damage impeding the search. Do you know what that means? *They don't have them yet.*"

"You mean——?"

"They don't have the body *or* the murder weapon."

"Murder weapon. See, that's the thing I'm trying to tell you. I don't own a gun. I've never had a gun."

"Don't tell me that now. We'll cross that bridge when we come to it. And unfortunately, we probably will come to it. Bodies wash ashore. They get sniffed out by curious dogs. Any clever place you hide a gun—wedged under a sofa, thrown in the gutter near your house—somebody finds it. So." She shrugged.

"But I don't own a gun, I said."

"We're not discussing the facts right now."

"Seriously. I don't own a gun."

"If and when they find a gun, we can argue it's not yours. *If* the facts support that argument. The point is, we can't rely on those things staying gone. You with me so far?"

"Yes."

"Okay, next point. Whether you're guilty or innocent, when they bring you to court, you'll plead not guilty. And we'll ask for bail. Depending on what evidence they have at that point, you may or may not get bail, but we'll ask. Okay?"

"Yes. Good. I would like to get out of here."

"Glad to hear it. That brings me to my next point. This is a corollary of don't confess, and it's the single, most significant thing I will ever tell you. *Keep your mouth shut.* You do not, under any circumstances, speak to anybody other than me about your case. That includes your brother, your mother, your cellmate, your best friend, your next-door neighbor. Not even your priest. You say you want to get out of here. I can tell you, the quickest road to life in prison is to shoot your mouth off. Do you understand?"

Aidan looked sheepish. "Yeah, uh, here's the problem. I might've confessed already."

She sighed loudly. "Oh, great. What did you say, Aidan, and to whom?"

"Mike Castro asked me if I killed the guy. Don't worry, I didn't say I killed him. But I might've said I wasn't sure."

"I don't understand. Who's not sure if they killed someone? You mean, you shot him, but you're not sure he died?"

"No. I'm not sure if I shot him. I remember being with Caroline at her house, and her husband was pounding on the door. But I don't, I can't—it's like I blacked out at some point. I don't remember anything after that knock on the door."

"You're telling me you blacked out and you don't remember whether you killed a man? I know we said not to talk about the facts of the case. But seriously? Come on."

Aidan closed his eyes, and the insides of his eyelids were red, like blood. He opened them again and looked at his hands. He could still feel the stickiness of the blood there. He could still see it swirling down the drain when he washed. But try as he might, he couldn't remember how it got there. He didn't recall doing the killing.

"I know it sounds crazy, but I don't remember," he said.

"That sounds like bullshit to me, kid," Lisa said. "You know, I've been defending homicide cases for fifteen years. You're the first guy who ever tried to pull that one."

"But it's true."

"I'm your lawyer, Aidan. If you lie to me, it makes it a lot harder for me to help you."

"I'm not lying."

"That remains to be seen, but let's move on. You say the husband came to the door. And found you with his wife."

"Yes."

"You didn't tell Castro that, did you? 'Cause if you admitted the affair, and being present on the night of the murder, you're halfway to screwed, and I'll tell your brother to save his money."

"No. Mike asked me if I did it, and all I said was, I'm not sure. I didn't say anything else. Not another word."

She exhaled. "Well, thank God for small favors, I guess. Saying you're not sure you murdered the victim is pretty bad. But admitting that you were at the scene of the crime at the time of the murder having an affair with his wife? That's worse, because it's so specific. The first thing, we can say you were confused, or didn't understand the question. The second thing looks like a motive. It makes the jury think you did it. Now, tell me, were you by any chance under arrest when Castro questioned you?"

"I was down on the ground with his knee in my back and the cuffs on. But he didn't tell me my rights yet. Is that arrest?"

She nodded. "It is, and since he didn't read you your rights, I should be able to get the 'I'm not sure' statement thrown out."

"Can I say something? If I did kill Stark, it wasn't because I wanted to steal his wife. Jason Stark is an animal. He cheated on her. Humiliated her publicly by bringing his mistress around. Then he threatened her life, and possibly hired a hit man to kill her. I don't remember killing him. But if I did, it was only to protect her."

Lisa Walters scribbled furiously in her notebook. She looked up at Aidan over her glasses.

"Aidan, what did I say? No confessing. *I only killed the guy because he was mean to his wife.* That's a confession."

"I'm saying *if* I killed him."

She paused, tapping her pencil against her notebook. Her fingernails were long and painted a deep crimson.

"Stark abusing his wife and hiring a hit man? That would be an interesting avenue of inquiry if it weren't so far-fetched."

"I know it sounds crazy. But I saw it with my own eyes. I followed Stark—"

"Okay, stop right there. You followed her husband?"

"Only because I was worried about her. And nobody knows I did it, that I'm aware of. Except Caroline. I told her."

"This is very bad for your case."

"I see how it might be."

"There may be things we can work with. Caroline Stark is their star witness, so if she had a motive of her own to kill her husband, we may be able to use that. The best way to convince the jury you're innocent is to convince them somebody else is guilty."

"Wait a minute. You mean, put suspicion on her? I don't want to get Caroline in trouble."

"She has no problem getting you in trouble. Your brother is spending his kids' college savings to pay for a lawyer for you. What are you, an ingrate? Besides, if she didn't do anything, they wouldn't actually charge her. It's just an explanation that we feed to the jury in your case."

"I don't think she did anything. She asked me to kill him at one point, then she changed her mind, and reconciled with the jerk."

The lawyer's mouth fell open. "Caroline Stark solicited you to kill her husband?"

"But I said no."

"But you discussed killing him. Is it possible that she recorded that conversation?"

"No way. She would never do that. We're in love. We're going to be together."

"Aidan, this woman is turning state's evidence on you. I assure you, she's not dreaming of a future with you. If she asked you to kill him, and you did it on her behalf, maybe we can go to the prosecution and make a deal. You testify that she solicited you—"

"No. Absolutely not. You're not listening. I didn't agree to kill him. I told her I would never do something like that. And she backed off."

"You say you would never do something like that. But I see in my paperwork that you have a prior manslaughter conviction. Are you being straight with me?"

"That wasn't my fault. Me and my best friend were down by the beach. We were fighting over a girl. Matthew hit me, and I hit him back. He fell and whacked his head on a rock, and he died. It was a terrible accident. I still have nightmares about it. I loved the guy."

"Okay, look. I think I can keep the prior conviction out of court. But I need you to be honest with me."

"I am being honest."

"I'm hearing a lot of excuses and frankly, some crazy stuff. This blackout thing," Lisa said, and rolled her eyes. "Maybe you killed him, but you don't remember?"

"I know you don't believe me."

"I don't believe you."

"So what do we do? Are you going to dump me as a client?"

Lisa sighed. "No. I promised your brother. I'll do my best to work with what you give me. On the blackout—do you have a history of seizures, neurological impairment, psychological disturbance, anything that would show up in medical records?"

"No," he said. "There's nothing."

"You're sure?"

"Positive."

"Drug addiction?" she asked.

"Nope. Never touch the stuff. Booze, yes, professional hazard. But not to excess."

"Were you drinking last night?"

"One shot of—what was it? Bourbon I think. With Caroline. It was kind of heinous stuff, but not enough to make me drunk."

"I'm going to request a psych workup and a complete tox screen of the blood sample they took at the time of your arrest. It's a Hail Mary, but you never know. Maybe there's something we can use to support a claim of a blackout."

She looked at her watch.

"All right, that's enough for our first meeting. You've given me a lot of information, Aidan. I need to get started right away following up on these leads. I'm going to remind you again, don't talk to anybody about the case. Understand?"

"Yeah, but—"

"No buts. You keep your mouth shut unless you want to spend the rest of your life in jail."

"But I need to talk to Caroline. She's the only one. I won't talk to anyone else."

"Ugh, don't you listen? What have I been telling you this whole time? Caroline Stark is the main witness against you. She's the last person on earth you should talk to."

"But she was there. She knows what happened."

Lisa threw her hands up. "Exactly my point. She was there, and she says you're guilty. If you talk to her, whatever you say, she'll rat you out to the police. It can only work against you."

"She wouldn't. She's not like that."

"She is *exactly* like that. I passed her in the hall before. She's in another interview room right now giving a statement to implicate you in a murder. Why can't you understand that?"

Aidan felt as if the air had been knocked out of him. His hands started to sweat in the manacles.

"Caroline's here? Now, in the police station? Please, Lisa, I need to talk to her. She can help me figure out what happened. I don't think I did it. But maybe I did. She knows the truth."

"If she knows it, and you're guilty, then she won't help you. And if you're innocent, then she's lying about what you did. This blackout story of yours is nuts, Aidan, but I'm starting to think the most far-fetched explanation is the way to go with you. Maybe there's something to it. Maybe you were unconscious, and she killed him."

"I need to talk to her."

"Is that what happened? Are you covering for her?"

"No. I—I mean, if there was something to cover for, I might. But I honestly can't remember if there is."

Lisa shook her head in frustration. How could he make her understand? Aidan could still smell the blood that had drenched his clothes. He could feel it on his hands. Something had happened last night, something terrible. Was it possible to kill someone and not remember? Could he have Jason Stark's blood on his hands, yet be innocent of his murder? Was Caroline involved in killing her husband? Did they do it together, and Aidan was blocking the memory somehow? The questions burned in his brain. The only way he could answer them was to talk to Caroline.

Lisa got up and pressed the call button to be let out of the interview room.

"Remember what I said. Don't talk to anyone about your case, *especially* not to Caroline Stark. Not that that's even possible. Believe me, they'll keep you a million miles away from her."

She left, and Aidan waited to be escorted back to his cold, dank cell. But he couldn't stop thinking about the fact that Caroline was here, in this very building. In the darkness of his mind, he could smell her perfume, hear the echo of her voice. Yes, his lawyer had ordered him not to speak to her. But he couldn't obey. He had to see Caroline. Nothing else mattered.

47

Lieutenant Jess Messina switched off the tape recorder.

"Thank you, Mrs. Stark," Jess said. "It was important that you started from the beginning, from when you first saw Aidan Callahan, and your details could not be clearer. You've been very brave. Your testimony will be the key to convicting this man of your husband's murder. I know that was a lot, and I don't want to burden you more than I have to tonight."

Caroline Stark hadn't cried a single tear in the three hours she'd spent in the interview room. But her hollow eyes and pale, clammy skin revealed a woman exhausted and in shock. Caroline was dealing not only with grief and trauma but with overwhelming guilt. A man she'd had a brief fling with had stalked her, stalked her family, broken into her house, held her prisoner, and slaughtered her husband in cold blood right before her eyes. Despite all that, some folks were going to blame Caroline for what happened. Blame the victim—too often, it was still like that. Jess didn't blame her; she admired her. To her mind, Caroline Stark was a rare truth-teller. How many witnesses were as honest about their own sins as she'd been? Not many. That should count for something. Not to mention that even if you considered Caroline's fling with Aidan Callahan a sin, she'd already been punished beyond imagining.

"I can keep going. We don't have to stop," Caroline said.

"You gave me a lot of information already," Jess said. "We now have on record that Aidan Callahan stalked you and your family leading up to the murder of your husband. That's extremely helpful testimony. When you discuss a trauma, you relive it, and that's very debilitating. You'll need your strength in the days ahead. I don't want to ask too much of you now."

"All right. Thank you for understanding, Lieutenant."

"I do understand. You can count on me. I'll be working this case all the way through the trial—if there is one. With the very detailed statement you gave, hopefully he'll plead guilty, and you won't have to go through a trial."

Jess was State Police BCI, brought in to assist the locals with major investigations they couldn't handle on their own. Normally, they worked side by side, but this case was different. The locals were tainted, because the suspect was the chief's kid brother. Jess had the file on Aidan Callahan's prior conviction, and it looked like the chief put his thumb on the scale for his brother on that one, too. That was *not* going to happen again, not on her watch.

"I want you to know, we're working every angle on this case," Jess said. "We've got people out searching the area where Aidan Callahan was arrested. We've got his truck. They're searching that. The forensics team will be going to your house to collect physical evidence. I'll need you to sign a form authorizing that."

"My house? Is that necessary? I already told you what happened. I'm an eyewitness. But my house—I want to get it cleaned and repaired right away."

"I understand, but it is necessary. We need corroborating evidence for your witness statement. What we get from the murder scene will bolster our case. Fingerprints, fibers, strands of hair, blood spatters, bullet casings, you name it. We want this case to stick. We don't want Callahan getting out."

Caroline went white as a ghost. "He could get out? But he'd come after me. My daughter, my sister. They're not safe."

"I don't think he'll get out. Callahan's in the holding cell right now, and they'll be transferring him to the state prison tonight, where he'll stay until he's brought to court. We're getting ready to file formal charges. Once the charges are filed, he gets a bail hearing. The more evidence we have, the more likely he gets remanded to custody instead of getting bail. That's why we needed to go through this lengthy interview tonight, and it's why I need you to sign this search form. Please, it's important."

Jess placed the form in front of Caroline, who seemed almost put out as she scrawled her name. Who could blame the poor woman? Her nerves must be shattered at this point.

"Thank you," Jess said. "And so you know, we're following up on other search locations as well. The murder weapon hasn't been found. Neither has—"

"You didn't find the gun? Did you look in his truck?"

"The truck's been towed to the lab. The lab is closed because of the storm. As soon as they reopen, our case is top priority."

"Can't someone go look inside the truck?" Caroline asked.

"There's a lot of blood in the truck," Jess said, as gently as possible. "That blood is evidence. They didn't want to disturb it, so when they didn't see a gun sitting in the open, they stopped searching."

"But if they would just look, I'm sure they could find it right away."

"The crime scene team is taking over because they have special training. It does mean a brief delay, but it's the best thing for the case. We need the blood, Mrs. Stark, because we haven't been able, we haven't—"

Jess looked down at the table, unsure how best to phrase this. But there was no right way.

"*Jason*. Jason hasn't been found. That's what you mean."

"That's right. I'm sorry. Callahan lawyered up. He wouldn't say what he did with the body. Based on your statement, I think we should be looking in the cave you mentioned, which is on the same beach where Callahan was arrested. Right now, it's not accessible due to storm surge. I promise we'll get inside it as soon as humanly possible. We want to find Jason before the evidence is literally washed away. And I know you want to bring him home."

Caroline's eyes were large, dark blue, and haunted. She was a beautiful woman, though how that would play in court under the circumstances, Jess couldn't be sure. A jury might hold it against her.

"He'll end up at the bottom of the ocean. It's cold there. So cold," Caroline said, and looked away.

"I didn't mean to suggest that. We don't know where he is, but wherever he is, we'll find him. I promise."

Caroline took a Kleenex from the box on the table and pressed it to her eyes.

"Mrs. Stark," Jess said. "I'm going to check if your sister came to pick you up yet. Apparently, there's some pretty bad flooding, but hopefully she was able to make it. In the meantime, can I get you something to eat or drink? Oh, and—would you like me to put you in touch with a grief counselor?"

"I couldn't possibly eat, and I don't need a counselor. Lieutenant, if you want to help me, *please*, keep Aidan in jail. After what he did, I'll never feel safe if he's out."

"You *are* safe. Mrs. Stark, your safety is our top priority. You have my word. Aidan Callahan won't get anywhere near you."

Mike Castro knocked on the door of the interview room.

"Your sister's here, ma'am. She's waiting in the lobby."

"Let me walk you out," Jess said. "I'd like to get Lynn's contact information and set up an interview about that incident where Callahan tried to run her off the road."

Jess and Caroline stepped into the hallway, which was much noisier and more crowded than it had been when the interview began hours earlier. The station house now appeared to be functioning as the town's emergency storm ops center. Firefighters and EMTs mingled with the cops. Several men wearing waders ran back and forth carrying equipment. Everybody looked tired and grim, and some of them were drenched. Jess looked at them and wondered whether her search warrants and labs tests would get the attention they deserved. Working a homicide case in the middle of a natural disaster was not going to be easy.

Jess took Caroline's arm and steered her through the crowd. As they reached the end of the hall, a door to their right swung open. An officer stepped out, leading a prisoner in a blue jumpsuit and manacles. Before anyone could react, he'd lunged forward, evading the officer's grip, and grabbed Caroline fiercely with his manacled hands.

"Tell me," he said, his eyes wild, his mouth working furiously. "I have to know. Did I kill Jason? Or did you? Did you kill him, Caroline?"

The officer threw his arms around Callahan's waist and wrestled him to the ground. But Callahan's grip on Caroline was so powerful that she went down with them, screaming.

"Get him off her!" Jess said, falling to her knees beside them.

She reached over and tried to pry the prisoner's hands from her witness's clothing. But Callahan refused to let go. It was like he had superhuman strength. In the middle of the scrum, he seemed almost calm, looking directly into Caroline's eyes.

"I love you. Please, help me. Don't leave me here," he said.

A second officer and then a third piled on. One of them pulled out a Taser and applied it to Callahan's side. Jess heard a rapid clicking sound and gagged at the burning smell. Callahan convulsed and then slumped to the side, his hands finally releasing Caroline's clothing. As the officers picked up his limp body and carted him away, Jess reached out to help Caroline to her feet.

"Are you all right? Are you hurt?"

Caroline wouldn't meet Jess's eyes.

"Are you hurt?"

She straightened her clothes, looking shaken. Her eyes were glazed. The poor woman.

"You said you would keep me safe," she said.

Jess's heart sank. Caroline was right. Jess had failed. The locals had failed. They'd failed in their first duty. They hadn't protected her.

"I'm so sorry. I can't believe they let that happen. I'm going to take this case completely away from the local PD. They're incompetent."

"You said I wouldn't have to see him. That he was locked up, that he could never get to me."

"This is inexcusable. I can't apologize enough. All I can do is promise that it won't happen again."

"I don't believe you. I don't trust you anymore. If the police won't protect me, I'll have to protect myself," she said, and turned her back on Jess.

Jess followed her to the lobby, buzzing around her like a fly, apologizing profusely. A blond woman who was sitting in the visitor area jumped up and came toward them. She held out her arms to Caroline, who walked right past them.

"Get me out of here," Caroline said to her sister.

The star witness marched out of the police station and didn't look back. Jess had the feeling she might never see her again.

48

Two days later, the storm had passed, and the sky was bright and clear. But Jess's mood was grim as she walked out of the courthouse following Aidan Callahan's arraignment. She ought to be happy. The judge ordered Callahan held without bail on the murder charge. The forensics team discovered a silver handgun wedged under the seat of Aidan's truck. (The gun was at the lab now, being tested for fingerprints.) The gun, combined with the blood on Aidan's clothes, was enough to back up Caroline Stark's statement. And when the prosecutor brought up the station house attack on Caroline Stark, the judge was convinced. She ordered him held without bail—*temporarily*. They now had ten days to get an indictment from the grand jury. That was the new deadline. Ten days. If they failed, Callahan would be released.

The prosecutor was a guy named Vernon Mays, who had blindingly white teeth and a political career in his future, and he didn't like to lose. This case was generating lurid headlines. BARTENDER KILLED MISTRESS'S HUSBAND, COPS SAY. FATAL ATTRACTION. ONE-NIGHT FLING LEADS TO MURDER. WIFE'S BOY TOY NABBED IN HUSBAND SLAY. And on and on. The press attention made it critical to get this right, Vernon said. He wanted the victim's body found—*yesterday*. He wanted a report that said Aidan's prints were on the gun. He wanted ballistics, and crime scene evidence, and every lab report on his desk by close of business tomorrow, no excuses. And most important of all, he wanted Caroline Stark in his office tomorrow morning, so he could sit her down, assess her credibility, and prepare her to testify before the grand jury.

There was only one problem. Caroline was missing.

Jess had been reaching out to Caroline ever since the other night, when Aidan Callahan assaulted her in the station house. Jess wanted not only to apologize, but to offer Caroline official protection. Yes, Aidan was in jail, but he might try to get to her through a third party. Jess had the paperwork in hand to have a security officer assigned to protect Caroline. She'd reached out over and over again, but Caroline wasn't answering her phone. When she didn't return numerous texts and voicemails, Jess got worried and went looking. What if something bad had already happened to her? Jess would be devastated to have a witness killed on her watch, and one she felt such profound sympathy for. Jess checked the beach house, but it was shuttered and cordoned off with crime scene tape. She had a colleague drop by Caroline's apartment in the city, but the doorman reported she hadn't been there for days. Finally, she reached out to Caroline's sister, Lynn, who said that Caroline was safe but didn't want to talk to the police. Why should she cooperate when they'd done nothing to protect her or her family? When Jess protested that she was calling precisely to offer security, Lynn's reply was basically *too little, too late*.

Jess reported to Vernon Mays that their star witness had gone into hiding, and the prosecutor refused to hear that. He flashed his campaign-poster smile and told Jess to have Caroline in his office bright and early the next morning to start preparing her testimony. If she was unable to accomplish that basic function of an investigating officer, he'd have to consider restaffing. Nothing personal, of course, but this was a high-profile case and he couldn't tolerate mistakes.

Hence, her grim mood on this sunny day.

"Jess, wait up!"

Mike Castro jogged across the parking lot toward her. He caught up to her by her car.

"I'm in a hurry," she said, and opened the car door.

Mike's face was flushed and shiny. He looked uncomfortable in his dark courtroom suit.

"What's going on? You're not returning my calls? How are we supposed to work this case together?"

"We're not working this case together, Mike. I don't trust your team."

"I noticed that when you wouldn't let me in the interview room with Caroline Stark."

"She didn't want a man in the room because she was discussing extremely personal matters. And she didn't want anyone from your department, for good reason. Your chief of police has a blatant conflict of interest."

"I hear you, but that has nothing to do with me. I don't play favorites, and especially not with Aidan Callahan. I'm the guy who's gonna be the hardest on him, I told you that."

"I don't need you to go hard on Callahan any more than I need you to help him. I want somebody who'll do the job objectively."

"That's me, swear to God. I'm totally objective."

"I'm sorry, Mike. After that fiasco at the station the other night, I can't work with you. I don't want your people anywhere near my case."

"That wasn't my fault either. You know it wasn't. I wasn't even in the interview room."

"I'm not saying it was personally your fault. But it makes the entire Glenhampton PD look incompetent, or like they're purposely trying to destroy the case. And you have to admit, that's a possibility."

"This was Keystone Kops shit. Incompetence. It wasn't intentional. Still, it never should've happened. Wayne Johnson's a good officer. The only thing I can think is, because it was Aidan, he let his guard down."

"That's exactly my point. You guys can't be trusted."

"Maybe they can't, but *I* can."

"It doesn't matter if it was intentional or not. Either way, it screwed my case."

"How did it screw your case? Nobody likes to see a witness attacked. But attacking the witness dirtied up Callahan good. Mays used it to get Callahan remanded. We can use it against him at trial, too."

"There may not be a trial. My witness disappeared because of the Glenhampton PD's incompetence. And I can't make a murder charge stick without Caroline."

"What?"

"Caroline Stark is in the wind, and there's no case without her. Do you get it now? She got physically attacked in front of a station full of cops. She's scared to death of Callahan, and she doesn't trust you to protect her from him. So, she ran. I don't blame her. Do you?"

"You can't find her? Did you try calling her?"

Jess slapped her forehead with the palm of her hand. "Duh. Why didn't I think of that? Call her phone."

"I'm sorry. That was dumb."

She rolled her eyes and slid into the driver's seat. He grabbed the door.

"What have you done to find her so far? I can help."

"I called her. I also visited every place she could possibly be. Either nobody's seen her, or they're not talking. And I don't want your help."

"Fine, I'll look for her on my own."

"Don't do that. And don't you go blabbing to the press, either. I don't need the whole world knowing my case is crap."

"The press? Why would I talk to the press?"

"Somebody is. Have you seen the headlines? They know all about the affair."

"Everybody knows about that. She picked him up on a busy night at the hottest bar in town."

"*She* picked *him* up?"

"Yeah. I was there. I saw it happen. So did everyone else. The place was packed."

Jess didn't like the implication that the affair was somehow Caroline's fault. Like she was some slut or something. Women always got labeled like that, and then their concerns were dismissed.

She tugged on the door. He wouldn't let go.

"Would you let go of my door, please? I have work to do."

"Jess, wait. I have a witness for you. An important witness."

"The only witness I care about is Caroline Stark."

"But this is an eyewitness from the night of the murder."

"No way. Who?"

"The next-door neighbor."

"Impossible. I had one of my guys canvass the neighborhood. Nobody was out at the beach that night. They all fled the storm."

"Not this lady. She's the type you'd have to carry out of her house. She stayed, and she's got an eyewitness account from the night of the murder that you need to hear for yourself."

"Wait, is this the old lady who lives next door? The one Caroline Stark told us about in her interview, who called to complain that the alarm was driving her nuts?"

"That's the one."

"I appreciate you telling me, Mike. I'll go interview her myself."

"She won't talk to you without me."

"I'll show her my badge."

"She didn't open the door for the guy you sent before, did she? I'm telling you, she's a crank, but I can handle her. She comes in to the station sometimes to file complaints, and I always give her the time of day."

"Great, so she's a nutcase."

"Nope. She's a pain in the butt, but her complaints pan out."

"I have to find Caroline."

"Interview Mrs. Eberhardt with me. Then I'll help you find Caroline. Jess, look, I want to nail this asshole worse than you do. I know this town. I can get people to talk who would never talk to you. Give me one more shot. Please? You won't regret it."

Jess hated to admit it, but Mike had a point. Small towns were always tough for the state police to penetrate. The locals stuck together and hated to rat on their own. And Aidan Callahan was more than a local. He was a bartender at one of the most popular joints in town and the brother of the police chief. His family had lived in Glenhampton for generations. What's more, it was clear to Jess after only a couple of days in this town that the locals despised the weekend people. Caroline and Jason Stark were as weekend as they come—city folks, with a big house on the water and fancy cars, who threw elaborate parties and didn't invite their neighbors. If you were investigating a crime committed by a local boy against snooty weekenders, it might help to have Mike Castro along to break the ice.

"All right. But I drive. I do the talking. And at the end of the day, if I'm not impressed by what you brought to the table, you're out."

"Deal," he said, smiling, and got in her car.

49

Francine Eberhardt lived next door to the Starks' oceanfront mansion. Jess had visited the Stark home the day before to walk through the crime scene with the head of the forensics team. The team was behind schedule, delayed by the storm and short of resources, and they had little of interest to report. As she and Mike drove past on their way to interview the witness, Jess was not happy to see the house shuttered and the police van gone.

"Where are they?" she said. "Vernon Mays is all over me to get the evidence together. It's only three o'clock. How do they expect to make this case if they don't put in the time?"

Mike was scrolling through his phone. "I got a text. They were called away to the beach. The tide went out, and they made it to that cave. They found something."

"Oh, thank God. The body."

"Nope."

"No? What did they find, then?"

"A blanket and a man's jacket, both soaked in blood, wedged behind a large boulder. It's possible that the body was there and got swept out to sea with a strong storm surge. But it's not there now."

"Crap. This case is getting worse by the minute," Jess said.

"They sent the items to the lab to be tested. But they took photos. We're supposed to show the pictures to Caroline Stark right away and ask if they belonged to her husband."

"Too bad we can't find her. Goddamn it."

Jess slammed the heel of her hand against the steering wheel, which made her hand hurt and didn't make her mood any brighter. Mike raised an eyebrow.

"Don't look at me like that," she said. "This witness better be good. She's taking time we could be spending looking for Caroline."

They pulled into Francine Eberhardt's driveway. The little house looked like it had taken a serious hit from the storm. The glass was gone from several windows, replaced by cardboard. The shutters hung askew, and most of the trees on the small property were twisted and mangled. An enormous tree branch lay across the small patch of lawn. A white-haired woman in jeans and muddy wellies stood over the downed branch with a chain saw. As Jess watched, she pulled the chain, making an ear-splitting sound.

"That's her, I take it?" Jess said, raising her voice to be heard over the ruckus.

"Yup. Don't get in her way while she's holding that thing."

They got out of the car. Mike introduced Jess to Francine Eberhardt, who put down her chain saw to shake hands. Francine looked to be in her late seventies or early eighties, but she had a killer grip and an impatient manner that made Jess think she'd be a handful as a witness— or as a neighbor.

"Michael offered to help clear this debris. That's the only reason I agreed to speak with you," Francine said.

Jess raised an eyebrow at Castro. "I see. Thank you, *Michael*," she said.

"Landscapers these days. It's highway robbery. They think everybody is a weekender and made of money. Well, I refuse to pay. Still, it's a lot for me to handle alone at my age, so when Michael offered, I figured it was worth my time to tell you what I saw the other night."

"We appreciate that. I'm glad we had something of value to offer you."

Castro winked at Jess behind the old lady's back as they went inside. The kitchen was cramped but cozy, with an old-fashioned gas range and a woodstove. A decrepit Chihuahua lay on a bed in the corner. He poked his head up and gave several high-pitched yaps.

"Don't mind him," Francine said. "When they say all bark and no bite, they're talking about Bandit."

They sat down at the small wooden table. Mrs. Eberhardt folded her hands and looked at them with a long-suffering expression. Jess took out her phone and placed it on the table in front of them.

"If you don't mind—"

"Oh, I mind. You can take notes if you like, but I don't like a microphone in my face."

"Of course. Whatever you prefer, ma'am."

Jess nodded at Mike, who took out a notebook and pen.

"How well did you know your neighbors?" Jess asked, to get the conversation going.

But she needn't have worried. For someone who resisted being interviewed, once she got started, Francine Eberhardt had plenty to say.

"Her, I saw all the time. Not socially, mind you. She's got her nose in the air, and I'm not good enough for her kind. But Jason Stark? Never. I saw his picture in the paper this morning in the article about Aidan Callahan's arrest, and that's the first time I ever saw his face. He was never here. I can see their driveway quite clearly from my bedroom window, so I know who comes and goes. He might have been here for that big party. I wouldn't know, because I don't know his car. She invited me, Caroline did. But it was just for show. I could tell she didn't really want me there, so I didn't go. It says something that she invited me, don't you think? How careful she is not to offend anyone, or raise suspicion?"

"Maybe she's polite," Jess said.

"Hmmph. I doubt it. Caroline Stark has something to hide."

"Okay. I'll bite. What is she hiding?"

"She was having marriage troubles, which is obvious from the fact that the husband was never here. *And*, she was having an affair with Aidan Callahan."

"Yes, ma'am, we know that. She told us herself. She's not trying to hide that."

"Well, then, she's hiding something else. Those two deserve each other. Aidan's been a devil since he was a boy."

"You *know* him?" Jess said.

"Of course. His grandparents lived next door. They owned the land that the Starks' house sits on now."

Jess looked at Mike sharply. "Did you know that?"

He shrugged. "Yeah. It didn't seem significant."

"I'd say it's significant. It could be a motive. Maybe he held a grudge against the Starks for tearing down Grandpa's house. What do you think about that theory, Mrs. Eberhardt?"

"If that's a motive for murder, every weekender in this town would be dead. I'm not saying Aidan wasn't obsessed with that monstrosity next door. He'd walk by and stare at it all the time. But more like he wanted it for himself than he wished it had never been built. He broke into it, too."

"Broke into Caroline's house? You mean, on the night of the murder?"

"Then. And there was another night a while back that I saw him sneaking around and then the alarm went off."

"But you definitely saw him break in on the night of the murder?"

"Yes. How many times do I have to say it?"

"I want to be clear. That is extremely important evidence. I want to make sure we understand you correctly."

"Yes. I saw Aidan Callahan break into Caroline Stark's house on the night of the murder."

"What time was it that Callahan broke in, Mrs. Eberhardt?" Mike asked.

"Around six o'clock."

"Six A.M. or P.M.?" Jess asked.

"P.M."

"But—are you sure?" Jess said. "We put the murder as taking place in the early hours of the morning, maybe two or three A.M."

"Put the murder wherever you like. Aidan broke in around six P.M. I wouldn't say it if I wasn't sure. I had just looked at the clock because I wanted to wait till the last possible minute to let Bandit out before the weather made it impossible. I took him right out in front of my house and saw Aidan's truck in her driveway. A couple of minutes later, the alarm went off."

"Okay. Caroline did say that her alarm went off earlier in the evening, and you called her about it. But she said it was only the wind."

"Well, you can't believe anything *she* says," Francine said, as if that were obvious.

It wasn't obvious. Jess *did* believe what Caroline had told her. Francine Eberhardt obviously disliked her wealthy, beautiful neighbor enough to discredit anything she said.

"You saw Aidan's truck, but you didn't see Aidan?" Jess asked.

"I'm getting to that. I saw his truck, very clearly. No mistake about it. He drives this beat-up old thing, bright red, with a big dent in the door. And I saw *him*. But not then. A little later. Normally, you know, alarms go off and they get shut down right away. Well, hers must be defective, because it wouldn't shut up. I called her to complain, and I said if she didn't do something about it, we'd have trouble. She must have called the police. Because, not long after my call to her, Tommy Callahan drove up in his police cruiser."

"Chief Callahan? Really?"

"Yes, really. My gosh, you people ask me questions, then you act like you don't believe the answers."

Jess and Mike exchanged glances. They both knew there was no record of Chief Callahan visiting the Stark residence that night, nor of any other Glenhampton officer doing so, for that matter. It was starting to look like Francine might not be reliable.

"I'm sorry. We're very interested in your answers. What did Chief Callahan do when he got there?" Jess asked.

"He went inside and hauled Aidan out by the scruff of the neck. The two of them went at it. Blows were exchanged. Then they both left."

"The chief left? And Aidan left?"

"Yes, that's what I said. And they left the alarm going, too. I couldn't believe it. At least turn the alarm off."

Jess and Mike looked at one another, openmouthed. Francine Eberhardt's information, if it was true, amounted to Chief Callahan covering up a felony. They'd reviewed the official GPD logs for that night with great care, to match them up to Caroline's testimony. After Caroline's phone call to the police, the dispatcher radioed for any patrol officer in the vicinity to respond to the alarm at the Stark residence. According to the official record, nobody responded, presumably because they were too busy dealing with the storm. If Tommy Callahan had actually shown up, found his brother in the Starks' house, and not reported it, that was a cover-up. It was also a crime. Jess could tell from Mike's face that he was as shocked by this as she was.

Mike shook his head, like he couldn't believe what he was hearing.

"Aidan left? Did he come back at any point?" he asked, trying to change the subject.

"Yes, he came back," Francine said. "I'm not sure when. I put in earplugs and went to bed. Hours later, I woke up to go to the bathroom, and I took the earplugs out. I don't like to sleep with earplugs in, generally. I find them quite uncomfortable, but between that infernal alarm and the noise from the storm—"

"Please, Mrs. Eberhardt, what did you *see*?" Jess said.

"It was what I *heard* that made me sit up and take notice."

"What did you hear?"

"Nothing. Dead quiet. It was as if the storm just left. The quiet was so strange that I went to the window and looked out, and then I realized, we were in the eye. The moon was out, and there was enough light to see clearly. Aidan's truck was there. He'd left in it, hours before, and now it was back."

"Did you see anything other than the truck?"

"Yes. There were two other vehicles. That big tacky SUV she has.

That monster must get terrible gas mileage. And a fancy, foreign-looking car. I don't know what brand. I saw the three vehicles, clear as day, as the eye passed. And then, within seconds, the storm was back, worse than ever, and I could barely see a thing. It was like staring into a whirl-wind."

"Huh. So, you never saw Aidan himself?"

"I saw three people. One of them was probably Aidan, but I can't be sure."

"What? Three people? When was this?"

"A couple of minutes after the eye passed. I was still at the window, only now, the rain was torrential. And I saw three people walking to Aid-an's truck. Well, two were walking. The third was being dragged."

"What do you mean, being dragged?"

"The two upright ones had somebody in between them, and they were dragging him by the arms. The person in the middle couldn't walk. His head was down, he was limp. He seemed to be unconscious."

"You say *he*. It was a man?" Mike asked.

"Hmm. I could see their forms, their shapes. I have the impression it was a man, with a man and a woman dragging him. But I can't be sure."

"Do you have an *impression* of who they were?"

"That's the sixty-four-thousand-dollar question, isn't it? The rain was so heavy, I couldn't make them out. But if I was a betting woman, I'd put money on that being Aidan Callahan and Caroline Stark drag-ging her husband's body. Wouldn't you?"

"Why didn't you tell anybody about this before now?" Jess asked.

"Who should I tell? The police? It's the police chief's brother we're talking about. They already think I'm nuts down at the station. Except for Michael. Michael, I trust."

"Thank you, ma'am. Much appreciated. I'll be back here bright and early Saturday morning, as promised, to handle your yard work."

Jess thanked Mrs. Eberhardt and said goodbye. She was lost in thought as they walked back to the car, pondering Francine's account of seeing three people walking to Aidan's truck. It didn't add up with what Caroline had told them about the murder, that much was certain.

They got in the car. Troubled, Jess turned to Mike.

"She's got to be wrong. She didn't see what she thought she saw. She's old. It was dark. The storm obscured her view."

"You don't like what you heard. I don't like it either, but I don't doubt her. She was very clear about what she saw. And when she didn't see something or couldn't answer, she admitted that. I think in your heart you believe her, but you're worried about what it means for the case. I say let the chips fall where they may."

"I'll take you at your word on that. Because, you know, there's another possibility for who the third person was."

"What's that?"

"Maybe Caroline Stark was pistol-whipped and unconscious inside the house, like she said. And maybe that was Tommy Callahan helping his brother dispose of Jason Stark's body."

Mike looked at her like she was crazy. "Where do you get that? She said the third person was a woman."

"She said she couldn't see."

"She could see shapes. A woman has a different shape than a man."

"Now you're the one interpreting the facts the way you want. Which scenario is more likely? Think about it, Mike. Francine saw Tommy pull Aidan out of the house after burglarizing it. She saw him let Aidan go. He let Aidan go years ago, on that manslaughter. He'll do anything to protect his kid brother."

"No way. Tommy Callahan would never cover up a murder. Not in a million years."

"Why not? He covered up the burglary. You believe that part, don't you?"

"Burglary is a whole different animal, especially since, as far as we know, Aidan didn't steal anything. I'm not saying it's okay, but that was their family's land. Aidan had a thing about that place since he was a kid. Tommy yanked his kid brother out of the house, read him the riot act, and decided not to turn him in. That's wrong. I think we should report it to higher authorities. But it doesn't mean he would cover up murder or, God forbid, help dispose of a body. I know the chief. He wouldn't do that, period. Besides, there's clear corroborating evidence to prove who the third person is. Francine already gave it to us. You just don't realize it."

"What are you talking about?"

"Follow the cars. Earlier that night, Francine saw Aidan's truck. The alarm went off. Then a little while later, she saw Tommy's cruiser. Tommy parked right in the driveway. He didn't hide. Two cars, two people. Aidan and Tommy arrive in their own vehicles, they leave in their own vehicles. You with me so far?"

"Okay."

"Later, in the middle of the night, Francine gets up to pee, looks out, and sees three vehicles. Aidan's truck. Caroline's Escalade. And Jason Stark's Mercedes. She didn't see Tommy's cruiser, or she would've said so. Then she sees three people—two walking, one being dragged to the truck, presumably unconscious or dead. Three cars. Three people. The people correspond to the vehicles. Aidan Callahan. Jason Stark. And Caroline Stark. Caroline Stark is the third person. She helped Aidan Callahan murder her husband."

Jess crossed her arms. "No way. Caroline is an innocent victim. Tommy Callahan was the third man. But you don't want to believe that your chief is corrupt."

"*You* don't want to believe that your eyewitness is a liar."

They glared at each other, at an impasse.

50

"I'm extremely disappointed in you, Aidan," Lisa Walters said.

They were in another cramped interview room, this one in the basement of the courthouse. Aidan had been denied bail and committed to the state prison, charged with the murder of Jason Stark. There hadn't been anybody in the courtroom to support him. Not Tommy, not Kelly, not even his mother, who'd taken to her bed when she learned of his arrest and hadn't gotten up yet. Only this lawyer stood up for him, and now she was on the verge of abandoning him, too. He'd thought Caroline would be his salvation. But she was his ruin.

"I'm sorry," he said.

"The only reason I'm not dropping you is that I'm the only person in your corner right now. I noticed your family didn't come to court. But if you want to keep me, Aidan, you have to listen to my advice. I said very clearly, don't go anywhere near Caroline Stark. And literally ten minutes later, you attacked her physically in front of numerous witnesses, in the police station. That's an incredibly stupid and self-destructive thing for you to do. It makes me wonder if there's a screw loose somewhere."

"I only wanted to talk to her. I would never hurt her."

"You heard the testimony in court just now, as well as I did. You physically assaulted her."

"No. When the guy jumped me, he knocked Caroline down. I didn't do that."

"You lunged for her. You grabbed her. It doesn't matter if a cop who was trying to stop you was the one who knocked her down. *You* caused that. The judge denied your bail because of it. He wouldn't even let me make my argument. I don't know what you were thinking."

"It was a mistake. I see that now."

"Too late. There's nothing I can do to fix that problem. And the gun. You lied to me about the gun. Another breach of trust between us."

"I didn't lie."

"You said you don't own a gun. They found one in your truck."

"I heard the prosecutor say that in court. And I saw the picture he showed of it. But that's not my gun. I never saw it before today."

"If it's not yours, then what was it doing in your truck?"

"I have no idea. I didn't put it there. Somebody planted it. Ask Mike Castro. He hates my guts."

"Hmm, you mentioned that grudge before. I'm no Pollyanna. I believe cops sometimes frame people, and I'd consider arguing that in court if there's a good-faith basis for it. So, what's the evidence here? Why does Mike Castro have a grudge against you? Give me something I can use."

"It's because of the Bosticks."

"Who are the Bosticks?"

"Matthew Bostick was my friend who died. The manslaughter charge? Matthew's dad and Mike are close. Mike thinks I got off too easy for that. He always resented me for it."

"So, in order to prove to a jury that Deputy Castro has a grudge against you that caused him to plant a gun, I have to tell them that you killed your best friend in a fight over a girl and got off easy for it, when that wouldn't otherwise be allowed in evidence? I said give me something that works. That doesn't work. It's a net negative. It plays right into you killing Jason Stark over his wife."

"Fine. But it's still not my gun."

"Who planted it, then?"

"I said. Mike."

"And I said, we can't use Mike. Other than Mike. Who else can we point the finger at?"

"Nobody."

"I'll tell you who. Caroline Stark."

"Why would she plant a gun in my truck?"

"For obvious reasons. She killed her husband and framed you for the murder."

"Caroline wouldn't do that to me."

"Oh, but she'd do it to him?"

"Maybe."

"You think she'd kill her husband, but she wouldn't frame you? What a sap you are, Aidan. People will go pretty far to get away with murder. My gut says this lady is no exception."

"Even if I agreed to use it, we could never prove that."

"I'm the lawyer here. Leave that up to me. I think there's a chance we *can* prove it. After our meeting the other night, I looked into the state of her marriage. There's a ton of evidence to show they were at each other's throats. Everybody at that party saw him show up with his mistress. They saw a big argument between the two of them. My investigator has a source at the county clerk's office who found out that Caroline actually filed a divorce complaint. She withdrew it, but we were still able to get a copy. It says he took all the money. Did you know that?"

"I did know that. That's why she asked me to kill him."

"Jason leaves Caroline for his mistress and takes all the money. She murders him and frames some poor schlub for the crime. You being the schlub in question. That's *good*. This is turning into a decent defense case. I'm actually starting to believe it."

"But——"

She pointed a manicured nail at him. "Don't tell me that you won't talk bad about your girlfriend. This is our best shot. We're using it, or else I really will think about dropping you."

51

Jess and Mike put aside their disagreements long enough to join forces to search for Caroline Stark. Jess believed Caroline with all her heart. She wanted to bring her star witness in from the cold and offer her protection. She also needed to reassure the prosecutor that Caroline could be relied upon to testify. Mike had a different agenda. He wanted to find Caroline so he could question her more aggressively about the night of the murder. He thought he could uncover discrepancies that would implicate her in the crime. Jess didn't like that idea, but she wasn't going to argue about it now. The important thing was to find Caroline, and quickly. For that, she needed Mike's help.

Jess delegated the technical side of the search to Mike. He'd serve subpoenas on the wireless companies to ping Caroline's cell phone regularly and monitor her sister's and daughter's phones. If Caroline used her phone, or if Hannah or Lynn communicated with her at a different number, they'd be able to track her down. Meanwhile, Jess would search for Caroline in the real world, starting with her sister's house.

It was getting dark as Jess pulled up to Lynn and Joe Lombardo's house on a quiet street in Massapequa. Jess remembered Caroline saying that Lynn had inherited their childhood home. The house was modest, with an older BMW sedan and a newish Ford pickup in the driveway. Lynn's husband supposedly owned a trucking business, and it looked like they did okay for themselves. But nothing lavish, and not anywhere close to the lifestyle that Caroline and Jason had enjoyed. Apparently, Caroline didn't believe in sharing the wealth.

The doorbell echoed inside the house and set a dog to barking. Lynn came to the door eventually, opening it a crack, keeping the chain on. Jess flashed her badge.

"Mrs. Lombardo, I'm Lieutenant Jessica Messina with the New York State Police. We spoke on the phone yesterday. I'm investigating the murder charge against Aidan Callahan. Can I come in and—"

"Hold on. I can't hear you with the dog," Lynn said, and shut the door.

The dog, which sounded big and mean, was barking wildly. Jess heard Lynn yelling for Joe to come take it away. She pressed her ear against the door. The barking stopped suddenly, and she heard Joe Lombardo ask his wife who was at the door.

"You better not talk to any cops," he said.

Jess heard that quite clearly, as well as Lynn's reply—

"What am I, stupid?"

Huh.

A second later, the door opened wide, and Lynn stood there with a smile on her face.

"Sorry about that, Officer. You were saying?"

The smell of spaghetti sauce wafted from the depths of the house. It was dinnertime already, and Jess hadn't eaten since breakfast. She wished this encounter would go smoothly, that she could find her witness with a minimum of fuss, that the case would fall into place and she could eat a good dinner and get a decent night's sleep. But that wasn't going to happen; she could see it just by looking at Caroline's sister. Lynn was armored for battle. Her smile was fake. She was shiny and untouchable, in capri slacks, a fancy blouse, high-heeled mules, with lots of jewelry and her hair carefully lacquered. Lynn's style was Real Housewife, while Caroline's was ladylike. Jess would have said they were nothing alike. But there was a toughness to Lynn that Jess had seen echoes of in Caroline. She remembered how dry-eyed Caroline had been during their interview. She didn't want to believe that Caroline was the third man. But she was starting to wonder.

"Could I come in to ask you a few questions?" Jess said.

"Sorry, it's not a good time."

"This won't take long."

"I said no. We're dealing with a tragedy here. My niece is with us. She's distraught. I have to take care of her. Your questions can wait."

Lynn pulled the doorknob, but Jess got her body in sideways, preventing her from closing the door.

"Mrs. Lombardo, I'm very sympathetic, but unfortunately it can't wait. I'm worried about your sister's safety. And beyond that, we can't pursue the case against Aidan Callahan without her. I'm sure you don't want him getting released for lack of evidence. If I could have a few minutes of your time to discuss Mrs. Stark's whereabouts, it would be a big help."

"I'm not telling you where she is. Didn't I say that when you called yesterday? Caroline doesn't want you to find her. She doesn't trust you to protect her."

"There are a lot of things we can do to protect a witness. If I could speak to her on the phone, I could reassure her about her safety."

"Be my guest. Call her."

"I have called. I tried many times, left messages, texted her. She won't answer. I was hoping maybe you could convince her to speak with me."

"Why would I do that? If Caroline doesn't want to talk to you, that's her business. She's scared. She just lost her husband. Go away and leave her alone. Leave *me* alone. I don't want you on my property. Unless you have a warrant, you need to go."

She moved to close the door again, and this time, Jess let her. But Lynn's behavior was odd enough to qualify as suspicious. Occasionally—*rarely*—the victim's loved ones refused to cooperate in a murder investigation, but that was in a specific kind of case. The kind where the grief-stricken husband initially reports his wife missing, but when the police uncover discrepancies in his account of events, he suddenly stops talking. Maybe even flees the jurisdiction, like O.J. in the white Bronco. This case had nothing in common with that scenario. Caroline Stark was an innocent victim. She'd been stalked by Aidan Callahan, and then he'd been allowed to attack her in the police station. Caroline had a reason to hide. It didn't make her guilty. It didn't. Mike Castro was wrong. Jess would keep telling herself that until she had hard evidence to the contrary.

Jess walked down the driveway toward the curb, where she'd parked, then stopped short, instantly on high alert. A shadow had flicked by the car as she came toward it, then disappeared. Somebody was there, on the other side of the car, hunkering down, waiting for her. Joe Lombardo maybe? Jess's hand flew to the gun at her waist. Adrenaline buzzed in her veins as she maneuvered around the vehicle, ready to defend herself.

52

A girl crouched on the ground near the rear door of Jess's car. "Get up," Jess said, holstering her gun. "I thought you were gonna jump me. I could've shot you."

"I'm sorry. Oh my God. I'm Hannah," she said, her voice shaky and breathless.

"Jess Messina. I'm working on the murder case. Are you all right? What are you doing down there?"

"I overheard you talking to Aunt Lynn and snuck out. I need to talk to you. My aunt and uncle can't know I'm here."

It was full dark outside, but a streetlight at the corner of the drive-way illuminated the area surrounding her car. The driveway sloped upward to the house, which sat on a rise. Somebody watching from a window would look down and see Jess standing there, but wouldn't be able to see Hannah, who was crouching. Hannah needed to stay down.

"Don't stand up, or they'll see you," Jess said to Hannah. "I'm going to open the rear door and lean in like I'm getting something from the backseat. Stay low and scoot past me onto the floor. I'll drive away, and we'll find a spot nearby where we can pull over and talk. Okay?"

Hannah nodded. They executed the maneuver smoothly. Jess drove until she spotted an elementary school several blocks away. She pulled into the parking lot. The school was dark, the playground empty of children, swings swaying in the strong breeze. Hannah Stark's childhood must seem very far away to her at this moment.

"Stay down there, okay, Hannah?" Jess said. "We're still in your aunt and uncle's neighborhood. I doubt they'll come looking for you, but you never know."

"Okay."

"Are you afraid of them?"

"Oh, no, nothing like that. Aunt Lynn and Uncle Joe would never hurt me. But I do think they're lying to me. I think Aunt Lynn knows where my mom is, and she won't tell me. She won't tell me *anything*. I told her I want to talk to you, but she said no. They don't want me talking to the police."

"Why would she do that? It's unusual in a murder investigation. Usually the victim's family is eager to cooperate."

"Aunt Lynn is trying to protect me. She and I are really close. Sometimes she's a little overprotective, but I don't need that right now. I need answers. My father is dead, and my mother's nowhere to be found. She may never come back."

"I'm sure she's coming back," Jess said.

Jess hoped she was right. If Caroline didn't come back to testify, the case would fall apart. But fear was a powerful emotion. After the station house attack, Caroline had reason to doubt that the authorities would protect her.

"I'm *not* sure. Aunt Lynn told me I can stay with them as long as I want. She said if I want to take a leave of absence from school until everything blows over, I could live with them. Why would she say I could stay with them indefinitely like that if my mom is coming back?"

"You think your mother told your aunt she's not coming back? That she'd tell your aunt that but not tell you?"

"She might. Mom and Aunt Lynn are really tight. Their father died before I was born. They got all the money and the other kids didn't. The other kids sued them. Ever since then, it's been the two of them against the world. And Dad and Uncle Joe follow their lead. So, I think Mom would tell Aunt Lynn anything. What surprises me is that Aunt Lynn wouldn't tell *me*. That makes me think it's something really bad."

"Bad? Like what?"

"I don't know. But I feel so alone."

Quiet sniffling sounds came from the backseat. It broke her heart to think of this young woman, at the start of her grown-up life, dealing with the loss of her father. And no ordinary death—but a brutal murder at the hands of her mother's lover, the salacious details of which were being splashed across the tabloids. Jess wanted to give Hannah a big hug and tell her everything would be all right. But she couldn't promise that—not when today's events had cast doubt on Caroline Stark's role in Jason's murder.

"I'll do my best to find her and try to convince her to come back. But you know she's doing this for a reason, right? She's afraid of Aidan Callahan."

"Shouldn't I be afraid, too?" Hannah demanded. "What about *me*? Did you know that Aidan came into the coffee shop at my school and pretended to be a student in order to meet me? It was definitely him. I saw his picture online and recognized him. Can you imagine how I felt when I found that out?"

"He was stalking your mother, Hannah. His approach to you was part of that. Your mother was beside herself when she learned about it, I can assure you. She blamed herself."

"She *should* blame herself. It was her fault. I actually thought he was cute. I invited him to my dorm room. I gave him my number. And then I see online that he slept with my mother and murdered my father? What kind of nightmare is that? *She's* responsible. She let it happen."

"I'm so sorry. That's truly awful. But you know, it may explain why your mother isn't returning your calls. She's ashamed of herself, and she can't face you."

"She's not ashamed. She has no shame."

"Why do you say that?"

"Everything that happened is because of her. Look at what she did. Cheated on my dad, and brought this killer into our lives?"

"I don't mean to defend your mother. I agree that her conduct was inexcusable. But your father cheated on her first. He brought a woman—"

"Yeah, I saw that reported online. It's a lie."

"Why do you say that? Were you at the party where the Russian woman showed up and made a scene?"

"No, I wasn't. But my mom told me about it, and I confronted my dad. He swore that woman was a business associate, and I believe him. He wouldn't lie to me, and he would never cheat on my mom. He adores her. *Adored*. Past tense. God, I can't believe she brought this *lunatic* into our lives and, and now . . ."

Hannah paused, her bitter sobs filling the car.

"*I'll never see my father again.*"

Jess passed a packet of Kleenex over the console. "Hannah, here. You poor thing."

"My poor *dad*," Hannah said, through her tears. "Everything he ever did was for her, to make her happy, to give her the things she wanted. The cars, the clothes, the beach house. That house cost millions of dollars. And yet I got a notice from the registrar's office two days ago that my tuition hasn't been paid. Something weird was going on with my parents."

"I can look into that. Is there anything else you can tell me? Anything unusual that happened? Anything you can remember that might possibly shed some light on your parents' circumstances?"

Hannah was silent for a moment, mopping her face with a tissue. Jess felt bad about leaving her wedged on the floor of the backseat.

"Hey, do you want to come sit in the front? There's nobody else in the parking lot, and you look so uncomfortable."

"I feel safer down here. And we should go soon, before they miss me. Aunt Lynn made spaghetti and meatballs for dinner because it's my favorite. I don't want her to think I'm ungrateful, or that I didn't listen."

Jess put the car in gear. "I understand. We'll go back in a minute. But first, think about my question. Anything unusual, anything that stands out?"

"Okay. Yes. One thing is, my dad started traveling for work a lot more in the past year. Like, a huge amount more. He was gone constantly, and that was new."

"Did something change at work? The nature of his job?"

"I don't know. But my mom probably does."

"She mentioned that he traveled a lot. But she never said it was a change."

"It was. And come to think of it, it was right around the same time that things, like, got weird, generally."

"Things got weird generally? What do you mean?"

"Nothing specific. Just a feeling that something was going on with them—something bad. Like they were in trouble."

"Can you be more specific? How did this come to your attention?"

"Dad was gone a lot. Mom was on edge, and even more of a monster to deal with than she usually is. When Dad was home, they'd lock themselves in their bedroom and whisper. And not like *that*. I could hear the tone. It wasn't happy, or romantic. It was like, urgent and troubled. I would ask what was going on, and they'd act like I was crazy. But I wasn't crazy. I knew what I was seeing. *Oh*. Another thing." She paused, thinking.

"What is it, Hannah?"

"Yes, this was definitely around that time. I saw a gun in my dad's briefcase. Now, maybe he'd had it before, but I doubt it."

"A—a gun?"

"Yes."

Jess knew what her next question had to be.

"What type of gun? Can you describe it?"

"I don't know anything about guns, and I only saw it once. It was silver and kind of clunky-looking. That's all I remember."

"Silver and clunky-looking" was an accurate description of the gun seized from Aidan Callahan's truck. Was Jason Stark murdered with his own gun? That wouldn't necessarily mean that Caroline had been involved. Maybe Jason pulled the gun on Aidan, and Aidan took it away from him.

Though that wasn't how Caroline said things went down.

Was she lying?

"Did you ask your father why he had a gun?"

"Yeah. He said it was for personal protection."

"Did he say what he was protecting himself from?"

"No. I wish I'd asked."

"You said they were behind closed doors, whispering, seeming unhappy. Do you think that might be because they were having trouble? Problems in their marriage?"

"No, actually. They seemed more like a team than ever. He was more adoring. She was more on top of him, always having him call to check in. They seemed so close. Like allies against the rest of the world. That's why I can't understand how this happened. I have so many questions. I'm lost, I'm mourning my father. She abandons me at a time like this? Why would she do that? There has to be something I don't know. What is she hiding from me?"

53

"Callahan. Get up. You got a visitor," the corrections officer said, rapping on the bars of Aidan's cell.

"Is it my lawyer?"

"Civilian."

"You sure?"

"Yeah, I'm sure. Get moving."

A civilian? Could that mean Tommy? The whole way to the visiting room, Aidan thought about what he would say to his brother. He wanted to proclaim his innocence, to reassure Tommy that he hadn't fallen that far, hadn't done what they claimed he did. That all of Tommy's efforts hadn't been for naught. But why would Tommy believe him? This wasn't their first rodeo. They'd been through it all before. Aidan remembered swearing to Tommy that what happened with Matthew Bostick was an accident. A fight over a girl in which Aidan hadn't even thrown the first punch. Tommy believed him then—and stood up for him, at some risk to his own reputation. And again, on the night of Jason Stark's murder, Tommy took a huge risk for Aidan, throwing him out of Caroline's house without reporting the break-in. Aidan promised to go to Tommy's house, to look out for his family, to stay out of trouble. Instead, he went back to Caroline's house, and now he was charged with her husband's murder.

How could he ask Tommy to believe that was a mistake? The same man keeps getting wrongly accused? Lightning doesn't strike twice. Anybody would laugh.

Besides, Aidan couldn't even be certain that the accusation was false. Try as he might, he couldn't remember the events of that night after he walked out into the storm. He was starting to think a piece of flying debris must've smacked him in the head, like Dorothy in *The Wizard of Oz*. The problem was, that left him not knowing what had happened. If they asked him to swear on a Bible that he was innocent of Jason Stark's murder, he'd have to decline.

As Aidan walked into the visiting room, he realized there was nothing he could say to excuse himself. He'd hold his brother's hand and thank him. Then tell him to go home and hug his kids and forget about Aidan. He was a lost cause.

He had that whole emotional conversation with himself. Then he got to the table and saw that his visitor wasn't his brother at all. It was Brittany Pulaski, Samantha's sister, the catering manager at Harbor Gourmet. He had no idea why she was here.

Aidan sat down across from Brittany and stared at her.

"Brittany. What are you doing here?"

Brittany was two years older than Samantha, and pretty, with the same gray eyes and curly dark hair. They'd been good friends back in high school. But after Matthew died, Samantha's whole family turned their backs on Aidan, including Brittany. In recent years, she'd thawed some. Brittany would now say hi when they crossed paths. She'd even hired him for that bartending gig at Caroline's house. Though, look how that turned out. The Pulaskis were bad luck for him, it seemed.

"Hey, Aidan. How you doing?" Brittany said.

"Uh. Not great."

"Yeah, well, I won't take a lot of your time."

"Whatever. I got nothing else to do," he said.

He squinted at her, puzzled.

"I came because Samantha asked me to deliver a message."

"Oh. Samantha knows about this? You told her?"

Samantha had gone away years ago, right after Matthew died. She moved to Pennsylvania, where her grandparents lived, and never came back. Aidan hadn't spoken to her since.

"I didn't have to tell her. She saw it on TV. You're famous."

He laughed bitterly. "Great, just what I wanted. What's the message? She's relieved they finally got me?"

"No, not at all. The opposite. She wanted me to tell you how sorry she is."

"I don't need her pity."

"It's not pity. She wants to apologize."

"What for? This isn't her fault. She broke my heart years ago, but that's water under the bridge now," Aidan said.

He realized he meant it. Finally, Samantha was in the past. The spell she'd cast over him had been broken by somebody else's spell. A more powerful witch. Did he never learn?

"Not for breaking your heart," Brittany said. "She's sorry she didn't speak up for you back in the day. She feels bad about that. When Matthew died, she was still a kid, and it was all too much for her. She freaked, she ran. She wants you to know she regrets how she behaved. That she left you in the lurch."

Right after Matthew died, Aidan had begged Samantha to come forward to back up his claim of self-defense. The prosecutor was coming after him with some ginned-up story of how he killed his best friend with his bare hands in a fit of jealous rage. It was a lie. What happened was Matthew's fault. Samantha and Aidan met in the cave down on the beach, where they'd always gone to be alone together. Samantha was tearful, apologetic, begging Aidan to take her back, begging forgiveness. Then Matthew showed up, and he wasn't looking to apologize. He was the one in the jealous rage, not Aidan. Matthew started the fight. Aidan only defended himself. Samantha could have told them that, but instead she abandoned him. That was truly when she broke his heart.

"It's true. She did abandon me. My life went wrong then. I went to jail when I should've gone to college. Never got a decent job since. And here I am again. I'm not saying that's Samantha's fault, though. Most of it's on me."

"Samantha can't change the past, Aidan, and neither can I. But she asked me to help you."

"*You?* How can you help?"

"There's something I never told you, that struck me as weird at the time. I thought of it again when I saw that woman's picture in the paper, and I told it to Samantha."

"The woman? You mean Caroline Stark?"

"Yes. I told my sister, and she made me promise to tell you. That's why I'm here."

"Okay. I'm listening. What is it?"

"Remember when I hired you to work a bartending gig at her party?"

"Yeah, but don't go feeling guilty about that. You offered me work, and I took it. The mess that came after—that was my own stupidity."

"Okay, *but*—I can testify that this lady was after you, Aidan. She had the hots for you back then. I know that, because she requested you for the party. Not just asked for you. She insisted. I don't know whether that helps or not. But, in the papers, they're making you out to be a stalker. I know that's not true. Caroline Stark came after you hard, and I'm willing to say that in court."

"It's true, Caroline came after me. But that was later. We didn't meet for real until she came into the Red Anchor for a drink one night, maybe three or four days after that party. Before the party, she saw me once on the beach, but she didn't know me from Adam."

"You're wrong. She definitely knew you before the party or she never would've asked for you like that. I had Eddie Morales lined up to work Mrs. Stark's job that night. He's my main bartender. Caroline Stark called me and instructed me to fire him and hire you instead, or else I wouldn't've done it. Aidan, she asked for you by name."

"That can't be. Caroline didn't know my name then. Well, wait a minute. She knew my first name. But not my last name, or where I worked."

"I'm telling you, she did. She said she wanted Aidan Callahan from the Red Anchor to work her party. She said she knew you from the bar and liked your style, thought you'd add flair to the event. I told her I had someone else slated in, but she didn't want to hear that. She told me to drop Eddie and hire you instead. It was like, if I wanted her business, I better honor this request."

"I'm certain Caroline didn't come into the Red Anchor until after the party. You're mixed up on the timing."

"How could I be? Something like that, I'd remember. You're not nobody to me, Aidan. With the history we have, I pay attention to what you do. Me and Samantha, we talk about you sometimes. We keep tabs. Some rich weekender chick comes in asking for you, I'm gonna remember."

"You thought I was sleeping with her?" he said.

She raised an eyebrow. "I wondered. I thought, maybe you got yourself a sugar mama."

"Well, I didn't. I wasn't sleeping with her."

He paused, remembering his lawyer telling him to keep his mouth shut. But he couldn't resist.

"Not *then*," he said, and wanted to kick himself. Caroline had her hooks in him so deep that, after everything that happened, he still felt the need to brag about their relationship.

"I don't know what happened between you and that woman," Brittany said, "but I want to help. Samantha's married, you know. She's having a baby in December. She feels bad that—well, she feels bad. And so do I. You should tell your lawyer what I said."

"I will. Thanks for coming."

As he watched her walk away, Aidan thought about what Brittany had said. He believed her now, but he didn't know how to process the information. Caroline had known his full name and requested him to work at her party. Why would she do that, and what could it mean?

54

Jess put on her power pantsuit for the team meeting at the prosecutor's office. She reminded herself to speak in a low register and not to fiddle with hair. People were always telling her that she looked too young to be a lieutenant, and Vernon Mays already wasn't satisfied with her work. She needed to appear mature and professional while delivering the bad news. Not only had Jess failed to locate Caroline Stark, but new evidence she and Mike had developed suggested that their star witness *might* be implicated in her husband's murder. It was really just a maybe. Jess still had faith in Caroline. She was hoping for good news from the crime scene team to shore up Caroline's credibility. Like Aidan Callahan's fingerprints on the murder weapon, or the recovery of Jason Stark's body with some forensic tell that Callahan was the murderer.

As Jess got off the elevator and marched toward the conference room, Mike Castro stepped forward to intercept her.

"You have a golf game after the meeting?" she said, looking him up and down.

He'd taken the opposite sartorial approach from Jess, dressing down in khakis and a polo shirt. Guys could get away with that, and people still paid attention when they talked.

"Give me a break. I worked late last night and went out early this morning to serve a subpoena. This was the best I could do," he said.

"Just kidding."

Vernon Mays walked by with Phil Nadler, the head of the crime scene team.

"You two joining us?" Mays said.

"Two minutes, boss," Mike said.

Mike waited until the others were out of earshot before speaking.

"Listen, I hit pay dirt, but you won't like it. Bad news about Caroline."

Jess blanched. "Is she all right?"

"I didn't find her dead if that's what you mean. I didn't find her at all. Her phone is off, and she removed the SIM card. Not only isn't she using it to make calls. It's not accessing data or pinging cell towers or anything. She's off the grid, and deliberately."

"That is bad news. But why do you think it's deliberate?"

"Because. There's something worse."

"Ugh, go ahead. Tell me."

"When I couldn't track her using her phone, I started analyzing the numbers she called for leads. The number she called the most in the days leading up to the murder? An *insurance company*. Two days before the murder, a new insurance policy was taken out on Jason Stark's life in the amount of five million dollars, with Caroline as the sole beneficiary."

Jess kicked the wall. "Two days. Two *days*?"

"I'm afraid so."

"Mike, two days. That looks like she killed him for money."

"Yeah. No kidding."

"Aw, shit. I really believed everything she told me. Hey, you don't think this could be a coincidence, do you?"

"Seriously? You can't be that naïve, right?" Mike said.

"Two days means she's involved."

"Uh, yeah."

"I can't believe she'd do it."

"Why not? The husband cheated. She's got a new guy. They get the insurance money and run off together. It's classic."

"I remember something. When Aidan grabbed Caroline in the police station, he asked her if she killed Jason."

"Why would he have to ask? He was there," Mike said.

"I don't know," she said, shaking her head. "But it suggests she was involved, right? We have to tell the team about the insurance policy. It's too big to keep it quiet. Mays will hate this."

"Or else he'll love it. More publicity."

In the conference room, Vernon Mays asked everyone to introduce themselves. There were more people present than Jess had expected, including officers from the crime scene team, an assistant prosecutor, and a federal prosecutor and an FBI agent. Jess had no idea why those last two were here, since there was no federal angle to the case that she knew of.

"We're going to start with a report from our colleagues from the feds," Mays said. "Assistant U.S. Attorney Vargas and Special Agent O'Reilly are working a Russian mob case that has a surprising connection to our murder. Their investigation is ongoing, so what they say doesn't leave this room."

He turned to the AUSA.

"Melanie, the floor is yours. I understand you have a PowerPoint?"

"Thank you, Vern. Good morning, everybody. Yes, one moment."

The AUSA stood up and walked to the lectern. She was early forties and confident, with sleek, dark hair, wearing a tailored dress and high-heeled leather boots—the sort of professional woman Jess wanted to be when she grew up. She put an organizational chart with photographs up on the screen. The heading read, KUNETSOV ORGANIZATION, NEW YORK CELL. Jess's gaze was immediately drawn to a photograph of a dark-haired woman in the second row. The woman wore heavy eyeliner, and the label under her picture read, GALINA MOROZOVA. *Galina*. The Russian mistress. Jess's eyes followed an arrow that led sideways from Galina's photograph to a picture of a handsome, dark-haired man. She looked at the name printed underneath that picture, and gasped.

Mike caught Jess's eye and shrugged. "What's the point of this?"

"It's *Jason Stark*," Jess mouthed, pointing at the screen.

"When I saw the reports of your murder case in the papers, I immediately reached out to Vern," AUSA Vargas said. "For the past two years, we've been investigating an organized cell of undocumented Russian nationals operating in the U.S. and Canada, led by a man named Victor Kunetsov. The Kunetsov organization primarily focuses on human and weapons trafficking. However, like all criminal organizations with substantial illegal proceeds, money laundering is a major part of their operation. Jason Stark, your murder victim, was one of our targets. We believe he laundered over fifty million dollars of the organization's money through his hedge fund, working with this woman, Galina Morozova."

Mike whistled. Jess raised her hand.

"Yes, Lieutenant," the AUSA said.

"Caroline Stark told us that her husband had a Russian mistress named Galina. Is it possible that this was simply a romantic relationship?"

"It may *also* have been romantic, but we're certain about the money laundering. Peter Mertz, who's the head of the hedge fund that Jason Stark worked for, reported Stark to the SEC several months ago when he discovered substantial irregularities in the accounts Stark handled. The SEC brought in a forensic accountant, who made the connection to our case through a complex series of transactions that I won't go into here. I assure you, the evidence against Jason Stark is very strong. Plus, there's more. We surveilled him."

The prosecutor clicked through a series of surveillance photographs. The man in the pictures was tall and handsome, with silvering dark hair and a chiseled face—far better-looking than Jess had imagined Jason Stark to be, based on Caroline's descriptions of a marriage gone dead and sour. Then again, Caroline had not been entirely truthful, had she?

"These are surveillance photographs of Jason Stark with Galina Morozova on three separate occasions in the past month," the prosecutor said, clicking through slides.

She stopped at a slide that showed Jason Stark getting into a blue Audi on a busy Midtown Manhattan street.

"I draw your attention to this photograph of Galina picking Jason up outside his office in Manhattan. On that day, we followed the two of them to an important meeting at an auto parts store in Queens, which you see here, and again here. Jason and Galina walked through the store to a small parking lot in the rear between the building and the garage. In that parking lot, they met with the top enforcer for the organization. We don't have great photos from the meeting because our operative was stationed down the street and would not have been able to access the rear parking lot except on foot. But he observed Mikhail Volodin exit the auto parts store not long after Stark and Galina left the place. Here's a photo of Volodin exiting, and here's his mug shot where you get a good look at him. Not someone you'd want to run across in a dark alley."

The mug shot on the screen showed a hulking bodybuilder type with a shaved head and a long, puckered scar on one cheek.

"We suspect Volodin of involvement in upwards of twenty homicides. We believe the purpose of the meeting at the warehouse was for Volodin to threaten Jason Stark's life. Your victim stole money from the wrong people. Stark skimmed several million dollars of the Kunetsov organization's money when it passed through the hedge fund. We intercepted phone calls between Galina Morozova and her boss indicating that they were threatening to kill him if he didn't pay it back."

Jess raised her hand again. "Wait, I'm confused. Are you saying these mobsters were involved in Jason Stark's murder?"

"That possibility is exactly why we're here. Right now, I can't prove that the Russians killed Jason Stark, but it would certainly be consistent with their MO to whack somebody who crossed them. And Jason Stark crossed them. I'd like to hear your evidence. If your evidence is weak, or could support my Russians doing this, I'd propose adding this murder to my conspiracy and racketeering case."

"Whoa, whoa, wait a minute," Vernon Mays said. "You want to take over?"

"Jason Stark's murder would become part of the Kunetsov case. I'd cross-designate you as a federal officer, Vern, so you could still handle the murder."

"Work with the feds. Okay, I like that," he said, nodding.

"Wait a minute," Jess said. "This can't be right. We have eyewitness testimony that Aidan Callahan murdered Jason Stark, and forensic evidence to back it up. So, Stark's murder can't be connected to your case."

"*Unless* Callahan worked for the Russians," Vargas said.

"He's a bartender in Glenhampton who was sleeping with Stark's wife," Jess said. "He has no connection to the Russian mob."

"That you know of. But take a look at this."

She clicked to the next photograph. It showed Aidan Callahan's truck several car lengths behind the blue Audi that carried Jason Stark and the Russian woman.

"This photo was taken by one of our surveillance agents on the day that Jason Stark and Galina Morozova met with the enforcer at the auto parts store. We ran the plate. The red truck you see here is registered to Aidan Callahan. He followed them to the meeting. It's *possible* that he attended the meeting. Here's a photograph of a man walking down the alley on the side of the auto parts store heading in the direction of the rear parking lot. We think this is Callahan, but we can't confirm it."

She put up another slide showing a man walking away from the camera, taken from a distance. The man's face wasn't visible, but based on height and hair color, it could very well be Aidan Callahan.

"This is the only photo we have of him," the prosecutor said. "We went back through all our surveillance material, and he doesn't show up in anything else relating to our case. We can't prove he worked for our Russians. But it is suspicious that he showed up at this meeting. Now, I'd like to hear about *your* evidence. What's your proof that Callahan was the shooter?"

"Our case hinges on a detailed witness statement from Mrs. Stark," Jess said. "She admits to having an affair with Aidan Callahan. When she ended it, she says he started stalking her and her family. That's why Callahan followed Jason Stark. It has nothing to do with any Russians. Caroline Stark claims that Callahan later broke into their home and shot and killed her husband. She saw it happen. Callahan was arrested in that same red truck. The truck was full of blood, and he was wearing blood-soaked clothing. A silver handgun was retrieved from the vehicle."

"We now have forensic test results on the blood and the gun," Vernon Mays said. "Phil, can you summarize?"

Phil Nadler was a storied crime scene investigator with a craggy face and salt-and-pepper hair, who'd worked some of the best-known homicide cases in recent history. A rumor was going around that he planned to retire any day now and start raking in the cash as an expert witness. Jess was excited to have this opportunity to see him in action.

"Afraid I forgot my PowerPoint," Phil said, drawing chuckles around the table. "But I do have some pictures to pass around, with extra copies for the feds if you'd like to take home a party favor. Okay, Callahan's truck, interior and exterior views. Notice the substantial amount of blood on the front upholstery. Photographs of Callahan wearing blood-soaked clothing, and the blood on his hands. Photographs of a silver-gray handgun, a Beretta APX RDO with bloody fingerprints. And photographs of a man's jacket and a blanket both recovered from a cave where we believe Callahan may have dumped Stark's body. The body has not yet been recovered. We believe it may have been swept out to sea by the storm surge from Hurricane Oswald. The good news is, we no longer need the body to prove the murder. The blood on the seat of the truck and on Callahan's clothing belongs to Jason Stark. We were able to develop a DNA profile for Stark based on a lock of hair taken from his daughter Hannah. That sample is one step removed, however. It's reliable. But I'd prefer a direct sample from Jason Stark for trial. We could get that from his hairbrush, razor, whatever. We searched the beach house based on Caroline Stark's consent. Unfortunately, Jason didn't spend time there, and we were unable to obtain a hair sample that we could confirm as his. We'd like to search their apartment, if his wife would give permission. But I've been told Caroline Stark is no longer cooperating with the investigation."

Everybody turned to look at Jess.

"Is that true?" AUSA Vargas asked.

Jess felt her face flush.

"She was physically assaulted by Aidan Callahan at the Glenhampton police station. He broke loose while being transported. After that attack, Caroline turned off her phone and stopped responding to my calls or texts. She claims she fears for her life and doesn't trust the authorities to protect her. Which could be the explanation for why she went AWOL. *But*—"

Jess took a deep breath. Her hands were clenched into fists. She made an effort to uncurl them and speak calmly.

"Deputy Castro and I have developed new information that causes us to doubt Caroline Stark's version of events. This information *may*— and I stress, this is preliminary—it may implicate Caroline Stark as a coconspirator with Aidan Callahan in her husband's murder."

There were some indrawn breaths around the table.

"This is news to me," Vernon Mays said. "When were you planning on telling me this, Lieutenant?"

"At this meeting, sir."

Mays was about to yell at Jess in front of everyone, but to her intense relief, Phil Nadler interrupted.

"I have evidence that undercuts Caroline's story also. Honestly, I dismissed it, but it could be read to say she's lying."

Phil hadn't brought his damaging evidence forward before, either. Jess was off the hook.

"Everybody wants to ruin my case today," Vern said. "Go ahead, Phil. What have you got."

"We went through Caroline's very lengthy witness statement and compared it to forensics at the crime scene, looking to corroborate. A few things don't add up. There was a lot less blood in the house than would be expected if an adult male was shot and bled out, even accounting for cleanup. There was *some* blood. But the blood belonged to Caroline Stark, not Jason. And that brings me to the forensic evidence most damaging to Caroline's credibility. The wound to her hand, which she claims she got by grabbing the knife away from Callahan, is extremely shallow. It's also on her left hand, and she's right-handed."

"What are you getting at?" Mays said.

"I believe that the knife wound to Caroline's hand was self-inflicted."

Jess drew back in shock. Hearing about the insurance policy, Jess had begun to accept that Caroline might be lying. That in fact she was *probably* lying. But to stage the crime scene, to fake an injury? That would mean Caroline had engaged in a carefully orchestrated, premeditated murder and cover-up. How could Jess have been so wrong about her?

"Lieutenant Messina, do you have anything further?"

Jess struggled to gather her thoughts.

"Um, yes. Okay. First, sir, the Starks' next-door neighbor, Mrs. Francine Eberhardt, who admittedly is elderly and was viewing the scene through the rain caused by the hurricane, says she saw three people leaving the Starks' house at or around the time of the murder. Specifically, she saw two people dragging a third. One theory is, that was Caroline Stark and Aidan Callahan dragging Jason Stark's body. Another theory is that Chief Thomas Callahan helped his brother dispose of the body, and he's the third individual that the neighbor saw."

"I strongly disagree with that," Mike said. "It was Caroline."

"There is some troubling evidence against Chief Callahan, who's our suspect's brother, which I will report through channels whether or not it impacts this case, sir," Jess said.

"The neighbor didn't say who it was? Just that she saw a third person?" Mays asked.

"She couldn't see clearly," Jess said.

"Could be anyone then. Might even be one of your Russians, Melanie. We simply don't know."

"Sir, there's something else. Something that does directly implicate Mrs. Stark," Jess said.

"Go on."

"Deputy Castro learned that Caroline Stark took out a five-million-dollar insurance policy on her husband two days before his murder. She is the sole beneficiary of that policy."

The room fell silent at that. Every eye was on Jess.

"Well," Mays said, "*that's* a problem. No jury would believe that's a coincidence. I don't see how we use her as a witness now."

Jess's stomach sank. "Shouldn't we at least ask Caroline about the insurance policy? Give her a chance to defend herself?"

"Ask her? You can't find her, Lieutenant. And this has got to be why. She knows she's guilty and she's on the lam. At any rate, she's now made herself useless as a witness. Callahan's lawyer would wipe the floor with her over that, and we'd be forced to disclose it."

Mays rubbed his chin thoughtfully. "Maybe the way to salvage this case is to go after *her*. Make Caroline Stark the centerpiece. Phil, do you see any forensic evidence implicating Caroline?"

"I do. Her fingerprints are on the murder weapon," Phil said.

Mays pounded the table. "Beautiful."

"*But*, so are Callahan's. And Callahan's fingerprints are bloody, which means he had blood on his hands when he touched the gun," Phil said.

"How does that make sense?" Mays asked. "Wouldn't the blood come *after* he shot Jason Stark?"

"Two possibilities. Either Caroline shot Jason, and Aidan handled the gun afterwards, during the cleanup. Or Aidan shot Jason without leaving prints, and picked up the gun with blood on his hands afterwards. As I'm sure you all know, it's possible to touch something and not leave a print if your hands are perfectly clean and dry."

"About the gun?" Jess said.

Heads swung back her way.

"Caroline claims that the murder weapon belonged to Aidan Callahan. She saw it in his apartment and she handled it there. That could explain why her prints are on the gun."

"She could be lying," Mays said.

"She could be," Jess conceded. "And there's evidence that she is. Hannah Stark contradicts her mother. Hannah says the Beretta recovered from the truck matches the general description of a gun carried by her father. She saw it in his briefcase."

"We have information on the source of the gun," Phil said, shuffling through some papers in a folder in front of him. "This is based on a query of the serial number to the ATF database. Okay, here it is. This firearm was originally purchased online three years ago in a batch of twenty firearms bought by a company that runs gun shows. No record of what happened after that, until six months ago, when the gun was reported stolen by its then-owner, a Joseph Lombardo of Massapequa, New York."

Jess sat up straight in her chair.

"Joseph Lombardo is Caroline Stark's brother-in-law," she said. "He's married to her sister, Lynn, with whom she's very close. Lynn knows where Caroline is, but she's not talking."

Mays leaned back in his chair and steepled his fingers. "What does this mean? You think Caroline stole the gun from her brother-in-law?"

"No," Jess said. "I bet Joe Lombardo gave the gun to Jason Stark. Gave it to him willingly. From what the AUSA said, Jason knew he was in trouble. That's consistent with something Hannah Stark told me. She said that in the months leading up to the murder, her parents seemed upset and worried, like something was wrong. About that time, her father started carrying the gun. Jason needed a gun to defend himself against the Russians. Joe Lombardo gave him his gun, but maybe he knew that his brother-in-law was dirty. He didn't want to be implicated if the gun was ever used in a shooting. So, he reported the gun stolen. And he was right to do that, because it *was* used in a shooting. It was used to kill Jason himself—somehow."

"Yes, but how, and by whom?" Mays said. "There are too many loose ends in our case. I'm uncomfortable. We need a witness who can reliably tell us what really happened. Somebody who was there."

"Caroline, obviously, once we locate her," Jess said.

"I said *reliably*. Caroline has no credibility. After the insurance policy? With her prints on the gun? Come on. She's toast. What about Aidan?" Mays said.

"*Aidan?*" Jess said.

"Why not? We flip him, get him to testify against her. Maybe he's the shooter, but she's the better target. Betrayed her own husband for five million dollars and the love of a younger man? It's classic."

"What makes you think he'd flip on her?" Jess asked.

Jess doubted it, personally. She'd seen the desperation in Aidan's eyes as he grabbed for Caroline in the station house. There was at least one thing Caroline hadn't lied about. Aidan Callahan was obsessed with her nearly to the point of insanity. Jess didn't believe he would talk.

"What's the alternative?" Mays said. "Callahan rots in jail while she lives it up on the insurance money? He'll flip, I guarantee it. I say we get a warrant for Caroline Stark's arrest. Put her in handcuffs, do a nice little perp walk into the courthouse. Oh, yeah. I'm liking this."

55

"I have some good news and some bad news," Lisa Walters said.

It was five days since Aidan's last court date, and five more until the grand jury would meet to determine his fate. Aidan and Lisa sat across a narrow table from one another in the small interview room that the prison set aside for attorney visits. The fluorescent lights buzzed. The carpet was dingy and stained. The room smelled of roach spray and damp. But Lisa, in a red suit and bold earrings, with her clear gaze and firm voice, brought a ray of hope.

"I could use some good news," Aidan said.

"All right. Good news first. And this is big. The prosecution wants you to cooperate against Caroline Stark."

"Cooperate? What do you mean?"

"Turn. Flip. Sing. Drop a dime. Call it what you'd like. They believe she killed her husband with your help, and they want your testimony against her in exchange for a reduced sentence."

"But—"

Lisa held up her hand. "Wait a second. I know what you're going to say. Waah, waah, Lisa, I can't remember. Waah. I love her, I won't talk against her. Well, stop right there, kid. You're gonna do this. You're going in there and agreeing to testify, but not with a guilty plea, and not in exchange for a reduced sentence. They're going to declare you innocent and drop the charges. I have a bombshell up my sleeve that changes everything. Your tox screen came back. You know how many Ambiens you took on the night of the murder?"

"Ambien? The sleeping pill? Zero. I never took a sleeping pill in my life."

"Wrong. You took *a shitload*. The tox screen shows an enormous concentration of zolpidem in your blood, which is the sedative in Ambien. Normally, zolpidem dissipates quickly. Your blood was drawn after your arrest, which by my calculation was about eight hours after you had that drink with Caroline—"

"The bourbon?"

"Yes. My expert says that to have that much zolpidem in your system that long after administration of the drug, you would've had to ingest up to four or five times the standard dose."

"You're saying Caroline drugged me?"

"That's exactly what I'm saying. Don't you think she did?"

Aidan cast his mind back to the first gulp of that bourbon at Caroline's house. It had tasted bitter and strange, but he'd ignored that and drunk the whole glass down, simply for the pleasure of drinking with her. Almost immediately afterward, he'd started feeling lethargic, dizzy and shivery. But the music was intoxicating and being near her was overwhelming, and he attributed his light-headedness to that. Yet, when he awoke in his truck the next day, his mind was wiped clean like he'd been bingeing for days, after only one drink. Aidan tended bar for a living. He had a high tolerance for alcohol. He never blacked out. Yet he remembered nothing after the singular moment of stepping out into the wind and rain. And then, to wake up drenched in blood with a gun he'd never seen wedged under the seat, and Caroline's husband dead, at his hand? He remembered telling Caroline he'd protect her from him. He even recalled wanting to jump the guy. But in his heart, he didn't believe he could do something like that and have zero memory of it.

"Maybe you're right," Aidan said to Lisa.

"I am right. Tell me about that drink, and how you felt afterward."

"The bourbon tasted funny. I passed out not long after drinking it. I woke up in my truck on the beach with my mind a blank and no memory of anything in between."

"There you go. Put that together with the Ambien in your blood, and it's obvious. But if you want to feel better about it, the prosecutor told me Caroline's fingerprints are on the gun."

"*Seriously?*"

Aidan's spirits soared. If *she* killed him, then Aidan's hands were clean. He hadn't realized until that moment how much he wanted not to be guilty. How much he *didn't* want to have another dead man on his conscience. He hated that Caroline would suffer. He wished he could carry that burden for her. But at least his own conscience would be clear.

"Though, you should know, your fingerprints were on the gun, too," Lisa said.

Crap. Aidan hung his head and rubbed his eyes. He couldn't handle much more of this stress, of this crazy roller-coaster his life had become.

"Which is it, then? Did I shoot Stark or did she?" he asked.

"I'll tell you what I think happened," Lisa said. "Caroline drugged you. She shot her husband, and then she stuck the gun in your hand while you were blacked out. She made sure your prints were on it, then she planted it in your truck."

"How did she get me to my truck? And dispose of Jason's body?"

"Somebody helped her. But it wasn't you."

He shook his head. "I don't know. I'm not sure I want to go in this direction."

Caroline was still a beautiful dream, one he couldn't give up. If she'd betrayed him that badly, it would be worse than anything Samantha ever did. He didn't want to face it. And yet—

"After all the proof I laid out, you still don't see that she set you up? I want to slap you, kid," Lisa said.

"There is this one thing."

He paused, afraid of what he was about to say, of where it would lead him.

"I'll bite. What's the one thing?" Lisa asked.

"Someone came to visit me the other day, and she told me a strange story. This girl Brittany? She works for Harbor Gourmet. She's the person who hired me to work at Caroline's party, the one where Stark's mistress showed up and made a scene."

"Okay, and?"

"Brittany says Caroline asked for me special, by name."

"Asked for you——?"

"Brittany says Caroline knew my first and last name, and where I worked, and that she insisted that I be the bartender assigned to her party. Brittany says she's willing to testify, to show that Caroline came after me. That I didn't stalk her. But I don't get how it's possible. I only met Caroline once before that party, in passing on the beach. We barely spoke. I don't see how she could've known my full name, or where I worked, and I don't understand why she would ask for me."

"You believe this woman's story?"

"Brittany has no reason to lie. She's not that good of a friend of mine. She says she's one hundred percent sure that it happened the way that she says it did. I believe her. And yet it makes no sense."

Lisa tapped her fingernails thoughtfully on the table. "Before Caroline requested you to work at the party, you say the two of you met once, on the beach?"

"Yeah. But just for a minute. I remember it was starting to rain. She was out for a run. She looked really beautiful. I remember she was wearing——"

"I don't need to know what she was wearing, Aidan. Tell me the things I do need to know. Where exactly did this happen? Did you speak? What did you say?"

"It happened in front of her house. I was standing there looking up at it."

"Looking at her house? Why?"

"I always look at it. That land used to belong to my family."

"You always look at Caroline's house? That isn't good. Elaborate, please."

"I go by there—I used to—to see how the house is coming along. To admire it."

"How often did you do this?"

"Few times a week, maybe."

"Was that the first time she saw you?"

"As far as I know. It was definitely the first time *I* saw *her*."

"But she could've seen you on other occasions?"

"Sure."

"Maybe she wondered who you were and why you were staring at her house."

"It's possible."

"Maybe she thought you wanted to rob it."

"I don't know why she would think that. I never did anything. Well, maybe, occasionally if nobody was around, I'd—"

He paused.

"You what?"

"I'd go in. I'm talking about when it was under construction, and it wasn't locked. I don't think she could know that. And one time after the party, when I set off the alarm by mistake. I'm sorry. Is that a problem for the case?"

"Of course it is. But maybe the truth is more complicated. How well-known is your prior conviction?"

"What do you mean?"

"Around town, do people know you were arrested for killing your best friend in a love triangle when you were younger?"

"Yes. Everybody knows."

"And how are you thought of? Violent? Unstable?"

"I don't know. Maybe. People are shitty. They don't give me the benefit of the doubt."

"So, if Caroline noticed you watching her house, and decided to ask around about you, she'd hear that you were an unstable young man, with a history of violence, with this, this *situation* in your past?"

Aidan sighed. "Yes. It's the first thing people mention if you ask about me."

"If you want my honest reaction, I think your friend Brittany is right. I think Caroline was playing a very long game."

"How so?"

"She knew who you were. She knew enough about you to think you'd make a good patsy. She asked Brittany to hire you to work her party in order to meet you. She wanted to meet you, so she could seduce you, kill her husband, and frame you for his murder. Do you see it now?"

No. Never.

Believing Lisa's theory would mean accepting that his love affair with Caroline had been a fraud from start to finish. A setup. And he knew that wasn't true. He'd lived it. He'd loved her. It was real.

"That's not possible," he said.

"You need to stop being so naïve, Aidan. People are liars. *Caroline* is a liar. You have to accept that."

"I thought this was the good news," Aidan said.

"Huh?"

"When you came in, you said you had some good news and some bad news. I asked for the good news first."

"This *is* good news. Not good. It's great. We have the Ambien in your blood. Caroline's prints on the murder weapon. And now your friend Brittany to explain how Caroline set you up. You're innocent, Aidan, and the prosecution is going to see that. I bet they dismiss the charges."

"Okay, what's the bad news then?"

"Nothing. Forget about that. Your only concern should be putting Caroline Stark behind bars where she belongs. That woman is evil."

56

The good news felt terrible. And the bad news was about to come bubbling to the surface like noxious gas rising from the bottom of a murky lake.

Aidan had been lying on his bunk, staring at the ceiling, reviewing in his head every moment he'd spent with Caroline. He was looking for treachery—and finding all too much of it. He'd assumed that he was the one who'd pursued her. He had it in his mind that she was above him, that he'd struggled to win her attention, that his charms had prevailed against all odds, that she gave in to her feelings for the guy from the wrong side of the tracks because she couldn't help herself.

He saw now that the truth was the opposite. From the first moment they met on the beach, it was Caroline who pursued him. She arranged for them to meet at her party. She came into the Red Anchor—twice—looking for him. She must've played drunk—had she drunk all the vodka tonics he poured for her?—in order to get him to drive her home. Once she had him in her house, she used a "tour" as a pretext to get him to her bedroom. To her *bed*. After that, he was lost. He would have agreed to anything she asked, no matter how extreme. Although he didn't, thank God. He had some moral boundaries. Almost immediately, Caroline—what was that legal word Lisa had used?—*solicited* him to kill her husband. And Aidan said no. So she was forced to kill Jason herself, but she made sure to set him up to take the fall. She acted afraid, so he promised to protect her. He followed Stark around. He put himself out there for anyone to see. Then she invited him to her home on the night of the murder, drugged him, shot her husband, and planted evidence of the crime in Aidan's truck. Aidan had delivered himself up like a sheep to slaughter. He was that gullible.

Now Aidan lay on his bunk, listening to his cellmate grunt as he did push-ups, trying to make sense of the disaster that was his life. He'd walked into a trap, and the door had swung shut behind him with a resounding clank. The cell smelled of sweat and urine from the toilet in the corner. The cellmate didn't speak to him and was in for armed robbery. Aidan didn't share Lisa Walters's optimism that the prosecution would agree to his innocence. He'd rot here forever, worrying that his cellmate would strangle him in his sleep. Wishing for that, even, to be put out of his misery. Things had never gone his way. Why would they start now?

The guard came up to the cell door and unlocked it, which could only mean one thing. It was visiting hours.

"Callahan. Visitor," the guard said.

"I saw my lawyer already."

"It's not your lawyer. It's a family member. Let's go."

Family. *Tommy?* Aidan scrambled down from the top bunk and presented his hands for the manacles. In light of everything that he'd learned this morning, he saw yet again how stupid he'd been to reject his brother's advice. The only person in his life who'd ever really looked out for him was Tommy. He walked down the long echoing corridor, his chains clanking, ready to throw himself on his brother's mercy. Ready to fight for his own future, if only for Tommy's sake.

But it was Kelly.

He sat down across from her. She took his hands. They both had tears in their eyes. Kelly, from seeing him in his prison blues, his eyes hollow and haunted. Aidan, from seeing how her familiar, pretty face had aged in the space of a single week. He could only imagine what Tommy looked like, and he couldn't stand it.

"Swear to God, Kel. I didn't do it. You've got to tell him," Aidan said, choking up.

"I don't want to talk about that. It's not why I'm here. I'm here for Tom."

"Yes. Can you tell him I love him? And that I'm innocent? This lawyer is going to prove it, and I can't thank you guys enough for paying for her."

"I'm here to tell you we can't pay for that anymore. I'm sorry, but we have legal troubles of our own now. Didn't the lawyer tell you?"

"Tell me what? What is it?"

The bad news. It must be truly bad, if Lisa couldn't bring herself to tell him.

"Tom got suspended. He's under investigation. The old lady next door heard the burglar alarm going that night. She looked out and saw you and Tom. She saw him let you go, Aidan, and she reported him to the state police. He's going to lose his job."

"My God. No. I'll tell them—"

"Tell them what? You can't say it's not true, because it is true. You know how I know? Tom can't sleep at night. That's why he hasn't been to see you. He can't look you in the eye. He believes it's his fault for letting you go. If only he'd had the guts to lock you up for burglary, you wouldn't be in for murder now. Tom thinks *he* ruined *your* life. Hah, can you believe that? My saint of a husband, always seeing the best in his screwup of a brother."

Aidan felt like he might vomit. Of all the things that had happened, Tommy taking this fall for him, blaming himself for Aidan's stupidity, was the worst of all. It was more than he could bear. He had to change this, to make this not happen to Tommy, because of him.

"You must hate me," he said, and instantly knew it was a stupid thing to say.

So self-pitying. He wasn't a whiner. He needed to fix this.

"I wish I hated you," Kelly said. "It would be easier. I love you, and so does Tommy. This is wrecking him. I fear for his health."

"I'll fix it. I promise."

"You can't fix this, because you *are* the problem. There's something wrong with you, Aidan. Bad luck, bad judgment. Call it what you like. Disaster follows you. You destroyed your own life, and now you're ruining ours, too. I don't see that changing at this point. Do you?"

57

Two officers showed up at the jail to transport Aidan to the sit-down at the prosecutor's office. One of them was a young woman he re-membered seeing with Caroline in the police station on the night he was arrested. The other was Mike Castro. Figures. Mike had been waiting for this for years. Two things he'd always wanted in one package. To see Aidan take a fall. And to steal Tommy's job. He must be licking his chops.

Aidan rode in the back of the patrol car, handcuffed, behind the mesh screen, looking out the side window. He'd been inside for a week, more or less, and had already forgotten the outside. The sight of it hurt his heart, because it was everything he was set to lose. The clear blue sky, the chill in the air. The leaves on the trees bright with autumn colors. Kids getting on a school bus, laughing. He didn't want to spend the rest of his life in jail. But if it was necessary to save his brother, Aidan would learn to live with it.

They entered the office building through a loading dock in the back. Aidan was then whisked upstairs in the freight elevator to spare the gen-eral public exposure to him. The world had always treated him like he was different. Now it saw him as dangerous, which made him feel alone. But then he saw Lisa Walters waiting for him in a small conference room and his spirits lifted for a moment. Until he remembered that he was about to disappoint her.

"Thanks, guys. You can uncuff him. And we'll need privacy," Lisa said, as Mike and the female officer escorted Aidan into the room.

"You sure about taking off the cuffs?" Mike asked.

"A hundred percent. You can stand outside that door if you like."

"Oh, believe me, I will."

"No eavesdropping though."

She winked. Aidan wanted to high-five her for taking his side, but antagonizing Mike right now, as good as it would feel, would be a mistake.

Aidan waited for the door to close. He kept his voice low, so the cops standing outside wouldn't overhear.

"Why didn't you tell me Tommy was under investigation?" Aidan asked.

"Because there's nothing you can do about it. You need to focus on your own problems."

"He is my problem. He's my brother, and he's in trouble because of me. Besides, there *is* something I can do about it."

"What's that?"

"I can plead guilty. Tell the prosecutor everything was my fault. Which it was. They got him on a charge of—what do you call it— obstruction? For not reporting me? But see, that was right in the middle of the hurricane. There was a state of emergency. Tom had to respond to calls. He couldn't take me to the station right then. He told me to turn myself in, and I promised I would. But I didn't. I went back to Caroline's house instead."

"That won't work."

"Why not? I'll take the fall if they dismiss the charges against Tommy. That's my deal."

"That might help your brother, but it won't work for *you*. You'll end up spending the rest of your life in jail. You saw the prosecutor in court. He's a real up-and-comer. Football hero back in the day, now a lawman. There's already a Vernon Mays for Congress committee. If you plead guilty, even if you agree to testify against Caroline, Mays will still ask for a significant jail sentence for you. He can't risk looking soft on a murderer. That's why you need to convince him you're innocent."

"Where does that leave my brother?"

"I'm not sure. Maybe if Mays believes you're innocent, he'll believe what you said about Tommy, too." She raised an eyebrow. "Even if it's not true."

"Say I do what you're telling me and claim I'm innocent. Is Mays gonna believe that?"

"In all honesty, I don't know."

"Did you show him the report that proves there was Ambien in my blood?"

"I did. He asked me, where's the proof you didn't take the Ambien yourself? And he's right. We can't prove that. It's only your word that she spiked your drink. As for her staging the crime scene, Caroline's phony hand injury and all, Mays thinks that if it was staged, you were involved. Mays is planning to ask you about it."

"What about Brittany's testimony? Doesn't she prove that Caroline set me up?"

"I told Mays about her, but he didn't bite. He thinks it's irrelevant when you met Caroline, whether she came after you instead of you going after her. In his mind, the only thing that matters is both of your prints on the murder weapon. That makes you coconspirators, and that's what he wants you to admit."

"You're saying he's already made up his mind that I'm guilty," Aidan said. "So, your plan won't work anyway."

"Maybe it won't. But the point of this meeting is to try to change his mind. Tell your story, Aidan. I believed you, and I'm as cynical as they come. Hopefully, Mays will believe you, too."

Aidan sat at the conference table with Lisa beside him, and the cops and the prosecutor across from him. Vernon Mays was dead center, stonefaced as he prepared to question Aidan about the murder. Lieutenant Messina was on Mays's right. She seemed kind and open-minded, but so young that she reminded him of the girl who babysat his niece and nephew. He doubted she would have much sway in deciding his fate. Mike Castro sat to Mays's left. Mike's expression didn't give anything away, but Aidan knew that Mike wanted Aidan to fry. He always had.

Mays handed Aidan an agreement guaranteeing that what he said today wouldn't be used against him in court, except to cross-examine him if he testified. Lisa explained it like this: If Aidan said he was guilty today, he couldn't change his story at trial. Whatever he said today would lock him in, one way or the other. It felt so final.

Aidan knew what he had to do. His hands shook as he signed the paper.

"Mr. Callahan," Vernon Mays said. "We're here today because the prosecution is interested in securing your cooperation against Caroline Stark. In order to do that, I need to hear your version of events. What you would testify to if called as a witness. This is a form of truth-testing. You need to answer my questions honestly. Do you understand?"

"Yes."

"Very good. Now, let's start with your relationship with Caroline Stark. From what I understand, that relationship was romantic in nature, is that correct?"

Aidan felt sweaty and tongue-tied, like he used to feel in high school when he got called on. Like everybody was going to laugh. But he had to go through with this.

"Yes, sir," he said, in a low voice.

"Speak up, please."

"I said yes."

"At some point, did Mrs. Stark tell you that she wanted to kill her husband, and that she needed your help?"

"She did."

"Did you agree to help her?"

All eyes were on him. His heart beat loudly.

"No, I did not agree. I refused."

Mays frowned. "Mr. Callahan," Mays said, "as the prosecutor, I have a duty to uphold the law and abide by ethical standards. When I put forth a witness at trial, I need to know that he is being truthful. Your lawyer has come to us with a story of you being drugged by Mrs. Stark prior to the murder. She claims that you're innocent, that Mrs. Stark murdered her husband and framed you. I find this story far-fetched to say the least. Our view of the case is that the two of you were lovers, and you conspired to murder Jason Stark, in order to take whatever money was left in the couple's bank accounts and collect on a five-million-dollar insurance policy taken out by Mrs. Stark on her husband's life. I need to hear the truth from you today if we're going to reach a satisfactory plea agreement."

The truth. Right. No matter what Aidan said, Vernon Mays would never believe he was innocent. Lisa was wrong. There was no point in going through this charade. Aidan should use whatever limited leverage he had to save his brother.

"You say, a satisfactory plea agreement. But what might satisfy you is different from what would satisfy me," Aidan said.

"If you want to know the sentence in advance, I can't make any promises," Mays said. "What I can do is tell you that, in similar cases, where truthful and effective testimony was rendered, defendants got somewhere between eight and ten years. That's a ballpark. It may sound like a lot. But compare it to the twenty-five-to-life you're facing now, and it's pretty sweet."

"That wasn't my question."

Mays spread out his hands. "Okay. I'm listening."

"I heard my brother Thomas Callahan, who's the chief of police in—"

"Oh, *come on,*" Lisa said. "Aidan. Don't do this. You're innocent. Tell him that."

Aidan didn't like to ignore Lisa's advice, but he had to. He would put Tommy first for once, the way Tommy had done for him his entire life.

"I heard that my brother is under investigation and suspended from his job because of something I did the night of the murder," he said.

"That's right. Because you broke into the Starks' house. We have a witness who says she saw him let you go."

"It wasn't like that. I can explain what happened, and you'll see my brother did nothing wrong."

"Fine, but what does that have to do with your testimony against Mrs. Stark?"

"I want to make a deal. I'll testify and say whatever you want. But my brother stays out of this. You drop his charges."

Mays leaned forward. "Let me make one thing clear. Don't ever tell me something because you think it's what I want to hear. You need to tell the truth."

"You said a minute ago that if I claim innocence, you'll think I'm lying."

"That's right. Because a claim of innocence is not consistent with the evidence as we see it."

"That's what I thought. If I claim I'm innocent, you won't make a deal with me."

"Correct, because I won't find you credible, and I can't call a witness if I believe he's lying."

"All right, then. What would you think if I said I did it? If I said I helped Caroline kill Jason Stark and dispose of his body? Would you believe me then?"

"That is consistent with the evidence we have. So, yes. I would believe you."

"What if I said I did it, and that I was willing to plead guilty, but only on the condition that you stop this investigation of my brother and drop his charges. What would you do then?"

"I would ask you to tell me truthfully exactly what Chief Callahan did that night."

"I can tell you right now. Tommy caught me inside Caroline's house. He was on his way to an emergency and didn't have time to book me. I promised him I would go to the police station and wait for him there. But I lied. I didn't go to the station. Instead, I went to Tom's house and helped my sister-in-law prepare for the hurricane, because I wanted to make up to him for what I knew I was about to do later that night. Then

I went back to the Starks' house and helped Caroline kill her husband and dispose of his body."

Beside him, Lisa was shaking her head in disbelief. Aidan ignored her and plowed forward.

"We left the body in the cave at Glenhampton Beach. That was my idea. I knew that place from way back. I took Caroline there. We were thinking we would come back later, when we had access to a boat, and dump him in the ocean. But the storm saved us the trouble. It washed him out to sea."

The room was silent. He felt Lisa watching him and couldn't turn his head. If he looked at her, he'd lose his nerve.

"What if I said all that?" Aidan asked. "What would the effect be on Tom's case?"

"If you said all that?"

"Yes. Would it fly? I plead guilty like that, and the case against Tommy gets dropped?"

"I think so. Not as a quid pro quo, you understand. But because I would then view you as a credible witness, somebody who's owned up to his guilt. Therefore, I would have no reason to disbelieve your testimony about your brother's actions."

"What would you do for his case?"

"Well. I could forward to the Internal Affairs people your account of the chief's actions, along with my assessment that you're credible and my recommendation that the investigation be discontinued."

"Would you do that? Would you put it in writing?"

"Yes."

"Okay, Mr. Mays. Then we have a deal."

58

Three days later, at the crack of dawn, the guards came to take Aidan to court. This time, there was no private ride in Lieutenant Messina's car. They put him in the windowless back of a prison van with five other guys who had hearings that day. Everyone looked pale and avoided eye contact. Nobody spoke. Maybe the others were going to plead guilty, too, and give up their freedom for months, for years, for life even. Aidan didn't feel much like talking either. He might not be able to see out of this van, but he still understood how much he was about to lose.

He'd been waiting in the cold of the holding cell for an hour when they came for him. He didn't know what to expect. Lisa Walters hadn't been to see him since the day Aidan told the prosecutor he was guilty. Maybe she'd given up on him. He wouldn't blame her. But they brought him to the attorney interview room, cuffed him to the chair, and locked him in. He sat there, thinking about how to explain to her. Then he realized he didn't need to. Lisa understood what Aidan was doing, and why.

Finally, Lisa showed up, wearing a purple dress and glasses to match, which made him smile. She didn't smile back. Her face was grim as she sat down across from him.

"Hi," he said.

"Hi."

"You look like you're going to a funeral."

"It *is* a funeral. *Yours.*"

"Mays says I'll be out in eight to ten years."

"No, in fact, he was careful *not* to say that. There's no specific sentence in your plea agreement. As of right now, Caroline Stark is still on the lam, and you don't even have anybody to testify against."

"That's good. I don't actually want to testify against her."

"It's not good. Without testimony, you're looking at twenty-five-to-life. For a crime you didn't commit. Oh—and there's no appeal from a guilty plea. It's *final*. Do you understand that?"

"I understand, Lisa. You explained everything. You did a good job."

"With this outcome? I don't think so. If you insist on going through with the plea, I can't represent you, Aidan. I'm sorry."

"I know you don't agree with what I'm doing. But you've been with me this far. I don't want to start with some other lawyer now. Won't you do this one last thing for me?"

"It's not that simple. I *can't* represent you. You allocute under penalty of perjury, and I can't suborn perjury."

"Can you talk like a human? I don't understand."

"You have to swear an oath on the Bible to tell the truth. Then the judge will ask what you did to commit the crime. If you say that you shot Jason Stark and helped dispose of his body, I'll believe you're lying. That's why I can't represent you. I can't stand beside you and give my endorsement to false testimony."

"You don't know that I'm lying."

"Come on, Aidan. We both know you are."

They looked at each other. He let out a breath.

"All right. If that's how you feel," he said.

"There is another way."

"What?"

"It's not too late. You don't have to plead guilty. You can go in there and tell the judge you changed your mind."

"And let Tommy take the fall? No thanks."

"I know you won't listen to me. But maybe you'll listen to him. Hold on."

"What? *No.*"

But Lisa was already at the door, knocking on it. The guard unlocked it. Lisa consulted with him in a tone low enough that Aidan couldn't make out the words. A moment later, Lisa left the room, and Tommy walked in.

Aidan watched as his brother lowered himself into the creaky metal chair. Tommy's eyes were red. His face was puffy, and for the first time, Aidan noticed that Tommy was losing his hair. If Aidan pled guilty, his niece and nephew would grow up while he was in prison, and his brother and sister-in-law would grow old. He needed to be willing to pay that price. He needed to stay strong and do what he knew was right—for once in his life.

"Hey, bro," he said.

"Kid."

"Thanks for coming to see me. Big day. Nice to have family in the courtroom to support me. And thanks for paying for the lawyer. She's a ballbreaker. It helped me so much to have her on my side," Aidan said.

Tommy took in a big breath and let it out slowly, like he was playing for time.

"I don't know where to start," he said. "There's so much to say, but the most important thing is this. Lisa Walters says you're innocent. She knows what she's doing, and she wouldn't lie, so I have to believe it's true. I can't let you take a plea when you're innocent."

"Guilt and innocence. Who's to say, right? It's what people believe, and nobody ever believes me, Tom. They're not about to start now. The prosecutor won't believe me. The jury won't. I'd go down and get nothing for it. This way, I get something I really care about. I get to make sure you don't suffer because of me."

"I can't let you do this. Go to trial, Aidan. I'll support you. And the jury will believe you. You'll see."

"At what cost? You losing your job? Wasting your kids' college money on my defense, only to see me get convicted? No, it's not worth it."

"You think I'll sleep at night, knowing you're locked up because you tried to help me? Don't sacrifice yourself for me. I can't live with that."

"After you sacrificed for me your whole life? It's my turn now, Tommy."

"I won't let you."

"My mind is made up."

"It's not just about what you want. There's also the truth. And the truth is, I cut you loose that night even though I saw you break into Caroline Stark's house. That was a dereliction of duty, a betrayal of my badge. I deserve to pay for it."

"You've been paying for helping me as long as I can remember. Enough."

"This woman is the one who should be taking the fall. From what I understand, they don't know where she is or when they'll find her. I could go look for her myself."

"Ah, she's probably in Mexico by now."

"I can't let her get away with this. She's a grifter. I could smell it on her when I saw her in the bar that time. She was working you, and you were eating it up. You always did have terrible taste in women. I should've said something. I should've stopped you."

"You said plenty, and I ignored you. Forget Caroline. Let me do this for you."

"I favored my family. That's not an excuse. It's the problem. I'm going to tell them the truth about what I did. Then you won't have any reason to fall on your sword for me."

"No. Don't you see? If you do that, my sacrifice is for nothing. I made my decision, Tommy. I'm pleading guilty. Go tell my lawyer. Take me to court. I'm ready."

59

ess and Mike were killing time, sitting in the courthouse cafeteria. They'd come to watch Aidan Callahan plead guilty to murder, but there had been an unexpected delay. They'd been told it could be an hour or two wait while a new lawyer was brought in to represent Callahan at the plea hearing. But it had already been over three hours, and when Jess checked in with the court clerk, he didn't have any new information.

Jess sipped her coffee and grimaced at the burnt taste of it. Mike scrolled through his phone, an herbal tea in front of him. She'd discovered he was a health nut. No surprise there.

"Hey," she said. "Do you think he really did it?"

He looked up at her. "Callahan? Of course."

"What about the Russians? They had a serious beef with Jason Stark, and they're known killers. Don't you think that's too much of a coincidence?"

Mike shrugged. "I agree that's strange. But truth is stranger than fiction sometimes."

"What about Callahan's claim that he was drugged? The test results showed Ambien in his blood."

"You think the Russians drugged him?"

"The Russians? No. Somebody else. Caroline, maybe."

"Or, Callahan took Ambien on his own that night. That's more likely."

"It was a lot. Who takes that much Ambien?"

"I don't know anything about Ambien dosage. I don't think you do, either. Anyways, he's pleading. Nobody pleads guilty if they're innocent."

"That's not true. They do if they think they won't be able to convince a jury, and the deal's sweet enough."

"If Callahan can't convince a jury, it's because he's guilty. And his deal isn't even that sweet. At this rate, we'll never find Caroline Stark. She's probably sitting on a beach with an umbrella drink in her hand, beyond the reach of the law. Without her to testify against, Callahan does a minimum of twenty-five. Say twenty with good behavior. Not exactly a sweet deal."

"I know. That troubles me. There's no appeal under his plea deal. What if he's innocent?"

Mike snorted.

"You thought Caroline Stark was innocent. Now you think Callahan is. I hate to break it to you, but if you want to be a cop, you need to start believing the defendants are guilty."

He went back to his phone.

"Okay, then," she said. "What about Caroline?"

He looked up. "What about her?"

"Why can't we locate her? We've been monitoring her phone. Her sister's phone. Her daughter's phone. Surveilling locations where we think she might turn up. It's been over a week with no trace. Where is she?"

"I told you what I think. She left the country."

"We checked. Customs and Border Patrol has no record of that."

"Maybe she used false documents. A false name."

"I don't buy it. If she'd made a big move, we would know. She went to ground. We need to search harder," Jess said.

"Okay. What do you suggest that we haven't already tried?"

"Follow her sister. We have every reason to believe they're in contact."

"Actually, their phones don't show any contact, Jess. Plus, I surveilled Lynn on two separate occasions. You read the reports. She went to the gym, the nail salon, the grocery store, and her husband's trucking company."

"Why her husband's trucking company?"

"I assume because her husband works there."

He went back to his phone again. Mike lacked imagination, in Jess's view. Something wasn't sitting right about this case, and she was running out of time to solve it. Mike didn't seem that interested in solving it, or maybe he just didn't feel the same nagging doubts. Callahan would plead guilty by the end of the day. Once that happened, the pressure to close the file and move on would only grow. They could say they'd solved it. The killer was in jail. And yes, maybe a coconspirator got away, but she was female. The public wouldn't view her as a serious threat. They could keep the warrant for Caroline's arrest open, but they'd be reassigned to other duties. Maybe one day, years from now, Caroline would get pulled over for speeding, and Jess would get a phone call. Or maybe not. Maybe Callahan would take the fall alone.

Mike would be satisfied with that outcome. Jess wouldn't.

She sighed, stood up, and went to the bathroom. When she came back, Mike was staring openmouthed at his phone.

"What is it?" Jess said.

"I think you might get your wish."

"What wish is that?"

"Caroline Stark."

"You have a lead?"

"I got a text from the claims adjuster at the life insurance company. We've been in touch all along. If Jason's death was foul play, they're not responsible for paying out the five mil, so she's been helping me. She just texted that Caroline filed a claim."

"When?"

"Five minutes ago. She filed electronically. I have to figure out how to trace that filing to a location. Do you staties have a computer forensics expert I could borrow?"

Jess thought about Aidan Callahan's plea. It would happen well before they could trace the claim, and it would be final.

"We can't wait to trace her electronically," Jess said. "By the time we get her location, she'll be gone. Call your insurance company contact. Tell her she needs to bring Caroline in."

"Bring her in where? How?"

"To her office. We'll be waiting to lock her up on the outstanding warrant. Tell her to make up some excuse. There's something wrong with the form Caroline filed. Or she has to sign it in person. Whatever the lady can think of."

"You think Caroline will fall for it?" Mike asked.

"With five million dollars at stake? Hell, yeah, she will."

60

The Long Island Mutual Life Insurance Company was located in a squat four-story office building on a busy street in Hempstead. There was a parking garage entrance to its left, a bank to its right, and a block of apartment buildings across the street. Behind the building, a fire lane allowed for deliveries and emergencies. Jess and Mike arrived in separate cars with less than ten minutes to spare until Caroline's four o'clock appointment with Lily Chen, the claims adjuster who'd contacted Mike. Jess set up in the alley, covering the rear entrance and the building's loading docks. Mike set up in front of the Regency Arms Apartments with a clear view of the building's front entrance and the entrance to the parking garage. They agreed on the need to assess every vehicle to determine whether Caroline Stark was inside it. Her Escalade and Jason's Mercedes had both been impounded as evidence, and they didn't know what she'd be driving.

They synced their radios and waited.

Three thirty came and went. Five more minutes passed, then ten. Jess was getting antsy.

"Anything yet?" she said to Mike over the radio.

"A couple people in and out of the front entrance. Two cars into the parking garage, one out. None of them was Caroline. You?"

"Nothing. It's dead back here."

They waited some more.

At four, Jess radioed Mike again.

"You think maybe you should check in with the claims adjuster?"

"Good idea. Hold on."

A moment later, Mike came back on the line. "Lily says she just left!"

"What? How did we miss her?"

"No idea."

"Do you have eyes on her now?"

"Nope. And I've been watching. Anything out the back?"

"Nothing. Do you think she's disguised somehow?" Jess asked.

"Huh. Hold on. I'll see if Lily has further information."

Jess waited. Mike came back on a minute later.

"You're right. Lily says she looked older than she was expecting. Short gray hair and glasses."

"Was it even Caroline?"

"I don't know. Wait. Wait, I think I see her. That might be Caroline in a wig. Yes. It's definitely her. Short gray wig. Nobody does that unless they're guilty as sin."

"Or, hiding from the Russian mob," Jess said.

"Come on. You can't possible still think she's innocent. Uh, she just pulled out of the garage. Proceeding southbound in a silver Nissan Rogue with New York plates. Pursuing."

"Got it. Moving out. I'm behind you but I don't have visual."

A couple of stoplights later, Jess spotted Mike's car in the distance. But she didn't see Caroline.

"I have eyes on you now," Jess said. "I don't see her."

"She's getting on the Southern State, eastbound," Mike said.

"Copy that. I'm behind you."

They followed Caroline for a good forty minutes, until she got off the Southern State Parkway and headed into Central Islip. Jess was familiar with the area from an MS-13 investigation she'd worked a couple of years earlier. But as soon as she saw the name of the street they were on, she realized there was another, more salient connection to this case.

"I know where she's going," Mike said, over the radio.

They were on a busy surface road in an area of warehouses, strip malls, and fast-food joints, not far from the LIRR station.

"Me, too. Lombardo's trucking company," Jess said. "Never been there but I recognize the address."

"I've been there, as you know, since I surveilled Lynn to that location. You said Lynn visiting her husband's company was significant. You were right. She went to the grocery store first and brought two bags of groceries with her."

"She was feeding someone. Caroline's been hiding out there."

"That's got to be it. Okay, the subject vehicle is pulling in to the Lombardo Trucking lot. I see two buildings. One is the main building, plate-glass windows. Looks like the office. Five passenger cars parked in front. The second is a hangarlike structure with four garage bays. To the right of the office building. The subject vehicle is entering that hangarlike structure, specifically, the third garage bay from the left. Door closing behind her."

"Should we pop her now?" Jess asked.

"The place looks busy. It's not even five yet. I say we sit on it for a while and see if it clears out, so we don't risk any interference."

"Got it. Pulling into the parking lot directly across the street."

"Heading around the back."

They sat and waited. At some point, Jess realized it was after five o'clock. Aidan Callahan had pleaded guilty by now. To Jess's mind, that made it more, rather than less, urgent to apprehend Caroline Stark. If Aidan acted alone, let Caroline convince them of it and explain the evidence to the contrary. And if he didn't, Aidan could testify against her, and Caroline would face the music.

More sitting, more waiting. Jess wished she had a cup of coffee, but she didn't. She didn't even have chewing gum.

It was nearly six thirty. The sun had set. Jess had watched five different men leave the Lombardo Trucking offices, departing in the vehicles that had been parked in front of the building with the plate-glass windows. Towering streetlamps lit the parking lot, illuminating several rows of tractor trailers and the large garage facility that Caroline's Nissan had disappeared into an hour earlier. But the lot was empty of people.

Jess radioed Mike. "Office lights out. No individuals visible on the lot. Time to move in."

61

Jess and Mike pulled up simultaneously in front of the garage building Caroline had disappeared into earlier. They each parked lengthwise across the bays, so that any vehicle inside would be blocked from exiting. The building had no windows and no doors on the front other than the garage bays, which were closed up tight. There was no way for anybody to look out and see them, though it was possible that their approaching cars might have been heard.

Jess checked her service weapon and returned it to the holster under her arm. She took a utility knife and a lock-picking tool from the glove box and put them in the pocket of her pants. When she got dressed this morning, she'd initially pulled out a dress and high-heeled boots in imitation of that AUSA who told them about the Russians. Thankfully she'd thought better of it and put on pants and a blazer instead, with leather brogues that she could run in. A cop really couldn't wear a dress, not even to court. You never knew where the day would take you, or what surveillances or chases it might bring.

She met Mike behind his vehicle. They crouched down and kept their voices low.

"There's a door on the back and another on the right side," Mike said.

"We hit both simultaneously."

"She could run out the front. She'd have to open a bay first, and we'd hear that."

"And she'd be on foot. I may not look it, but I'm fast. I bet you are, too. We'll get her," Jess said.

Mike nodded. "I'll take the back."

Jess looked at her watch. "Okay. We hit in five minutes, so we have time to set up. That'll be six seventeen."

"Got it."

Jess went around to the side door. It was elevated about five feet above ground, accessed by a short flight of concrete steps. There was some kind of skylight above it, but no window that would afford someone inside a direct view of Jess's approach. She climbed the stairs. The door itself was metal, with a flimsy knob. The knob was locked, but she was confident she could breach it. She took the metal pick from her pocket and got started. It was harder than it looked, or maybe she'd forgotten what she'd learned in the academy about lock picking. She checked her watch. She had two minutes before they were supposed to enter. But that time slipped away as she wiggled the tool in the lock, her hands sweating in the cold, wondering if Caroline could hear her. She started thinking about shooting the lock, but the door was metal, and bullets could ricochet.

"Police!" Mike Castro shouted from behind the building.

Shit. Mike was in, but Jess was still locked out. As she started down the stairs, intending to go around and support him at the back entrance, the metal door flew open. Jess whirled to see Caroline Stark standing there, a shocked look on her face.

"Stop right there!" Jess said.

She was back up the stairs in an instant. Caroline ducked inside, yanking the door closed, but Jess managed to grab the handle. They played tug-of-war until Caroline let go and fled back into the building. Jess ran in after her.

Inside, the lights were out. Jess stepped forward quickly, and her foot hit open air. She grasped at the emptiness in front of her, struggling for balance; then she plummeted. The fall lasted a millisecond, and then she hit hard, landing on hands and knees on a concrete floor with the breath knocked out of her. Pain radiated through her wrists and legs. She managed to shift to sitting, and looked back. In the darkness, she'd walked right off a concrete loading dock and fallen about five feet to floor level.

Jess staggered upright, shaking her extremities and patting herself to assess the damage. Nothing was broken.

There were skylights above each side wall, and the rear door stood ajar, adding up to enough light to see outlines. Her eyes were adjusting. She saw the silver Nissan that Caroline had been driving. Two cots and a plastic table and folding chairs. A closed door that presumably led to a bathroom. But no people. Where was Caroline? Where was Mike? Either they'd run out the back exit, they were hiding inside the car, or they were in that bathroom. Jess took out her gun and moved cautiously toward the Nissan. She peered in through the side windows, but in the dim light, she wouldn't be able to tell if there was someone lying on the back floor. She holstered her gun and took out her phone, flicking on the flashlight to shine into the car.

In the reflection the light made on the windows, she saw the man standing behind her. She heard him chamber a round in his gun and saw him point it at the back of her head. She recognized him immediately from the surveillance photos taken in Queens of him meeting with Galina and the Russian enforcer.

"On the floor, *now*," Jason Stark said.

62

Jason Stark knelt beside Jess and patted her down, taking the gun from the holster under her arm. His sour smell and heavy five-o'clock shadow told her that he'd been holed up in this garage for days, hiding from the mobsters who wanted to kill him. And hiding from the police, who would blow his cover by telling the world that he wasn't actually dead. Jason wore a thick bandage on his left hand. It was gray and dingy and snaked up his arm, its bulk puffing up the sleeve of his shirt. Jess knew how he'd suffered that injury—opening a vein, spilling enough of his blood to fake his own murder and hang it on an innocent man. Aidan Callahan was a patsy. He was innocent of the murder of Caroline's husband, who was alive and well and currently pointing a gun at Jess's head.

Caroline must've been in on it with Jason all along. Jess had followed Caroline to this garage, which proved that Caroline knew that Jason was here, and knew he was alive. Of course she did. She'd been hiding out herself, waiting for the plan they'd set in motion to play out. The two of them stole millions from the Russian mob, enough to support their lavish lifestyle, to build a fabulous oceanfront house, and presumably to fill the coffers of the numerous offshore bank accounts that Jess would now spend years attempting to trace, assuming she got out of here alive. Stealing that money wasn't the sort of crime a person should expect to get away with. Not because the police would find you. The police were busy; they missed a lot. But the Russians weren't so easily distracted. They were ruthless and relentless. They wouldn't stop until they got every penny of their money back and took the interest payments in blood. The Starks knew what was coming. Jason would end up in a shallow grave with a bullet in the back of his head, and there was no escaping. Mexico wasn't far enough to run. The only way out was to die before they got to him—credibly, believably, with someone else to take the fall. Someone who'd walk into the trap willingly and play his role to perfection because he didn't even know he was playing. Someone gullible and vulnerable, like Aidan Callahan.

"Up," Jason said, and yanked Jess to her feet roughly.

He stood behind her, pressing the gun into her back. They were alone in the garage as far as she could tell. The rear door was open; Mike had gone in pursuit of Caroline. The building was large—fifty or sixty feet wide by thirty long—and sparsely furnished. The SUV Caroline had been driving was parked in the middle of the floor. The Starks had set up camp along the far wall, with cots, table and chairs, and a workbench that functioned as a makeshift kitchen, complete with microwave, hot plate, and groceries. There were tools on the workbench that Jess might be able to use as weapons, if only she could reach them.

Jason wasn't about to give her that chance. He pulled her around to the driver's side of the SUV, opened the front door, and shoved her in. Then he jumped in the seat behind her and stuck the gun against her neck.

"Turn the car on. I'll tell you where to go."

There existed a real possibility that Jason was planning to take her somewhere and kill her. She replayed the moment when Jason came up behind her. He'd emerged from behind the closed bathroom door. Mike Castro presumably hadn't seen him. Mike didn't know Jason was here. Jess was the only one who could blow Jason's cover and prove he was alive. If she got away and told her story, word would spread. The case against Aidan Callahan would be dismissed, and the Russians would come looking. Jason wasn't about to let that happen. In order to stop it, he'd take her away from here, to somewhere remote, and put a bullet in her head.

"I said, turn the car on."

The coldness of his tone confirmed her assessment. He'd be capable of it, when the time came.

Jess pushed the ignition button. The garage door was down, and Jason was too distracted to realize that. She was about to ask him whether he intended her to drive right through it, but then she realized this was her chance.

"*Go*," he said, waving the gun.

She stepped hard on the gas and crashed into the metal door. There was a terrible crunching sound as the front of the SUV crumpled. Jess wasn't wearing a seat belt, and the impact tossed her forward. The airbag deployed, so fast and hard that it felt like a punch to the gut. She felt a searing pain in her chest and couldn't breathe. But she forced herself to reach for the door handle. Managing somehow to open the door, Jess rolled sideways out of the car onto the concrete floor. And in the nick of time. Jason, who'd been thrown around in the backseat, righted himself and fired at the spot where she'd been, an instant too late. The bullet punctured the airbag with a loud popping sound. He fired again and shattered the windshield. Jess struggled to her knees and crawled around to the back of the car. He'd be coming for her any minute. She tried to get up and run, but whatever the hell was wrong with her chest made it impossible. Her breath came in wheezes. She saw spots, felt light-headed. Her side was an agony of pain. She must've broken a rib, punctured a lung. She heard Jason get out of the car behind her. He got off a third shot. It hit the concrete floor beside her, sending up a spray of chips. She rolled aside. But his feet were coming. There would be no escape.

"*Drop it now!*" Mike said.

He stood inside the back door, moving forward, his weapon out. The shots came too fast for her to keep track. Jason was down on the floor, his blood spreading toward her.

"He's got a second gun," she said.

Mike crossed to the spot where Jason lay and felt his pulse. He reached down and took Jess's gun away.

"He's alive. I'm calling an ambulance."

"I need one, too," Jess said, and passed out.

63

One month later

Aidan walked into the hushed lobby of the federal courthouse. Caroline and Jason Stark were scheduled to plead guilty to criminal charges this morning, and he wanted to be there to see it happen. He stepped up to the security line, placed his phone and belt in the bin, and walked through the metal detector. As he retrieved his belongings on the other side, a woman who'd just done the same turned around and gasped.

"What are *you* doing here?" Lynn Lombardo said.

The security guard was right there watching. Aidan didn't need to get into some confrontation with Caroline's sister. If nothing else, the past weeks of chaos had taught him to keep a tighter grip on his emotions.

"I'm here for the guilty plea. It's open to the public," he said calmly, and walked away.

Lynn's high heels rang out on the marble floor as she pursued him.

"Aidan, *wait.*"

He turned. She caught up with him by the elevators.

"I didn't mean to sound so hostile. Can we talk for a minute? Please," she said.

"All right."

They moved out of the stream of people to a bench against the wall.

"I owe you an apology," Lynn said.

"That's an understatement," he said.

"Caroline lied to me, like she lied to you," Lynn said. "She told me you were stalking her and her family. That's the only reason I came after you at your job. I'm sorry. I should have known better than to believe anything she said."

"Wait, you're apologizing for yelling at me at the bar? I don't give a crap about that. I almost went to jail for life for killing a man who was still alive. You knew about it and did nothing. Try apologizing for that."

"Yes, I'm sorry for what happened to you, and my part in it. You have to understand, though—Caroline told me you were trying to kill Jason. I knew nothing about the Russians or the money laundering or any of that. She told me you were a jealous lover, and that she had a way to make it look like Jason was already dead, so the police would finally arrest you. It made sense to me at the time. But she was lying, like she lies to everyone."

"I heard Caroline is living with you. If she really put one over on you, then why take her in?"

"Because she's family, and she had nowhere else to go. The judge let her out on bail, but only on house arrest with an ankle bracelet. The feds seized all their assets. Not only their money. The beach house and the apartment in the city, too. My place was her only option."

"They seized the beach house?"

"Yes, it's going on the auction block next month."

The idea flashed into Aidan's mind that this was his chance to get Gramps's land back for his family. But, no, it was impossible. Even heavily damaged by the hurricane, that house would sell for a bundle at auction, and he barely had a dollar to his name. He could try to talk to Tommy. Maybe if they pulled together, they could raise the money somehow. It was something to hope for, anyway.

"Caroline won't be staying with me after today," Lynn said. "Once she pleads guilty, they'll take her straight to jail. Her lawyer thinks she'll get one to three years. Jason's looking at ten, and that's only if he testifies against the Russians, which is like a death sentence. So, you see where Caroline's greed got them."

Aidan looked away. He nursed a cold fury at what that woman had done to him. But her hooks had sunk in deep enough that it still troubled him to think of her in jail.

"I'm sorry to hear that," he said.

"Are you? If I was you, I'd want to see her punished. Isn't that why you're here?"

Aidan didn't answer.

"Court is about to start. We should go," he said.

As they waited for the elevator, he thought of something.

"Lynn?" he said. "Would you tell Hannah I'm sorry for the way I approached her at her school? I thought she was in danger. In my mind, I was there to help. It seems far-fetched now, but Caroline had me so confused."

Lynn nodded. "I understand, and I'll tell her. I talked her out of coming to court today. It upsets her so much to see her dad in handcuffs. She's back in school now, and I want her to focus on herself. I don't know if she'll ever forgive Caroline for what happened. But Joe and I are there for Hannah, always. We'll make sure she comes out of this all right."

Aidan watched from the back of the courtroom as Jason Stark entered guilty pleas to conspiracy and money laundering and was led away by two guards. It was jarring to see the Wall Street titan in prison blues, manacled and unshaven, his once impeccably trimmed hair looking gray and disheveled. As Stark reached the holding cell door, he turned, raised his fingers to his lips, and blew his wife a kiss. In the front row, Caroline was too busy consulting with her lawyer to notice—or else she didn't bother to respond. Aidan wondered where things stood between them now that their perfect life had been destroyed so completely.

Aidan stared as Caroline huddled with her lawyer. She wore a dark suit and had her hair pulled back in a twist. Her face in profile, the fine tilt of her head—everything about her still called to him. But he was wiser now. He leaned into his anger to fight the attraction, and it worked, mostly. Aidan had come close to spending his life in jail for a murder he didn't commit because of this woman. She'd used him; she'd played to his weaknesses and set him up for a terrible fall. His deliverance had come at the very last moment and as a matter of sheer luck. His new lawyer didn't get to court on time, which meant his plea hearing got postponed for a day. In the meantime, the police found Jason Stark alive, or else Aidan would be in jail for a murder that never happened.

The judge walked off the bench, and the court clerk announced a fifteen-minute recess before Caroline's case would be heard. Aidan watched as she went over to hug her sister, who sat in the front row. Then she turned, and before he realized what was happening, Caroline was coming up the aisle directly toward him.

He'd come to watch her take her punishment. He'd never really imagined that they would speak. But now that it was a possibility, he wanted that closure. He had questions. He would demand an apology. He stood up and went toward her, expecting her to back away. But she stopped.

Their eyes met, and words deserted him.

"Aidan," she said. "I'm so glad to see you."

He hadn't been expecting that.

She looked to the front of the courtroom. Her sister and her lawyer had noticed that they were talking and watched them with worried expressions. The lawyer stood up and started walking toward them.

"Let's go outside for a minute," Caroline said.

"Are you allowed to?"

She looked like he'd punched her.

"I am, until I plead guilty. This is actually my last chance for a while. Come on."

He held the door for her. She glanced back over her shoulder. They took the elevator down to the lobby and walked out onto the busy

Brooklyn street. There was a park across the way, and they crossed to it. Aidan noticed the lawyer following a discreet distance behind them. He obviously didn't trust his client not to up and run.

It was a gray November day. The leaves were off the trees and the wind was bitter. As the air filled with fumes from a passing bus, Caroline breathed in with a longing that Aidan recognized. He'd felt it himself not that long ago, staring out the window of the patrol car as they carted him off to jail. That desperate love for the outside world, right when you were about to lose your freedom. He wanted to take some satisfaction in this moment, to feel a sense of triumph at her fall, but he couldn't. Caroline had lost in the end, as she deserved to. But that didn't mean that Aidan won.

"Why did you come today?" she asked, as they walked.

"I want to see you pay for what you did to me," he said, and realized how true that was.

She turned on him angrily. That wasn't the answer she'd been looking for, apparently.

"What *I* did? Here you are, walking free. Jason and I are both going to jail. My daughter hates me. My sister hates me. I've lost everything I ever owned. I'm the one who's suffering."

He stared at her in disbelief.

"Are you serious, playing the victim here? I *went* to jail, Caroline. You would have let me rot there forever for a crime that didn't even happen. You branded me a murderer. What did I ever do but love you, and try to help you? I thought we had something real. But you set me up. What I thought was the start of an incredible relationship was just another con job to you."

"No. I honestly did care for you, Aidan."

"Don't lie. You lied enough already. This whole thing was a setup from the beginning. You went to Harbor Gourmet and had them put me on your bartending gig, so you could lure me to your bed and use me as your patsy. You got me to follow your husband, so you could tell people I was stalking your family. Then you drugged me. You planted all sorts of evidence to frame me up for murder. You even defaced your own car.

That 'Die, bitch' thing? You did that yourself, to make it look like I was crazy, didn't you?"

She crossed her arms over her chest and glared at him. But she didn't deny it.

"You're not even sorry," he said, and he was shaking with anger.

"I did what I had to do. Jason was in a lot of trouble with the Russians. I was trying to save his life. Besides, Aidan, you brought this on yourself. Do you know how I found you? You would stand outside my house, casing it. You scared me. I thought you were one of the Russians. So, I investigated. I asked around about you."

"And found out I was an outcast with a criminal record. The perfect fall guy."

"You put yourself in this situation."

"By looking at your house? That land belonged to my family. It's no excuse for what you did to me. You're evil, plain and simple. I wish you would admit that to yourself."

"Oh, please. You made your choices. Everything that happened, you wanted. I wanted it, too. We had real chemistry. We're more alike than you think. Remember that. From the beginning, I felt like I knew you. We were never really strangers."

She took a step toward him, looking up into his eyes as she leaned in to kiss him. Her soft, warm lips, the sweetness of her mouth, were as intoxicating as ever. Time stood still as he breathed in the scent of her perfume. He could have held her forever. But there was only one thing left to say.

"We're strangers now, Caroline."

And he turned and walked away.

Turn the page for a sneak peek at
Michele Campbell's new novel

The Wife Who Knew Too Much

1

NINA'S DIARY

July 4

I'm writing this to raise an alarm in the event of my untimely death. This is hard to admit, even to myself, let alone to the world. My husband is planning to kill me. For obvious reasons. He's in love with someone else. And he wants my money.

I'm sitting in my office in the tower room at Windswept as I write. I look out over the ocean. The waves pound the beach as dark clouds sweep in from the east. A storm is coming. This house belonged to my first husband, Edward. On the day we met, I was twenty-three, working in an art gallery, barely scraping by. Edward was fifty and one of the wealthiest men in New York. People said I was a gold-digger. But they were wrong. Edward might not have been the perfect husband, but I loved him. When he got sick, I nursed him. When he died, I grieved him. A year later, I met someone else and fell in love. And I married again.

That was Connor, my second husband. On the night we met, he was thirty. I was fifty and one of the wealthiest women in New York. Connor didn't have a penny. People took that to mean he could only be after my money. I didn't see it that way. People had been wrong about me. I assumed they were wrong about him, too.

But they were right.

I just finished meeting with the private investigator, and I'm writing this with tears in my eyes. A photograph sits before me on the desk, incontrovertible proof that the two of them are together—and have been for a very long time. I don't know how far it goes, or what they're capable of, but I fear the worst. As Connor well knows, we have an airtight prenup. The prenup says he gets nothing if he cheats. I can divorce him and throw him out on the street. Everything I gave him—the cars, the clothes, the expensive watches, that boat he loves so much, the jet—I can take away. And I will. He knows I will. How far would he go to prevent that from happening? I hope I'm being alarmist, but I fear he'd go to extremes.

I'd throw him out right this minute, but I'm expecting three hundred guests. I'll be holding my annual Fourth of July gala tonight, here at Windswept. It was at that very same party two years ago that I first saw Connor. Infatuation at first sight. I should have slept with him and left it at that, but I'm too much of a romantic. Or just a fool. Well, I won't be foolish tonight. I'll be extremely careful. As soon as my guests leave, as the fireworks fade from the sky over the ocean, I'll confront him. I'll tell him it's over and kick him off my property. I won't do it alone. I'll take precautions. I'll have security with me, because I fear what Connor might do if he knows he's about to lose everything. I'll be careful. I'll do it cleanly, quickly. And this marriage will be done.

It's going to be so hard, though. I still love him. I love him so much that I have to fight the urge to give him another chance. To ask him to explain the things the investigator found. I can't do that. It would be a terrible mistake. It could even put my life at risk. I don't trust myself with him. That's why I'm leaving this diary where it's sure to be found. If something goes wrong, I want an autopsy. If I die unexpectedly, it was foul play, and Connor was behind it. Connor—and *her*.

2

SOUTHAMPTON, New York, July 5—Noted businesswoman and philan-
thropist Nina Levitt was found dead early this morning. She was 52.

Mrs. Levitt was discovered unresponsive, floating in the swimming
pool at Windswept, her mansion in Southampton, where she had just
thrown a lavish party attended by hundreds of guests. She was rushed
by ambulance to Stony Brook Southampton Hospital, where she was
pronounced dead upon arrival. Cause of death is believed to be drowning, to be confirmed by an autopsy, the results of which are pending.

Mrs. Levitt was best known as the widow of real-estate tycoon
Edward M. Levitt, the founder of Levitt Global Enterprises, Inc., which
maintains offices in New York, Hong Kong, and Dubai. Mrs. Levitt
served in various capacities at Levitt Global, including most recently
as chairwoman of the board.

During Edward Levitt's lifetime, the couple were fixtures on the
social scene in New York and Southampton. Mrs. Levitt was famous for
her lavish parties and fashion sense, and appeared frequently in pub-
lications such as *Vogue*, *Town & Country*, and *Avenue*. Her ethereal

beauty—she was known for her pale skin and red hair—made her a favorite subject of fashion photographers.

The Levitts' accomplishments as developers of commercial real estate in the U.S. and abroad, and as collectors and donors of late-twentieth-century contemporary art, were often overshadowed by scandal. The couple were frequent subjects of tabloid stories concerning Mr. Levitt's extramarital affairs. In the years since Mr. Levitt's death, Mrs. Levitt was believed to have found happiness with her second husband, Connor Ford. Mr. Ford is currently an executive at Levitt Global, having enjoyed a meteoric rise within the company since his marriage to Mrs. Levitt.

Mr. Ford did not respond to repeated requests for comment in regard to this story.

3

TABITHA
Memorial Day weekend

The night Connor Ford walked back into my life, I was waitressing, just trying to make ends meet.

I was standing by the bar at the Baldwin Grill, waiting to pick up drink orders for my tables, when I happened to glance out the window. A sexy black sports car with New York plates was just pulling into the parking lot, and I remember thinking, *That guy must be lost.* We don't rate the jet set, and that car screamed money. Don't get me wrong. The Grill is right on Baldwin Lake, one of the prettiest spots in New Hampshire. This area used to be ritzy back in the day. But not anymore. We draw a rowdy crowd in the summertime, folks from Massachusetts, New York, and Jersey who can't afford the shore. Partiers and big drinkers. They come for the local microbrews scrawled on the chalkboard and the big-screen TV tuned to the game. But they're not the rich and famous, no way.

As I watched, a man got out. A tall, gorgeous man. And it was *him.* He glanced at the restaurant with an air of purpose and started walking toward the entrance. I couldn't believe it. My heart was pounding. I started to sweat.

Connor and I were together for just one summer, back when I was seventeen. It was a tumultuous summer for us both. We fell into each other's arms and stayed there, clinging for dear life, until they pried us apart. To this day, nobody has ever reached me like he did. I'd been married and divorced, in and out of my share of half-assed relationships. But I'd never gotten over him.

Now, there he was, looking cool and gorgeous in dark jeans and a crisp white shirt. And here I was, pushing thirty, makeup melting off my face, my clothes smelling like food, as the love of my life walked through the door ten feet from where I stood. What did I do? I panicked. I backed into a customer, knocking his half-empty beer out of his hand and onto the floor, where it rolled around and splattered people's shoes.

"Oh my gosh, I'm so sorry. Let me take care of that," I said.

In the ensuing chaos, as I raced to get paper towels, mop up the mess, and replace the poor man's drink, I lost track of Connor in the crowd. On this Friday before Memorial Day, the Baldwin Grill was jammed to capacity. You couldn't turn around without bumping into some beefy, red-faced guy who was sloppy drunk. Which made me wonder—what the hell was Connor doing here, anyway? His family sold their lake house years ago, after his grandmother died. The lake had gone downhill since then, while Connor had only come up in the world. He'd married a woman who was rich and famous, and their pictures were constantly in the tabloids. Shouldn't he be on a yacht somewhere with Nina Levitt, instead of at a second-rate sports bar, rubbing elbows with the common people?

Unless.

Could he possibly be looking for me?

"Hey, Tabitha, I just sat a hot guy in your section," the hostess called out as I passed by with my tray of drinks.

And I knew it was him.

I almost turned around and told her to give him to somebody

else so he wouldn't see me like this. Let's face it, even if I wasn't wait-ressing, I'm not what I was at seventeen. Who is? But, we were fully booked tonight, and short-staffed. There was nobody to cover my table. I'd have to face him, whether I liked it or not.

Out on the terrace, it was a party scene. The sun hadn't yet set, but everybody had their buzz on. Music blasted from the speakers. Motorboats raced across the water, and somebody was shooting off Roman candles from the dock. I saw Connor out of the corner of my eye. He was seated at a table along the railing, facing the restau-rant, his back to the lake, scanning the crowd like he was looking for somebody. A woman, presumably. His famous wife must be joining him, and he'd saved her the chair with the view. A gentleman, as always. That gave my heart a wrench.

It took awhile before I could get to him. I had two tables waiting for drinks, three ready to order, two with food sitting in the kitchen that I needed to get out, and two others ready to pay. I was glad for the delay, which gave me time to collect myself. I'd dreamed of this moment so often. Sometimes it ended with us in each other's arms. Sometimes with me telling him off for letting his family come be-tween us. Never once did it involve me taking his drink order.

When I couldn't avoid it any longer, I grabbed a pitcher of water and headed for his table. And found myself looking right into his eyes. Those hazel eyes I'd loved so well the summer I was seventeen.

1. How do you see Caroline's nervousness about Hannah fitting into her character? Does it make her more sympathetic? Less?

2. When you learned more about Aidan's backstory partway through the novel, did it change your opinion of him? If so, in what way?

3. Early in the novel, Caroline talks about the difference between thoughts and actions. What's your opinion on this topic? Do you think that bad thoughts inevitably lead to bad actions, or are people entitled to think whatever they want? Explain why you think that way.

4. In chapter one Caroline says, "The thing about being rich is, there's always someone richer." Can you see this statement as a kind of foreshadowing for her actions later? Why do you think wealth is so important to someone like Caroline?

5. How did the dual-narrator format affect your reading experience? Do you think it worked well within the novel?

6. Halfway through the novel a huge storm hits the coast and rattles Caroline's beach house. How did this contribute to the atmosphere and mood of the second half of the novel? Can you point to specific passages where the writing created this atmosphere?

7. Whose perspective did you believe (or believe more) while you were reading? When did your allegiances shift, and why?

8. In chapter 33 Caroline says "The reckoning was coming for all of us. I could feel it." What kind of reckonings does this book leave us with? Do you think that justice was served by the end of the novel?

*Discussion
Questions*

9. Given the dual narration and the unreliable narrator in the novel, who do you think is actually the protagonist—Aidan or Caroline? Can you make an argument for both?

10. Did you see the ending coming? If yes, when did you start to figure it out? If not, what *did* you think was going to happen?

About the Author

Nina Subin

A graduate of Harvard University and Stanford Law School, **MICHELE CAMPBELL** worked at a prestigious Manhattan law firm before spending eight years fighting crime as a federal prosecutor in New York City.